# The Ancient Whisper

Book One
A Whisper of a Mystery
Trilogy

# M.A. APPLEBY

The Ancient Whisper
By M.A. Appleby
Printed in U.S.A.

ISBN: 978-0692921296

2nd Edition Printing 2017

Information regarding permission, contact: info@maappleby.com
Visit Author website: www.maappleby.com

Cover, graphics, layout design, and all inserts by M.A. Appleby
Photo by V. M. Little

Fictional Novels by Author: *A Whisper of a Mystery Trilogy*:
 *The Ancient Whisper*, Book One ~ ISBN: 978-0-6929-2129-6
 *Whispered Dreams*, Book Two ~ ISBN: 978-0-6929-2133-3
 *Journey of a Thousand Steps*, Book Three ~ ISBN: 978-0-6929-2134-0
National Award-Winning Non-Fiction: ~ ISBN: 978-1-4984-9873-9
        *RAISING DAVID AGAIN*
    *A Guide To Understanding The Uniqueness of Brain Injury
        And How Our Faith Sustains Us*

# *Dedication*

This book is dedicated to my son, David.

It was his traumatic brain injury and subsequent recovery,

that allowed me to forge ahead.

His incredible determination, fortitude, and humor,

helped me understand what *'the other side'* is like,

and we are grateful to have him in our lives.

# *Testimonials*

*Ancient Whisper is a compelling story entwined around a woman who is abducted after her husband mysteriously dies. Ellen is a strong character you want to cheer for as she untangles the clandestine circumstances surrounding her abduction and the effect it has on her family. M.A. Appleby keeps you guessing, as the story weaves its way through an interesting cast of characters. It takes the reader to a horse farm in Virginia where we get an up-close view of a racetrack, then segues into a web of deceit and intrigue.*

~Karen Hansen, PhD, LMHC (Settle, WA) www.transpersonaltherapy.com

*Have you plunged into a paragraph to be immersed in intrigue, challenges, and mystery within minutes? I found exciting mini stories embedded in the main story on pages of M.A. Appleby's book, Ancient Whisper. You are compelled to keep reading to find out the next part of the story. I found it hard to find a good place to stop reading. Unsurmountable problems begin to happen, and financial challenges seem to be met through high stakes horse race wagering, but can you really win that way? Could an antique garage sale buy enough time? Is it possible a ghost could possibly whisper a secret to Ellen on the Ashwood Farm? Ellen's son is targeted for murder. It is hard to put this entertaining novel by a promising star writer down. The greatest news is whether or not this book opens the door to a possible sequel.*

~Don Paullin (author and speaker)

*In The Ancient Whisper, M.A. Appleby takes the reader on a wild ride. This story opens as Ellen Andress wakes slowly from a drug-induced stupor in a Middle Eastern country. How she got there is a mystery to her. The last thing she remembers is being in a bathroom at the Kauai airport as she and her husband were returning to their children after an island vacation. Over time, her captors reveal that her husband is dead and that she cannot return home for reasons no one will explain. Eventually, she does return to the United States, where two people, who identify themselves as FBI agents, immediately sweep her into a witness protection program. They leave her in a decrepit Virginia horse farm which she owns in partnership with some questionable characters. Within months, Ellen's mother and children change their identities and join her on the farm. However, the story does not end here, as both strange occurrences and amazing good fortune continue to follow this family. Appleby has written a very entertaining story that draws the reader in and pushes him or her to finish in order to understand how the author can tie together so many loose ends. A sequel could prove to be promising.*

~ Annie Peters (The Portland Review)

# Table of Contents

*"The greatest good is what we do for one another."*

~ Mother Teresa of Calcutta

# Chapter One

## The Narrow Windows

*Ravi, I'm having a nightmare and I need you. Where is everyone? You know I panic when I can't get in touch with Mother...is Jason still in bed? Melanie will be angry if she misses our trip to buy jeans and Curlie has a recital tonight. My family is an essential part of my life. and I can't seem to find them.*

I am in a dreamlike state and struggle to wake. In the semi-darkness, the shadows of unfamiliar objects take on an ethereal look, but I can't make out what they are. A soft buzzing sound is coming from inside my ears, as if a tunnel surrounds my head. This feeling is accompanied by a dull pounding that runs along the top of my skull. It's as if little hammers are hitting the felt pieces on a piano, but there's no sound.

Nausea surfaces when I turn my head or try to lift it. I'm unable to move, as nothing is working--arms, legs, or fingers. The drubbing in my head is so intense—that darkness pulls me under again.

Someone opens one of my eyelids, then the other, as the sensation of something cold is being dropped into them. Is it daylight or twilight?

My mouth is sandpaper dry, and a strange odor is lingering in the air. I won't move to keep nausea that lurks under the surface from emerging. Am I in a hospital? It smells like one. Who is that in the shadows? Are you a nurse?

Fighting to wake, I will my eyes to open all the way, but it's hazy—as if a gauze veil is covering my face. My fingers can move a little now. Pinching on my right hand makes me want to bring it to my face, but something is preventing me from lifting it.

Focusing better, thin strips of adhesive are on both hands where purple/blueish spots are spreading out on either side. My right hand is attached to a board.

Is there someone here? Who are you?

I cannot keep . . . my . . . eyes . . . open.

Ravi, are you here?

Migraines are like that sometimes, often disorienting—even hallucinogenic to a point.

*I must be suffering the monster of all migraines!*

As I open my eyes, there is movement as a dark cape swirls toward me to set something on a tree stump. As the caped person moves closer to me, I squeeze my eyes shut, as this frightens me. The caped person begins to speak and then lifts my left hand. When the caped/person moves away, I bring it closer to my face. My fingernails are short, cut straight across. My wedding rings and wristwatch are missing.

Disorientated from a headache, it continues to pound in my skull, as the annoying buzzing and sharp pain returns, pulsing at the back of my head. Something is pricking my arm and euphoria takes over, allowing me to fall into a pleasant dream of floating on the ocean in a little blue boat.

When I open my eyes again, someone is setting a tray on a thick table. My brain slowly comprehends that I don't know where I am or how I got here. The unnerving awareness that the table is not a tree stump surprises me. Then I realize, this is not, a hospital room.

My mouth will not form the words I'm thinking. It's as if I woke up in someone else's body and the sensation is both repulsive and alarming!

The cape/person is now bending over me speaking gibberish, pointing to things in the room, but my brain understands little. Is the person a large woman or a man?

Wanting to hide under the blanket, I can hear soft classical music playing in the background, but the sleepiness and nausea overwhelm me, and I drift back to sleep.

Waking again, I fight to stay awake. A headache and nausea are still present when I try to lift my head, although it isn't as intense as it was.

How much longer will this go on? I need to find Ravi. He must be here somewhere. I must call Mother. Ravi and I should have been home hours ago. Mother will need to stay with the children until we get back and they'll be very concerned we aren't there.

Time is difficult to judge. It might be early evening, as the room now has a soft glow of unnatural light from something my brain can't describe. Looking around, I'm lying on a mound of pillows, then realize these are not the clothes I put on yesterday!

*Why is my brain so scrambled?*

*Why can't I form a cohesive sentence?*

My mouth is dry. Is my tongue swollen? My hand brushes something. It's a bottle of water, so I guzzle it down when the cap comes free, then comprehend moments later what a mistake it is. The sea of nausea floats back as it blots out all thought. Grabbing a towel near the edge of the pillows, holding it over my mouth, I try to stand up but my legs will not support me, and I fall back onto the bed.

After several attempts, I move as quickly as possible toward a door on the far wall, hoping it's a bathroom. I slump to the floor, grateful to rest my head on the coolness of the commode. Cold chills suddenly replace hot flashes. Content to sit on the stone floor, nausea rises again. I struggle to get my head above the bowl, but my head hits the porcelain.

*What is happening to me? Ravi, where are you?*

A voice brings me out of my delirium as a shadow hovers above me. Moments later, I feel a cold cloth passing over my face and neck. It feels so good that I don't want to move.

*Thanks, Ravi, you are here.*

*You won't believe the dream I'm having.*

*You're not Ravi! Who are you?*

No words are coming out of my mouth! The shadow gently picks me up and carries me to the outer room. My eyes close without my permission as something soft brushes my forehead.

CLICK.

Waking with a shudder as the room has cooled, I use my t-shirt to wipe my eyes to clear away any ointment that is distorting my vision. As things begin to focus, the large cushions are a coverlet on top of a huge bed. All other furniture seems bulky and heavily upholstered. A faint glow is coming from a single lamp, and it's either the same or maybe the next night. Judging time without a clock is difficult.

*Where am I and why do I feel so awful?*

The dreadful pain in my head and nausea seems to have abated for now, but my body aches in every joint. What is most distressing, besides the purple marks on my hands, is the appearance of pink prick marks on the insides of both arms.

*Am I half in or half out of a waking/sleeping dream?*

Touching my hair, it feels atrocious. The tender spot on my forehead reminds me of hitting my head on the commode.

*Did I change my clothes in my sleep?*

Now that I can see better, the room is exceptionally designed and large by most standards. The fabric on the square pillow/coverlet consists of vivid shades of orange, magenta, rose, gold, and blue.

*Have these been here all along?*

I'm suddenly hungry, then hesitate to make sure there is no nausea before moving off the pillow/bed. A tray is sitting on the thick table I thought was a tree-trunk. Lifting the shiny dome cover to inhale the aroma, it makes a clunk sound when I drop it back onto the tray. It's not something I wish to eat.

CLICK.

The doorknob slowly turns, so I move quickly back to the bed with the intention of throwing the covers over my head, but not before the door swings open and a large man enters the room carrying a tray. He's smiling (nice white teeth), saying something I can't understand.

He sets the tray down near me, and when he bends his head, there is a large tattoo on the inside of his arm, and a smaller one on his neck. It looks like the astrological sign of Gemini. A brown leather strip holds his dark hair away from his big face; a mustache is on his upper lip. He then points one of his large fingers at the tray, and then at me.

*Is he the cape I imagined swirling into the room? Could he be the shadow in the bathroom?*

The man moves to a side wall that magically slides open. From where I'm sitting, there are mounds of colorful bolts of material vertically stacked in what appears to be a large closet. He touches several before extracting one, where he places it near the end of the pillow/bed. Moving toward a chair, he picks up one of my sneakers from the floor. Glancing at me, he points to the tray, and then at me again.

"I demand to know why I'm here. Where is this place and what have you done with my husband? Don't I have the right to know where I am?"

Ignoring me, the man goes back to the open closet to pull out several shoeboxes. Rummaging through several more, he tosses a pair of slipper-looking shoes onto the pile.

"Where is Ravi? I demand to know why you are holding me here!"

The man makes a loud 'tsk' sound with his tongue, then steps forward to remove the silver dome cover on the tray near me. He proceeds to pile food onto a small plate, then thrusts it into my hands.

"I'm not eating that. It smells disgusting." As I spew these words at him, the man mumbles something in my direction, then points at the mound at the end of the pillow/bed. "And you want me to change my clothes, is that it?"

The food reminds me of couscous with large and small pieces of vegetables mixed in with it, but the meat looks suspect, so I'll avoid that. My first impression is that it doesn't taste good, but the fruit seems safe. Laying the plate back on the tray, I pick up what looks like a pear. The man looks somewhat pleased with this (smiling briefly), and then points toward the bathroom, and again at the mound of fabric.

"Get out, and I'll change my clothes," I mutter at him.

Gesturing for him to leave the room, he picks up the old tray and shouts something at the door, at which time, it opens, and then closes swiftly behind him with a thud.

CLICK.

*Did he lock the door? Is this a psych-ward? Have I gone mad?*

Narrow windows are located high up on a stone wall, where faint, yet distinctive sounds filter in through the opening. I can't determine whether the window is open, yet it seems that the sounds are coming in through there. Is this the music I imagined was classical? Where is my wristwatch? Why is my mind jumping all over the place?

*Could this be Turkey?*

Crawling over the cushions and picking up the mound of fabric, I admire not only the color but also the fine weave. When I open the bundle, it turns out to be a long-sleeved blouse with a matching skirt. The skirt is so large that I could wrap it around my body twice.

*Could this be India?*

Steadier now, as nausea seems to be gone, I slowly move toward the bathroom. The usual items are present, except there is no bathtub or window. The floor is white marble, and the countertops are a complimentary white flecked granite. The shower area at the far wall has matching tile with the addition of colorful mosaics. The shower is large with oversized water spigots and handles. Set into the walls on three sides are high-tech shower jets. It is so massive that it could hide several people.

*Is this Morocco?*

The towels are fine Egyptian cotton and have a familiar scent, reminiscent of my fabric softener back home. Do I imagine all this? Am I still dreaming? My red carry-on case is next to the vanity with the airline tag still attached. Where is the rest of my luggage?

My brain suddenly flashes a picture of a woman in a restroom at the airport. Something is familiar and yet not familiar about her. She has a red carry-on case like mine. Did we laugh about that?

Opening the case to pull out the items I know are in there, I nearly panic when I can't find my purse. Where is my passport? My laptop and cellphone are also gone!

A quick inventory reveals a pair of jeans, pajamas, a t-shirt, two pairs of underwear, my makeup, toiletries, two paperback novels, a crossword puzzle book, and a deck of playing cards. Where are my sketchpad and camera?

A plastic bag that contains a rolled piece of material reminds me that it's my swimsuit; wet from the quick dip in the swimming pool the morning we left. Tossing it into the wastebasket, I wonder how odd that it's moldy after only a day.

*Ravi and I left the Kauai Airport yesterday!*

*Where is Ravi? Why am I here and he isn't? Is he home taking care of the children?*

Maybe a hot shower will clear my head? I must force myself to remain calm. It won't help the situation if I become hysterical before knowing all the facts. Ravi surely would have made sense of this if he were here. Maybe he's in another room, and this is a grand hotel.

Stripping out of my clothes, I step into the shower hoping to wash away the cobwebs that are muddling my brain. The water feels good as it hits my aching back. Automatically reaching for the shampoo and conditioner, it's within reach. That someone has thought of everything is puzzling and a little disturbing. The water is soft-jetted and hot, and I start to feel better when more flashes occur, but they don't make sense. Are these actual memories or are they leftover bits and pieces from the dream/state?

Turning off the water, I clutch one of the large towels to wrap around my body. Sitting on the toilet, it occurs to me that someone could be watching. Keeping the oversized towel wrapped around me, I switch off the light, and grab my clean clothes. When I switch the light back on, I absently glance into the mirror and ponder my apparent weight loss. I gained a few pounds on vacation, but this is a strange way to lose it!

Taking the clothes from the floor, I place them under the spigot, lathering them with shampoo to scrub away whatever lingers on the fabric. The towel bar will do as a dryer.

*Where is Ravi?*

*Without my laptop or cellphone, how will I contact my family? They must be in as much of a snit as I am by now.*

An anxious feeling begins to wash over me as I try to apply makeup with shaking hands—more to the reddish/purple mark on my forehead. Then, out of defiance, I leave the mound of fabric on the counter with the slipper-shoes, because I'm not about to put them on.

Back out in the bedroom, there's no sign of how the big man made the closet open. Now I'm not only annoyed but frustrated! Was it all a dream or was I drugged? How is that even possible? *The Wizard of Oz* floats into my head, and a familiar phrase pops into it-- I'm not in Kansas anymore.

The Persian Carpet under the sofa is exquisite. Is that gold leaf on the picture frame? Are those antique tapestries on the wall? My, what I wouldn't give to have my camera!

Severe headaches can distort things and leave a residue. The only thing that ever helped mine was to sleep it off. The odd thing is that I don't recall being this ill and this muddled with a migraine before. This one must have been a real doozy!

Suddenly, my mind starts to race as images flash past. They slow down, speed up again, stand still, then move quickly again. "NO," I hear myself scream as my legs give way and I feel myself fall to the floor.

Someone picks me up and gently lays me down on the pillow/bed, covering me with a coverlet. Something soft touches my forehead and the pounding returns along with nausea. The only thing that will help now is sleep.

"Oh God," I hear myself moan.

CLICK.

I open my eyes to see a young girl who is tiptoeing around the large chairs. How long have I been out this time? Has it been hours, could it be days?

*I'm wearing the clothes I just put on.*

A silver tray is on the pillow next to me. Near the door, the big man is sitting cross-legged on the floor with his arms across his broad chest. Studying his face, I realize he's dressed entirely in black.

Why is he here? He reminds me of Lawrence of Arabia. I was at the Kauai Airport in the Hawaiian Islands with Ravi. How could this be Arabia?

The man opens his eyes as if he senses that I'm staring at him. Blinking, he opens his mouth to speak, but doesn't and closes it again. As memories begin to flood my mind, I make a gesture for him to leave. I'm now so furious that my first impulse is to scream at him.

"You-Son-of-a-bitch! What happened at the airport? Why did you drug me? Where am I? Where is my husband? I demand an explanation!"

The man rises quickly as the young girl darts out of the room. As he reaches full height, I grab whatever's on the tray and fling it at him. He must anticipate this, as he puts his hands up to deflect a cup and saucer that has narrowly missed his head. He backs quickly out of the room.

CLICK.

A brown liquid is now making its way down the partition near the door. It is forming a sickly yellow puddle on the floor where the broken china lays shattered. I start to shake uncontrollably.

*How did I get here? Are my children all right? I need to call my mother! Who is responsible for this?*

Trying to squelch the panic that is threatening to engulf me, my thinking becomes erratic. I'm hoping my mother will take care of the children until I get back. Indignation then surfaces at the fact that unseen hands have touched my personal items in my carry-on, removing them without my consent.

Moving to the bathroom, I throw water on my face and start to cry uncontrollably. When I return to the outer room, nothing remains of the mess. Everything is correctly in its place, as if nothing happened. Even the beautiful carpet is devoid of the food and plates I threw.

"Is this some sick joke?"

I start to laugh at the absurdity. It's an irrepressible, jerky kind of laugh that won't stop. Then hiccups take over, and I wonder if I'm going mad. I was sane a few days ago, wasn't I?

A tray is sitting on a rollaway cart near the door. Under a shiny lid, there is an envelope with my name written in fancy script. It contains a single folded hand-printed note. I suddenly start to weep so hard, the words on the paper begin to blur.

*My Dearest Ellen,*

*Please accept our sincerest apologies for your present situation. It has never been our intention to detain you. Unfortunate circumstances brought you to us. Please join us for dinner this evening so that we may discuss your options.*

*Sincerely, His Royal Highness,*
*Crown Prince Akdemir Halim Abdul Obagur*

Are my captors summoning me to dinner? It's beyond ridiculous! I don't intend to have dinner with these people!

*PUT THE PIECES TOGETHER! I tell my brain. Try to think!*

KNOCK. CLICK.

"DON'T COME IN HERE!" I scream at the open door, "STAY THE HELL AWAY FROM ME! *Do you hear? Does anyone hear me? I want to go home!"*

The door closes quickly. CLICK.

A day or so passes, and there has been no word from the Mr. Prince person or his big man. They could have slipped another note under the door! The odd thing is that food trays mysteriously appear and disappear when I go in and out of the bathroom. The only logical explanation is that there's a camera hidden somewhere within the room.

*I don't care as long as they feed me.*

I'm feeling better now, but not ready to meet my captors. Could they be as curious about me as I am of them? Within minutes of thinking this, there is a knock on the door.

CLICK.

The door opens slowly as a mature-looking woman walks in with something draped over her arm. She is almost my height of five foot five inches but outweighs me by at least forty pounds. She's wrapped in colorful material like the bolts in the hidden wall closet, loose in places, tight in others. It's difficult to judge how old she is, as her face is hidden by material until she pulls it aside to smile sweetly at me.

The woman takes my arm to get me to rise, pulling me with her as she opens the wall/closet without effort. It reveals the colorful fabric where she makes a quick selection. Then she leans down to pull out a shoebox, turning to yank at my jeans. I back away from her because I don't know what she's about to do.

The woman utters a string of words I don't understand and comes at me again, but this time she reaches to pull up my t-shirt. I gently bat her hand away, and she says something else, then hands me what looks like a bodysuit.

Pulling off my jeans and t-shirt, I put the bodysuit on over my underwear, which elicits a laugh from the woman. She comes at me again, so I let her do whatever she wants this time. Taking the most substantial piece of material, she motions for me to step into it, then adjusts the waist with pins. She smiles, picking up the matching long sleeved blouse-type top, she fits this on my torso. The skirt part is loose enough to walk.

When she tries to wrap a scarf around my head, I put my hands up to protest. Defiantly standing with her hands on her hips, she then walks forward to put a piece of material (that resembles a napkin) over my head and face. Pulling it off, I toss it on the table.

The woman begins to shake her head at me, then pulls at her veil, tucking it in and out, while mumbling something. When I don't do what she expects, she picks up the piece of material to drape it over my head again, covering my face.

*Good God, why is it necessary to cover my head and face?*

When the woman is satisfied, she pushes me gently into the bathroom. When I stick my head around the corner, she's gone. Turning toward the mirror, I pull the material off my head, touching the red spot on my forehead to feel the bump that remains. I don't look like myself and wonder if my mother would recognize me. Would my children be scared? Punctuated by dark circles, my eyes look too big for their sockets.

As I come out of the bathroom, there is a knock on the door, which is followed by the loud CLICK sound. The door swings open and the big man enters. He is smiling (there are those nice white teeth again), which quickly turns into a frown. Pulling the napkin piece of material out of my hand, he plops it awkwardly on top of my head. It's weird to look through the veil, as it gives an unnatural appearance to things.

Gesturing toward the door, he attempts to take my arm, but I back away from him, cognizant of the form-fitting skirt. He shakes his big head, making a loud 'tsk' sound, waving toward the door.

"How far do we have to walk?" I ask. Expecting him to ignore me, I'm surprised to see a chair with wheels outside the doorway where several men snap to attention. He points to the chair, and I sit down. Everyone is similarly dressed, but are not as dressy as the big man. Except for the length of their hair, they look like shorter clones of him.

The men are quick to surround me. Someone pushes the chair while the big man taps the back of my head. When I look at him, he's waving a piece of material in my face. Is he threatening me with a blindfold? A silver ring with a blue stone is on one of his fingers. Does this mean he's royalty?

The men navigate down hallways, around corners, up staircases, and down more halls. If the big man thinks I will escape, how would I possibly know where to go? Wouldn't you think a place this large had an elevator? Three or four of the men hoist me up and down each set of stairs as if we weigh nothing. Still, it seems so outrageous.

It's difficult to judge how long it takes; it could be more than twenty minutes or so before we finally stop at ornately carved wood doors. They appear to be at least twelve feet tall and about eight feet wide. The decorative hammered steel hinges must be at least four feet long!

When the big man pushes the doors open, it reveals an enormous room. Turning toward me, he gestures for me to rise, and reaches to take my arm. When I stand, the chair thing and the men begin to shuffle noiselessly away.

With a hand on my shoulder, the big man guides me into the room. We walk around a large wood table that is surrounded by at least thirty heavily upholstered brocade chairs in a beige/blue hue. More chairs line the room at intervals. Matching fabric adorns the walls, and three sparkling chandeliers are hanging over the table, perfectly aligned.

*Is that Swarovski Crystal?*

The wannabe architect in me admires the solid white/pink marble columns that have dimly lit alcoves on either side of the room, which gives the entire space a grand, balanced appearance. A massive fireplace with an immense mantle is at the opposite end.

Positioned directly above this mantle is the most significant portrait I've ever seen. A man is standing next to the fireplace with his back to us. From here, he looks a lot like my Ravi, which makes me gasp at the possibility. I want to run to this man, but think better of it, as the material gathered around my torso makes fast motion impossible.

Waiting at the doors, the big man says something loud enough for the man near the fireplace to hear. His voice echoes slightly, and the man turns in our direction. At this distance, it's impossible to see his face. The man waves for us to come forward and my escort asserts slight pressure on my shoulder again.

When we get closer, I can see right away that it isn't Ravi, and it disappoints me, yet triggers a déjà vu feeling. Something is familiar about the Prince, but I don't know what it is yet.

Deliberately set with care, the three place settings of exquisite Lennox china are in a fluted pattern with gold trim. The silverware is of exceptional quality that is accompanied by Waterford Crystal. It looks strange that only three will dine here, but at this point, I'm grateful there are so few because, in a little while, I might be screaming at these people if I can't control my temper!

*My captors seem unruffled. They act as if I'm their guest. Have they contacted my family to demand a ransom yet? What could they possibly hope to gain by kidnapping me?*

The Prince motions with his left hand for me to sit down to the left of him. A sizeable silver ring set with a blue stone resides on this hand, larger by far than the one the big man wear, It glitters in the glassware as he moves his hand.

As the big man pushes the chair into the back of my legs, the Prince says, "Please sit down, Ellen." He speaks in a perfect British accent with a slight inflection. Meanwhile, the big man is waiting for me to sit down, but I don't.

"How do you know my name?" I say rudely. The big man pushes the chair more forcefully into the back of my legs again, and I have no choice but to sit down. "Who are you? How do you know my name? Why am I here? Where is my husband? I want to go home. You have no right to hold me here. Who are you?" I say to them both.

*Why is he so calm?*

The Prince reminds me of Ravi, because he has an exotic face that is a similar bronzed color, he's trim, but not skinny. He must have been educated somewhere in the west, along with training in the more delicate points of social graces.

"My dearest Ellen, we will answer all of your questions in due time. Allow me to introduce myself first. I am Prince Akdemir Halim Abdul Obagur. I am at your service."

Having decided his name is excessively long and complicated to pronounce, I'll call him Abdul. It's the only name I'll be able to remember.

"Why am I here? How do you know my name?" I demand.

Ignoring my rudeness, the Prince says, "This is my First-In-Command, Captain Jamaile."

When he pronounces the big man's name, it sounds as if he is saying Gee-Male, so that's what I'll call him. Mr. Prince gestures toward the big man, who nods his head. He does not look happy to be here.

"He will see to your every need," he adds politely.

The person named Gee-Male smiles for an instant, showing his beautiful white teeth, then clamps his mouth together in a sneer as Mr. Prince claps his hands together. Seconds later, servers dressed in starched white jackets and black pants shuffle silently around the columns and into the room. As they place platters of food on the table, others fill goblets with liquids of different colors.

Mr. Prince murmurs with Gee-Male, which promptly leaves me out of their conversation. While they converse, someone from behind me places two rolls on a little plate near my right hand. When the servers leave the room, the Prince turns toward me.

Unraveling the scarf, I've decided that there is no polite way to eat with it on and ask, "Can I dispense with this?"

The man named Gee-Male makes a disgusted sound as the Prince starts to laugh. "There is no harm in that. It is quite all right for now. Mrs. Andress is not used to our customs, and she is excused tonight."

*What is the courteous way to speak to one's captors?*

"Gee thanks! Where am I exactly?"

The Prince replies politely, "As I said in the note you were sent; we regret detaining you. We saw no other alternative at the time."

"How do you know my name? Can you please tell me how I got here? I need to contact my family and you call *this* detained? And where is my jewelry?"

*What I want to do is throw one of the rolls at his face. Is it too much to ask for a simple, straightforward answer?*

The Prince turns toward Gee-Male and he shrugs. "You were not the Target, dear Ellen. What jewelry are you referring to?"

"What do you mean by the word Target? And I'm talking about my wedding rings and wristwatch. They're missing, Mr. Prince. I would like them returned, along with my laptop, cellphone, and all the other things you took. Where's the rest of my luggage?"

The Prince gazes at the big man, then says, "I am afraid that a mistake was made, which I am not at liberty to discuss with you. The particulars are of a high-level intelligence operation, and we shall keep it to a minimum. You are not to concern yourself. I do not know anything about your jewelry. Jamaile, do you know of these things?" The big man doesn't answer, and instead, merely grunts.

The Prince's feeble explanation makes no sense to me. When I start to laugh, both men turn toward me with an alarmed expression. Then a jumbled memory begins to flash across my eyes, which triggers a feeling of déjà vu. Was this at the Kauai Airport? Did an airplane explode in a thunderous fireball as it was taking off? Then my brain starts putting it all together, and then I blurt out, "I saw a jet explode!"

The Prince's eyes flicker oddly, and he blinks several times. He takes a forkful of food and puts it into his mouth. In the next moment, his face begins to turn red, and I realize he's choking. Before Gee-Male has time to react, instinct kicks in. I push the heavy chair backward, pulling up the skirt in an un-lady-like manner and reach around the Prince to administer the Heimlich maneuver.

The room suddenly fills with people. Someone pushes me out of the way, and my thoughts go to my children. How many times have I used this life-saving technique on them? I should be home with them right now. Maybe Ravi is home, and I was the only one taken.

When the room empties, Gee-Male notices that I'm still standing and shoves me roughly back onto my chair. Reaching for a goblet to take a big gulp, what else could this be but wine?

As the Prince regains his composure, he clears his throat and reaches for a glass of water. "Thank you," he says weakly. "I will forever be in your debt, Ellen."

"Ma'dame," Gee-Male says, comically patting his head.

I don't understand until I look down to see that I have mistaken the head/veil for my napkin. Was it a sacrilege to wipe my mouth on it? Should I be more careful? Watching as the two men exchange a millisecond of comprehension, there is silence for several minutes.

"Did a plane explode in the air?" I ask.

"Yes," the Prince says, glancing first at Gee-Male, then at me. "You were taken to safety and awoke during transportation." Putting his hand to his breastbone, he presses lightly. Mr. Gee-Male mutters something toward him, but the Prince responds, "I am fine, Jamaile."

"My thoughts are all jumbled up right now, but the last thing I remember is that I was in a car. What happened to my husband?" The Prince has a pained look on his face. "If you know something, you need to explain it to me."

Panic is starting to take over when I realize that Ravi was on the plane and I wasn't. It is painfully evident that the Prince is struggling with something, as he won't look directly at me.

"Where am I and when can I go home?" My voice begins to falter and sounds far away and raspy.

The Prince bows his head, glances toward Gee-Male, then begins to whisper. "Your husband was on the plane. He was with the Target. I wish to convey my sincerest sorrow at your loss. We did everything we could to prevent it."

Gee-Male nods his big head in agreement. My throat begins to constrict as tears run down my face. Reaching for a goblet of red liquid, I decide it isn't a wine I'm familiar with, but drink it anyway. "I wanted to believe he was home with our children."

"Please accept my condolences for your loss," the Prince reiterates. "We truly had no way . . . to avoid it."

"I want to go home!" Gasping for air, I'm now sobbing in waves.

"That will not be possible," the Prince says softly. "We will help you to return you to your country when it is safe. Jamaile, should we consult the doctor for Mrs. Andress?"

Trying to compose myself, I say, "I don't need a doctor; tell me when it *will* be possible?" My body is starting to shake in alarm. "How long do I have to stay here?"

"We hope that we convinced our enemies that they succeeded in their mission," the Prince says. "You will be safe here as long as you remain out of sight."

"Wait a minute, how am I involved with your enemies? How does this affect my family and me?"

"Ellen, they may exact revenge upon us should they find out that you are here. You need to remain out of sight until the threat no longer remains and things settle down." Abdul stops to rub his throat.

"How am I involved with this? I get it, you're asking for a ransom."

Abdul looks stunned for a moment. "My dearest Ellen, we do not intend to ask for a ransom. We did not kidnap you."

"If this isn't a kidnapping, and you don't expect a ransom, and I'm not involved with the jet exploding, then why can't I go home? If I'm here against my will, it's called kidnapping! What will happen to my children? And that drug you people gave me was God-awful!"

"Ellen, we meant no harm . . . ." Abdul says, shaking his head.

My brain suddenly registers disbelief as thoughts turn to words. "You talk about enemies, but why would your enemies be *my* enemies? Did they kill my husband? Why would they do that? Are you saying they think I'm dead?"

"I do not know how to explain this to you," Abdul whispers. As the Prince and his accomplice glance at each other, I start to resent this annoying gesture.

"What does Ravi have to do with any of this? We were on vacation! Can't you get in touch with my government?"

The Prince shakes his head from side to side as Gee-Male says in broken English, "We cannot do this for you. We must wait."

"You speak English? And you ignored me all this time?"

"Ma'dame, I did speak to you, you did not talk back. I could not explain, so did not explain to you," Gee-Male mutters.

I'm trying to control my temper. "Why can't you contact my government? I'm not your enemy. I don't even know who you people are. God knows Ravi didn't have anything to do with whatever you're accusing him of, and what are you accusing him of anyway?"

"We accuse him of nothing," the Prince says emphatically. "We cannot contact your government. They do not know you are here. We are hopeful that no one knows you are here with us."

It's becoming more challenging to keep my thoughts in check. "How did I get here? Why haven't you answered my questions? How do you know my name? And where *is* here again?"

The Prince begins to frown. "We will make a workable plan, dear Ellen. It will take time to implement that plan as things do not go as quickly here as they do in your country. The less you know, the better it will be for your safety."

"What do you know about my country? You brought me here, so take me back where you found me. I won't say anything. How simple a plan is that?"

The Prince barely makes a gesture with his hand. When the practiced hands of those in service enter the room, all conversation ends until all traces of dinner is gone.

Once the servers leave the room, he says, "The time will present itself, and then we will act on that plan." The Prince nods in the big man's direction. "You are probably tired and need to rest after your ordeal."

As the Prince stands, Gee-Male responds by coming around the table behind the Prince to pull out my chair.

"You better come up with a good plan, Abdul, because you have no idea who you're dealing with!"

Gee-Male makes a disgusting sound behind me, then grabs my arm to escort me toward the large wooden doors. We are about halfway past the big table when the Prince starts to speak, and we turn toward him.

"We did not give you the drugs, Ellen. Our medical people say whoever did this gave you too much of an experimental drug. We will talk about our plan tomorrow. Good night, Ellen."

"That's it? Thanks for coming and no you will not answer any of my questions? Maybe I should have let you choke!"

The Prince starts to walk toward us. "In the meantime, please enjoy your peaceful surroundings. I am pleased you were able to join us for dinner. I am glad that you are feeling better. Thank you for helping me, I am sincerely grateful."

"You're welcome." *But am I?*

"Let Jamaile know what you need. Please trust us, Ellen. We are not your enemy." Putting a hand to his mouth, he coughs lightly. "I must take care of some pressing matters. Good night, Ellen." He turns to walk away again.

If he's not the enemy, then who is? Who would do this to my family? I need to ask one more question. Shrugging off Gee-Male's hand, I turn around. "Can I contact my family to at least let them know I'm alive?"

Prince Abdul continues to walk away, the back of his head moving from side to side in that universal language that means 'no.'

"Why can't I contact them?"

Prince Abdul continues to walk toward a door near the fireplace as Gee-Male grips my arm to pull me with him.

"Come," he says gruffly. "His Highness will talk about the plan tomorrow."

"You can't dismiss me like this. You have not explained why I'm here! My family must be out of their minds with worry by now! Those drugs nearly killed me!"

Somehow, Gee-Male has the piece of material, which he clumsily attempts to stretch on top of my head. When he opens the door, his army is waiting in the hallway with the chair contraption.

I'm shouting at no one in particular. "I want you to return my laptop and sketchpad. Do you hear me? I want my cellphone. Am I a prisoner here?"

The big man pushes me into the waiting chair and turns to close the ornate doors. As if in rewind, we go back through the maze of corridors in silence. The only sound is the muffled echoes of the men's boots on the stone floor.

Suddenly overcome with emotion, I start to weep for Ravi, my children, and the endless questions the Prince didn't answer. I don't know any more than yesterday or was that today? Perhaps it was days ago! I'm so preoccupied with my thoughts that I don't realize we're back at my room. Gee-Male pulls at my arm, then backs out of the doorway once I'm inside.

CLICK.

The sound of that lock is starting to grate on my nerves. If I'm not a prisoner, then why is the door locked? How can Prince Abdul expect me to trust him when I don't know who he is or why I'm here?

Alone with my thoughts, they start to collide with one another. Trying to make sense of my situation. I'm more aggravated by what was not said. The Prince sidestepped my questions to babble on about making a workable plan. I'm sure that they deliberately withheld information and it's unnerving when they do that silent thing! I want to know where I am. Is that too much to ask?

"All I want to do is go home to my family!" I yell.

Sadness begins to overwhelm me as the memory returns of the exploding jet, plunging me into a deep sorrow as panic returns. How can these total strangers be trusted?

"Where in the hell am I?"

Sound begins to filter in through the narrow windows that let in dim light. Without a clock to mark time, what am I supposed to do, read the shadows on the walls like a sundial?

My thoughts go to my children. Will they understand when I explain what happened to their father? Is Mother able to step in to be both parents for a while longer?

What is the reason they took my camera?

What happened to my luggage?

*Oh, now I remember, it was on the plane.*

Suddenly remembering a meditation technique, I'll use it to help clear my mind. In the past, when faced with a severe problem or design issue, it usually helped to focus on something opposite of the problem. But concentration is difficult right now, and I start to weep instead.

Could this be a side effect of the drugs?

Are they mood swings, or merely grief?

I don't feel like reading.

There's a deck of cards in my carry-on; I'll play solitaire.

*Isn't that appropriate!*

*"Time is strange.*

*A moment can be as short as a breath,*

*or as long as eternity."*

~ Cornell Woolrich

# Chapter Two

## Luxurious Captivity

Light filters through the narrow windows, giving the room a soft glow. The deck of playing cards lay scattered across the coverlet. It has been several days since dining with the Prince, and I am grateful that the food trays mysteriously appear and disappear at regular intervals.

Why haven't we talked about his plan yet? Perhaps he is punishing me for asking him so many questions when we first met.

I scramble off the pillow/bed and head to the bathroom, aware of watchful eyes, and keep the light turned off while I dress.

CLICK.

Poking my head out of the bathroom, a young girl is placing a tray on the table I have nicknamed the tree trunk. She smiles when she sees me staring at her, and I attempt to engage her in conversation, but she doesn't respond. The girl walks to the door, knocks on it, and leaves when it opens.

CLICK.

Digging into what looks like a mound of potatoes and onions, I discover that it isn't a familiar taste, but eat it anyway. The hot brown liquid must be what they think is our version of coffee. It's too bitter. To compensate for the taste, I add several teaspoons of coarse brown sugar, wondering how I'll ask for cream.

Maybe Prince Abdul and I will work on his plan to get me out of his country today. When does he think this will be, a week from now? A month from yesterday? Questions keep ruminating in my head. Why was I taken in the first place? If they don't answer my questions, how will I know things?

The jeans and t-shirt I scrubbed yesterday are finally dry. Putting these on, I wash out the dirty ones. Thinking that I should have put more underwear in the red case, I absently look in the mirror to examine the mark on my forehead; it appears mostly blue and yellow now, but I still look dreadful!

When I pull my hair back from my face, the dark bags under my eyes give me a skeletal appearance. My hair is a lack-luster auburn in need of highlights and a good haircut. I want to curl up and go to sleep, so this nightmare goes away. But I know that if I do that, it's an admission of defeat.

Something occurs to me that there might be one or more cameras hidden in either the large bedroom or bathroom. It's the only explanation for how people can move in and out of here so quickly. A search turns up nothing in either room; there are no hidden cameras and no listening devices. Just because they are not visible, doesn't mean that they aren't here. It merely means I haven't found them yet.

Muffled rustling, followed by a loud knock, startles me and I freeze with anticipation.

CLICK.

Suddenly, the door is flung open, and Gee-Male walks into the room. He is frowning. He pats my head making a motion across his face. Shaking my head pretending that I don't know what he means, he makes a 'tsk' sound with his tongue.

"You don't like what I'm wearing? Are my clothes not acceptable?"

I half expect the big man to slap me, but he doesn't. The tiniest bit of satisfaction at his lack of approval makes me smile. After all, they could have provided other clothes besides the long skirts and blouses. Some extra underwear would have been nice, too.

Gee-Male walks to the wall that is closest to the door and touches something. I'm too far away to see what he's done, but a panel slides open. He begins to rummage through the bolts of fabric and turns toward me, shaking his big head.

Handing me a colorful scarf, he says brusquely, "Come, we meet His Royal Highness to talk about his plan. Put on your head and cover your face."

Taking the scarf from his hands, I attempt to wrap it around my head, but he's impatient with my lack of quickness, and he reaches down to cross the ends over my nose, then tucks the sides in near my ears. Then he gestures toward the open door, and his army of men stand quickly at attention, discretely averting their eyes. I'm guessing they think I don't need the chair today as it isn't in the hallway.

"You walk!" Gee-Male growls.

"Sure, I guess I need the exercise. What's got you all riled up today?"

The man is big, basketball player and linebacker large. "Hump," he thunders.

From what I can gather, we aren't going toward the dining room but in the opposite direction. It's difficult to breathe with the scarf across my face, but it is easier to see where we're walking without sitting in the chair.

Although Gee-Male pushes at the back of my head to look downward, more things are visible at this height. As we move along the hallway, stone color walls in beige and tan are visible where there are glimpses of beautiful dark carved doors and tucked away alcoves with furniture every so often. I begin to crave my sketchpad as we pass large artwork in heavy frames, colorful pottery, and lamps on ornate tables. The alcoves themselves have glazed ceramic tile on the wall facing the corridor.

On either side are intricate metal screen-type hangings, but all I can see are the lower half. Perhaps they go all the way to the ceiling. It reminds me of some very private place in which to meet a clandestine lover. The amazing part is that they all seem to be different, different tile, various furniture, and in different colors.

We stop at a pair of double doors, like the ones near the dining room, but not as ornate. Gee-Male knocks on the door which he enters, leaving me in the hallway with his men. Lifting my head to look around, I can't help but marvel at the richness of the colorful tiles that frame the archway.

Moving forward to touch the wall, I'm thinking that the men aren't paying attention, but as soon as I do this, they close in automatically, and I get a whiff of their body odor. A moment later, Gee-Male opens the door, letting out what sounds like a laugh. He motions to me as the men step back into formation, escorting me inside. Prince Abdul is sitting at an enormous dark wood desk toward the back of what must either be his office or the library.

What is it about him that seems familiar? When he smiles in greeting, it triggers a déjà vu feeling, but I push it to the back of my mind because it doesn't make sense.

"Welcome, dear Ellen, welcome. Come, sit here," The Prince says, gesturing toward a chair near his desk.

"Can I take this thing off, it's hard to breathe." Unraveling the scarf, I leave it around my shoulders.

"Of course, Ellen, you may dispense with it for now," he says smiling.

The room smells slightly musty with a lemon scent. The walls are mostly heavy dark wood with bookcases along the walls stocked with all kinds of books and massive volumes. A ladder is attached to a rail that runs the length of one windowless wall.

Narrow windows are on the opposite wall, spaced between other bookcases. The windows appear glassless, but from this angle and distance, it's tough to tell. The windows might be set into thick walls, anywhere from one to two feet thick and reminds me of old buildings and castles in Ireland, where the walls were three feet thick. The tour guide mentioned that buildings constructed in this fashion had dirt and gravel sandwiched between some types of hard cement material. The thicknesses kept arrows from penetrating the walls and were meant to keep their enemies at bay.

*I do not believe we are in Ireland!*

The library is a cavernous room, but not as large as the dining hall, but like that, it has incredibly high ceilings, but the echo that was dominant there, is not present here, only a humming sound from overhead fans.

My brain is working better as it registers every nuance and color in the room. Thick Persian carpets anchor the comfortable looking furniture to the space. What might the rest of this fortress look like, that is if they allowed me to see it?

Sofas, chairs, tables, and lamps are strategically placed in the center of the room, giving it a comfortable feel. Although the furniture doesn't take up the entire space, it seems ridiculous in scale, overstuffed and large in comparison to the delicate upholstered dining room chairs.

Will I be told something of substance today? Suddenly, and without warning, the sadness of a few days ago overtakes me and I start to weep. The big man surrounds me with his arms, guiding me to the chair, sticking a box of tissues in my face, dropping it into my lap.

"My dearest Ellen, again, I am saddened for your loss," he says in a quiet tone.

*It doesn't make sense that he cares. I'm also mindful of his deadly game.*

"I wish you wouldn't address me like that. What would you know about my loss?" I snap at him.

Prince Abdul nods his head. "We have been in conference with various parties. We think we have an equitable solution; however, we must wait until we are certain it will work. The right time will come for your departure, I assure you."

"How long do *we* wait, Abdul? You don't mind if I call you that, do you?"

Glancing at Gee-Male, his expression is ghastly as he makes a 'tsk' sound. I'll bet he doesn't approve that I call His Royal Highness by one of his names. Maybe he's trying to control his temper because he's opening and closing his large hands.

"You may call me whatever you like, Ellen," he says quietly. "It takes time to put a plan of this magnitude together. It is no easy task to set into motion. There are many things to consider."

"Will you contact my government now?" I ask sincerely.

"That is not possible until you are safely out of my country." Abdul comes from behind the desk to sit half on, half off the edge, looking a little dejected. "My hands are tied in this matter. I cannot explain this to you right now."

Silently praying that he'll answer, I ask, "Can you at least explain how you know who I am?"

"I am not at liberty to discuss anything further. It could jeopardize our plan," the Prince says softly. "We cannot compromise your safety, under any circumstance."

I'm trying to be polite. "In other words, you're not going to tell me anything."

"It was luck that brought us to you. I understand that you have children, how old are they? What are their names?" the Prince asks.

"How do you know I have children, Abdul?"

"I cannot divulge this information, Ellen. You must trust me. What do they like to do with their time when they are not in school?"

*What would it hurt to talk about my family?*

"Jason is fourteen, Melanie is twelve, and Curlie is eight."

He must think this is funny, as he begins to laugh. "You named your daughter Curlie? How did you come by such an unusual name?"

*Two can play his game.*

"How do you know that Curlie is a girl?" I ask.

Abdul smiles broadly. "Perhaps she had curly hair when she was born?"

"That, and no one could pronounce her name."

Abdul seems amused. "In other words, Curlie is not her name. It is your nickname for her?"

"Yes. Why are you asking such personal questions of my family?"

Abdul half-laughs, asking, "You are not going to tell me, are you?"

"Why should I tell you anything? You haven't answered any of my questions. After all, you're treating me like a prisoner."

When the Prince cocks his head to the right, it triggers a feeling of déjà vu. "You are not our prisoner, dear Ellen, on the contrary."

Gee-Male, is impatient with the conversation. "Woman got on the plane instead of you. Our people see two women, wearing same clothes, you both have red case."

"Are you telling me that someone took my place on the plane on purpose?"

"She gave you the bad drug. She got on the plane before the door close," Gee-Male says. "You were found in the restroom."

"Now how would you know that, Gee-Male? Were you there?"

Gee-Male winces as Abdul says, "Our people took you away before the others found you, Ellen. We did not set the explosion, but rather, we tried to prevent it. We could not avert what happened." As soon as he mentions explosion, tears begin to form, then run down my face before I can wipe them away. "Our objective was to save your husband," he continues. "When that became impossible, we found and rescued you."

*This mediocre explanation doesn't sound remotely plausible!*

I'm sniffing into a tissue. "Was I supposed to die with my husband?" My voice is a high-pitched wail, and I can't seem to control it. "Ravi would never have left me in Kauai. Maybe he thought I was sitting next to him."

Abdul starts to pace the room, weaving in and out of the furniture where he stops short of the desk. "It was a terrible mistake, Ellen. Our operative was sure. . ."

Gee-Male hands me a bottle of water. "We took necessary precaution. Our man not in the right place." As they glance at each other, there is a practiced, unspoken understanding between them.

"That makes no sense. What does this have to do with my husband or me? We had a wonderful vacation. We were on our way home."

"I will try to explain," Abdul offers. "When our people found you, your life was in danger. As Jamaile said, we had no choice but to extract you from the situation. We had no way of knowing what the effects of the experimental drug she gave, would do to you. My people pulled you out to transport you to safety."

"What were your people doing there in the first place? What do my husband and I have to do with this? How are you involved?"

Abdul is thoughtful. "You began to wake up. One of our people noticed as the jet exploded. Our man administered something to aid your discomfort. Accept our sincerest apology as there was no way of knowing it would make you so ill."

"Did you know the plane would explode?"

Abdul reaches for my hand, but I recoil. "That is all we can tell you at this time."

"I demand to know who is responsible for turning my life upside down!" I'm shouting now.

Abdul blinks, saying, "You demand, but we cannot comply."

"Contact my government and get me the hell out of here!" I must be shouting louder than I suspect because Gee-Male has placed a hand on my shoulder. Does he think this will keep me quiet?

Abdul walks away from me, turning to touch the spines of some books where the shiny lettering is visible.

"You are welcome to spend as much time as you like here in the library, Ellen. You may read here or take books back to your room. Whatever you wish to do with them, will be your choice. I require three things from you: 1. There will be no contact with anyone while you are here. 2. You cannot go outside of this building unless Jamaile accompanies you. 3. You must keep a veil across your face when you are in the hallways and do not wear those jeans outside your room again."

"That's four things," I mumble.

Dropping his head in a motion that reminds me of a father who has scolded his child and is sorry afterward, then adds, "Yes, I agree that is four things. Do you understand this request, Ellen?" Abdul lifts his head, as softness comes back into his eyes.

"Oh, yes, perfectly. Where and how would I get out of here? I'd need a map to find the front door. You do have a front door, don't you?"

Laughing, Abdul says, "Then we will wait to put our plan in motion. In the meantime, please accept our hospitality while you are here and enjoy your peaceful surroundings." Making an imperceptible nod, this must mean our audience is over.

"That's it? You're still not going to answer my questions?"

Gee-Male, the ever-vigilant hulk that he is, reaches over the chair to take my right arm, yanking slightly.

"How do you know my name? Can you at least tell me that? And what is this great plan of yours, Oh Great and Powerful Oz?"

Gee-Male leads me toward the door, as my thoughts turn to my children and family; will I ever see them again?

"I bring you tomorrow. Cover head." Gee-Male pulls at the scarf, then waits. When he becomes impatient, he leans forward to take the scarf sides, and the surprising thing is how adroit he is in crossing them over my nose and mouth so expertly, tucking them near my ears. For someone with such large hands, he is quite dexterous, except for one problem.

"I can't breathe or see . . ."

Putting a big finger close to the material, he yanks it downward to uncover my eyes. Then he puts a hand on my shoulder to guide me out the door. His army of men snaps to attention where they take their usual place.

As we make our way down the passageways, more extraordinary items are visible along the corridors. Intricate ironwork blends with colorful tile in unexpected places and I catch a glimpse of a pair of colossal cloisonné vases. I peek at the treasures until Gee-Male taps the back of my head.

*Where am I? Why does my brain hurt?*

When the army stops abruptly, we are back at 'my' door. A small wood plaque with a symbol is attached to the wall near the doorjamb.

I'll try to memorize it for all the good it'll do. Gee-Male throws the door open, but I anticipate he will say something snide, so I put my hand up and walk in without his help, because, by now I know the drill. The familiar CLICK then follows when the door closes.

How long will this fiasco continue, or more pointedly will it ever change? Sadness begins to overtake me again, and I think of Ravi. What have they told my children? Are they devastated? Can we fix this? I need to contact them.

*What will they do when they find out I'm alive?*

Abdul hinted at it, but he didn't say what Ravi was involved with, but he was a good man who loved his family. We loved each other, and although our marriage wasn't perfect, it was good.

The only person who can shed light on this mystery is dead, and nothing will bring him back. My heart is breaking. A pounding headache returns, and I slump into the pillow/bed to cry myself to sleep.

I wake to motion at the peripheral edge of slumber. Someone has entered the room. A young girl has turned on a small light, where she pulls items out of a box to place them onto hangers. After she does this, she puts them into an open closet. The girl doesn't look familiar, nor does the cabinet. It isn't in the same place where mounds of material are, but further down along the same wall.

The girl smiles at me, then returns to her task as I slowly rise. The items look familiar, but they are not mine. I move closer to examine them to find the tags are missing. The girl thrusts a bundle at me, then gestures toward the bathroom.

A persistent dull ache near the base of my skull keeps me from moving quickly. After a nice hot shower, I turn off the light, because I'm very sure someone is watching. Could they also be videotaping? The clothes I plan to wash are no longer on the floor next to the vanity.

*What little elf snuck in while I was taking a shower?*

Reaching into my red case, I'm grateful the migraine tablets are in a side pocket. When I return to the outer room, the girl is gone, and so are the new clothes.

Searching for something to activate the wall panels, I'm both frustrated and annoyed that it won't open. Picking up the nearest object (the lantern thing), I fling it at the wall. Three things happen simultaneously; the glow goes out of the room, a sound like a cupboard opens, and the door of the room bursts open after the all too familiar CLICK.

Gee-Male's face says it all. He asks if I'm hurt, then notices the mess on the wall. Humorously, he pinches the bridge of his nose, then puts a huge hand on his forehead. The light from the hallway shows the consequences of throwing the lamp. The splatters slowly darken as they roll down the wall. It has narrowly missed what appears to be the secret closet.

*Surprise, there are all the new clothes!*

Gee-Male motions to someone in the hallway, and in what appears as one full motion, people fill the room to scrape up the oil. The big man shakes his head from side to side, then says, "I will return. Dress for the meal." He then points at my jeans, mumbling, "Not that." Pulling out a long-sleeved, high-necked evening gown, gruffly saying, "Wear this."

CLICK.

Who is the Prince entertaining tonight, the King of Siam? There's no way I'm putting that dress on! To my surprise, the closet contains several long wool skirts and several long-sleeved tops. Along with shoes and socks in built-in drawers near the bottom, where I discover another drawer that holds underwear and PJs.

Then I wait for what seems like hours. I've already read the second paperback and don't want to do another crossword puzzle. There is no TV, no radio, and no magazines, only my deck of playing cards. Irritation begins to surface, as I think how utterly stupid it is that they won't give me back my laptop! I'm about to throw something else at the door when there is a knock.

CLICK.

*That sound is making me edgy.*

Gee-Male throws the door open, saying, "Come, His Royal Highness waits." His face is telling me that he's not pleased with my choice of evening attire but doesn't say anything. His men are not in the hallway, and there's no attempt to hide my face. I don't know if these things alarm or surprise me. Maybe it *is* to confuse the enemy!

He does not attempt to conceal where we walk, nor is there a hand on the back of the head or any threat of a blindfold. Did they finally get the memo about not being able to navigate these hallways without getting lost?

"Don't you have a better way to get to wherever we're going, Mr. Gee-Male?"

"You like walk, we walk," he says gruffly.

"Yes, I like to walk. I could use the exercise. Where is your army tonight? I assume it's night. Without my wristwatch, it's a little tough to tell what time it is."

"No need," the big man says crossly.

"Who do you mean are not needed, my wristwatch or your men? Where's the fire, Big Guy? Can you slow down a little? You're walking too fast! Are you mad at me for throwing that lantern against the wall? If you had told me how to open the closet thing, maybe I wouldn't have thrown something at it."

I try to engage him in conversation, but Gee-Male does not want to talk. Maybe the Prince yelled at him when he found out I threw a temper tantrum and was destroying stuff.

His reaction is a surprise. "You have a hot temper," he says in a clipped tone of voice.

"That's because you people make me crazy. Why do you lock me in that room? I don't deserve this treatment and certainly not your rudeness!"

Gee-Male abruptly stops, and his face contorts when he presses his big face down to mine. Grabbing my arm roughly, I am suddenly terrified.

"No, you do not deserve this. You deserve to go out of this country. You create a nightmare for the Prince. You will go out soon! Keep walking."

He is in a foul mood tonight. It must be awkward being mean all the time. Despite his demeanor, I try to keep my composure as we walk. What I want to do is run away and move one of the heavy chairs to wedge under the door, but I probably wouldn't be able to find the room or move the chair without help.

*Oh, God, I pray silently, please deliver me from this evil!*

Gee-Male stops again. "You must. . . I account for you and guard you. I cannot allow anything to happen to you! I account for His Royal Highness and you. I account for you both. You and he must remain safe."

"I thought you were going to hit me."

"Come, he waits for you." Gee-Male opens and closes his large hands when he starts to walk again.

An involuntary shudder runs through my body. As a child, whenever this happened, my sister Terre and I would say that someone was walking across our graves. I never fully understood that, but maybe it's a prelude to my life now as a dead woman.

*Dear God, everyone thinks I'm dead!*

"We are late. I do nothing to anger His Most Royal Highness." Looking down at me, he slows a little and seems more composed. It appears he must not enjoy talking (or maybe he's unsure of his English). "I am sorry for busting out."

I want to laugh at the way he says this, but he's volatile right now, and I shouldn't anger him further. "That's okay, Gee-Male, we're all a little edgy these days."

"His Royal Highness is a good man. He does not harm you in any way. You are safe here," he says.

Without saying another word, we walk until we reach the dining room doors where Gee-Male opens them to escort me inside. The Prince is already in the dining hall, standing near the enormous fireplace. I immediately get a déjà vu feeling when we approach him. Although we've never met before the other day, this feeling will not go away. The table is set once more for only three people.

"Good evening, my dearest Ellen." He has a quizzical look on his face, then glances at Gee-Male. What transpires between them when they do this annoying thing? He indicates the chair to his left, "Please sit down. Thank you for joining us this evening. I trust you are well?"

"I'm fine, thanks for asking." The chair hits the back of my legs as a large shadow falls across my plate, forcing me to sit. "Thanks, Big guy."

Abdul waits until Gee-Male sits down. "Are you comfortable, Ellen?" The Prince signals his staff and servers enter with platters laden with food I can't quite identify. Hands reach from behind us to pour lovely colorful liquids into our goblets, exiting quietly.

I want to ask the hundreds of questions that keep ruminating inside my head, but instead say, "Yes, I'm most comfortable."

"Do you require anything?" he asks politely.

Gee-Male eyes me cautiously. "Yes, thank you for asking. I require something to do!" Would the big man bodily remove me from the room if I say something he doesn't like? What do I have to lose if I say it nicely?

"What are your interests?" Abdul asks courteously.

"I have many interests, but for starters, there's nothing to do. Without my sketchpad and laptop, I can't do anything constructive. There's no TV, no radio…no movies, no National Geographic magazines."

The Prince cocks his head to the side and gazes at Gee-Male, then back toward me. "I do not understand, Ellen. You have the whole of the library at your disposal. My dear Ellen, there is much to do here."

"I can't work on anything without my laptop." Probing what appears as fish, I then stick my fork into yellow-looking rice, noticing something that resembles stir-fry vegetables. When I look up, they're both smiling. "Why are you looking at me? It's a little creepy."

Abdul laughs lightly. "It is good to see you eat so…heartily. You will need your strength for what lies ahead."

"What lies ahead for me, Abdul? Do you own a crystal ball? How about a magic lamp where a Genie grants three wishes? It's annoying when you two do that!"

"What do you find that is annoying, Ellen?"

They look from one to the other. "You did it again!"

"I do not understand why you are requesting these things," the Prince says, pushing food around on his plate.

"As much as I love to read, my dear Prince, I can't read all day. A person needs stimulation, people to talk with, a shopping trip maybe. I feel like your prisoner locked up in that room all the time."

"That is not our intention. We certainly do not want you to feel like a prisoner. There are other things you can enjoy; however, this shopping is out of the question."

Abdul gestures and servers stream back into the dining room with different platters and bowls filled with steaming contents. He picks up one of the goblets, sips slowly, eyeing Gee-Male over the rim, and says, "You are our guest while you are here. You should have everything you need."

"That's a laugh. I don't feel like a guest, and no, I do not have everything I need."

Abdul changes the subject. "Our plan progresses nicely, Ellen. We have a fine group of compatriots who are willing to put their lives on the line for you."

Trying to keep rudeness out of my voice, "How *soon* will that be, Mr. Prince?"

"We must wait for the right time. Jamaile has many men involved, and it is their responsibility to see to it that our plan follows a certain path, shall we say. I assure you that we will achieve our goal quickly, and your journey will begin soon."

"Can you give me a hint of when that might be? Should I pack for a trip tomorrow, maybe next week, or the week after?"

"As I have told you, we must wait," he says softly. Turning toward Gee-Male to talk, this rudely leaves me out of the exchange. Do they know how irritating this is?

Moments later, Abdul turns to face me. "We know your family has buried you and your husband." When he says this, tears start to roll down my face. "Perhaps we will talk about this another time."

We eat in silence until Abdul gestures and servers remove the platters of food, plates, goblets, and silverware, while others quickly replace them. Someone sets a tray of tiny pastel delicacies near me. *They make my mouth water just looking at them.*

"Go ahead, Ellen, enjoy them," the Prince says, grinning.

"Speaking of family, don't you people have large families? Where are all your brothers and sisters? Who are the people in the painting?" I'm stuffing another delicate pastry into my mouth as they are so good they seem to melt on my tongue! Did I moan with pleasure?

Blinking, he says, "The King is out of the country and the people in the portrait are my family. They are not involved in delicate matters that don't concern them."

It sounds a little too rehearsed, yet he offers nothing else in the way of explanation. I can determine that he's lying because the vein at his temple is visibly pulsing. Gee-Male then slurps, and I catch him glaring at the Prince; did he roll his eyes! They play a deadly game with my fragile psyche. I resolve here and now to beat them at their own game.

"These are wonderful, not too sweet, but very tasty. Would your chef give me the recipe?" I ask warily.

"You may come to the library to select as many books as you wish, Ellen, if you need something constructive to do."

"That would be great. May I come tomorrow?" I'm stuffing another morsel into my mouth, trying to decide if I'll shove several into my napkin or ask if I can take some to my room.

"You may come late morning if you wish, or we can have books brought to your room. We have gathered an extensive selection from around the world. We will talk more about our plan then."

*It appears that the library will be my only form of entertainment.*

Pointing to the tray of goodies expecting a negative response, "May I take some of these with me?"

Abdul seems amused at this. "Of course, Ellen, they will be delivered to your room."

Since he's in such a good mood, perhaps I should ask for other things. "May I also request some fruit, a coffee pot, some ground coffee, maybe a few crackers?"

His eyes widen in surprise. "Jamaile has already taken care of this for you," Abdul sighs.

"Let me guess. Is it hidden in a secret compartment in the wall like everything else?"

Gee-Male does not look happy. Did he show this to me when I was under the influence of the monster drug headache?

"I will show you," Gee-Male says glumly, "one time more."

The Prince stands to signal that the meal is over. "We will talk again tomorrow. Thank you for coming to dine with us this evening, Ellen, I hope you have a good evening."

As Abdul turns to walk away, Gee-Male moves to my side of the table to pull my chair away.

Pleading as gently as possible, I ask, "Would you please answer one question?"

"Questions will have to wait as it has been a rather long day. Good night, my dear Ellen," the Prince says smiling.

Something in his voice or demeanor has me wondering why he is so guarded tonight, but I can't quite put my finger on what it is. "How hard would it be for you to answer one question?"

As Gee-Male takes my arm to lead me toward the door, Abdul says, "Good night, Ellen." He remains standing near the fireplace watching us leave.

Pulling away from Gee-Male's grip, I turn toward Abdul. "I would like to come to the library tomorrow. Tell your chef the pastries are delicious. Would you answer one question?"

Gee-Male is tugging at my arm when the Prince shrugs his shoulders. "One question, then."

"How long have I been here? You owe me that much!"

The Prince is quiet for a moment. "I owe you that much, that is true. You have been here approximately two months." He says this so quietly I almost miss it.

"Did you say two months?" Glancing at Gee-Male, he nods his head. "But that's impossible!" In my mind, I've only been missing (or dead) two weeks, three at the most. The cold fingers of panic start to grip my chest. "What do you mean I've been here two months?"

Gee-Male's hands are restraining me. "Come, Ma'dame," he insists.

I'm not one to let go easily, so I plead, "Please explain this to me!"

Abdul calmly walks toward us but stays a good ten feet away. "The woman that assumed your identity was placed there by our enemies. The date of the explosion was 17th of March. You arrived here the 18th; it is now the 20th of May."

It has not been a few weeks as I thought, but two months! "Nooooo!" Slipping out of Gee-Male's hands, he latches on quickly to prevent me from hitting the stone floor. As my brain starts to register these facts, my mind won't reconcile the time frame.

"You cannot go home to the life you once had, dear Ellen. We will talk more tomorrow." Abdul nods in Gee-Male's direction and then walks away.

Gee-Male picks me up as gently as a rag doll, carrying me back to my room. Something about how he moves is comforting. He must be aware of this as he relaxes his stiff arms. Then I realize that his job is to protect, not harm. Touching my head with his in a gesture that is so tender it makes me weep, he then whispers, "not to give up" and "you will go when it is safe."

On the long trek back, he doesn't appear to either sweat nor alter his stride. Standing me upright in the hallway, he opens the door, and says, "I will take you on the journey when the time is right," he says, walking toward the secret wall. Moving to the left of the oil stain, he looks down at the floor. Pointing, he says, "Two steps to left, press here."

The undetectable depression opens to reveal a complete kitchen.

"You must be kidding," I mutter.

"No kid is true," he says calmly.

Moving to the opposite wall and looking down at the floor behind the sofa, he says, "Press here."

It reveals a large flat-screen TV that is sitting on an equally big credenza with doors. He then bows slightly and leaves the room.

CLICK.

Temporarily distracted, and afraid the walls might swallow up the kitchen, I search for how to open the secret wall panels and study where two of the stone tiles come together precisely where the wall slides away. An almost invisible indentation makes the kitchen disappear behind it.

With the kitchen fully open, I inspect the contents. Each cupboard is full of dishes, glasses, boxed and canned goods, all products that are from the U.S. Further down is a full-size refrigerator, microwave, stove, sink, dishwasher, washer and dryer, iron and ironing board. Opening the cupboard above the machine, I find a box of laundry soap that I use at home.

The refrigerator is stocked with bottles of water, juice, iced tea, and an assortment of fruit, while the freezer contains packaged food. Is this someone's apartment? The TV catches my interest, but there's no regular TV and no cable. Rummaging through the credenza, it contains movies I don't recognize.

What does Abdul mean that the life I knew is gone? How are my children getting through this horrible ordeal? How are Mother and my sister, Terre, coping with all this?

Suddenly overcome with grief; I start to sob uncontrollably. In the bathroom, I throw cold water on my face. When I return to the large room, there's a plate of tiny desserts on a tray on the tree-trunk table. Irked that people slip in and out without detection, I leave the kitchen panels open, leaving the light on over the sink for security.

Grief descends upon me as I remember that it was twenty years ago today that Ravi and I were married. We were going to celebrate by taking the children to a hotel to have a wonderful weekend together. That will never happen now.

The light diminishes through the narrow windows, and the room grows dim, and it's too dark to play solitaire. I wait for the music or chanting to start. What time is it? Is it eight o'clock? Is it nine?

Too exhausted from crying, I get ready for bed determined to form my plan. Tomorrow, May 21st, I will make a calendar to track this plan, as soon as I find paper and a pencil. I know there will be challenges along the way, but I'll keep my wits about me, observing anything and everything.

My thoughts turn to my family once again. When my parents were children, they had to overcome great odds. Born during the late

1930's, they lived in France during a war-torn Europe. Their world was turned upside down by nighttime bombings, lack of food, and clean water. What a miracle to have survived when most or all of their family did not.

They also made a point not to dwell on their past, saying that Aristocrats took them out of orphanages, and on to Argentina. They grew up in different areas, Mother in the small landlocked province of Tucuman and Daddy near Buenos Aires.

Terre and I traveled with Mother and Daddy extensively during our youth. They exposed us to a multitude of cultures, performing arts, museums, and grand openings.

We sipped tea at the Russian Tearoom; saw the Rockettes at Radio City Music Hall, numerous plays and live performances. We chowed down on some of the world's most exquisite cuisine and learned firsthand what most students only collected from books. We then shared this with our classmates in the form of journals and photographs.

Daddy and Mother took us to such grand places as Versailles in the spring and Venice in the fall, where we marveled at the architecture of St. Mark's Cathedral and the city built on water. We walked the same cobblestone streets as Shakespeare!

Then, during one great summer of travel, we strolled on one part of The Great Wall of China, took cruises down the Seine and Danube Rivers, and touched many Mayan Ruins. Mother's passion for Renaissance Art took us to France and Italy's renowned museums where we saw humidity-controlled rooms filled with vibrantly colored portraits from the Twelfth and Thirteenth Centuries.

My mind wanders back to Ravi and our first years together. What will my life be like without him? I can't believe he's dead. We had such plans for the future. Now all of its gone and I'll never see him again!

Waking with the exciting prospect that my plan will begin soon, the light over the kitchen sink illuminating the space gives me comfort. Could the monster of a headache be attributed to the months without caffeine?

Searching through the cupboards to locate the coffee pot and can of coffee that I discovered last night, I settle in to make myself some breakfast.

Pressing the indentation that opens the closet to reveal the new clothes, I choose some that look cheerful. Trying the door handle to see if it will open, it doesn't.

A quick rummage through the drawers produced nothing to write on, let alone a pen or pencil. Without these items, there's no way to capture my ideas. Anger is beginning to cloud my thoughts.

Two months is a long time. Will my children freak out when I finally contact them? Please God, help me be strong for what lies ahead; give me the strength to persevere. How will I get out of here and get back to my family? I don't have a cellphone, so I can't call for help.

Deciding to play along with Abdul for the time being, I begin to formulate questions in my head, repeating them until they're committed to memory.

1.   *Why were Abdul's people at the airport?*
2.   *Who is this other woman? Why did she take my place?*
3.   *Why am I here? Does Prince Abdul know Ravi?*
4.   *How does Abdul know my name?*
5.   *Who is responsible for blowing up the airplane?*
6.   *Who are Abdul's enemies and why would they be mine?*
7.   *What does this have to do with Abdul and his country?*
8.   *Why would they take me to keep me safe?*
9.   *Why can't I go back to my life?*
10.  *Lastly, why do they lock me in this blasted room?*

Spending the rest of the day playing cards and crossword puzzles, I rummage through the movie cabinet. I'm not surprised that it contains an odd array of DVD selections. Alice in Wonderland looks interesting. Inserting the disc, I stretch out on the over-sized sofa, making a mental note that there are no music CDs of any kind. When the movie ends, I sit up, realizing that my mind has cleared sufficiently.

Pounding on the door every so often and yelling at it produces nothing. It soon becomes apparent that today is not the day to visit the library nor discuss my departure.

There's nothing to write with except my lipstick, and I won't sacrifice that, so I try to come up with what I could use. Would the back of a can of soup work? What are the facts? Just the facts Ma'am. Sargent Friday, from the old *Dragnet* TV series, pops into my head.

A shudder runs through my body, which morbidly makes me think someone is walking across my grave again. It's the second time in as many days that this has brought back this memory. What must my children be enduring, having to bury not one, but both of their parents?

The most frustrating thing is the locked door; is this to keep me in or to keep others out? Do they think this is the proper treatment for a guest? Determined to survive this ordeal, I try to squelch negative thoughts.

Mother said to make lemonade when you have lemons, be positive, and take control of the situation. Daddy taught us other things; when bullies threaten, be smarter than they are, wait, and listen. Somehow, I'll get through this and go home. I'm a strong person! Or at least I was a few days ago.

A childhood prayer comes to mind about a guardian angel. Mother and Daddy used to recite it to my sister Terre and me at bedtime, then Ravi and I recounted it to our children as we tucked them in at night when they were little.

'*Angel of God, my guardian dear; to whom his love, commits me here, ever this day, be at my side, to light and guard, to rule and guide. Amen.*'

By hook, or by crook, tomorrow, I start *my* plan!

*"In three words I can sum up*

*everything I've learned about life; It goes on."*

~ Robert Frost

# *Chapter Three*

## The Plan Is Formulated

The next morning, when the room floods with light, I put a DVD into the player. Each DVD is approximately one and a half to two hours long which helps with the passage of time.

Mid-morning, I start pounding on the door with the back of a metal spoon as no one has come to take me to the library.

"Is anyone out there?" I yell at the door.

*There is no answer.*

Pounding on the door again, yelling louder, "Can you hear me? Please get Gee-Male!"

*There is still no answer.*

Pounding on the door for the third time, I scream, **"Can you hear me? Please get Gee-Male!"**

A short time later, a familiar KNOCK is followed by a loud CLICK as Gee-Male flings the door open. "What do you require, Ma'dame?" he snarls in greeting. He's standing inside the doorway with his feet between the doorjamb and the hallway.

"Abdul said I could go to the library. That was yesterday. Would you take me there now?"

The only sound is the static-charged air that is rustling in deafening silence around his big head. I'm disappointed, as there is no semblance to the sensitive man who carried me to this room the other night. What did I expect from this unpredictable, prickly person?

"Come," he says in a flat tone. "Where is a head cover?"

Holding up the scarf, throwing it around my head, saying, "It's right here, Big Guy." To which he makes a guttural sound that resembles a chuckle.

One man guards the hallway, and he averts his eyes quickly when I look in his direction.

"Aren't you afraid I'll try to escape?" Panting behind him, I'm trying to keep up with Gee-Male's long strides. "Is Abdul ready to go over his plan yet? Why didn't anyone come for me?"

"Plan not ready," he says curtly.

"Why am I locked into that room? I couldn't find my way out of here if my life depended on it!"

He's in no mood to talk, so we go up and down, over and around until we reach the large double doors of the library. No one is guarding the entrance, and when Gee-Male throws the wooden door open, the only thing that greets us is the heady aroma of lemon and leather that mingles with a musty odor that permeates the room.

"Get books. Do quick," the big man says brusquely. "I have much to do." Is his facial expression telling me that he's tired of babysitting me?

As Gee-Male stands near the door, I wander around the large room, moving toward the bookcase at the farthest wall. Something catches my eye on Abdul's impossibly large desk. Glancing away, I direct my attention to the extensive sets of matching volumes that take up the lower shelves. Oversized, heavier atlas-type books take up residence on most of the bottom ones.

On a shelf about chest-high, there are tiny books as small as four inches. The script-like writing along with colorful animated pictures depict life in the desert. Some are worn and tattered; some appear brand new. Running my finger across many of the other books, I pull some of them out, push them back in, then glance at Gee-Male occasionally to see if he's watching.

At the next set of shelves, there are books of various sizes and colors that take up much of the space above the larger ones. The sheer number of them is surprising, as is the fact that most of them are leather-bound with gold lettering. Abdul and his family spent a small fortune to fill the shelves with such wonders. I can't read most of the titles, and the layout of this library seems disorganized.

An odd-sized Italian book catches my attention. It's an ancient and very rare book titled: HIERONYMI Cardani Medici Mediolanenfis DE SVBTILITATE. Part of my degree was studying Historical Italian Architecture and Literature. Medici is an ancient Italian family name associated with great wealth. Setting this book on Abdul's desk to start the pile to take back to my room, it occurs to me that this library might contain other rare and first editions.

Navigating through the titles is difficult as they're mostly script. Further along are many English titles. Pulling *To Kill a Mockingbird*, I can't shake the feeling that I've touched this book or seen its twin recently. Reaching for another commonplace book, *For Whom the Bell Tolls*, I add these on top of the Italian volume. They have extra blank pages that will come in handy later.

Several other titles look familiar: *The Origins of Species, The Wind, and the Willows, The Art of War,* and *The Lord of the Rings: Book 1*. My hand lands on a pristine volume of *Moby Dick*, and I confirm it's the 1st edition. The famous first sentence, "Call me Ishmael" is a familiar one. A memory flashes of the first time I read it, making me laugh. It's as if Mr. Melville used his chapters for topics-of-thought rather than chapters. This little book also has several blank pages both front and back.

To forestall going back to my room, I continue to wander around, occasionally sneaking glances at Gee-Male to gauge his mood. He hasn't moved from the doorway, although he now appears angry.

A world globe with a brass ring around the middle is sitting on a carved wood stand near Abdul's desk. Giving the ball a little shove, and moving in to get a better look, I can't decide whether the letters are numbers or the numbers are hieroglyphs. Although the continents are in the right places, I can't read their names. Gee-Male mumbles something and has an amused look on his face, but gives no hint as to why he finds this humorous.

"Where is Abdul this morning?" I ask nonchalantly, loud enough for Gee-Male to hear. I lay the books on the desk, pushing something close to them, being careful to conceal what I'm doing. Either he can't hear me, or he chooses to ignore my question. "Where is Prince Abdul this morning? Why isn't he here?"

Gee-Male looks displeased. "His Royal Highness meets with official peoples. Are you done? We go."

"He said he would be here when I came. Oh, I forgot, that was yesterday." Walking toward him, I stop near the sofas.

"Men are part of plan to...it takes great plan..." he seems to struggle with the words or perhaps he's angry that he's here. "It is a big plan for you."

"Can you tell me about this plan? If it involves me, shouldn't I be consulted about it?"

The big man shifts slightly, then uncharacteristically raises his eyebrows, saying, "You must wait for His Royal Highness to talk about the plan. We go now, come."

"I'm not finished."

"You have books, come, we go now, Ma'dame," Gee-Male says, waving his hand.

"Is there some paper here, maybe a pen to write with?" When he doesn't answer, I walk back to the desk and turn to stare at him. "Gee-Male..." Right after I say his name, he closes his eyes and his face contorts. It's odd behavior, and I don't understand it. "Gee-Male, I will not use the paper to send a message. I can't even see out the windows, let alone throw anything out one of them. I want to make a list, so I don't forget things."

"No," he mouths, shaking his head from side to side.

"You can watch me; you will see I'm only making a list. Please, Gee-Male, as a favor to me?"

His expression softens, then returns to the stony face of a moment ago. His eyes flicker an acknowledgment, but his mouth forms the word NO again. He must take great pleasure in torturing me.

Sliding the pile of books toward me, I'm careful to keep the stolen items in the space between the bottom volume and my body. When the full weight is in my arms, the books nearly tumble to the floor. Gee-Male moves to open the door when I approach but doesn't offer to help. "This is heavy," I snap at him. "Can you at least take the ones on top?"

Holding onto the bottom book pressed tightly against my body, he reluctantly takes the top three books and escorts me back to my room in silence.

Then I chuckle that the stolen pen and pencil taken from Abdul's desk will unite with the extra pages from the volumes to create my journal. My plan can now begin. I need to document this bizarre experience, and with a calendar, it will be easy to count down my journey home, or at least back to the United States. It'll help me to stay focused and sane, or at least that's the immediate plan.

During my search for electronic bugs, I checked the kitchen and surrounding surfaces, flushing what I found down the toilet, but I know I'm being watched. Taking *Moby Dick* into the bathroom, I turn off the light. With a little coaxing, the pages come away easily. Doing this to a book is a particularly heinous crime on a literary work-of-art, but under the extenuating circumstances, there's no choice in the matter.

Returning to the outer room and pretending to read, I print as small as possible to conserve space. Since there's little privacy, a kitchen towel, draped across my arm over my hand, should disguise what I'm doing.

Moving backward to the date Ravi and I started our trip on March 8th, I draw a grid using a plastic movie case. When I'm not working on it, I'll hide the pages in the red case under the plastic that forms the bottom. Then I'll put the pen and pencil in the coffee tin in a kitchen cupboard.

My feet are suddenly cold from walking on the stone floor without my sneakers, and the air feels damp. How is this place heated without a fireplace in each room?

*Something hot to eat or drink would be nice right about now.*

Homemade soup will do, but a rummage through the kitchen drawers didn't produce a knife. Trying to cut vegetables with a plastic one is useless as it doesn't take long for the blade to break.

Hoping to arouse the guard in the hallway, I pound on the door, but there is no answer. "Anyone out there?" Have they dispensed with the guard? "**Please get Gee-Male. I have a problem**!"

Perhaps ten minutes later, there's a familiar KNOCK, followed by a loud CLICK. An uncharacteristically out-of-breath Gee-Male flings the door open.

*Have I taken the big man away from an important task?*

Gee-Male passes one of his large hands over his face in an exaggerated manner, then sniffs the air. The meat I found in the freezer is simmering on the stove, and it's becoming aromatic.

Waving the carrots, narrowly missing his big nose, I say, "How am I supposed to cut these without a proper knife? I can only eat the food by overcooking it. It's darn time you gave me a decent knife."

"I will return," Gee-Male says as he backs out of the doorway, pulling the door shut.

CLICK.

Filling in what I remember, starting a grid for April, I wait for the big man to come back. Sometime later, he presents me with a small, but dull paring knife which will at least cut vegetables, adding them to the already thickening meaty broth. Much to my delight, there's a supply of homemade biscuits in the freezer.

*They were not there yesterday.*

Picking up *Moby Dick*, I read it in case someone questions me. As I reacquaint myself with the character, Queequeg, I laugh aloud as it's almost as difficult to understand as Shakespeare; one needs an interpreter (such as an English Literature Professor) to ascertain the meaning of Mr. Melville's words. But then, reading is not the objective, the blank pages are.

I wonder what the terrain looks like outside. If I can see it, it might give a clue as to where this citadel resides. The only noises I've heard are muted sounds that filter up from below at different times of the day. Perhaps it means there's no activity going on.

What's the climate like outside? Is this an oasis in the desert? It does seem to be warm during the day and cool during the evening. Are we near a mountain? That might account for the dampness that continues to seep into the room.

Deciding that I need to look out the narrow windows, I wonder if the oversized monster chairs, might support my weight; however, they're too heavy to move. Hoping the tree-trunk table might work, half rolling/half pushing it under one of the narrow windows, I gingerly step onto the middle with one foot at a time, grasping the base of the window with my fingers.

The windowsill is about six feet off the floor, and it would take a ladder to reach it. But if I use three cushions from the pillow/bed one on top of the other, it could help me to gain elevation. After stacking them I notice that it's warmer the higher I rise, but without more height, the only thing visible is the top of a wall and clouds that drift past. Add another cushion, and it could all topple over.

*Is this the Sahara Desert?*

The soup sputters, startling me back to the room. My mind begins to wander as I stir the soup/stew. Maybe I can attach a long spoon handle to a mirror. Retrieving a sewing kit and a small mirror from my red case (minus the tiny scissors that someone removed), I attempt to attach the mirror to the spoon. When the thread breaks for the fourth time, I give up, putting the furniture back.

As I'm about to take a bite out of my biscuit, there's a knock on the door. When I don't respond, Gee-Male unlocks the door and propels himself into the room. The quizzical look on his face reminds me of the character named Kramer, who comically burst into Seinfeld's apartment in every episode of the sitcom. Unlike Kramer, when Gee-Male does this, it's not funny.

"You know; I find that very offensive when you do that! I would appreciate it if you would stay out in the hallway until I permit you to enter! You open the door and walk right in. Did it ever occur to you that I might be in a compromising position?"

Gee-Male does not come into the room nor does he shut the door. "His Royal Highness asks if you are well. Do you require any thing?" he says sniffing the air.

"Yes, I require that you return my possessions. Then ask the Most Royal High & Mighty Prince to give my cellphone and laptop back."

"His Royal Highness wishes you join him for the evening meal," he says through clenched teeth.

"Tell his Most Royal Pain in the kumquat that I've already eaten my dinner. And you may tell his Most Royalness that I won't be accepting his invitation for this or any other night unless of course, he returns my things."

*He can jump in the sea, for all I care!*

Gee-Male frowns, saying, "Ma'dame, many peoples work on your plan. It does not go quick. His Highness will not like that you do not come. Would you come now?"

"No. How much longer will I have to wait for this great plan to be put into action, Gee-Male? My family is likely going crazy right now without me!"

The big man flinches. "Almost done; plan almost done. Do you require anything more? Do not ask for items!"

"I require that you contact my government."

"You ask for what we cannot give you," he says, shaking his head.

"I require that you allow me to go home! Pass that little tidbit on to your High and Mighty Mr. Prince for me, would you?" Taking a bite of the biscuit, I continue to eat my stew.

I must be testing his patience today as Gee-Male bends his head slightly, saying more gently this time, "Almost time for the plan. Be patient longer. Come to the meal. He will tell you."

"I can't possibly accept his invitation, because I have to wash my hair tonight."

With that, Gee-Male backs out of the doorway and closes the door with a thud.

CLICK.

Why does he lock that stupid door? I wouldn't be able to find my way out of this labyrinth of a place if I had a map! Will Gee-Male get in trouble for not coercing me into coming to dinner? Will Prince Charming come in search of me? Maybe he'll send Gee-Male to slay a dragon or two.

*I do not care!*

As the escapades of Captain Ahab and his cronies continue, *Moby Dick* becomes tedious to read. Now I'm wondering why I picked this, of all books to read from the myriad of wonders from the library!

As I'm about to rifle in the cupboards for a treat, there's a knock on the door.

CLICK.

Abdul walks in ahead of a server who carries a large tray. Setting this on the tree-trunk table, he averts his eyes, and backs out of the room, shutting the door behind him. The server could be anyone from the dining hall or any number of Gee-Male's men dressed as one.

"You were missed at dinner this evening, Ellen," Abdul says, in a quiet voice. Sitting down on one of the upholstered chairs, he gazes at the TV screen and the animated movie that's on with no sound. "You are perhaps upset with how long it takes to implement our plan? Is that why you do not come to dinner?"

"That and why the door is locked. And whenever anyone wants to talk with me, you all waltz in without my permission. I have absolutely no privacy!"

"My dear Ellen, I did not realize it was offensive to you. It is for your protection. Gee-Male has the only key. He is keeping you safe."

"Really? A prisoner has more privacy than I do. What if I was in the middle of dressing and Gee-Male walked in on me? Oh, I forgot, you have spies that watch, so you know what I'm doing all the time, don't you?"

"Ellen, this can be explained." The Prince is giving me a sincere look, but I have learned that this is a tactic of his. "I am curious. Do you often read and watch a movie at the same time?"

"It helps me think. Why don't you install an intercom?"

"Intercom?" Abdul repeats the word as if he has never heard of it before. "That is an excellent idea, Ellen."

"And why would I want to have dinner? It's not as if we have stimulating conversations. You don't answer any of my questions. You made these *peaceful surroundings* so comfortable, why would I want to leave them?"

"Ellen…my hands are tied, so to speak. I am not at liberty to discuss most of the things you question." Abdul sniffs the air, as the soup/stew lingers.

"What happened to us discussing *the plan*? I waited for days and then had to pound on the door until someone went to get Gee-Male."

Abdul stands abruptly. He starts to walk around the room, stopping to finger the binding on *Moby Dick* on top of the pile of books. "Are you enjoying the books? You have chosen some rather diverse titles; *DE SVBTILITATE* is an odd one. It would be an interesting book to read?"

"Yes, if you have an affinity for architecture, science, and old things, which I do. They correlate to one another. You probably haven't read a fraction of the books you have in your library. Do you even have time to read?"

The Prince continues to walk. "I see that you have discovered the kitchen." He touches the cabinets, the tapestries, and then stops for a moment to look at me. "My pastry chef has made something extraordinary for you tonight." When there is no reaction from me, he lifts the lid off the plate to reveal mounds of chocolates, fresh fruit, and what appears to be whipped cream. "I had hoped you would join us, nonetheless, here they are," he says quietly.

"What is it you want from me, Abdul?"

"I came to see if you are comfortable, Ellen. You have not been to dinner for several days. I wanted to tell you that we are working out the details of your journey home."

"Cut the crap, Abdul. I'm comfortable for a prisoner."

An uncomfortable silence ensues for several minutes until he begins to speak. "As I told you several times, you are not a prisoner, my dearest Ellen. You are our guest. I trust you are well?"

"Then why do I feel like a prisoner?"

"You are free of the headaches now?" Abdul asks, changing the subject.

"Why on earth, would you care whether I have headaches or not?"

"Have we not provided everything you need?" Abdul persists.

"Sorry to disappoint you, Royal Highness, sir, you've essentially taken everything I value and refuse to return them to me. When the hell can I go home?"

"There is no need for the use of profanity, Ellen. It is regretful, but we cannot take the slightest chance of your discovery here. It would mean a terrible consequence for me, for my country, and for you," he says sternly.

"What are you talking about?"

"I cannot discuss this further," Abdul murmurs.

"Will you return my things when I leave here?"

"No, Ellen, we cannot return your items," he says soberly.

"I can understand why you would restrict access to the internet, but what do you think I'm going to do with a sketch pad? I'm a designer. I'm always thinking of new things and combinations. I design stuff."

"Again, Ellen, your safety is our priority," he sighs.

"This conversation is making me crazy. What does that have to do with anything? Why didn't you leave me in the restroom and let the authorities take care of things?"

"We could not do that. We made a promise." Abdul appears sad and then looks down at his hands, rolling the big silver ring with the blue stone around his finger. "We took a great risk in doing so."

"If it was such a great risk, you should have left me there!" My eyes fill, and all attempts to stem the flow of tears seem lost. "Why is *your* problem *my* problem?"

"We were honoring a promise, Ellen." Standing abruptly, he walks toward the door. "I have said too much."

"Wait! I have questions. If you don't want to answer them, say you can't, and we'll move on."

Abdul turns to face me. "Alright, provided you do not ask how and why again." He seems very sober tonight, and it continues to bother me that he reminds me of Ravi.

"How do you know my husband?"

Abdul walks back to the chair and sits down. Detecting a slight twitch along his jawline, he clenches his teeth and finally says, "I am not at liberty to discuss anything to do with your situation at present."

I guess it's not a lie to him if he skirts the truth. "You mean that at some time in the future, you'll discuss it with me?" I'm trying to remain calm anticipating his answer will be an emphatic no.

"That possibility exists," he smiles pleasantly. "Perhaps sometime in the future."

"UGH!" I say in frustration. "Will you give me a straight answer?"

"Will you stop asking me questions I am not at liberty to discuss?" he says in retaliation, as a little laugh escapes his throat.

Without thinking, I say, "Touché."

"Do you fence?" he asks with unexpected enthusiasm.

"No, do you bowl?"

Abdul's face splits into laughter, showing his perfect white teeth, and his demeanor instantly changes. "You seem like a worthy opponent to parry with, Ellen," he says lifting his eyebrows.

"Funny, I thought we were sparring, as in boxing."

"Would you like to have a fencing lesson? I could arrange it. A Master comes to the Royal Palace several times a month," he says quickly. He is the one who taught…"

"I'm not interested in fencing, but thanks anyway. What I want is my sketchpad, cellphone, and all the other items you took."

"Sadly, I cannot do that," he says softly.

*Then I don't feel guilty about the missing pages used for my notes.*

"What do I have to do with this promise you spoke of?"

"That, I cannot answer at this time." Abdul appears sad again, then he stands, bids me goodnight, and abruptly leaves the room.

"Wait, I want to ask…"

CLICK.

Abdul made a promise, but what does that have to do with my family? Trying to distract myself, I start a May calendar, filling in what activities or appointments that come to mind, sad when I print Jason's birthday in one space and almost lose it when I write my wedding anniversary in another.

What is the mystery between Prince Abdul and my family?

What is the thread connecting Ravi and the woman on the plane?

Since there has been no contact for days, I work on my calendar and watch old movies, but then it dawns on me that the Prince might be upset with me for being so rude to him the other night.

*Pounding on the door brings only silence no matter how loud I scream.*

Finally, a note slips under the door to ask if I will come to the library. Two can play this game! I'll not comply unless they return my possessions. I write this on the paper and slip it back under the door. This behavior goes on for two additional days, and then I start to worry they won't replenish the food.

Starting the month of June, hiding it with the other notes at the bottom of the red case, I'm sad about what I've been missing by being absent from my children's lives.

Tired of this lack of interaction with others, I consent to go to the library when Gee-Male comes to the door. His mood is difficult to judge. Is he exasperated, or relieved my self-imposed exile is over. He insists on the headscarf, asking me to change into a long skirt and long-sleeved blouse, refusing to budge until I do.

We walk the hallways in silence until Gee-Male turns to inform me of the meeting that's taking place in the library. In his broken words, he does his best to tell me that His Royal Highness feels it's in my best interest to be present.

Before I go in, there are a few rules. I'm not to speak unless someone addresses me personally and I'm not to move once I'm sitting down. Gee-Male will touch my shoulder if I'm supposed to respond, and squeeze my shoulder if I'm doing something wrong or I'm to keep quiet.

"Show me what you mean by a touch on my shoulder."

Gee-Male thumps his index finger one time on my left shoulder. "If I give signal, you can speak. Do not speak if you do not get signal."

"What's the signal if something's wrong?" I ask.

"This," he says, squeezing my shoulder hard.

As we reach the library door, he turns to face me, putting a big finger to his lips in a gesture to remain quiet, coaching me on what to say. When Gee-Male is satisfied, he escorts me to a chair near the Prince, where he stands behind it with a hand on my shoulder. Several men are sitting around in a large circle near Abdul. Each one eyes me suspiciously. Even though the skirt is long and proper attire, the denim jacket must be offensive to them.

They have no idea how ridiculous they appear to me. In my opinion, the men occupying the seats are a motley looking group. Some of the men are in regular street clothes, while others wear flowing robes. Still, there are those who wrap their heads in scarves, but most all of them have either beards or mustaches or both.

"Thank you for joining us, Mrs. Andress," Abdul says politely. "These Royal Alliance Ministers deal with my government."

Introducing them one by one, I promptly forget their names, as I can't pronounce them anyway.

Abdul continues by saying, "They have come to discuss the issues surrounding your coming to be with us. They will be instrumental in helping you to return to your country."

Gee-Male thumps his finger on my shoulder, indicating that I may now speak.

"Thank you, Your Highness. I am pleased to be here."

"We have a suitable plan that might work well for you," Abdul says cheerfully.

Moving forward a tiny fraction, I'm about to blurt something out when Gee-Male applies pressure to my shoulder.

"It is quite a delicate situation," says a large man sitting closest to the Prince.

"We wait for the right time. We cannot take a chance and be wrong again," another man says in broken English.

A rather robust man, who dresses in something that resembles a caftan, inhales loudly and starts to talk in their language. All the men lean forward to hear his words. After several nods and conversation, they resume talking in both English and what I have determined is Arabic. They pause briefly and then continue to speak all at once.

*Whatever is happening in the room appears phony and staged to me.*

All conversation ceases when two of Gee-Male's men open the doors to allow servers to carry in large trays. Prince Abdul flicks his hand, and in the blink of an eye, the first man both assembles and pours the contents of a shiny teapot, while the other man uncovers domes to reveal tiny square sandwiches.

As servers work, an uncomfortable silence floats in the air like a balloon. When the servers finish, they follow the guards out the door, and the animated conversation resumes.

Meanwhile, Gee-Male has removed his hand from my shoulder but remains behind my chair. The Prince turns toward me. "It is teatime. We thought it would ease the tension if food were present. Please help yourselves gentlemen, Mrs. Andress?"

*Is he kidding? There's no polite way to eat without smearing food all over this headscarf!*

Gee-Male thumps my shoulder, and I respond, "No, thank you, Highness."

As the group of men talks, they simultaneously wipe out the contents on the tray. When Abdul sets his cup and saucer down on the table in front of him, all conversation ceases. The men turn in his direction and he begins by saying, "We have been working on a plan that we think will work for your safe return, Mrs. Andress."

The men nod in agreement, then begin to mutter to each other. Do they understand English and are pretending to speak in their language to frustrate me?

"Prince Akdemir, we commend you for what you have done so far. We had a great concern to handle this situation we have been presented with, as delicately as possible," the man to the far left of the Prince declares.

"Sadly," Abdul begins, "We have been in contact with your government, and they have informed us they do not wish involvement at this point. We are trying to…"

*Did he say my government doesn't want to help me?*

Gee-Male's big hands are on my shoulders to keep me firmly in the chair, but the words come out of my mouth anyway. "Excuse me? Would you repeat that, Your Highness?"

When the men all start talking at once, Abdul raises his hand, saying a string of words, then turns to me with a pained look on his face. "I'm afraid that your government does not want to be involved with your situation. Do not worry. We have worked out an alternative solution."

"What do you mean my government won't help me? Did you tell them what happened to me?" Gee-Male's hands tighten their grip on my shoulders, and I squirm uncomfortably trying to shrug off the pain of his fingers.

Abdul speaks again when the others remain silent. "We now have to revise our plan to keep you safe. It is not a simple plan. There are many factors to consider that you cannot possibly understand. It will take an army to achieve what we need to do for you."

"Who did you contact? Did you go to the Attorney General? What exactly did they say?"

Abdul looks stricken as if I have slapped him across the face. "I cannot discuss this with you, Mrs. Andress."

"So, they think I died, figure out a way to get me back to Kauai, and I'll convince them who I am. My mother will vouch for me, after the shock of course."

The men begin to talk to one another. It gets quite noisy as the words bounce around the room. Abdul closes his eyes for a moment, clamps his mouth shut, calmly raises his hand again, and everyone instantly grows silent. They are now looking at me as if I have two heads.

*Did they think I would sit here and say nothing?*

Gee-Male's hands are now squeezing both of my shoulders. "It doesn't seem all that complicated to me," I say quickly. "Maybe you shouldn't have taken me in the first place!"

Abdul recovers to pass a finger across his lips as another man finds his voice.

"We try many things, but no good luck comes of it. We try another in several months when things…um, how to say…get settled out." He makes a gesture as an umpire would to a player when he calls him safe.

The man directly to his right, who has said nothing so far, leans in with, "This is the best we can do for you right now. You should be grateful we do so much under the circumstances. His Royal Highness and the Alliance Ministers have gone out of their way for you."

The person across from him says, "You are not happy with our plan, you come up with a better one!"

My shoulders are now in extreme pain. "Would you loosen your grip, Big Guy? You're hurting me!"

Abdul nods at Gee-Male, and his hands immediately release their grip. "Gentlemen, please… Mrs. Andress is understandably upset her government will not help." Turning toward me, he says, "We need time to work out the rest of the plan. We ask for your patience. It is important that you remain calm while we negotiate this delicate matter."

My face is burning with rage, but I give it one more shot. "You haven't said what this plan is yet! I've been patient and have been calm. I certainly won't wait a few more weeks. If I'm not your prisoner, then I want to go home, NOW Abdul!"

Abdul shakes his head and in an open-palm gesture, glances at Gee-Male, and then at me. "We have done everything we can, and your government does not want to help you," he says. "You will have to wait until we can come to some equitable solution, Mrs. Andress. We will work as fast as it is possible."

"Why would my government not want to help me? I'm a United States citizen! I have rights."

Abdul addresses this by saying, "We do have an alternative to this, but we cannot discuss our plan in case it does not go well. It involves many people that will be difficult to execute, as it requires the utmost secrecy."

"You take me out of my country, and now you can't take me back?"

A man with a big round face, who has not addressed the group yet, raises his hand to speak in perfect English. "The authorities are not convinced there is a problem as the woman who sat next to your husband on the plane had your identification. They think you died in the explosion. It is very dangerous to take you back at present. It could jeopardize…"

"Do all of you know my business? How did you take me in the first place?"

"If we take you back without thinking this through, it could be seen as an act of war on our part," Abdul adds. "And we wish to avoid that at all costs."

The large man turns, forcing the bulk of his body forward to speak directly to me. "You should be grateful we help you at all," he snarls, waving his hand in the air.

"Grateful! Are you kidding? Isn't this a fine howdy do!" Knowing Gee-Male's ability to shut me down, I figure he can't keep me from speaking unless he covers my mouth, (which is a distinct possibility, if he's angry enough). "I did not ask for your assistance. You make it sound as if it's my fault. It isn't pal, the way I see it, it's yours."

My ace in the hole is the information tucked safely away in the red case. It'll go a long way when used as exculpatory evidence when the authorities confront me, once I get home. Abdul quickly raises his hand to stem the flow of conversation, lest they all start a ruckus because by now, we are all talking at once, some are even shouting.

During a moment of silence, I add, "I don't know anything about foreign policy. I did not ask for you to remove me from my country, and I sure as heck didn't ask for you to rescue me."

"My dear Mrs. Andress, distinguished guests," the Prince says calmly. "We will stop now and come together again when we have an agreed upon plan. Until then, please accept our sincerest hospitality while you are in the Royal Palace." Turning toward me, "We will do everything we can to honor your request. We will do this as quickly as it is possible."

Mr. Snarly mumbles something in their language as another man begins to chime in, then the rest of the men do the same. Abdul raises his hand yet again, and the men grow quiet. "Thank you all for coming today," he says softly. "We will come together with the finalization of our plan."

"I am sure we can do nothing else now but wait, your Highness," one of the men says in English as the others nod in agreement. The meeting is over when Abdul waves his hand, and they all stand up. They bow slightly toward him and do something with their hands by their faces. Abdul then presses something near his right side that is part of his chair. Does the Prince have a panic button? The wood doors at the end of the room open quietly, and the jabbering men quickly leave.

Is smoke rising from my headscarf to let him know how livid I am? Abdul gives Gee-Male that imperceptible nod of his, and he moves to stand next to Abdul's chair, where I can finally see his face. He doesn't look at all happy.

Yanking the scarf off my head, I'm trying to choose my words wisely. "That's probably gonna leave bruises, Big Guy!" My mind is sprinting through scenario after scenario in its bid to right this incredible wrong. Abdul says something, but I hold my hand up as if to say STOP. "I need to think about things right now. Can you give me a few minutes?" It will buy time to come up with something. It needs to be quick, and apparently without my government's involvement.

Gee-Male is making his irritating 'tsk' sound, and when I gaze at him, he's rolling his eyes. Abdul motions for him to sit down.

"Why don't you take me back to where you found me? You slipped me out, so slip me back into the Kauai Airport. No one will know you're involved; no one needs to know I was even here. It's not an elaborate plan; it needs to be simple, right? It can't get any simpler. You can even drug me, so I don't know where I came from, which is a joke, because I don't know where I am."

Abdul and Gee-Male converse for a few moments.

"Please don't give me the same drugs, because they were appalling! My government thinks I'm dead, right? When I show up claiming I'm Ellen Andress, I'll tell them I hit my head and have amnesia. They can call in someone who has experience with that sort of thing. Homeland Security must deal with this stuff, the FBI or the CIA. There will be no mention of your government and no implications for you, so it's the end of the story."

The plan sounds simple enough, but will they buy into it? Again, Abdul and Gee-Male discuss this between them.

"I honestly don't know who you are or where this place is so that it won't be a lie, will it? It's a simple plan. It could work! My government can always check my dental records to prove who I am. Think it over, but don't take too long, because I'm running out of patience." This time I stand up.

"Please sit down, Ellen." Abdul is thoughtful for a moment, resting his elbows on the chair. "We must exercise caution around the logistics of such a plan. Even though it may appear simple; there are things we must consider. Your safety is still our priority. We need people on the other end who are willing to take up our cause."

"What do you say, Big Guy? Do you think my simple plan will work?"

"Not sure about the plan, Ma'dame. Many things to worry about in transport. Many peoples to work this out," Gee-Male responds thoughtfully. "It is more difficult than you know."

"Do you think they will believe your story?" Abdul asks politely.

"It's so bizarre the authorities will have to believe me because I couldn't have made it up. Besides, it won't be your problem any longer. I'm fairly certain that the authorities will help me figure it out once I'm back on U.S. soil."

"We will talk again..." Abdul stands up.

"...tomorrow?" I say, finishing his sentence. "Gee-Male, can you smuggle out as you can smuggle in?" I don't know that he was involved in my rescue, but he hasn't denied it, either. "Abdul, no more talking. I want action, and I want out of here as soon as possible."

"You must be patient," Abdul says quietly. "You must trust us."

My wounds are too fresh, and the pain of what happened invades my thoughts to the point that I'm now getting them under control. "Why should I do that?"

"We are men of our word. We will see that you come to no harm, Ellen, this is my promise to you." He struggles with some unseen thing, but I already know he's not willing to share what it is.

Gee-Male's expression is indecipherable, and it's a silent walk back to my room. Is it my imagination, or is this great hulk of a man lost in thought?

"Can it work, Gee-Male?" He winces when I call him by his name, so I don't expect an answer, and I'm surprised when he speaks.

"It might, little one," he says almost apologetically. "His Royal Highness and I will talk more about it tonight. We will come up with the right plan for you."

"May I ask what time the chanting starts in the evening?"

He looks stunned, asking, "What does chan ting mean?"

"It sounds like this." I feebly attempt to copy the sound coming through the narrow windows at night.

"Does not sound like any thing I know. Sounds like a wounded dog, after a fight," Gee-Male says, shaking his head.

"Why do you scrunch up your face when I call you by your name?"

Gee-Male shakes his head from side to side. "You do not say it right. Every time you say my name, you say it wrong. Is bad, Ma'dame, very bad."

"Then how is it pronounced?" It never dawned on me that I was mispronouncing his name other than calling him Gee-Male or the Big Guy.

"Jee-ma-ale," he says giving certain syllables emphasis. He repeats it a little slower for me to absorb how he pronounces it. "Jee-ma-ale. You say it better now?"

"Jam-ale, Jam-ale, Jam-ale. How's that?"

"Close enough," he says.

When we get to my door, he opens it, saying, "His Royal Highness wishes that you accept invitation to join him for a meal this night."

Walking into the room and turning toward him, I say, "Let me think about that for a moment."

"May I tell him you come?"

"NO!" Then I push the door closed in his face. Ah yes, there is the familiar sound of the CLICK.

What do they think this is? I'm *not* at the Prince's disposal, and I declare myself thoroughly emancipated, vowing not to lose control over my own life.

*Something is nagging at my subconscious.*

Usually, there are little twinges or flashes of future things or events that pop into my head. It drives my children bonkers because they typically band together when I ask who broke a vase or walked across the kitchen floor with mud on their shoes. I can usually pick the culprit with accuracy. The odd thing is since I've been here, there have been no flashes.

*Did the drugs take that away?*

The possibility exists that my journey may take place any time now. In preparation, my red case holds a change of clothes, four pairs of underwear, pajamas, toiletries, and other items needed for my return home. I'm a light sleeper. Should anyone enter the room, I'll know right away.

I'm confident that the information written on the pages removed from the books will explain what happened to me. They are my salvation to this extreme insanity.

Anticipating a quick departure, I've put my red case on the bed next to me. I want to go home, even if it is to a different life. I miss my children more than they will ever know. If I ever see them again, I'll make a concerted effort to spoil them.

The chanting begins, and I fall asleep.

*"The journey of a thousand miles*

*begins with one step."*

~ Lao Tzu

# *Chapter Four*

## The Journey, But Not Home

**T**wo days go by, and there have been no invitations to dine with his Most Royal Pain-in-the-ass! It's okay with me because food magically and inexplicably appear. Could someone have access to the kitchen cabinets and refrigerator through a secret wall out in the hallway?

The essence of my nightmare is now tucked safely under the bottom of the red case. I had enough paper to complete it. Who would know, besides me, that it's there? As confidence returns, peace and the need to stay positive follows. Will Jam-ale follow through on his promise to take me home soon?

A light knock on the door announces a visitor. The familiar CLICK sounds and the door opens after I give permission to enter. The Prince strolls in and sits down on a chair next to the sofa. Wearing khaki pants and a blue and white striped long-sleeved shirt with the collar turned up, he appears oddly casual.

Acting as if we are old friends, he says, "My dearest Ellen, how are you this evening?" Stretching his hand out to me, he withdraws it quickly, triggering a hair-raising sensation.

"Why are you here? Don't tell me you miss me?" I say sarcastically.

"I trust you are well?" He glances around the room, and it suddenly occurs to me that he found out about the missing pages from his network of spies.

"Unless you have some good news that I'm going home soon, we have nothing to say to each other!"

Abdul appears hurt, almost as if I've struck him, much as he did that last time we were in the library with his compatriots. "You must be patient, dear Ellen. Many people are working diligently on our plan to return you to your country."

"I have been patient, Abdul. Have you found my wedding rings and wristwatch yet?"

"We have conducted an inquiry about your missing jewelry. We had determined that your rings and wristwatch were not with you when you arrived here. Perhaps the woman in the restroom took them after she drugged you."

*That is not what I expected him to say.*

"Will you give my laptop and other things back to me when I leave?"

The Prince shakes his head, sighing heavily, bowing as if his head is deflating. "You have been told many times that we cannot do that. We are doing our best, Ellen," he says, looking at me sternly. "It is difficult to put this plan together. It is of great magnitude. You need to trust us." Almost as an afterthought, he smiles, "You need to trust me."

"And why would I do that? What is this great plan of yours? How do you know my name?"

It's unclear whether he is unhappy or if he's thinking of what to say next because he doesn't answer for some time. Then he reaches to push a strand of hair away from my face, and I flinch as the odd gesture unnerves me somewhat because Ravi used to do that.

"I am not at liberty to discuss the particulars with you, Ellen. It could jeopardize the undertaking of what we must do to get you back to your country. It is one that requires precision military execution."

"What are you trying so hard *not* to say, Abdul?"

"I am honor bound, Ellen. You will be taken back to where we found you because I feel that I owe it to you to do this."

"When, Abdul?"

"I assure you, it will be soon. You are not happy here? Are you not comfortable? We tried to give you everything you need. I hoped you would not be in such a rush to leave. We could get to know each other better; perhaps bring your family here. Would you like that?"

I start to laugh. "You can't be serious. Why would I want to stay here? I miss my family, and I want to go home! No friggin way would I stay here, pal, and there's no way I would allow my family to come here, either. Where is here, again? You haven't shared that with me! Never mind that you took my identity, my passport, my wallet, my purse, and everything in it. Then you refuse to return them."

Abdul stutters, "My dear Ellen, there are…there are so many things I cannot discuss with you right now. You are in my country by default. At some point, I am quite certain that it will be straightened out. You must trust that when the time is right, we will return you."

"Do you have a magic lamp and a Genie? Can you grant me three wishes and fly me the hell out of here on a magic carpet? Do you honestly think you could make me happy? Do you want me to be grateful for keeping me a prisoner? I'm not, Mr. Prince! Thanks, but no thanks!"

Abdul, the quintessential gentle person that he is, seems extraordinarily calm in the face of my insults. "I understand," he murmurs, "I quite honestly do. Someday, I hope that you will know that I did my best to honor the promise I made."

"I will never forgive you for rudely removing me from Kauai and bringing me here against my will."

*If I close my eyes, will he go away?*

"Ellen, I have enjoyed your company. Perhaps one day, you will forgive me. Perhaps you will know all that it took…"

"You did this without my permission, and that is unforgivable. What is this mysterious thing we keep avoiding, Abdul? And don't pretend you don't know what it is!"

*There is no mistaking the disillusionment of our conversation.*

"It is understandable that you are angry. We did what we thought was right, Ellen. Our main objective was to keep you safe, and that is what we did," he says almost apologetically. "Whether you forgive me or not, it was the right thing to do."

"I don't know what kind of game you're playing, but I'm quite certain my family and I want no part of it!"

Leaning toward me slightly, talking almost in a whisper, he says, "I have grown fond of you, dearest Ellen. We did not mean to cause you pain."

Before I can react, he reaches for my hand and tenderly kisses it. Then he straightens, bows slightly and leaves the room before I can hurl another insult at him.

Nothing in the world will keep me from going home to my family, except my real death! Dear Lord that didn't sound right in my head. If I ever do get back, I know there will be obstacles to overcome. It'll be rough for a while for all of us, because of what happened. I brood over what is and envision what might be. The decision is quite clear. I want my life back!

It won't be the same without Ravi, but we'll adjust to that. We are each strong individuals as Mother taught Terre and me to buck up in the face of disappointment while Daddy taught us other things about life. He made us aware of the advantages of growing up in the upper class of Chicago business deals along with the apparent politics surrounding the local racetrack. He taught me to know the difference between a good deal and a bad one.

*It is not a good deal.*

I want my children, my house, my career, and our dog back. If I have to dig my way out of here with that dull kitchen knife, I will go home!

Trying to fall asleep, I think about the words written on the pages stashed in the red case, then drift off mentally willing my captors to move this along a little faster.

I'm not asleep very long when the hairs on the back of my neck trigger a spine-chilling feeling.

CLICK.

Fully awake, Jam-ale is close. He whispers to hurry and get dressed. The pile of clothes that are at the end of the pillow/bed is waiting in anticipation of this very moment. Putting them over my pajamas, Jam-ale tries to usher me forward, but I reach for the handle on my red case. I half expect him to say leave it behind but grab it anyway, glad that he hasn't asked about the headscarf.

Jam-ale's guards are out in the darkened hallway, their shadows somewhat visible, but they don't move. He fumbles with a blindfold, placing it clumsily over my eyes, tightening it, so there's no way to see. As soon as he does this, a sensation of closeness activates a feeling of helplessness. Someone grabs my arm, pulling my red case away from my hand. My protest goes unanswered as a hand covers my mouth.

*Are they taking me home?*

"Come," Jamaile whispers close to my ear, "remain quiet, there is a threat."

We might be in a small elevator, as the air feels close, and the floor moves under my feet. I feel a slight breeze and another sensation that we're in a tunnel because the closeness feeling returns. It's damp and smells musty, and it's difficult to gauge our direction.

Jam-ale's long strides make it challenging to keep up, so he half carries/half drags me along. At a series of staircases, we descend slowly. Is it to keep the men from falling over each other or on top of me?

I can identify several sounds, while others are unidentifiable; a whistle off in the distance, muffled clatter close by, creaking leather, a sneeze, or a cough. Distinct snorts from horses, along with mumbled chatter makes me wonder if we're near a stable, or outside near one as familiar odors grow stronger the lower we go. How many people have assembled for this event? Is this the whole of Jam-ale's army?

The sudden thought of traveling by horse makes me pull away from Jam-ale's grip, but he hangs on tightly. Chirping crickets are now mingling with muffled stomping, while something jingles like a cluster of tiny bells.

Suddenly I'm airborne, lifted roughly under the arms, my body comes down hard across something firm. I'm now sitting side-saddle across Jam-ale's legs.

The horse sidesteps, then quickly calms. Jam-ale softly reassures us that everything is all right. He asks me to put one arm around his waist while he pulls the other arm through something that he tightens. He then whips something (that feels like a cape) around us. Leaning forward, it feels as if he is moving his right arm giving hand signals.

Jam-ale whispers, "It will be a long journey. Try to sleep."

"Are you kidding? Can anyone sleep like this?"

Not long into our little adventure, there is such pain from the strain of being in this position that I want to scream! All feeling has gone out of my legs as they come down hard on the big man's legs every time the horse canters. The saddle-horn is chafing my thigh, which will probably result in a substantial bruise there!

Hoping he has an alternative travel contingency other than horseback, I try to say his name correctly. "Jam-ale, I can't take this anymore. I can't breathe, and I can't feel my legs. Can we change positions?"

Jam-ale somehow unties the blindfold to snarl at me, saying, "Certainly, my little Princess." He shouts something, and the big horse slows as the bells tinkle again. Moving his cape aside, he unfastens the piece holding me to his chest, lifts me up and practically throws me into the waiting arms of one of his men, who drops me to my feet.

Without warning, I am airborne again, and my legs are pushed open so that I now face Jam-ale. It isn't humiliating until he asks me to wrap my legs around him! Grateful to be wearing jeans; now I'm glad they're still loose. Jam-ale refastens the straps but doesn't put the blindfold back on. He whips the cape back around us in so practiced a move; it makes me wonder how many times he's done this. Without hesitation, we start to move fast again as the feeling slowly returns to my limbs.

"Thank you! That makes all the difference in the world, Jam-ale."

Are we miles from where we're going? Are they taking me all the way by horseback? Was I brought here this way? At least they are trying to honor my request. Breathing is a little easier now, the motion of the horse lulls me to sleep. Then I wake briefly, then fall sleep again, but for how long, it's difficult to judge.

As dusk comes upon us, something jars me awake as the horse slows down. Waiting for what feels like a half hour, there are muffled sounds and the faint tinkle of bells every so often. Occasionally Jam-ale lifts an arm or moves his body, while the horse shifts under us. I can only imagine how large this stallion must be to accommodate our combined weight.

Jam-ale rips away the cape and puts the blindfold back across my eyes. As luck would have it, light is visible under the blindfold as it's not tight this time. He then lifts me up as someone catches me like a sack of potatoes! I can smell smoke along with a familiar scent. Judging from the aroma, it might be meat.

*Are we camping in the desert?*

Dropped abruptly on what feels like cushions, Jam-ale removes the blindfold. I am in a tent-like structure that does not look like tents we camp with as a family. It reminds me of a circus tent with a large center pole. A brass tray with foldable legs is sitting near the cushions while lanterns placed along the inside of the tent at intervals give off a soft light.

Laughter leaves my throat before I can stop it, because the tent is set up like every movie I've ever seen about nomadic life in the desert! It elicits a grunt-like sound from Jam-ale as he stretches out on the cushions next to me, then closes his eyes before kicking off his boots.

The pillows look eerily like my pillow/bed, but the cushions are not as colorful or of the same delicate fabric. How did all this stuff get here? Was it by train, camel maybe? Did it drop from the sky at this predetermined destination? Is this an oasis? Perhaps it's rented for special occasions. I start to laugh again.

"We will eat," Jam-ale says after a while. "We will sleep. DO NOT GO OUT OF TENT!" Opening his eyes to shake a big finger at me, he adds, "My men will carve you up for a meal!"

"You expect me to believe that? And by the way, where is my red case?"

"Try, and you will see. The red case is here, no worry," Jam-ale says smiling. In his feeble attempt to make a joke, he still sounds gruff, but I know he has a tender side, too, although it doesn't show up very often.

"How much further is it, Jam-ale?"

Jam-ale doesn't answer, so I move closer to see if he's sleeping. His breathing has slowed, and he must be exhausted. How do they know what time it is? Do the guards study the stars or something, as astronomers or navigators once did?

The tent flap opens a short while later, and someone places my red case inside the doorway. Something is sticking out of the zippered top that looks like a package. That's odd. I know it was fully zipped last night. As I tear away the paper, all three of the books I could have sworn were left behind, tumble to the sand.

Jamaile opens his eyes as if an unseen hand is poking him. Sitting up slowly, he then abruptly stands. As he pulls the tent flap aside, he says, "You have the case. I will return." Pointing his big finger at me, he snorts, "DO NOT GO OUTSIDE OF TENT!"

"Where would I go, Big Guy?"

Jam-ale returns a short time later with a tray piled with food, drink, and goblets. I'm so hungry I'll eat anything on that tray, and I'll make my mind think it's steak. The rice is somewhat spicy. As I reach for a goblet, Jam-ale puts one in my hand. Watching me closely, we both eat in silence. His expression is unreadable. Tears fill my eyes as the reality hits that I'm going home.

"I'm going to miss you, Jam-ale, although I'm not going to miss being a prisoner in a faraway place, I can't name. Thank you for your kindness. I do appreciate your taking me back."

He reaches to wipe a tear that is flowing down my cheek. This tender thing makes my eyes overflow.

"You have lost...You must grieve," he says quietly.

"How much farther will we travel, Jam-ale?"

Before he answers, the tent flap moves aside as one of his men enters. I've learned to watch for nuances between these men who must know each other so intimately that a flick of a finger or the nod of a head speaks volumes when no one utters a word.

"You will be home soon, Ma'dame." Taking the goblet out of my hand, he stands up.

I'm suddenly woozy. Flopping onto the cushions, I realize there must have been something in the goblet beside the juice. Something covers my body as something else tenderly brushes my forehead.

"Jam-ale...what...have...you...done..."

A familiar pain pounds in my head as the foul taste of bile makes me gag. I open my eyes to see that I'm sitting on a cold floor, and it looks like a restroom stall. I am furious when nausea rises like a thunderstorm up my gullet and out my mouth. It's a gurgling sound followed by a disgusting splash, as it hits the water. Sweet Mother of Jesus, I'm so thankful the commode is here!

*Those dirty bastards*!

The sound of the outer door of the restroom opens, and someone begins to murmur, "Are you okay, Ma'am? Do you need help?"

"Yes." I manage to say.

Two women have come into the stall. One of them is flushing the toilet while the other is trying to help me stand up.

"Are you alone, Ma'am?" A woman in a uniform is handing me a moistened paper towel. "Did you miss your flight?"

"No," I manage to say.

Then many hands reach out to help me onto a table with wheels. It moves quickly down a hallway and into a dimly lit room. Someone places a mask over my mouth and nose, and I quietly drift off.

"There's no identification," a disembodied voice says.

"That's odd," someone else says. "We'll check the bag the woman had and run this through Homeland Security to see if we can identify her. I don't see an airline tag."

A young man is whispering as he pricks my left hand. Vaguely aware of movement over my head, people are coming in and out of the room, asking questions. But a pounding headache prevents me from answering. When it finally dulls, it leaves me a bit light-headed. I know the consequences of sitting or standing too quickly and will remain motionless until I'm sure the nausea is gone.

"How are you feeling, Ma'am?" The woman who helped me in the restroom is leaning over me. "Are you feeling any better? The paramedic thinks you're dehydrated and started an IV drip. You need to rest now until we can figure out how to help you, okay?"

"I'm a little better...my family! Did you contact my family?" Tears flow uncontrollably into my hair. Is this happiness that I'm back to my universe? Or sad that I feel so dreadful?

"That's good you feel better. I'll be back in a little while."

"What's the date today and where am I?"

"It's June eighth," she says. "Don't you know where you are? Did you have a purse? It's not here, and there's no wallet, boarding pass, or anything else that we can use to identify you. So, no, we didn't contact your family."

I'm near the panic stage. "What? There are papers in the bottom of my red case. They will prove who I am."

"I'll get someone who can talk with you. You rest now, okay?"

*I'm not thinking good thoughts right now!*

After all that talk about promises and trust, it's almost too much to take! I clench my teeth, digging my nails into the palms of my hands. They've managed to put me back all right, but they didn't include my purse! The papers are in the red case, but I can't reach it hooked up to this IV thing.

When the door opens again, two people walk toward me. One is an attractive sandy-haired woman in a light green blouse and navy-blue skirt, and the other is the young man who inserted the needle for the IV. He's back to rip off the tape and remove the mask. He smiles as he helps me off the table and onto a sofa.

"Okay, we'll take it from here. Thanks so much, Johnny." As the young man pushes the gurney out of the room, the woman pulls a chair away from the table to sit near me. "My name is Jennifer Holmes. I'm with Homeland Security. I'm going to ask you some questions." Poised with a small notepad a police detective would have, she taps her pen on it impatiently waiting for me to answer. "Please state your full name."

"Ellen Peters Andress."

As I answer, she scribbles on her pad, then looks up in surprise. "Did you say, Andress? Spell that for me, please."

"A n d r e s s. My husband and I... his name is Ravenalt Andress."

"Answer my specific questions, if you would. It will save time. What is your home address?" Jennifer is giving me the impression that she's bored and not at all interested in what I have to say.

"We live at 1734 Elmhurst Drive, Evanston, Illinois; it's north of Chicago."

"What were you doing in Kauai? What was the length of your stay?"

"My husband and I..." Choking on the word husband, it reminds me that Ravi is dead.

"How long were you here, Ma'am?"

"A week, we were supposed to be here a week."

"How did you come to be in the women's restroom throwing up?" she asks blandly.

"I was on vacation with my husband." Tears are spilling uncontrollably from my eyes. Jennifer hands me a box of tissues and motions by circling the air with her pen.

"Where's your husband now?" she asks impatiently.

"It's complicated, you see... my husband is dead. Does my name sound familiar to you? Have you been searching for me?"

Jennifer stiffens, stands abruptly and says that she'll be right back. Moments later, she returns with a man she introduces as her colleague. "This is Devon Michaels, also with Homeland Security. Please repeat what you told me."

Jennifer no longer has an amused expression. She hands me a bottle of water as a memory flashes of drinking too much too fast after being drugged! I regurgitate my story in between sips of water.

Both agents begin to question why I showed up out of the blue in the restroom with no identification, airline tickets, or luggage.

"We'll be right back," Devon says, abruptly ending the questioning. They both leave the room, but a few moments later, Devon returns without Jennifer. "Would you please state your name again?" Devon asks.

"I told you, I'm Ellen Andress."

"That information could have been obtained from any number of sources. The real Mrs. Ellen Andress is deceased. She has been for almost three months, and so is her husband," he says solemnly. Sitting on one of the chairs, he nods for me to go ahead.

"Look, I have proof. My name *is* Ellen Andress. I do live in Evanston. I was on my way back home with my husband on March 17th after spending a week here in Kauai."

Jennifer steps back into the room, bending to whisper to Devon. He makes a sound like agreement, then she says to continue and sits down next to Devon.

"I already told Ms. Holmes here that I went to the restroom before we were supposed to board our plane. I had a stomachache. As you know, the lavatories are..."

"Please answer our specific questions." Devon seems impatient.

Jennifer asks, "What flight were you supposed to be on?"

"I can't remember the flight number. I went into the restroom. Some lady that looked like me, drugged me. I realize how odd that sounds."

"We have proof that Ellen Andress died in an explosion alongside her husband on March 17th," Devon says. "But do go on."

*Are they playing good cop, bad cop?*

"Ravi and I were flying to Houston before going on to Chicago O'Hare. Right after someone took me, I woke up to see the explosion. I was in a car...hand me my red case, and I'll prove it to you. The proof is in there, I swear it."

Devon is reluctant to do this, but picks up my case, setting it on the sofa next to me. Jennifer's cellphone chirps and she leaves the room. As I begin to pull out the contents, a feeling of dread threatens to overpower me when I pull up the bottom flap, and there is nothing there.

*A feeling of betrayal grips me.*

Mortified at this discovery, I'm now shouting at Devon. "What did you do with the papers that were in here? Why did you take them?"

"We searched your bag, but there was only what you see in there. You've concocted an elaborate story, haven't you?" Devon utters.

"I'll agree that it's an extraordinary story, but one I did *not* fabricate! I had proof. It was right here. You must believe me. Someone removed it."

Devon is shaking his head. "There were no papers in your case, except those three books and those items."

Jennifer steps back into the room, immediately launching questions at me. "What do you know about the explosion, Ma'am? It would seem that there is nothing to substantiate your claim to be this person named Ellen Andress."

"I think I saw it from a car before I passed out."

Devon responds by saying, "We asked for anyone who witnessed the explosion to come forward, but that was months ago. We talked with everyone. You don't appear to be who you say you are."

The sharp pain in my chest suggests that fright is progressing to a full-blown panic attack. "I am Ellen Andress! Please, call my Mother, she'll tell you. Call her, 775…wait a minute. Yes, it's 775-992-8970."

Jennifer's cellphone rings, looking down at it, she clicks her tongue, saying, "I have to take this. Be right back."

"Please, call my Mother. Call my dentist and check my dental records. You must believe me. Someone gave me a drug. They kept me there all this time."

In the meantime, Devon looks blankly at me. "Now you're saying someone kidnapped you? Who took you?"

"Yes, I'm saying that exactly. I don't know why but the person who took me is called Prince Abdul. It's Prince something, something, Abdul, something. I'm begging you to believe me!"

"Jennifer is making calls right now," Devon says, apparently not amused by this latest information.

Overwhelmed, I start to sob, unable to catch my breath. Realizing that without my notes, it's going to be very difficult to prove who I am. Devon moves toward me, handing me the box of tissues.

Why would anyone believe me? Abdul and his people must have been watching more closely than I thought. Why did they give me the books? Is this Abdul's way of paying me back for ruining them?

Jennifer returns, asking Devon to join her in the hallway.

"Sure," he says.

Devon moves toward the door, motioning to someone outside in the hallway. "Don't leave her alone. Stay with her until we get back."

The door closes after the woman in the uniform comes in to sit down next to me. "You must be scared right now, honey. I'm sure we'll get this all straightened out soon."

"They don't believe me, do they?"

"It appears that you might be in shock. Why don't you close your eyes and rest?" the woman murmurs.

A few minutes later, Jennifer and Devon step back into the room and excuse the woman.

Devon starts with, "Try to answer our questions as honestly as you can, Ma'am. You said a Prince Abdul abducted you. We can't find a Prince Abdul anywhere. Try to recall the rest of his name. Surely you can tell us what country you were in?"

"That's just it, he told me his whole name, but it has maybe four or five names. The Abdul part is near the end of it. I couldn't write it down. They took everything in my case except some clothes and makeup. They took my laptop and sketchpad. I had nothing to write on except the pages I tore out of some books I took from his library. Even the note he gave me is gone. You mean you believe me?"

*Hope begins to return.*

"That might be a premature assessment." As Jennifer glances at Devon, she says, "We're not saying that yet."

"Then, what are you saying?"

"We called in the authorities," Devon mutters. "They advised us not to contact your family at this time and instructed us to sit tight until the Cavalry gets here." Devon is abrupt while Jennifer sits down next to me on the sofa.

"Are you able to describe this Abdul person?" she asks.

"He looked tan, wavy dark hair, about 5 foot nine or six feet tall. They held me in some type of fortress or palace that was very big, like a hotel or castle. It had stone type walls with marble floors."

Neither Jennifer nor Devon writes anything down, but they continue to ask questions. "Do you know what country it was?" Jennifer asks.

"No, but it was some arid climate, a desert perhaps. I don't know exactly where it was because the Prince said I was not to go outside. The papers are where I wrote everything down. They would have proven everything." Weeping again, I grab for the tissues.

"Okay," Jennifer says. "No one touched your case in the restroom. We've already gone through it twice, and there are no papers inside."

Devon reaches over to grab my left arm. He must be noticing the faded marks. Motioning to Jennifer, he says, "We'll be right back."

I get the impression that they think I'm a drug addict and have imagined my little adventure. Could they toss this up to some hallucinogenic drug I gave myself?

*They could be right, and I've already lost my mind!*

How could Abdul and Jam-ale dump me here? Closing my eyes, I lean my head against the back of the sofa as the pounding returns.

"Ma'am, can I ask you some questions?" Someone says quietly, touching my arm.

When I open my eyes, it's not Jennifer, but someone else. The woman is pretty. She has shoulder length brown/blond, highlighted hair. She's wearing a smart blue suit with a white blouse. Her nametag identifies her as Special Agent Andrea Simmons, FBI. She is smiling; but it doesn't look sincere.

"Ma'am, can you hear me?" she asks again.

"Yes, I can hear you."

Sitting down on one of the chairs, Agent Simmons asks, "Can you help me understand something? You told Homeland Security that you couldn't remember some things, is that correct?"

"Yes, I was drugged. Can I contact my family now? They're…"

"Answer my questions so we can move this along quickly, all right?" she says tersely. Her demeanor seems rough around the edges. "It sounds like you have had quite a time. We are in the process of running your fingerprints and photo through our system to see if there is a match."

"Why would you run my fingerprints? I'm not a criminal. I know who I am…I'm Ellen Andress. I live at 1734…"

"Hold a moment." Agent Simmons opens a folder and thrusts a picture in my face. "Here's a recent photograph of Ellen Andress, married to one Ravenalt T. Andress, on May 20th, 1987."

*Oh, these people are good!*

"Let me see that!" The people responsible for the original mystery concerning my husband's death has somehow managed to cover their tracks, that I'm starting to doubt myself. It is unbelievable! Although the person in the photo looks *like* me, it's apparent that it's *not* me.

"That doesn't look much like you, does it?" she says.

"I don't know how they did this, but this is wrong. Agent Simmons, please help me. I *am* Ellen Andress. This woman is a phony. She's the one who drugged me! I'm sure it was her. How can I prove it to you?"

"Frankly, I don't know if you can," Agent Simmons says flatly. "Our records indicate that she died in the explosion along with your husband."

I slowly shake my head. "They took everything that would have helped me prove who I am. Can you please contact my family? Mother will vouch for me. She's probably staying with my children."

"Who are *they*, Ma'am and we can't contact your family yet," Simmons says without expression.

For the next hour or two, we go back and forth; Agent Simmons questions me as I repeat my story, pausing to drink the water. I continue to tell her as much as I can remember, all the way up to and including when the woman found me in the restroom. Without my notes, it's impossible to recall everything, but bits and pieces emerge the longer she persists.

Agent Simmons stands. "Okay, that's enough for now. By the way, there is no record of your fingerprints. There is no record of you, anywhere," she says in a smug tone.

As I take another swig from the water bottle, the door opens, and three men walk in. They are all dressed in dark suits and wearing sunglasses. It instantly reminds me of the movie *Men in Black*.

"I told you, I'm not a criminal."

Agent Simmons suddenly becomes animated. "Hello Lenard, Gene. These men are from the FBI, Special Agents' Unit. They'll be taking over the investigation from here. You will tell them your story, again."

"Thank you, Agent Simmons. I'll catch you later, okay?" As Simmons leaves the room, the one named Lenard throws a manila folder on the table. "I am Special Agent Lenard Casings, this is Special Agent Gene Thornburg, and that's Agent Tom Spalding."

As he says this, he dramatically takes off his sunglasses, planting himself on a chair opposite me, flashing his badge in my face, while licking his lips in a repulsive manner.

I sense a negative vibe coming from all three because something is not right about their demeanor. Lenard is about five foot nine or ten in height, has short, neatly trimmed dark brown hair, a narrow nose, and is clean-shaven. He has brown eyes, semi-bushy eyebrows, and a noticeable scar on his upper lip. Agent Lenard looks like he works out some, his annoying mannerisms will be problematic.

"We have been called in to assist Homeland Security deal with your situation," he murmurs.

"You believe me? You believe I'm Ellen Andress and I can go home now?"

"Not yet. The local office here could not locate certain information about you, and it raised a red flag. We followed the reports for some time. They had you highlighted from the start."

"What reports? What exactly does this mean?" I ask.

Agent Lenard smiles, saying, "Don't get excited. Highlighted is a term the local authorities use to contact our office. They are duty-bound when there is a threat to National Security. In this case, you do not exist anywhere on the planet. We call this a breach of security and a clear threat to our National Security."

Special Agent Gene Thornburg interjects, "One we take seriously, Ma'am."

Special Agent Gene is as blond as Agent Lenard is dark but shorter and somewhat stouter. His southern accent is skewed, some twang and something else unidentifiable. When he removes his sunglasses, he begins to blink a little too often as if he's wearing the old hard-type contact lenses. It doesn't look like he works out, as his midsection suggests.

Unlike the other agents, Agent Tom is taller and broader, and his suit is tight in certain places. His eyebrows are bushy over his dark sunglasses; his mouth is a tight line. Agent Spalding, remaining near the door, has his hands clasped in front of him.

"What kind of security breach have I caused? I want to talk to someone who can help me. I'm a US citizen! Call someone at the Pentagon. Call the Attorney General. Call my mother! I'm real!"

As I move toward the table, the words *The Andress Document* is hand-lettered on the manila folder. "What's this?"

Agent Tom moves to grab the folder before I can reach it, returning to his position near the door, cradling it in his beefy arms. He reminds me of a bouncer in a nightclub, or worse, Jam-ale.

"Why is my name on the folder?"

"That does not concern you right now," Agent Lenard says, licking his lower lip. "Care to start from the top?" For the next hour or so, I repeat the story of who, what, where, and the whole of my previous dissertation, as Agent Gene paces the room.

When Agent Lenard's cellphone rings, he steps out but returns a moment later. Signaling to the other agents, he says, "Let's go."

*I hate surprises! What should I expect from these total strangers?*

Fear is replacing panic. "Where are you taking me? I'm not going anywhere with you."

"Unless you'd rather go with Homeland Security for lockup, we are taking you to a hotel," he says briskly. "They do not believe a word you have said, but we do."

"Does that mean you know that I'm Ellen Andress and you're going to help me get home?"

"It is quite possible that the people who took you are watchin your family right now, Ma'am," Agent Gene says taking my red case.

Agent Lenard then escorts me out of the room, down the hall, and out of the airport so fast, there's no time to wave to the woman who was so nice to me. There's no sign of Agent Simmons, Jennifer, or Devon. Exiting the building, we walk toward a shiny black limousine that's waiting near the curb. The trunk opens, and Agent Tom takes my red case, as Agent Gene holds the rear door open for me to enter the vehicle.

Agent Tom gets into the front seat and drives us to a hotel located within or near the airport grounds. Bypassing the lobby via a side door, we go up the stairwell to a room on the third floor where Agent Gene gains entry with a plastic key card. It's a typical hotel room with a single queen-sized bed, dresser, TV, etc. and it looks comfortable.

Agent Lenard doesn't miss the opportunity to go over the rules he recited in the limo, insisting that I repeat them back to him several times.

"It is a matter of National Security. You need to be patient while we work out all the details. You will stay here tonight. We will have more information in the morning to go over with you."

"Can I contact my family?"

Agent Gene smacks Agent Lenard on the arm.

Agent Lenard's compassion vanishes. "Mrs. Andress, it is imperative that you do not try to contact your family. After all, they are still trying to recover from your funeral. Until we get things in place, we ask that you refrain from the urge to use the telephone, except to order room service."

"Wait a minute. How do I know you're real FBI agents? How about I call them and ask for verification."

Lenard is shaking his head, saying, "That is not advisable. It is not safe for you. Do you understand the severity of the situation, Ellen? Any slipups could spell disaster. You know what happened to your husband. Do you want the same thing to happen to the rest of your family?"

"I understand. May I ask what the significance of the folder might be that you brought with you today? It had *The Andress Document* written on the cover." They look from one to the other, reminding me of Abdul and his giant sidekick.

"Let us say there is more to this than we can share with you right now. We will be back in a little while. We still have information to check out, and there is much preparation to do for tomorrow. Order yourself some dinner and make yourself comfortable until we return."

The agents let themselves out. When the door closes, there's an unmistakable CLICK.

*THEY DID NOT LOCK THAT DOOR!*

I'm furious. I'm so irate that I can't focus. How does this differ from Abdul's fortress? Running to the door, I pound with one hand and pull with the other, but the door remains closed.

Flipping the deadbolt, because there is one, we'll see how this game goes. When I pick up the telephone on the desk, fully expecting to punch in numbers, I'm surprised when a female voice answers.

"May I help you?" The voice sounds familiar, then remember Agent Lenard's words of warning that this could be a deal-breaker where my family is concerned.

"Is this Room Service?"

"Yes it is," the soft voice says. "What would you like to order?"

A clock next to the bed reads three thirty, so I order a steak dinner to be delivered around five thirty. Removing my sneakers, I start to laugh when I remember pulling my clothes on over my pajamas. Pulling down the comforter, I flop down on the bed and fall fast asleep.

A loud pounding on the door wakes me; the digital clock reads 5:45. "Room Service!" Looking through the peephole, a young man is standing in the hallway looking rather annoyed. Knocking again, he yells, "ROOM SERVICE!"

I ask him to leave the tray out in the hallway, but the server stammers that he needs a signature. He finally relents when I promise he'll get a tip. Anger begins to cloud my judgment, and I wonder when the FBI men will return, as I like my food hot!

Ten minutes or so later, there's a knock on the door. "Ellen, can we come in?"

CLICK.

The door handle turns as I release the deadbolt. Agent Lenard strolls into the room as Agent Gene comes in holding my dinner tray. "You waitin for this?" Gene asks, setting it down on the desk.

*Is the third agent guarding the hallway?*

"Looks like you have made yourself comfortable, Ellen. Eat while we tell you about our plan," Agent Lenard says, flopping down on a chair. Suddenly, déjà vu strikes. Did Agent Lenard say he has a *plan*?

Savoring my dinner, I listen as the agents take turns like the Bopsie Twins reciting a poem on an invisible stage. "It was something you said during the conversation with Agent Simmons," Lenard says, taking a paper out of his pocket.

Gene adds, "It triggered a computer search and we b'lieve most of what you say, but I have to tell ya, little lady, there are some big holes in your story."

"Oh, my God, you believe me? I can go home now. Can I call Mother?"

Lenard is frowning. "That will not be possible," he says.

"At least not yet anyway," Gene adds, smiling.

"Why isn't it possible? I need to let my family know I'm alive!"

Lenard walks toward the window, and peeks through the closed curtains. "Some things need to be in place before you can see your family again. It is a matter of National Security, Ellen." His eyes flicker as if he's not telling the truth. "After all, they think you're dead."

My body starts to quiver with alarm. "I know, but I need to talk with Mother. I need to know my children are all right. Are they in danger?"

Turning slowly toward me, Lenard says, "They are if you try to call them! There are dangerous people out there, Ellen! You, of all people, should know that!"

"Look, if it's a matter of identification, call for my dental records or exhume that woman's body. That'll prove she's not me!"

Gene's face flushes, then he says, "That will not be possible."

"Why not?" I ask.

"B'cause nothin much was left of the bodies before cremation," Gene says quickly, glancing at Lenard. "There was not much left of 'em to begin with."

"Oh, that's horrible." Shock tries to creep in, but I squelch it quickly.

"Look, Ellen, we are working on the details, but you have to be patient."

Lenard seems frustrated, and I've already decided they're going to give me a hard time with or without all the notes written during my incarceration with Abdul.

*A cloud of silence hangs in the air.*

Lenard sighs heavily. "Ellen, we are doing everything as quickly as we can. There is a team of Special FBI Agents working on it right now. They will be at it into the wee hours if need be. It is..."

Gene takes over by saying, "It is gonna take some time. We were only aware of your situation. It probably seems like an eternity to you, but be patient. Trust us, okay?"

As those words reach my brain, I laugh at the absurdity of this. "Yes, the Most Royal Highness and General-Pain-In-The-Ass said those same words. And you expect me to believe and trust you, perfect strangers with what's left of my life?"

Gene looks sympathetic. "We are tryin to solve what must be an unbelievable ordeal for you, Missus. Our teams are only gettin started."

"I want this to end! I want my life back! It's a freaking nightmare!"

Lenard's face is reflecting the seriousness of the matter. "Your old life is gone, Ellen. What we can offer you is a new one."

"What do you mean my old life is gone? I don't want a new life, I happen to like the old one, thanks very much, and I want it back!"

"To protect you and your family, we have to put certain things in place," Lenard says, glancing at Gene as he takes over.

"We are gonna put you in a program to shield you and your family from the fallout that is sure to happen if we do not get this under wraps soon." Gene is smiling, blinking a little too often.

"What if I don't want your help?"

They both look a little stricken when I say this.

"Too late for that, Ellen! You asked for our help," Lenard says, rather brusquely.

"And we are givin it to ya," Gene adds.

"Things were set in motion when that plane exploded. We have some damaging information that points to--we can talk about that another time." Lenard stops talking.

"What information are you referring to?" I ask.

"We do not want to get into that now," he says turning toward the window, reaching to fidget with the wand. "There will be time to talk tomorrow."

I wish for the *get-a-grip* attitude Mother instilled in me to show up, but apparently, I'm wailing instead. "What about my children? They must be part of my new life, too! I think I know how this works, but maybe I don't want to go along with your plan. I need to know what your plan is before I agree to it!"

"Ellen! For Christ's sake get a hold of yourself!" Lenard is visibly irked now, licking his lips repeatedly. "You have created a nightmare for our people!"

"How exactly did I do that?"

"We are still working out the details. At some point, your children will be allowed to join you..." Gripping Lenard on the arm, he looks embarrassed and pulls away. "But we have no definite timetable for that yet."

"Thank you, oh thank you. You do believe me!"

"We will contact you tomorrow," Lenard says moving toward the door.

"Do you have to lock it? They did that where I was being held, and it makes me crazy."

Sighing heavily, Lenard says, "It has everything to do with National Security and your safety, and it's only for tonight. Good night, Ellen."

CLICK.

*A strange panic washes over me when I hear that sound.*

What if there was a fire in the building? How would I get out? Lenard's attitude is getting on my nerves. He seems impatient, not as concerned with my welfare as he first did. How can either of them be trusted? The people who I've encountered the last day are the ones who scare me the most.

*Aren't they supposed to be my people!*

Bolting the door from the inside, it makes me feel more in control. Leaving the TV on for background noise, it makes me chuckle--all that's missing is microwave popcorn!

It's been a long day (or days) so a hot shower will feel good. When I remove my pajamas, there's a large bluish/yellow bruise on my left thigh where it rubbed against the horn of Jam-ale's saddle.

81

I climb under the comforter, fully appreciating the softness of the mattress, but sleep does not come quickly. I'm still a long way from home.

How will Mother and the children react once they know I'm alive? Will I have the strength to keep things together?

Or will I fall apart without Ravi?

Where will we end up if we can't stay in Illinois?

*I must think more positively, and pray for the guidance we're all going to need!*

*"They always say time changes things,*

*but you actually have to change them yourself."*

~ Andy Warhol

# Chapter Five

## A New Life, a New Identity

In the last several hours, I was able to reconstruct most of my original notes along with a list of questions for Lenard and Gene. I don't know what to expect today, but whenever I find myself in sticky situations, Mother's sage advice comes back. She would often say, "When faced with adversity, one must adjust their attitude and look on the bright side of things."

*Whatever these two goofy men throw at me today, I'll deal with it.*

I wonder when the agents will come as it's nearly eight o'clock. A few minutes later, Lenard knocks loudly on the door asking if I'm up yet. As he unlocks the door from the outside, I release the deadbolt.

Gene is pushing a cart as Lenard strolls in after him. "Morning, Ellen," he says, taking a bagel out of a basket, plopping himself on the desk chair. They must have ordered this, as I have no recollection of calling room service.

"Hello Lenard, Gene. Come on in."

"We have a workable plan put together for you, Ellen," Lenard states candidly. Standing to pace, he pulls the curtains aside slightly, then refills his coffee mug from the large carafe and sits down on the chair again.

*Should I worry that Lenard is using the same words Abdul used?*

Lenard and Gene act as peculiarly as Abdul and his giant sidekick. The absurdity of this makes me laugh aloud, and they both stop to gape at me.

Expressing his concern, Lenard asks, "Is this funny to you?"

"No, it reminds me of a, never mind, tell me about this wonderful plan you've come up with, Lenard."

Lenard takes a swig from his coffee mug and says, "There is only one little hitch. It has to do with a silent partner we want to bring in. So far, it looks like he and his associates will agree to our terms. Our Special Team worked on this nearly all night."

Gene reaches for the carafe and offers me a cup, and then waves his hand at the basket of pastry, "Are you eating?"

Lenard gulps his coffee, then licks his lips. "We have to make sure anyone involved understands what the plan entails and some things need more work."

"Can you get to the point, Lenard?"

His manner is exasperating this morning. It's unclear how these two have the distinction of a special agent because so far, I don't see anything special about them.

"You do not have to snap at me, Ellen!" Lenard says, licking his lips again. "Our teams worked on an extensive plan after putting several models together. It was not a simple thing!"

Gene smiles sweetly, blinks, and says, "We let 'em go at it to see what they could shake out. We all feel it is the best way to go for you and your family."

Lenard slams his mug down on the desk. "How do you like horses?"

"Do ya think you can manage a horse farm?" Gene asks.

*They can't be serious!*

It has been a dream of mine for many years. Ravi and I talked about moving to the country where we could grow vegetables, living semi off-the-grid, and raising horses. As time went on, and because Ravi traveled so much, life intervened, and it dropped by the wayside.

"Lenard, what exactly are you saying?"

"It is part of a bigger picture, Ellen," Lenard says. "We are going to relocate you."

Gene quickly adds, "On a great big piece of property with a barn, and pastures, and outbuildings, and you will see it for yourself very soon."

"Our teams think it is genius," Lenard says in a smug tone. "They are quite pleased with themselves."

*If this is their actual personalities, they are giving me a headache.*

"You will have a new life with a new identity, Ellen. The only catch is that you have to share this venture with…" Lenard stops to take a bite of his bagel, slurping his coffee, which allows Gene to finish his sentence.

"The silent stakeholders are open to the idea, though, once it was on the table," Gene says. He glances at Lenard as if he is deviating from an invisible script, or he has forgotten the next sentence.

After a few seconds, I wonder if they might have said something they shouldn't, or did they mean to say something to throw me off for some reason?

"The one person who can pull this all together is mighty special," Gene finally says.

"Who are these silent investors you're talking about?" I ask.

Gene chuckles, "One of 'em was lookin for this very thing, only he needs a person he can trust to take care of his half of it while he is out of the country. It's where you come in."

"He needs *you*, Ellen," Lenard mumbles. "We have a meeting with this person and his people at one o'clock day after tomorrow."

As if on cue, Special Agent Andrea Simmons waltzes in with two large, bulging, unmarked department store bags, and a large wheeled suitcase. She greets the men in a somewhat friendly way saying, "Good Morning, Lenard, Gene." Then doesn't bother to acknowledge my presence.

"Mornin Agent Simmons, let me get that for ya." Gene takes the suitcase and throws it awkwardly onto the bed.

"Thanks, Gene." Andrea smiles at Lenard, where a millisecond of comprehension passes between them, but I'm not privy to what it might be.

*Could they have been lovers at one time? That can't be right!*

"Agent Simmons went shopping for you," Lenard says, touching his tie and licking his lips in Andrea's direction.

Agent Simmons unceremoniously begins to dump the contents of the bags onto the bed. Holding up one of the dresses, she turns to me saying, "Yes, these will do."

*Is she wearing a wig? Is it even the same style or color it was yesterday?*

"I had a lot of fun spending someone else's money," she chuckles.

As the agents talk, I rummage through the piles, noting that the clothes are not something I'd wear, but would certainly appeal to my teenage daughter.

"Where are we going?" No one answers. "Hello, where are we going?"

The agents reluctantly stop their conversation, but it's Andrea who speaks. "First, you are going to the salon; your persona needs changing. Then you are going on a little trip. I would get going if I were you; there is not much time!"

"Thank you, Agent Simmons. I could use a haircut. What else do you want to change?"

"Ellen, you cannot look like your old self. You need to be more..." Lenard snarls.

"You want me to look more what, Lenard?"

"You cannot be the person you were," he retorts. "That needs to change!"

Picking through the pile of clothes, I choose something that looks comfortable. They are of good quality, but there are no tags. The clothes at Abdul's palatial digs had tags removed, too.

About thirty minutes later, I'm ready for my new adventure. When I step out of the bathroom, Agent Simmons has left the room.

"We packed the clothes for ya. Are ya ready?" Gene asks. "We have a long flight today. We need to stay on course." Gene hands me an envelope with ELLEN D. THOMPSON written across the front. "That is your new identity; passport, driver's license, and social security card."

The passport and license elicit a chuckle as my weight, height, and color of hair are entirely wrong. "I have no memory of posing for this photo. It looks like one of my mother's."

Lenard sighs heavily, "It is best you let us take care of things right now, Ellen. You will need to trust that we made good decisions for you." He seems a little nervous this morning as he continuously licks his lips, unnervingly impatient, and more than a little snarly.

"The last time I heard those words I was drugged and held prisoner! I'm almost ready. I need to find a sweater."

Lenard and Gene exchange glances, reminding me how this leaves me out of their club, much as Abdul and Jam-ale did. How long will the events of the last several weeks come crashing through my thoughts every time there is a similarity?

I open a small purse to find a wallet with a fake ten-dollar bill with photos of people I've never met. Also, inside is a beautiful watch! It strikes me so funny I start to laugh, but the dynamic duo doesn't know what to do when this happens. As I regain my composure, Lenard says, it would be funny to him too, if this had happened to him.

"I had five hundred dollars in my wallet, but the Great Oz didn't give it back. Do you intend to give me any to tide me over?"

Lenard harrumphs loudly. He then walks out of the room without saying anything. As Gene watches him leave, he turns to me. "We will take care of that later. Right now, we need to get going."

Gene wrestles the suitcase off the bed and pushes it toward the open door. In the meantime, Lenard stands rigidly at the elevator motioning to us when it opens. He appears angry when he glances at Gene. They each grab bags that were in the hallway, and we go down in silence.

They brusquely escort me through the lobby, passing a girl at the desk who waves, and mouths the words, 'have a nice day.' A shiny black car that looks like the limousine from yesterday is waiting at the entrance to the hotel near the curb.

Agent Tom is sitting in the driver's seat. He gets out when the trunk flies open and reaches to help with the luggage. As the bags go into the trunk, Gene tries to grab my red case, but I won't hand it over. He finally gives up as Lenard takes my arm, practically pushing me inside the vehicle, sandwiching me between them.

New-car smell is noticeable, and I wonder if this is our government dollars at work. What does an elaborate plan like mine cost? How many projects do we taxpayers unknowingly fund? How many more are in the works right now?

Several minutes later, the limo stops at a salon where Lenard says Anna is waiting for me. Hours later, the transformation is remarkable, and it's amazing how a new style and hair color can make a person look completely different. Even the boys comment, but it's uncertain whether it's a compliment or a polite acknowledgment.

Agent Tom drives for approximately twenty minutes to the airport grounds. A large hanger comes into view where a small jet aircraft is waiting on the tarmac. A young man waves as he descends the stairs and opens the car door when the limo comes to a stop near him. His name badge identifies him as Michael. He informs us that the Captain is waiting for us to come aboard and we follow him up the stairs as Agent Tom takes the luggage out of the trunk.

"Take any seat you want, Ma'am. Relax and enjoy the flight." As we take our seats, Michael pulls the stairs up, locking them in place, and then goes through a pre-rehearsed spiel, pointing to the exit, the mini-bar at the back, and magazines in the rack up front. "We will take off in a few minutes."

He gives a little salute to Lenard and Gene and a small wave to me as he goes through the cockpit door where a faint click signals he has locked it. The plane jostles slightly when our luggage goes into the compartment under the aircraft. Since I'm toward the back, it's easy to reach the mini-bar where I grab some snacks and a few bottles.

A crackling voice says, "Welcome aboard, I am Captain so and so, and we will be leaving as soon as clearance comes from the tower."

Settled in a comfortable dark leather seat, I reach into the case to pull out a book, deliberately ignoring *Moby Dick* as the exploits of Ahab or his sidekick are no longer of interest.

Casually opening the front cover of *For Whom the Bell Tolls* expecting to find the pages removed, I'm startled to see they are intact, but lightly glued together. A wafer-thin note falls into my lap when I pry the pages apart. It is from none other than His Royal Highness Crown Prince pain-in-the-ass!

Looking around quickly, I half expect one, or both of those lunatics to be close. How did the note get into this book? What do they want from me? I thought this part of my drama was over.

Turning the book over, fingering the embossed lettering on the cover, it doesn't look quite right. Somehow, it seems thicker, and it appears that the page glued to keep the leather edges in place inside the front cover, is shifted.

What do I do? Try to pry the cover off now, or wait? Do I tell Lenard and Gene, or keep my mouth shut? Are they in on this, or is someone else responsible? I decide to wait for another time, so I place the book into my case and put it between my legs. Reclining the seat when the light goes off on the seat-belt sign, I'm quickly lulled to sleep by the motion of the jet.

Michael strolls down the aisle to ask if I want lunch. Since I don't know when the next meal will be, I accept the tasty offerings and devour everything on the plate. Pulling out a sheet of paper to write down my thoughts, I lightly sketch Michael's face.

Sometime later, the jet pitches to the right as we begin to decelerate. Lenard and Gene wave, asking if I'm okay. A crackling voice says that we're experiencing turbulence, fasten your seatbelts, bring trays to their upright position, and remain in your seat.

It isn't too much longer when I drift back to sleep. Hours later, the crackling voice says, "We will be down to earth shortly as soon as we have clearance."

Lenard and Gene are involved in an animated conversation as their heads bob up and down above their seat backs, which reminds me of bobbleheads. They often have their heads together either discussing or arguing, and their incessant finishing of each other's sentences is unnerving. Perhaps it's years of working together, but they act more like an old married couple, and it's beginning to grate on my already frayed nerves.

The ground below, sectioned into squares and circles, could be any number of states viewed from the air. It could be Maryland, New York, Massachusetts, Kentucky, or Timbuktu for all I know!

"Where are we fellas?" When they don't answer, I ask again. "What state are we going to?"

Gene pops his head up, waving his hands in the air, saying, "It's the great State of Va'ginia. The great land of the Thoroughbreds!"

The crackling voice says we have permission to land, and the ground comes up to meet us. Our landing is surprisingly smooth, and we taxi to a hanger that looks strangely like the one we left in Kauai. A shiny black limousine, sans Agent Tom Spalding, is waiting on the tarmac. Did we fly in circles all these hours and are back at the same airport? Are these two numskulls messing with me?

When the jet comes to a complete stop, Michael comes out of the cockpit. A faint click means that the Captain of this airship and owner of the disembodied, crackling voice, will remain out of sight. Michael unlocks and pushes the stairs out, then turns to talk with Lenard and Gene, but with the engines winding down, their conversation is not audible.

Holding on to my red case, I follow Gene down the stairs as Lenard brings up the rear. Gene takes the luggage from the underbelly of the jet to the trunk of the waiting limo. He tries to grab my red case, but I refuse to relinquish the handle. Lenard asks what's so important it can't go into the trunk. I'm not about to part with my notes again and simply say, it's personal.

Lenard clutches my arm and pushes me inside the limo. A short time later, it stops at a large hotel where Gene and Lenard orchestrate our luggage through the lobby and into the elevator. When we arrive at the sixth floor, we walk to the end of the hall and stop outside a Presidential Suite. Gene inserts one of two plastic door keys he holds, then turns to hand one to Lenard.

The square foyer is stunning in mahogany paneling. A vase filled with faux flowers sits on a table blocking the view into the suite. As we walk around the table, Gene throws the double French doors open and asks me to follow him as Lenard stops to deposit his duffle bag at the first bedroom. As we pass the second bedroom, Gene drops his suitcase at the doorway.

Moving through the living room area, we navigate around several overstuffed chairs. It looks regal and tasteful. A marble fireplace with a beautiful wood mantle displays Lladro porcelain and Wedgewood plates. Two Stiffel lamps are precisely placed on end tables while silk embroidered throw pillows are grouped on a multi-pieced sectional.

A large muted landscape painting, in the same hues as the accent pieces completes the room. It's an exciting mix of fabric and décor, and it looks quite elegant. Beyond this is a dining room containing a large table, upholstered chairs, a hutch containing china and delicate Dalton knickknacks.

Has a president stayed here? A counter and bar stools on the opposite wall are under a cutout that gives a glimpse into a full-sized kitchen.

"This is your room, little lady," Gene says, stopping at a door off to the right of the dining room. Disappearing with my suitcase, he comes out of the room saying, "This should be real comfortable for ya."

"I'm feeling a little dry. Do you think there's some juice in the kitchen?"

Lenard sticks his head out of the cutout opening, gruffly saying that he'll see what there is and bring it to me. As I touch the drapery fabric,

Lenard startles me by noisily placing a small tray of bottled juice and water on the dresser.

*Why is he acting so strange today?*

"I will order dinner for six thirty, if that suits you. Gene and I have details to go over, so you should rest. I will let you know when the food arrives."

Lenard closes the door, and I wait for a CLICK, but it doesn't come. Since I don't trust him, I lock the door from the inside. Reaching for a bottle of water and looking around the room, I'm pleasantly surprised there is a small desk. On top, there's a box of stationery that must hold at least a hundred pages.

Searching through the drawers produces several pens. Suddenly drained of energy, the digital clock on the nightstand reads 4:30, but now I'm too tired to deal with anything and stretch out on the bed.

"Ellen? Dinner is here." The digital clock next to the bed reads 6:55!

"I'll be out in a minute." Shaking off the drowsiness and splashing water on my face, I quickly change clothes.

Is this a parallel universe? There are three place settings. Although they have different names and faces, it strangely reminds me of the dining hall, Abdul, and Jam-ale.

Lenard and Gene have also changed their clothes and are now wearing jeans and polo shirts. We make small talk as we eat where Lenard yaks on about protocols and rules and what is required now that the program is mostly in place. He says there's nothing to worry about as their teams worked day and night to pull this together for my family, and we should all be happy with the outcome. Here, have some more wine.

After dinner, Lenard suggests that we move to the living room so he can go over the details of what the significance of having a new identity entails. From where I'm sitting on the sofa, Gene is clearing the table, stacking the dishes on the bar counter, clumsily clinking the glasses together. Has Lenard told him he has kitchen duty? It doesn't appear that he likes it.

Meanwhile, Lenard outlines the protocols that are the most significant to the plan. He does this apparently from memory where he closes his eyes to recall the next one, then begins speaking as if he's delivering a lecture to a crowd of people.

I try to interrupt him several times, but he ignores me and licks his lips in that nervous habit of his. By now, Gene has joined us with a tray of sweets, fruit, and coffee. Gene pours as Lenard continues, repeating what it means to be in the Federal Witness Protection Program along with the rules that go with that.

"We have these rules in place for a reason, and you will follow them to the letter! Do you understand the gravity of what that means, Ellen?"

Opening my list of prepared questions, I say, "Before I agree to anything, I have some questions I want to ask."

Lenard and Gene glare at me. "You wanted our help and our protection. You do not have a choice in the matter any longer. You and your family are already in the program, right, Gene?"

"Yessiree, as soon as you accepted the passport and driver's license, you became Missus Ellen D. Thompson," Gene adds. "You are no longer Ellen Andress."

"You never told me that!"

Lenard is abrupt. "I am quite sure that we did, Ellen. You were a bit upset yesterday and probably a little groggy from the drugs they gave you. We certainly told you. How about it, Gene?"

Gene nods his head, yes, but his face suddenly flushes a deep crimson.

"What I asked was for someone to contact my government and family. I didn't ask to be part of this program! You never gave me a choice. What does the D stand for?"

"Dillon; it stands for Dillon, your new maiden name," Lenard says in a terse tone. "You are now in the program, Ellen, whether you like it or not! That is how it is." His tone changes as fast as a storm blowing in.

Gene says, "Yup, there is no question about this. It is a done deal all right, and there will be no going back now."

Lenard retorts, "I am quite certain we told you all about that last night."

It seems a bit unfair, but there's no way to prove it. Dillon? It can stand for ***determined*** because I'm resolute to retake control of my life. "And I'm quite certain you did not! What if I don't like your plan, Mr. Lenard; what happens then?"

Lenard stiffens, then glances at Gene. In a dramatic gesture, Lenard closes his eyes, as if he's trying to compose himself to keep his anger in check.

"You will like it plenty once you get used to it. Everyone that goes into the program does. By the way, Ravenalt Andress is not the person you thought he was."

"Yeah, in fact, it was not even his real name," Gene sputters. "Did you know that?"

"What are you two talking about and what do you know about him?"

"The only thing he told you that was half-way true, is that he worked for Stahlman Industries." Lenard bends to pick up his coffee cup, moving around the room, he stops at the window to peer out.

"That's a bunch of hogwash! He went to work for them right after he graduated from college. I certainly would have known if he was lying to me!"

"He is not the person he told you he was," Gene says. "Did he ever mention what he did for them?"

"Didn't you ever wonder why he traveled so much?" Lenard asks, watching me over the rim of his coffee cup.

Gene shifts forward in his chair. "Didn't you wonder where he went when he left you and the kids alone for so long? He told you more than one lie. They were whoppers, too." He starts to laugh, then Lenard rudely tells him to shut up.

"This is preposterous. I don't believe you! He told me right from the beginning his job would require him to travel. You two are as loony as a three-dollar bill. You have the wrong person. I trusted him. Why would I question him? He told me where he was going and called us every night. He gave presentations to groups of people all over the world, for Stahlman Industries."

"Yes, that is what he told you, but did you know what he was doing?" Lenard sneers.

I'm becoming agitated. "Stop this insanity right now. I don't have to listen to this nonsense. Ravi isn't here to defend himself, now is he?"

"Ellen, I did not make this up," Lenard sighs.

"Are you sure you have the right Ravenalt Andress? He trained people, and it had something to do with electronic thingies."

Gene asks nonchalantly, "Were you a little curious about those odd markings on his body?"

"Oh, stop this. Everyone has a birthmark here and there."

"Ellen, calm down. We have irrefutable evidence to suggest that he was into something we are not at liberty to discuss. Our bureau has been watching him for some time now and the authorities want him in conjunction with a serious crime that was committed a few years ago."

It's the most absurd accusation yet. "Are you trying to convince me that my husband was a criminal when I know he wasn't? You have the wrong person."

"Do you remember the movie called *True Lies*? Are you familiar with the characters who were undercover agents?" Lenard grumbles.

It takes everything I can muster to keep from jumping over the coffee table to choke him. "My husband was not an agent. I went to Stahlman Industries on many occasions, and I traveled with him. We went to Christmas parties, company picnics with his coworkers, met his boss, his boss's boss. He couldn't have faked all that, I would have known!"

"That is the person he wanted you to see. That is *not* who he was. By telling you now, we thought it would save you embarrassment later. We are looking out for your future," Lenard says smugly.

Gene is more sympathetic of the two. "He was a very clever man, Ma'am. He was a highly trained individual."

*Are they playing good cop, bad cop, as Homeland Security did yesterday?*

"He was highly trained in electronics or something. But you aren't saying that kind of training, are you?" Both men are quiet, nodding in agreement. "And, of course, you aren't at liberty to tell me, because it's a matter of National Security."

"Your husband was killed for a reason. Until we have all the information, it might be best to leave it for another time," Lenard says changing his tone.

Gene adds, "It's for your protection; need to know basis, you know the drill."

"No, I do not know the drill! I have no intention of leaving any of this alone. I have questions, and I want answers."

"That will have to wait. We can pick this up again tomorrow morning," Lenard sputters.

"I don't want to wait; I need to know things right now."

"You will have that opportunity tomorrow. Gene and I still have hours of work yet. We need to finalize what we are doing, so it goes smoothly at our meeting with the investors tomorrow. I suggest you go to your room and let us finish up here. We will see you in the morning. Good night, Ellen." Lenard walks toward the kitchen as Gene starts to clear the coffee table.

"Are you dismissing me, Lenard?"

"We will talk in the morning," he snaps, sounding much like Abdul when he excused people.

Walking toward my room, I stop near the kitchen cutout. "What are your intentions about my family, Lenard? When will they be able to join me? And I want to see this proof you have about Ravi!"

Lenard sticks his head out and says, "My dear Ellen, you will have to trust us, because all that is being worked out. We have a lot of work to do. Go to your room and let us get to it, okay? Good night."

"Don't ever call me dear Ellen again, do you hear me?"

Lenard glares at me for a second, and then a slow, condescending smile replaces his sneer. I am beginning to dislike him.

After I shut and lock my bedroom door, it dawns on me that there should be sketches of everyone I met since my little adventure began. It might come in handy if I ever want to prove my bizarre story to other people.

I'm bothered by Lenard and Gene's attitude. Is my imagination playing tricks on me? Something is holding me back from sharing things about the books in my case. And why were they trying so hard to convince me that my husband, Ravi, was not who he told me he was?

*Have I been sleeping with the enemy?*

Will this nightmare ever end? Will the truth ever be uncovered? Curiosity gets the better of me, and I put my notes and questions aside to retrieve Abdul's note. Taking a closer look at the other two books, I determine that the covers on all three have the same type of alteration, which is an exciting twist. I don't dare disturb the leather yet, not until these two dimwits are no longer with me.

*Is there a secret under the book covers?*

The day begins when a sliver of light slips through the room-darkening draperies and hits my face. Thoughts drift across the miles of challenging terrain that is now my life. Is this a vacuum? Perhaps I fell through a black hole into a new universe!

Will my children be able to leave their old lives behind without too much stress? Will Mother come with them? Will I ever see my sister and her family again? Lenard and Gene said there would be no contact with anyone we once knew, with the emphasis on NO ONE.

Unlocking the door, the aroma of coffee beckons. Lenard and Gene huddle over papers spread across the coffee table in the living area. Waving, they go back to what they're doing, ignoring me for the most part. Fresh-squeezed orange juice, several chafing dishes, and a mound of pastries line the counter.

After getting a cup of coffee, I sit down at the dining room table to observe Lenard and Gene as they gather their papers to shove into folders. They refill their coffee cups, scoop out generous portions of eggs and bacon, and then sit down at the table near me.

"Hope you slept good, Ellen," Lenard says in a tone that is off-putting to me. Is it condescending or his normal obnoxious self? "Is that all you are having? You might be hungry later."

"We got a big day ahead. Not as long a trip as yesterday. There will be lots to see. You are goin to love it. Can I get you some eggs or somethin? You gotta fill up on more than that."

"I'm not very hungry. Look, I've been doing some thinking about what you said last night, gentleman. You can't be talking about the Ravi I knew."

"We disagree with you," Lenard states, shoveling food into his mouth.

"Will you answer some questions now?"

"Let me see," Lenard says grabbing my list, then raising his eyebrows, then hands it back. "Okay, go ahead."

"My first question is; When can I see my children?"

"As soon as we settle everything, Ellen. There is no timetable."

"My second question is; are they with my Mother?"

Gene answers, "Yes."

"Has she been contacted? Do you know if she and the children are okay?"

Talking with his mouth full, Lenard says, "No, we have not contacted her yet. I am sure everyone is alright."

"Who are the people we're meeting today? Do they know my circumstances?"

Lenard sighs heavily, "Ellen, our teams say that these people wish to remain anonymous. They are private investors who will act as silent partners. You will be one of them."

"My next question is; do you know who is responsible for blowing up the airplane and why that Prince person took me?"

Lenard looks disgusted and then says, "Those are two completely different questions, Ellen. No, we have no definite answers or proof at this time."

"I asked you for some cash. May I have some?"

Lenard rolls his eyes, sighing heavily. "Not this again. I thought you took care of this, Gene."

Gene stops eating. "I was going to...you know, after..."

"After what?" I ask.

"Do you have another question, Ellen? We have things to get to before we leave here today," Lenard says, stuffing his mouth with food again.

"Yes, how do you know my husband is not who he says he is?"

Lenard looks pensive. "I told you. We have irrefutable evidence to support our claim. No, we will not share that with you at this time."

"Last question; any chance this thing will backfire, guys?"

Lenard and Gene stop eating and appear dazed as neither one answers. Then Gene blinks as Lenard recovers to say there will be no more questions.

"What does she mean, Lenard?" Gene stammers.

Lenard abruptly grabs his plate and walks into the kitchen. When he clears his throat loudly, Gene glances his way. His face whitens and then flushes a deep crimson. An unpleasant picture starts to emerge about these two. Have I caught them between the proverbial rock and hard place?

"You should have contacted Mother by now, Lenard. Won't she have a decision to make whether she'll join my children or stay in Illinois?"

"It is not safe right now. It could jeopardize everything." Lenard is a bit evasive, his nervous lip thing is increasing with frequency, and he won't look directly at me when he talks.

"Why can't you get her a message that I'm alive? What would that hurt? You are both acting as if I've said something wrong. Are you ignoring me?"

Lenard moves back to the living room, making a motion for Gene to do something, but he has a vacant look on his face. "We will contact her at the right time. It isn't the right time yet. Come in here so we can revisit the protocols."

*What has thrown them for a loop?*

Lenard's narrative is not as smooth as it was last night. He runs through the lists of items the newly-formed Thompson family must now follow, once we are all reunited. He says I will receive a complete dossier as soon as all pertinent information is available. It will be my job to tell both my mother and children that they *must* abide by it.

"Lenard, I thought you said no one contacted her yet."

"Ellen, stop interrupting. *If* your mother wishes to join you, she must abide by the same rules we have set down for you and your children. It is a matter of National Security. It is your duty as American Citizens to accept these rules and regulations unconditionally. They are for your survival and for those who made this possible for you."

"They are the b'hind the scenes people. It is the fruits of their labor," Gene says smiling.

Lenard adds, "They worked very hard for you and your family these last few days and nights. It will take us a couple of hours to get where we need to go today. You will need to be ready in about thirty minutes. We are on a tight schedule. Gene, may I have a word with you?"

"Let me know when you want me to come get your suitcase, Ma'am," Gene says thoughtfully.

"Lenard, you didn't say anything about moving to another hotel."

"We swear that you were told last night that we would be in a different place tonight," he says.

"No, you didn't." The realization suddenly strikes me that my life has changed in the blink of an eye.

*What if I don't like their plan, how will I get out of it?*

Gene calls from the dining room asking if I'm ready. Zipping the suitcase, remembering that I wanted to open the small white envelope he gave me yesterday, I decide it can wait. Leaving the relative security of the suite, we go down in the elevator where we walk across the empty lobby to the predictably shiny black limo parked near the curb. A chauffeur drives us today. He doesn't look familiar.

Thinking once again of the mysterious bulge of the book covers, but not so paranoid as to attract attention to them or my notes, I allow Gene to put the red carry-on case in the trunk. We drive for about two hours in a south or southwest orientation along a mostly deserted four-lane divided highway. Lenard and Gene are deep in discussion, and I try to tune them out to look out the window.

The limo slows to turn right onto a two-lane road where rural landscape comes into view. My heart skips a beat as we pass pasture after pasture, with miles and miles of fencing. Some are white, some plain planking, still others have fancy shiny metal between posts.

A sign welcomes us to a little Village called JASPER, population 1,220, est. 1801. We pass large farmhouses with dull red, white, or green barns that have large Oak trees, pickup trucks, and rusting farm equipment abandoned in fields. We slowly pass horses of every color in pastures of brown and green.

The limo slows to turn left onto a road where we follow a three-tiered fence that looks as if it were white at one time. A sign announcing ASHWOOD FARMS appears to be new. It has black letters on a red and gray background. A small, two-story red brick structure sits on one side of the driveway. It appears occupied, as curtains are apart and the windows are unbroken. Beyond and to the extreme left, is a massive red brick rectangular country-style mansion that looks like a small hotel.

A bay picks up his head when we roll down the gravel driveway, and his tail swishes from side to side as we pass. It reminds me of a memory lodged deep within my subconscious; it emerges, then quickly fades.

The limo continues past a row of garages where a grey SUV is parked. Beyond the garages, and presumably downwind, is a convoluted red and white barn, part of which is listing precariously to the left.

"Welcome to your new home, Ellen," Lenard announces, as the car stops under a portico. "We have some time before our meeting with the silent partners this afternoon so that we can tour the house and grounds. I know what you are thinking. It is a little overwhelming, but you will get used to it."

Gene leans in to say, "Ain't it beautiful? You will like it, Miss Ellen, honest you will. You need to give it some time."

A large woman in a mauve suit and bright magenta blouse motions from the front door. It's obvious her pumps are a tad too small as her feet are puffy. She has the biggest hair I've ever seen. A collie rests on the front landing near her, reminding me of our Sheltie named Sassy. The collie moves toward the car and lets out a soft woof in greeting.

"Are you serious, Lenard? What if I don't like it here? It looks like it's in need of a lot of repair and renovation. All I can see are dollar signs!"

"Keep your voice down and say nothing. Let me take care of it." Lenard throws the car door open, saying, "Gladys, it's so nice to see you again."

The woman juts her hand out, pumping Lenard's arm like an old pump handle. "Hello, Lenard, greetings to everyone! I'm so glad you're here. Come inside; we've been expecting you. Oh, what a glorious day it is. Welcome everyone; it's a great day for a tour. Follow me; there's so much to see. You must be Ms. Thompson. Howdy, to you all. Shoo Rosie, Ms. Thompson don't want you sniffin around her," the woman says to the dog. "Go lay down somewhere else, will ya?"

"How are you this fine day, Gladys?" Lenard roughly takes my arm to pull me toward the front door and the woman who hasn't stopped talking. She has a high-pitched voice that immediately grates on my nerves.

"Who is this woman, Lenard? You should have warned me about her." As we stand on the crumbling front steps, the dog begins to nuzzle my hand, and I absently pat her head. Glancing around at the landscape, the buildings, and then up at the sky, I question what God's Plan might be...does He think we'll be happy here?

I must trust that although there are real doubts about Lenard and Gene's intentions, I must get through the next couple of days for my family to be reunited. If there are frogs to kiss along the way, then I can do that too. But, please God, make it quick, won't you?

"Ellen?" Lenard is licking his lips and pulling at my arm. This lip thing is annoying, but he's now talking in a more progressive condescending tone of voice. "Ellen, come! We don't want to make Gladys wait!"

Rosie stays by my side even when the woman tells her to go away again. When we enter the house, the dog disappears through the doorway.

"Do the owners intend to do repairs? The steps look dangerous. It's not at all what you described. I don't know if I can do this!"

Lenard stares daggers at me. Hissing loud enough for me to hear, he says, "Keep your voice down; Gladys has no time to go over this kind of stuff with you right now."

Gladys has moved into the vestibule and may or may not have heard our conversation. When she turns around, she walks past Lenard to take my arm to pull me closer.

"What do you think of the weather here, Ms. Thompson? Bet you won't miss your mid-west winters. It's mild and wonderful here almost all the year through. Oh, my, I'm forgettin my manners. I'm the local Real Estate Agent outta Jasper; name's Gladys Mogador. A warm welcome to you." When she smiles, I notice her capped front teeth. "You're going to love it here! Please come in; you've been expected. There's a lot to see, and you don't have much time, so come right on in."

Gladys explains the cleverly concealed cloakrooms the original owners used when they gave fancy parties, delighting in the nuances of the details, the way the wall opens to become a counter. She then goes on to expound on the beautiful trim, the flooring, and the quality of the workmanship.

"Isn't this facinatin Ms. Thompson? There's so much detail here. Let's move along quickly, shall we? Don't you agree it has some great features, Ms. Thompson?"

"Yes, it has countless features, Gladys."

"We don't have much time before you go to your appointment, isn't that right Lenard?" Gladys stops dead in her tracks, glances at Lenard, as he pulls me ahead of her and into the main house.

Things are not adding up. What has Lenard told her? How would she know about my mid-west winters or our appointment today? I was under the impression information like that was carefully guarded.

As we walk through the French doors leading into a grand hallway, it looks like a hotel lobby, minus the bell hop station. A grand staircase is in the middle which flows up to an expansive landing on the second floor.

Glossy brochures are on a small table in the hallway. As Gladys talks on, I browse through one wondering how many tours with potential buyers have already come through this place. There's no selling price, so the old saying that, 'if you have to ask how much it is, you can't afford it,' must apply here.

Gladys probably hopes I won't notice the squeak of the floors as we walk across them or the odd musty smell of a house shut-up for extended periods, but I do. Pointing to the left and right, she gives little snippets about the house, spreading her arms wide in an arc, which elicits comments from either Gene or Lenard.

She drones on about the walnut wood floors, hewn from the trees on this very property, then segues into the history of the expensive wool rugs, going on *ad nauseam* about the antiques that seem to be everywhere.

Next is the library that has a large fireplace positioned on an inside wall, which is large by most standards, but not as massive as the one in Abdul's dining room.

*Why did that memory come back now?*

Gladys mentions that the original Mrs. Ashwood was very particular when it came to the fireplaces. Both the one in the library and the one in the living room had to be open to the main hall to heat the house during the winter months. She laughs heartily and says that both the builder and the architect went back and forth about that part of the design.

A door leading into Mr. AJ Ashwood's office, which became his son's office, then his grandson after him is at the far end of the room. Custom built-in bookshelves are everywhere we look, which contains more knickknacks than books.

The original house plans are open on the long library table. Each Ashwood generation looked for ways to improve the manor house, moving walls and such to satisfy each wife's love of all things functional. All the renovations and reconstructions are there, Gladys insists. Did she wink at Lenard?

"Oh, there's this handy little elevator installed for Old Miss Abigail. She was the last of the Ashwood's to live here. It looks like a closet, but it's a real working elevator! I wouldn't tell your kids about it right now, though. They might think they can ride up and down in it all day. I'd keep this a secret for now. Miss Abigail got feeble toward the end of her life. It was a real Godsend for Mrs. Murdock and the nurse who came to care for her."

"And Mrs. Murdock would be?" I ask Gladys as we walk.

"You'll meet her soon enough, her husband too. So that you know, Mr. Murdock won't go near that elevator. Someone else had to bring Miss Abigail up and down from her bedroom, b'cause he didn't want anything to do with it. Got a scare of some kind."

Gladys rambles on, with what is turning out to be an epic oration. Rosie appears and then disappears into another room as if she is chasing an invisible ball. We continue to follow Gladys, who never slows down in her descriptions and I can't shake a nagging feeling that something ominous is about to happen. Maybe it's nerves, or perhaps I'm a little hungry.

We troop after Gladys, going through a paneled archway from the library into a billiard room, but we don't linger here. As we enter the kitchen, my first reaction is utter disbelief.

"Oh, Lord!" tumbles out of my mouth before I realize I've said anything. Everyone stops as Lenard shakes his head at me. "Did I say that out loud? Please continue."

Gladys is pointing out the spacious butler's pantry that is within easy reach of the country kitchen that is stuck in the fifties. Near the back door are a mudroom and two small bedrooms that share an antiquated bathroom.

This area was the hub of activity when the farm and dairy were in its heyday. The workers came to eat here or congregated on the back porch until 1954. That's when Mr. AJ Ashwood the second passed away, and his son took over. Things changed drastically after that, and the farm passed into troubled times.

"Gladys, where is the laundry located?" I ask, not wanting to know the answer.

"It's in the basement, Ms. Thompson. Will that be a problem for you?"

"No, no problem." It will take bazillions of dollars to restore this place to its former glory. How much can we generate if both Mother and I sell our houses? Imaginary numbers are crunching in my head.

"Ellen, I told you to let us take care of everything. Gladys will think, loose that awful expression, will you? We can talk about this later."

"I wonder how I can afford this, Lenard. I don't know if I can do this."

"Stop causing trouble," Lenard says, as the others move off in another direction. "Of course, you can, there is no need to worry; our team worked everything out."

"Oh? What exactly did they work out, Lenard, you haven't shared that with me."

"Keep your voice down. Ellen, you need to trust us. Come on; we need to catch up. We have little time."

Passing a stairway leading to the second floor from the kitchen, we go through a doorway that takes us into what Gladys describes as the Morning Room. The Ashwood family would eat their breakfast and mid-day meals here, not in the kitchen. Beyond this room, is Mrs. Ashwood's office.

Gladys then directs us through a set of pocket doors into a massive formal dining room containing a large table with matching upholstered chairs. Centered over the table is a gleaming chandelier with two large built-in glass-fronted china cabinets along one wall; each filled with a bevy of glassware and assorted dishes.

Two highboy hutches (on rolling casters) are flanking the double pocket doors. Gladys mentions that the architect, Mr. Saxby, and Mrs. Ashwood vehemently argued over this detail. They could move the highboys easily when the doors were folded into the wall along the sides for the living and dining rooms to combine as a ballroom for large parties.

It must have been a splendid house at one time. Now, the furniture is old and worn, and it's difficult to determine what the wallpaper pattern might have been. There's little evidence that anything changed during renovations in either room or the whole of the downstairs, for that matter.

*Dare I speculate what we'll see when we visit the upstairs?*

As we walk into the living room, a man is sitting on one of the sofas. Standing when he sees Gladys, she makes quick introductions.

"Glen Murdock will tell us about the history of Ashwood Farms in a little while."

He lets out a chuckle after Gladys asks him about lemonade and cookies, then says, "Be right back."

Gladys then directs our attention to the large fireplace, asking for us to make ourselves comfortable on the deflated sofas, prattling on about the configuration of the rooms.

The library and living rooms are the same width and length, and unlike the wood mantle in there, this one is made of a lovely Italian cream-colored marble.

Gladys continues to chatter on about the custom-made, built-in window seats, the exquisite crown molding, and the beautiful full plank baseboards. She segues into the abundant antiques and other items that distinguish this from all the other rooms. Then she stops midsentence, and glances at Lenard.

Mr. Murdock steps into the room, telling Gladys that Mona will be with us shortly. As we wait, I can't help but wonder if the beams in the two-story hall run through the floors and into the attic, because the engineers must have needed something massive to hold up this monster of a roof!

Do I feel a headache coming on now?

*Maybe I'm hungry.*

*"Kind words can be short and easy to speak,*

*but their echoes are truly endless."*

~ Mother Teresa of Calcutta

# Chapter Six

## The Struggle Within

**A** woman enters the room pushing a tea cart. Pastel aluminum tumblers are tinkling as a forgotten memory surfaces of lazy summer picnics by the shores of Lake Michigan. She sets cookies on the coffee table that give off a fragrant vanilla/cinnamon scent and proceeds to pour each of us a glass of yellowish liquid from a matching pitcher. When she's finished, she sits near the man on the sofa.

*My stomach is growling so loudly, Lenard glares at me.*

Gladys introduces Glen and Mona Murdock as the remaining employees of Miss Abigail Ashwood. Mona is wearing a gingham dress with a clean white apron. Her facial features are delicate, framed by wire-rim glasses. Her gray-streaked brown hair is clipped on top of her head, giving her a grandmotherly appearance. She is squeezing her folded hands together as if she's waiting to visit the principal's office for a scolding.

In contrast, Glen Murdock looks quite at home on the sofa. He pats Rosie's head, and she must be his dog by the looks of how comfortable the dog appears. Glen's face is rugged and tan. His hefty wiry whitish/reddish mustache puts him somewhere near to be a ranch hand, judging from his large, calloused hands.

Murdock is wearing a plaid shirt with a bolo, faded, but comfortable looking jeans with a shiny buckle, and tall hand-tooled cowboy boots. His dishwater blonde/red hair appears mashed down on his head as if he just took off a hat.

Standing up when Gladys nods to him, he's lean and lanky as a Willow tree. Placing an elbow on the mantle, he embarks on the history of Ashwood Farms, speaking in a slow Southern drawl, reciting from verbatim from the brochure I hold in my hand.

"The house was built in 1889 for Mr. Attwell Jacobs Ashwood, AJ as he was known around here. It was for his bride, so that makes the house 122 years old this year. The house is part of the National Register of Historic Homes, as you can see by the plaque near the front door," Glen says confidently, glancing at Gladys.

"AJ met and married a young woman named Sarah Burchfield Cunningham. They both came from prominent families near the Chicago area. He wanted a Frank Lloyd Wright House, but Ms. Ashwood wanted somethin else, not Victorian or Prairie, but somethin in b'tween, like a country manor."

"May I ask a question?"

Lenard's hand lands on my arm, shaking his head, he says, "If there is time, you can ask questions later, Ellen."

"They found an architect firm in the Chicago area called Wallingford & Desmond, who had a young apprentice by the name of Joseph Lindeman Saxby. He impressed Mr. AJ so much that he brought him out here ta gander at the property. AJ was big on wantin ta breed and race horses, and he felt this was the perfect environment ta do so. As they talked and walked around the property, Mr. Saxby sketched. Together, they came up with mostly this design. Then they all went back ta Chicago ta put their plans down on paper."

"If I may ask…" Lenard is thumping my arm, giving me a stern look.

"Since this was a new design structure, engineers had ta figure out if it would hold up such a gigantic roof. The first one was flat-out rejected, and they ended up with the roofs ya see taday. The basic footprint of the house was rectangular, with wings on either side." Murdock makes a square with his fingers for emphasis.

"When the plans were finally approved, they braced the roof from inside with those beams out there in the hallway. They go all the way through the basement and inta the bedrock under the house. Then it goes clean on up inta the attic where the beams form the ceiling. It's the only one like it in the whole country!"

*Does the FBI have a contingency plan if I refuse to live here?*

"Miss Sarah did have definite ideas of her own, and they were quite smart for the time. Mr. Saxby sometimes had ta go back ta Mr. AJ with the strange requests his wife wanted done here. AJ indulged her, as he made his fortune in the railroad business alongside the Rockefellers and Moores.

"Ashwood Farms not only had a dairy, they farmed fields, owned cattle, and bred horses, which they trained and raced at the local racetrack. We had a champion that went all the way ta the *Little Brown Jug* by the name of *Charlie's Delight*. That was a little b'fore my time, though."

When there is no reaction, Glen volunteers that the *Little Brown Jug* is part of the Triple Crown of Harness Racing for Pacers.

"That was some time ago when AJ's son, Attwood Jacob Ashwood Two had his hand in racin. I think that if AJ Three were still around, he'd have even gone ta the Breeder's Cup, as his reputation was that good. Or if we woulda kept up the farm, things mighta been different." Glen deviates from the brochure somewhat, ad-libbing that last part.

"What about the other buildings, Mr. Murdock?" I ask out of curiosity.

"The house near the end of the driveway was built in 1891, as was the double set of garages used for the first AJ's prized carriages, and then his cherished automobiles. The valets, trainers, and even some of the jockeys and drivers all lived above the garages 'til '54."

Out of curiosity, I ask, "Are blueprints for the garages and barns, with the original drawings?"

"I don't rightly know, Ma'am," Glen says looking at Gladys.

"Those might be with the original plans we found and put in the library," she says calmly. "Go on, Glen."

"When AJ Three passed, everything went to his sister, Miss Abigail, b'cause AJ did not have an heir. By then, the rest of the family was mostly scattered around the country and none of them wanted the responsibility for runnin the farm, so Ole Miss Abigail stopped farmin altogether. She did the best she could with what she had." Glen stops talking, looking down at his boots.

"It's okay, Glen, please continue," Gladys encourages.

"Right. Miss Abigail went off ta college ta learn about birds, nature, and such, not farmin and horses. Everyone was all let go, except for a cook, housekeeper, and property caretaker. She didn't know how ta train or breed horses. I think she got terrible advice from folks 'round here, but that's only my opinion.

"Miss Abigail was an accomplished Equestrian. She sold off most of the other horses and stuck with ridin her beloved *My Little Joy*, her prized quarter horse. We boarded horses for other people for extra cash, but she never raced or tried ta breed 'em again after she had that awful fall."

Leaning forward to snatch a cookie, I say, "May I interrupt you for a second, Mr. Murdock? I'm curious about something."

Lenard sticks his elbow in my arm. "Let Mr. Murdock finish what he has to say, Ellen. We don't have time for this."

"Please continue, Mr. Murdock. Sorry for the interruption." Slowly building to the explosive stage, I'm sure that there will be an opportunity to exact my anger onto him. It may come out at an inappropriate time, if he's not careful. Reaching for another cookie, I marvel at the exquisite taste.

"Now where was I?" Glen mumbles. "Oh yes, the barn was rebuilt and enlarged late in 1960 after an unexplained fire destroyed the front half of it. That's why there's two colors. There are trophies, ribbons, and stuff stored in the attic, put away when all the Ashwood men raced their horses at the local racetrack. This place has only been owned by one of the Ashwood's, the last remainin bein Miss Abigail and she's been gone now goin on three years.

"This here is Rosie, our farm dog. We have six horses; one is ours the other five are boarders. We don't do much else besides keep up with the horses with a lesson here and there." He seems sad; could he be missing something else besides Old Miss Abigail?

"Mona and me," he says looking lovingly at his wife, "we live in the Gate House near at the end of the driveway."

"How long have you and your wife been here Mr. Murdock?" I ask before Lenard can stop me.

"We've been here since '78, Ma'am. We were kinda young, but we learned ta do what it took ta get the job done. We raised our two boys here. Mona takes care of the kitchen and the house, and I take care of the barn, the boarders, and pretty near most of the property."

Glen looks at Gladys, where she nods at him. With that, he slumps back to the sofa to sit next to his wife. Rosie sticks her snout under his hand so he'll pet her head as Mona reaches for the pitcher to pour more lemonade into our glasses. As Lenard, Gene, and Gladys talk, Murdock leans forward a little.

"Know anythin about horses, Ms. Thompson?"

"I have a working knowledge of horses, Mr. Murdock."

"Have ya ever been on one? Know anythin about farmin?"

"Does it matter, Mr. Murdock?"

"Only wonderin is all. You look like a city gal ta me, not the horsey-type." Murdock is eying me warily over his glass of lemonade, taking a bite out of his cookie.

"Can't a city gal know how to ride a horse, Mr. Murdock? Many women ride professionally."

Lenard's hand is on my arm again. Does he wish me to be polite and keep my mouth shut, much as Jam-ale did?

Gladys appears a little nervous, glancing at Lenard, her big hair doesn't move when she talks, and I chuckle because there must be a lot of hairspray on it to keep it that way. Her high-pitched whiny voice nearly unravels me when she clears her throat.

"Mr. Murdock? Is that golf cart ready to take us around the property, b'cause we'd like to see it now if you please?"

"That is a good idea. We should get going," Lenard says. "We have a little time left."

"I'll see to it right away, Ma'am," Glen says quickly. "Won't take but a few minutes. Needs a little juice and we're good ta go." Towering over the demure Mrs. Murdock, Glen and she looks comfortable together as he takes her hand as they leave the living room.

"Why don't we take a look upstairs until Glen gets the cart ready. If you'll follow me; it's such a wonderful house. The Ashwood's brought in contractors from all over the country to work on it. There are many wonderful pieces of furniture left from the first Mrs. Ashwood's era and a lot of the others. I honestly don't know why no one took them; they stayed with the house. They all come with it; you know, all the antiques, all the furniture and furnishins, everythin you see here, turnkey, you know?"

*How Gladys talks without taking a breath, is beyond me.*

As we go up the front staircase, Gladys points out the wings by making finger quotations. We follow her into the three bedrooms in the middle, located on the left side of the house.

"The original Ms. Ashwood was a great planner. These rooms are part of the nursery designed for the Ashwood children. She wanted at least six, designing each side with a bright playroom set into the middle. Ms. Thompson, your side has the bonus of havin Miss Abigail's elevator. There's a large bathroom for each of the three child's rooms on both sides."

Turning to Lenard, I ask, "What does she mean by my side? Will the other people live here too?"

"Not now, Ellen. We will talk about that later."

Gladys is on the move again, saying, "There are two front master bedrooms per wing, used by prestigious guests. Rumor has it that General Grant and his wife stayed here at one time."

"Are you talking about Ulysses S. Grant, Gladys?"

"Yes, Ms. Thompson."

"Why are you interrupting? Let Gladys continue."

"I'm no historian, but I'm reasonably sure that the house was built after Grant died."

Gladys seems a little rattled, and then resumes her chatter without addressing my remark. "The rear master bedrooms were for the owners. Mr. and Mrs. Ashwood had separate bedrooms because Mrs. Ashwood loved her privacy. She wanted it decorated in a style that was not to Mr. Ashwood's liking. It's on your side of the house, Ms. Thompson."

*Aren't I the lucky one?*

"Mr. Ashwood's is far more masculine. . ." Gladys pauses for a moment. Perhaps Lenard is hoping she will finish her sentence with the appropriate conclusion, so he doesn't have to. "Anyway, it's located on the right-side wing," she finally concludes. "This way, please."

Gladys chuckles when we walk into the children's bathroom. She says that the Ashwood's were one of the first families in the State of Virginia to have a toilet by Thomas Twyford. However, modern ones have long since replaced them. Little evidence suggests there has been anything of significance done here, as the old-style water closets are still above the toilets.

"Do you know when the renovation upgrade of the bathrooms took place, Gladys?"

Gladys appears a bit stunned. "Are you askin  when the renovations were done, Ms. Thompson?"

"You mentioned the bathrooms were renovated and upgraded. When do you think that was? They look fairly old to me."

Gladys stares at Lenard so long that I get the feeling she doesn't know as much about this house as she thinks she does.

Lenard reacts, by saying, "Do you need to know that, Ellen?"

"Have you ever purchased a house, Lenard? It's important to a potential buyer. I doubt this house will pass an inspection."

"Some of the toilets were replaced during a renovation maybe in the 50s, 60s maybe? The owners left some of the original pieces intact, for posterity's sake. They're quite interestin, don't you think? I mean, they still function, see?" As she flushes a toilet, a loud groaning sounds somewhere within the house.

*In a pig's eye! How can these be considered modern?*

They probably ran out of money, which anyone will do if they buy this money pit! At first glance, the bathrooms are indeed quaint, but the pedestal sinks have noticeable chips, and the claw foot tubs have dark stains. The one thing they all share is the missing or broken floor tiles.

Gladys prattles on. "Your kids are gonna love this next thing! It's a dumbwaiter! It's so clever b'cause it's better than an elevator. It zips right up here, but I wouldn't tell your kids about this, they might want to ride up and down inside it as one Ashwood child did years ago." For an instant, her eyes glaze over. "Oh, I didn't mean to mention that. . ."

"Come along," Lenard says. "What else do you want to show us, Gladys?"

"Thought-provoking," I mutter to myself. "Did someone die in there?"

Gladys turns away quickly to sidestep my question, moving on to another room. "This house has many clever things about it, don't you agree?"

Trying to tune her out, I'm pondering the endless possibilities that start to emerge, mentally taking notes as the imaginary numbers continue to crunch in my head. Most of the draperies and wallpaper are faded, yet the rooms contain some lovely antiques.

Opening a drawer on one of the dressers to examine the construction, they are all made with dovetail joints. The flat handles will shine up quite nicely with a little spit and polish.

Lenard makes a little noise when I run a finger along the top of a chest of drawers in one of the bedrooms. He moves closer to me and says, "You have already decorated this room. I told you that you would like it here. I told you to trust me!"

Now I understand why his team chose this place. He knew how important my work was to me and this is a veritable designer's dream, or nightmare, depending on how you look at it. Even if Mother and I combined estates, will it be enough to bring this wonderful old place back from the brink of demolition? The other investors will need to step up with some big money very soon for that to happen.

"What does the other side of the house look like, Gladys?"

Before she can answer, Lenard jumps in with a snide remark that it's the same as mine and it's the other owner's, so why would I want to look at it?

"Trying to hide, something, are we?"

"Why no, Ms. Thompson, why ever would you say somethin like that? We aren't tryin to hide anythin, are we Lenard?"

Gladys then declares how time flies when you don't have any, steering us down the back stairs where we come out in the hallway near the kitchen. As we traipse through, I take a closer look at the uneven floor. When it gives more than a little when Gladys walks across it, I wonder if it could have something to do with termites. Cha-Ching, go the dollar signs. The floor joists will need replacing no doubt, and short of a stick of dynamite, it will take a major renovation to help this outdated and nonfunctional kitchen!

We are directed to the screen door and out onto the back porch. As we walk toward the barns, it's evident that both are color-washed to cover bare spots. It looks splendid from far away, but up close, it's a different story.

As Gladys heads off to find Mr. Murdock, the rest of us are standing outside to wait. The bay comes trotting from the opposite end of the barn, then immediately heads for the open pasture on the far side where he stops near the fence with its rump toward us. It makes me laugh. Is this his way of saying he doesn't want our company?

Mr. Murdock drives out of the garage moments later with Gladys in the backseat of a six-passenger golf cart. Steering it toward me, he stops, missing my feet by mere inches.

Pointing to the front seat, he says, "Sit here, where I can keep an eye on ya. Hang on and I'll try ta steer clear of the bumps. *Lightnin's* a little touchy since the old mare died."

"Are you referring to the horse that ran out of the barn, Mr. Murdock?"

"Yeah, real name's *At Lightnin Speed*, but we call him *Lightnin* for short."

"Ms. Thompson doesn't want to hear about that kind of stuff, do you, Ms. Thompson? She wants to hear about the farm. Tell her about the farm, Glen," Gladys says laughing.

Ignoring her, Glen launches into a triad of his own. "Ole Miss Abigail's mare used ta run with 'em, but *Lightnin's* not been too happy since the mare died. He was only a colt at the time. I think he misses her more than he misses Miss Abigail. He's none too friendly with the folks anyway. You might want ta steer clear of that one until he gets ta know ya better."

I'm beginning to get overwhelmed when Gene starts to talk about his childhood in rural Mississippi. It doesn't ring true, but it makes us all laugh, which temporarily gets me to focus on something else.

Gladys mentions a school system a short bus ride away, located in one of the first campus-like settings constructed in the area. A drive north will take us to a new ultra-modern museum, along with several restaurants that are within a few miles of the farm. If we're into boating or fishing, there's even a lake not far away. Glen and Gladys then take turns telling us about the neighbors who live in the Village of Jasper. Everyone is friendly and welcoming to strangers. It's as if they are describing the fictional town of Mayberry.

*Does Sheriff Andy and Barney Fife live here too?*

The local drama association puts on plays once a year, and the cinema has the latest films. A County Fair happens in July, and local stores offer anything from hobbies to knick-knacks. Stores along Main Street offer a modern beauty salon, Gladys' real estate office, a bakery, a sporting goods store, and electronic gadgets are all mentioned. A miniature golf course, bowling alley, and a large bank are all located around a central park where they hold summer concerts.

The only drawback is the fact there's no large shopping mall, but plenty to do, otherwise. I'm hoping my teenagers can be resourceful at finding things to keep themselves busy. I'll have my hands full with renovations, that is if I take on this enormous project.

After the tour of the property, Glen returns us to the barn where he shows off his small office. It reminds me of a fox's den because it's dusty and smells of stale coffee.

Remnants of days gone by are evident everywhere we look. The horse stalls look as if they might collapse any minute. A faded blanket dangles on a hook near a washbasin with a hole so large that my head could fit through it. Lenard's hand reaches to grab my wrist as I'm about to touch an old saddle hanging from a peg. Shaking his head, he puts a finger to his lips. Cha-Ching, go the dollar signs again.

Murdock talks on about the horse called *Lightning*. "He lets himself out so I gotta lock him in at night. *Lightning's* a free spirit that some said would never be broke, but Ole Miss Abigail sure did love him. She bought his mama and didn't know she was in foal, so it was a surprise ta all of us. He was born here. Miss Abigail used ta come out every day. Then she had that fall and stopped comin."

Rosie runs into the barn, stopping next to me. Wagging her tail and woofing, she nudges my hand as if we're old friends. I'm getting overwhelmed at the thought of how much might be needed to get this place back to its former magnificence, and the *flight or fight* syndrome threatens to overtake me.

Excusing myself, I walk out of the barn to get some fresh air with Rosie at my side. We're near the fence at the driveway, and it seems sturdier than the ones inside the barn, so I climb up to sit with my back to the bay as Rosie lies down in the grass, settling her head on her paws.

It must have once been an architectural masterpiece, but from where I'm sitting, a general shabbiness is apparent. Several patches of mix-matched roofing materials are also evident of roof issues. Under all that weight, I can only speculate what the attic might look like from the inside.

How did the owners let this house get into such a deplorable state? Since the house is over 100 years old, we're likely to find knob and tube wiring when a contractor opens the walls. The plumber might need to replace all copper tubing, and we didn't go down into what is probably a dungeon of a basement. The thought of having to do laundry down there makes my skin crawl.

Cha-ching, cha-ching, cha-ching goes the cash register in my head. It will take millions of dollars to renovate this place! Where will we get the money? I'm annoyed with Gladys, who should know as a real estate professional, that this is not a weekend fixer-upper! And that barn! A gust of wind could push that leaning section down with the rest of it! A pounding starts at the back of my head; the stress is getting to me.

*How can I bring my family here and tell them this is where they're going to live now?*

I want to go home to Evanston where I belong. How can my children give up their friends and their lives to come here to this dilapidated old house? Tears start to roll down my cheeks as I reach for a tissue.

Rosie lifts her head off her paws, woofing once, dropping her head back down. Something soft begins to nudge the top of my head. *At Lightning Speed's* warm breath is on my neck. Reaching up with my right hand, I stroke the right side of his neck. *Lightning* makes a soft nicker sound as if he's been waiting to meet me.

"Aren't we a pair, both forced into a situation we have no control over. You and I have suffered incomprehensible loss, but maybe we can work this out."

Rosie woofs her approval until a voice off in the direction of the barn breaks the spell. *Lightning* jerks his head up, then backs away.

Murdock is running awkwardly towards us. "I don't believe it," he says when he reaches us.

"Everything is all right, Mr. Murdock. *Lightning* came to say hello," I say, jumping down off the fence.

"I gotta tell ya, Missy; he don't ever do that. Ole Miss Abigail had ta have sugar cubes or carrots in her hand b'fore he would come ta her. And I don't believe this dog; she hasn't left my side since Miss Abigail died! I thought you didn't know nuthin about horses!" he stammers. "What did ya do, hypnotize him? I've seen stuff like that at the County Fair, but this is odd behavior comin from these two critters."

"Mr. Murdock, I believe what I said was, I have a working knowledge of horses. There's nothing odd about it, and no, I didn't hypnotize them."

It's not such odd behavior as we probably have more in common than anyone suspects. Maybe that's why we're here. Perhaps this *is* God's Plan for us.

As we walk toward the barn, he says, "I came ta tell ya the fellas are ready to leave, Ma'am."

"Mr. Murdock, I don't know very much about running a farm or training horses to race, but I do know that I can learn. Anyone can learn if they apply themselves, don't you agree?"

"Yeah," Murdock takes off his hat and runs a hand through his hair. "That sounds 'bout right."

"You said those same words a little while ago."

Murdock nods his head, "Yes ma'am, I surely did."

Gene is motioning to our driver as Lenard reaches out to shake Mr. Murdock's hand, "We must be on our way now, Glen. Thanks so much for the tour." Then he yanks at my arm trying to steer me toward the limo.

"You're comin back here later today, right?" Glen asks.

"Sure," Lenard says moving past him. "We will be back after . . ."

"You said our new owner would be stayin after taday."

Trying to keep my voice low, "Lenard, we have to talk about things. I'm not sure I want to live here. Why does Murdock think I'm coming back here today? I haven't agreed to anything."

Lenard glances at Gene as he opens the rear passenger door. "Not now, Ellen, we cannot be late for our meeting." Turning, he takes Gladys' outstretched hand. It's odd that they don't say anything. It's as if they might be sharing a little secret.

As the limo drives away from the farm, Lenard and Gene must be struggling to contain their curiosity when Lenard blurts, "How did you get that horse to come to you?"

Gene, howling like a wolf, says, "Woooeee, we all could not b'lieve it. After what Murdock said about that horse. What did he say the horse was doing, Lenard?"

Lenard shrugs his shoulders as if he's annoyed with Gene.

I offer a simple explanation by saying, "The horse nuzzled me. It's a way to show affection, much like a hug from a human."

"I thought you said you knew nothing about horses!" Lenard looks angry, spitting a little when he talks.

"I never said that. You asked if I could manage a horse farm."

"OH," they both say at the same time.

*What idiots! It's sad to think that these men work for our government. Did they pass through the rigors of FBI training the first time? Or did they get their badges out of a Cracker Jack box?*

On the drive to meet the mysterious investors, Lenard and Gene are conversing around me, as if I'm not in the middle. They don't need to know that I have more than a working knowledge of horses.

As Lenard talks, I only half listen, when he starts poking my knee with his finger. "You need to let us handle this today, Ellen. You are not to ask any questions like you did back at the farm. No one needs to hear your concerns right now. We are meeting for the express purpose of the agreement, which is all they are here for, do you understand?"

"If you gave me information, Lenard, I wouldn't have to ask so many questions. Give me a hint as to who these people are."

"All I can say is that we are meeting with a Mr. C and another gentleman who shall remain anonymous." As he says this, his cellphone vibrates. Putting it to his ear, he doesn't say anything, presses a button, and squints at Gene, and then they continue as if there was no interruption. Licking his lips repeatedly, I wonder if he is aware that he does this annoying thing.

"Did you hear me, Ellen? I must insist that you keep quiet and go along with everything. Our teams worked into the night to get everything set up for today. Are you listening?"

"Yes, Lenard, I hear you." This drill is getting tiresome, and I want to punch him in the face. "I'm hungry. Will we be having lunch soon?"

Lenard lets out a loud sigh as if a balloon is deflating. "You should have had a bigger breakfast, Ellen. Or more of those cookies."

We drive for about a half hour when the limo turns into the entrance of a restaurant that appears closed. Draped over the sign is a blue tarp. Two vehicles are in the parking lot, a white stretch limo, and a red foreign-made car that reminds me of an Italian movie, one that has lots of intrigue, action, and gunfire. I'm hoping it's more the former, not the latter.

*The scene strikes me as quite humorous.*

Lenard and Gene want to know what has made me laugh. I doubt they will think it's funny, so I don't say anything. When we get to the door, Lenard gives the door three knocks, which opens when a young man unlocks it. He silently escorts us through the restaurant into a room at the rear.

I fully expect to see the Godfather and his minions, as there are three chairs set in front of a booth that is in complete darkness. As our eyes adjust to the light, a waiter plunks down five glasses of water, pushing two of them into the shadows. He lays several menus on the table and leaves without saying a word.

"Oh, good, I'm hungry." As I reach for one of the menus, Lenard's hand prevents me from picking it up.

"Later, Ellen," he snarls. "We are not here to eat."

A deep voice in a foreign accent asks us to sit down. Both Lenard and Gene steer me to the middle chair, pushing me down onto it, then sit on either side of me. The voice says to go ahead, and Lenard starts an odd, animated conversation with the darkness. Reaching for the menus, Lenard pushes them out of my reach.

"We have seen the house, the property, and the barn. Mrs. Thompson has agreed to act as the manager for you." Lenard pauses, while I stomp on his foot under the table because this can't be further from the truth! "Ellen, that was not necessary!" Both he and Gene grab my arms.

"What are you smoking, Lenard? I have agreed to nothing of the sort." Turning to the dark booth, saying, "Have you seen the house? It honestly looks like Camp Run-Amuck!"

Lenard hisses for me to be quiet and looks embarrassed.

Not knowing to whom I'm speaking, I talk to the dark booth. "Have you seen it? It's in a despicable state of disrepair, and the barn is falling! Have you seen that kitchen? I nearly fainted when I walked in there! Happy Days called and they need it for their reunion show."

"Please be quiet, Ellen," Lenard grumbles. "When we said silent partners that is what we meant, *silent!*"

A voice on the right side of the booth says to let me talk, but the boys have not released their grip. As I glance at each of them, Lenard's face contorts, while Gene's face slowly turns red.

"Let go of me! That place will never pass a home inspection. It will take thousands of dollars to bring things up to code. It will take millions more to restore that place to its former glory."

"Lenard mentioned you are an expert with that sort of thing," the voice on the right says.

"We can't go in and gut the place; it's on the National Register of Historic Homes. It must be restored to their standards if you want to keep that plaque near the front door. Do you have a lot of money to sink into it? I sure don't."

The deep foreign voice on the left asks, "How do you know it needs that kind of money to fix it up?"

"It's what I do for a living. One part of the barn is leaning so far to the left it could fall any minute. I got a glimpse of the windows, but they look like they're an odd size and probably single-paned. Is the waiter coming back to take our order?"

Through clenched teeth, Lenard sputters, "Ellen, we are not here to eat."

The voice on the right side of the booth says to continue.

"I thought the roof had a third story until I looked at it again. It's a mighty hip roof with patches all over it. No telling what damage you'll find up there. The whole thing is a bit overwhelming! Do you have any idea what a new roof for that hunk of junk would cost?"

Lenard continues to plead. "Ellen, you must stop. We are not here to debate the merits of the house or the barn or anything else for that matter!"

I continue to ignore him. "Will you take responsibility for half of it? Is this a partnership or not? I don't care if you people want to remain silent, but it's supposed to be equal, right? Split right down the middle?"

Lenard seems nervous as if he's trying to impress his boss and I've thrown a bomb on the table. The shadows in the booth shift slightly. Are they uncomfortable with what I'm saying or do they agree with my assessment?

My stomach growls loudly. "This is ridiculous. If we can't talk about this openly, then we have wasted each other's time. I don't think this will work out. What is this cloak and dagger stuff! Is there a hidden camera in here somewhere?"

As I stand abruptly, my chair falls backward onto the floor. Lenard and Gene scramble to stand up as they grab my arms again. Where would I go, they could easily overtake me. Shouting at the shadows, "I demand to know who you are!"

Soft laughter floats from the right side of the booth, as Lenard loudly asks me to sit down, while Gene leans back to pick up my chair.

"We can work this out!" Lenard stammers. "I am very sorry; hope this doesn't jeopardize our deal in any way, sir. Mrs. Thompson is under a lot of stress right now, and she does not mean what she says."

"So it's a *deal* now Lenard? You know, there's a big difference between a deal and a plan. It's from one extreme to the other! You said it's a great plan worked out for my family. It's not a good plan! It doesn't even come close to a good plan. Let go of me, you idiots!"

An even louder laugh comes from the right side of the booth as more whispering occurs as the shadows shift in the darkness. "She's right, it feels like cloak and dagger stuff to me, too," says the voice on the right (assuming it's Mr. C). "Please take your hands off Mrs. Thompson and allow her to sit down. We would like to continue our conversation and ask her some questions if you don't mind?"

Lenard and Gene release their grip, and I sit down.

"Your voice sounds familiar, but without seeing your face, I can't be sure. What would it hurt if you showed me?"

"I asked you to be quiet, Ellen," Lenard rudely says. He glances at the left side of the booth, as Gene looks down at his hands.

The person on the right side says, "May I call you Ellen?"

Is this the parallel universe talking, or Déjà vu? "Humph," I manage to say.

"Does that mean you'll stay?" he asks kindly.

"We are not finished with our questions," says the strange voice on the left. It is difficult to identify, Spanish, Portuguese maybe? "We don't want to make this any more difficult than it is. Lenard told us of your situation. It must be confusing for you after your ordeal."

"And what has Lenard told you about me? Please identify yourself." I turn to Lenard and mentally accuse him of breaching the '*need to know rule.*' The rule that he went over repeatedly, the one he made me swear to uphold!

"He needed to know, Ellen. He's part of the de--I mean plan. They are both parts of the plan!"

"You are such a dork, Lenard."

"That may be, Ellen, but without these people, it is essential that we bring you all into this together, right Mr. A?"

"Oh boy, we have a Mr. C and a Mr. A, so is there a Mr. B back there too? Come on boys, is this necessary?"

Before Mr. A responds, Mr. C says, "Lenard is right, Ellen. I have seen the house and the barn, and agree that the kitchen seems stuck in the 50s. I also agree that it needs a lot of work. We can do it little by little. Lenard says you're a decorator, so you know how to be resourceful."

"First of all, pal; I'm not a decorator, I hold a bachelor's Degree in interior design with minors in both business and architecture. I ran a business for eighteen years, and there are few, if any, complaints." It's probably a little more forceful than it needs to be, then realize my old credentials are worthless unless Lenard magically provided new ones in that white envelope.

"Thank you, Ellen. I didn't mean to insult you, merely wishing to say that as someone with your qualifications knows, there are tricks of the trade you can use to our advantage. Maybe something that requires little or no money?"

"From what I can gather, Murdock probably doesn't break even with the horses he boards. Do you have any idea what it takes to feed and care for one horse, Mr. C?"

"No, not really," he answers.

"Or run a farm, for that matter?"

"No, I don't," he murmurs.

Turning to Lenard, I ask him, "Can't imagine what Mrs. Murdock needs to run that house. Lenard, you're so smart, why don't you jump in here with some details?"

"I did not want to get into that right now, Ellen. These men are very busy and cannot be bothered with this stuff. We can talk about it later, okay?"

"I want to talk about it now! How much does the Ashwood Estate contain? They should know what they're getting into because it's not fair to lead them into this mess without. . ."

Mr. A's deep foreign voice interrupts, "Ms. Thompson, we know what is at stake here. We are willing to take the chance with you. There are factions at work that must be kept secret at all costs, and we will do everything in our power to make this a smooth transition."

Mr. C adds, "Things will work out, you'll see. Lenard has no doubt explained all that to you. We know the importance of keeping you and your family safe, and we feel we can do that by offering you the partnership of our combined funds. We would like to ask you some more questions if you don't mind?"

"Lenard explained certain things, but nothing about how or who will manage the farm, so I can't help you there. Please ask your questions."

"Would you have a problem if we send an occasional guest or two out to the farm?" Mr. C asks quietly. "You know, to spend a week or two here and there?"

"No, I suppose not. Give us a heads-up of at least a week before you do, so that we can get things for you or your guests."

"How about during a major holiday, say Thanksgiving or Christmas?"

I'm a little annoyed. "Why are we doing this? I haven't agreed to anything. Don't think I'm going to run that eyesore like a hotel!"

Lenard lets out a heavy sigh. "Ellen, please go along with this. I told you, I will explain things later, okay?"

"You keep saying that. You do have a lot to explain, Mister. If you stay on *your* side of the house, Mr. C, we shouldn't have a problem, but honestly, is this what you want to talk about; isn't anyone else hungry?"

Lenard asks, "Any more questions, gentlemen?"

"Yes," Mr. C says. "I have a few more."

I glance behind Lenard to see if the waiter is lurking in the shadows near the kitchen when a thought occurs to me. "Wait a minute, shouldn't we be discussing how we're going to *pay* for this monstrosity? May I please have something to eat? Where's the waiter?"

"Ellen, let Mr. C ask his questions. Then we can move on with the business at hand!" Lenard pleads.

Mr. C clears his throat, "Thanks, Lenard. Ellen, how much do you anticipate it will take per month to keep the farm going, financially?"

"Now we're getting to the brass tacks. I honestly don't know as no one deemed it relevant to show me any paperwork while we were at the farm today. But I can take a wild guess."

"She is right; we did not talk about that," Lenard volunteers.

"I do know that it takes thousands of dollars per horse for the simple necessities, like grain and hay."

The shadow on the left coughs and then the shadows seem to merge slightly as the whispers occur again. "I'm starting to get the picture," Mr. C says quietly. The whispers continue, but they're so quiet I can't make out what they're saying. "Mr. Murdock is the caretaker for the farm, correct? He takes care of the barn and the property?"

"Yes. Where are you going with this line of questioning? I already told you he didn't share what his expenses are, but from what I can gather, he isn't generating what he needs to cover his costs. Isn't anyone else hungry?" They must not intend to have lunch here; there's no smell of food cooking.

"But they have boarding horses that pay for that part of the farm, correct?" Mr. C asks.

"Why are you asking such asinine questions? I told you he's probably not making enough to cover his costs."

"Indulge us, Ms. Thompson," the strange voice on the left says. "It will help in the end, I assure you."

Suddenly wondering what I've got myself into, I politely say, "No one mentioned expenses, upkeep of the farm, or allowed me to take a gander at their books, Mr. A. I don't know what is keeping them going. They can't be far from shutting off their credit, from what I can gather. I'm hungry, where is the waiter?"

Moving to stand up, Lenard clutches my arm, asking me to sit down. "I told you, we are not here to eat, Ellen."

Mr. C says, "Can you give us an idea?"

"We saw the property an hour ago. It's beyond ridiculous! Are we not in a restaurant? Is it not lunchtime?" Lenard lets out a huge sigh as my stomach grumbles. "Will you contribute to half of the expenses?"

"It will be taken care of," Mr. A's deep voice says. "We will provide anything you need."

Mr. C changes the subject abruptly. "Ellen, what do you plan to renovate or fix up first?"

"What do you have in mind?"

"I was thinking a wine cellar to store my extensive collection would be nice," Mr. C replies.

"I'm done playing your little game; show your face! I want to see who you are. There's a lot at stake here!"

Lenard sucks in a breath; not only places his hand on my arm again, but he also applies pressure. It doesn't deter me from spewing more words. "Come on; let me see your face! I'm going to see you anyway when you come to the farm unless of course, you wear a disguise!"

The shadows shift, and the one on the right moves forward. In the millisecond he does this, his face becomes quite clear.

"Oh, it's you." It changes the playing field somewhat.

"You're a little surprised?" Mr. C asks.

The voice now has a name, and it's one of Hollywood's most notorious bad boys. But it comes nowhere near his real name, and although I've been in the presence of many, I'm not impressed by celebrities. The only difference between us is the amount of money we earn.

"Yes, a little and maybe a smidge overwhelmed after seeing that atrocious house and barn. How did *you* get mixed up with these guys? Don't you have like a billion-dollar estate in California or something and a ranch in Wyoming? What do you want with this money pit? Why do you want to be in partnership with me?"

Mr. C laughs. "Have you considered being an actress, Ellen? You do have a comedic flair."

The left shadow shifts, coughing roughly, as his baritone voice says, "Understand that this venture is for both of your interests, Ms. Thompson; things are not always what they seem. You will have the whole estate mostly to you and your family. We only ask that you follow a few rules. One, consider everything that comes with the house belongs to all the investors. Two, under no circumstances, are you to sell any of the antiques. Thirdly, you will need to vacate the house when any of the other investors are present."

"Wow, this keeps getting better and better. Is there anything else?"

"Yes, there is a quaint Bed and Breakfast called Dover Inn that will accommodate you and your family when one of us comes to stay at Ashwood. You might like the get-away it affords," Mr. A adds.

"I have some rules of my own. One, I will not inconvenience my family to accommodate you and your guests when you feel like dropping by. Two, you will give me proper notice, and three, I will expect funds from each of the investors if you want the house restored. The freaking house is big enough for all of us! *YOU* go to the B & B, because I'm not leaving! Let's see who *you* are, Mr. A."

Lenard grabs my arm and says I'm *never* to know his identity. It's for my safety as well as his. Loud laughter floats from the right side of the booth while the left side remains quiet.

"I like your spunk, Ellen. Don't worry; we can work it all out," Mr. C says, laughing again. "Here is my card." Mr. C pushes his business card into the middle of the table as Lenard pushes one toward him. "You have good business sense, Ellen. You already have a handle on what it might take to renovate the house and barn. If there is anything else you need, please contact me."

The left shadow's meaty hand pushes a card forward; a broad silver ring with an enormous red stone is on one of his fingers. As I reach for Mr. C's card, Lenard is quick to intercept both cards, saying all contacts will go through him, if that's all right.

"No, it isn't! How will they know if I need something?"

"All requests will go through me, Ellen," Lenard snarls. "That's how this will work."

Lenard and Gene stand up, pulling me out of my chair. Mr. C's right shadow moves slightly, but he remains in the dark. "Thank you for coming to talk with us, Ellen. It was nice to meet you. Give it a little time for things to work out, okay? We'll contact you in a few weeks to see how you're doing. Give it three months."

"I thought we were having a nice little lunch over drinks and what, a conversation where we discuss something of substance?" Lenard is pulling me away from the table. "Nice meeting you both."

As we walk through the empty restaurant toward the front door, Gene starts lamenting, "She wasn't supposed to see him, Lenard!"

"Shut up! You are such a senseless man! He wanted her to see him," he retorts.

"Lenard, I'm hungry. Can we at least get some fast food?"

Gene opens the limo door as Lenard pushes me inside. "Get in. We do not have time. We need to get back. You should have eaten more for breakfast."

"What do you mean we don't have time? What do we have to get back to?" I inquire of a stony-faced Lenard.

"Our special unit team is so sure this will be a successful endeavor, they put bets on it. They are seldom wrong about these things."

Gene snickers, saying, "Yeah, they ain't been wrong yet, have they, Lenard?"

"Give it three months, as Mr. C asked, okay?" Lenard growls.

"What kind of odds have they bet, Lenard? I'm curious; do you know how to bet?"

"What?" Lenard sputters. "What do you mean?"

"You know, like odds in betting on things."

He and Gene shake their heads. "Why would I care about that?"

"Odds, Lenard, like five to one, twenty to one, that type of odds, like in real betting?"

*Perhaps it should bother me that he doesn't have a clue.*

Gene asks, "You mean like a football pool or somethin' like that?"

Lenard is shaking his head. "I do not know what you mean by odds; they took bets. Are not all bets the same? Gene, help me out here."

"Yeah, a little like that or something. I can't believe you two; I'm talking about odds as in racetrack betting. Have you two ever been to a racetrack? Haven't you ever gambled?"

*Did they fall from the sky and land on their heads?*

"Not everyone knows how to gamble, Ellen. We do not have time to do this thing called gambling. Our time is valuable. Our employers do not want us doing stuff like that."

Lenard stops talking, as Gene takes over. "They would not like us doin things like that, right, Lenard?"

"What planet are you from, guys? Isn't the US Government your employer?"

When the limo pulls into the long gravel driveway at Ashwood Farms, a sinking feeling comes over me. The grey SUV is gone, and there is no one to greet us at the front door, not even the dog.

"Why are we back here? Lenard? Why are we here? I thought we had to talk things over before . . ."

"Let's talk in the house, Ellen."

Lenard and Gene share an imperceptible nod which reminds me of the other two people whom I have tried to keep out of my head! Do they practice this stuff or is it part of FBI Special Agent 101 training?

Lenard takes my arm to lead me through the unlocked front door into the paneled vestibule. "Give it three months. I promise it will feel like home to you by then."

"What are you saying, Lenard?"

"You will get used to things and your children should be here by then, too."

"You are *not* leaving me here! Lenard, you can't leave me here!"

"Keep your voice down; eyes and ears, remember the protocols?" Lenard says tersely.

"Do I have to go over your head and call your superior to discuss my displeasure at your mishandling of my case?"

Lenard stiffens, "No Ellen, you do not want to do that! My boss, our boss, is counting on us to take this to the end. Give it a little more time, and you will see that things work out, I promise you."

"You better be right about this!"

Gene opens the front door, pulling my large suitcase along with my red case. He sullenly shifts from foot to foot.

"Remember, it's a matter of National Security," Lenard mumbles. "You need to promise that you'll keep your mouth shut."

"And ya need to keep the low-down on this, so your family stays safe," Gene adds, as he opens the French doors to the large hall, leaning my suitcases against the newel post.

"I have questions!"

"Keep your voice down." Lenard is practically pushing me toward the stairs. "Ellen, we are not going to debate this now."

"Why not? You said we would discuss everything later. You can't leave without answering my questions."

"I'll call you in a day or two when you've calmed down, and we can talk then."

"We are gonna have to leave ya now, but we will be in touch, okay?" Gene says sadly, hanging his head.

"How can you dump me here? I didn't sign anything. How can I live here without signing anything – LENARD!"

"As far as anyone knows, Ellen D. Thompson and private investors, who *will* remain anonymous, have purchased and paid for this property. It's already yours."

"How can that be?"

Lenard tries to take my hand, but I don't want him to touch me and back away. "As Gene told you, it's a done deal."

"How could you have done this without my signature? It didn't come with a small price tag. What did you do, Lenard? Do we have a mortgage?"

Gene looks away, as Lenard leans in to whisper. "No. We did what we had to, Ellen. To the world, you are dead. You and your husband's life insurance policies no longer exist. Your bank accounts are closed and so are your 401Ks. Everything is wrapped up in this property."

*I'm speechless.*

"We had to, Ellen. We had to make it look like you did not exist and that meant wiping out . . ."

". . . My life and everything Ravi and I worked so hard to achieve all these years? What about my children? What are we going to live on in the meantime? Do I have any money? What about my business?"

Lenard genuinely looks remorseful for a change. "That is gone too."

"This farm will not run by itself. The Murdock's are only getting by!"

"You are a very resourceful person, Ellen. I guarantee that you will be okay in three months. I know Mr. A said not to sell the antiques, but I'm sure he wouldn't mind if you sold one or two. There's so many of them, he'd never notice." Reaching as if to hug me, I back away from him. "Remember to follow the protocols to the letter. Your family's safety depends on it. We are not the enemy. We are here to help you."

Rosie pushes the door open leading from the kitchen and wanders over to me, sitting at my feet, nuzzling my hand.

"What happened to the money you said you would give me?"

Lenard grumbles at Gene and his face flushes. "I thought you took care of that already? Come on Gene, let's get going."

"Lenard! You have *two* months. If my family isn't here with me, I will go over your head and report you, National Security or not! You can count on that!" I say to his back. "Not a day over that, or I go over your head!"

In an awkward gesture that borders on gentleness, Gene says, "You are home now Ellen. Call if you need anythin." He also makes a feeble attempt at a hug, but I back away from him, too. Reaching for my hand, he puts a rolled wad of tissues into it along with a large white envelope. He walks away, then closes the front door behind him.

The envelope probably contains the endless protocols Lenard went over repeatedly, but when I peel away the tissue, there's a roll of money, a business card, and a large key. Rosy woofs, as the kitchen door opens, and I turn to see Mrs. Murdock.

*How much has she overheard?*

"May I get you anythin, Ms. Thompson? Would you like some lemonade?"

I can't allow her to see how distraught I am. After all, she has no idea why I came to live here today, other than the fact that I'm one of the new owners.

"Please, Mrs. Murdock, that would be very nice."

Following her into the kitchen with Rosie close by my side, I secretly wish for more of her delicious cookies, but I'll settle for anything right now.

"I missed lunch. Got anything to eat?"

*"Generosity is giving more than you can,*
*and pride is taking less than you need."*
~ Khalil Gibran

# Chapter Seven

## Power Struggles

The chrome chairs at the fifties-style table are in exceptional shape, but the gold refrigerator and green avocado stove add to my growing dread as I follow Mrs. Murdock into the kitchen. The monster of a sink takes up most of one wall, which I'm guessing is nearly six-feet long. All that seems to be missing is the pump handle that I've seen in old farmhouse renovation books. As I wash my hands, I notice there are no stains in the sink. Mrs. Murdock must be a stickler for cleanliness.

As she shuffles around the room, I take a closer look at what I must contend with first. This kitchen needs a total transformation. In its present configuration, it takes too many steps to reach the refrigerator, located in an alcove across the room. A large center island, with additional cabinets under it, would certainly help the flow.

The hospital green paint on the cupboards contributes to the appalling feel of the room, along with the cracked yellow linoleum floor. The brown, worm-like paths crisscross from the pantry to the sink, around the table and chairs, meander out to the mudroom, and roam down the hallway to the Morning Room where it stops at the hardwood floors.

Setting a glass of lemonade and a plate of pie in front of me, she stands behind a chair waiting.

"Won't you sit with me?"

"Yes, Ma'am." Mrs. Murdock says, sitting down on one of the chairs, but she doesn't look comfortable.

Placing the key on the table, asking her, "Do you know what this might go to?"

"It might be the one Miss Gladys took. The other one is in a drawer near the sink. We keep the front door locked; everyone knows to come to the back door. Miss Gladys told us you was comin today, but it don't look like you was ready to stay," she says quietly.

"I didn't know I was coming to stay here either until this afternoon. It will take some adjustment, but I'm sure it'll all work out. I know I'm hungry, but this is very tasty. Did you make this pie? And you must have made the cookies you served us today, didn't you?"

"Yes, Ma'am," she says quietly. "Oh, Ms. Thompson, you're gonna find out sooner or later," she blurts. "Sos I might tell ya now. I use the kitchen to make pastries and bread for the bakery in town. It was only supposed to be one day a week, but then it turned into three. We needed the money, Ms. Thompson. We pleaded with Mr. Yancy at the bank, but he said there's no money left in the Ashwood Estate. Glen only gets enough to feed the horses."

Putting a hand on her arm, she stops to stare at me. "Mrs. Murdock, are you receiving a salary for taking care of the house?"

She shakes her head no. "Not for a long while, Ms. Thompson."

"How about your husband? Does he get a salary for taking care of the barn and the property?"

Again, she shakes her head no. "That all stopped kind of sudden like."

"Then you did what you thought you had to do to survive. Does the baking you do cover all your costs?" Yes, she nods her head. "Do you like to bake?" She nods yes, again. "Then you keep on doing that because I'll find a way to straighten this out."

Reaching into my pocket, I extract the wad of money and hand her two fifty-dollar bills, then ask, "How on earth can you work in here without counter space?"

Mrs. Murdock's face registers surprise and is thoughtful for a moment. "I use the table in the Morning Room to mix everything up and set all the pans out in there. Then I use the oven at the Gate House and the one here and bake everything. It takes about eight hours or so, done that way. I use the golf cart to get back and forth."

"I'll bet you're tired at the end of the baking day." She nods her head. "Do you need more money for food?" Yes, she shakes her head. "How much do you need?"

Mrs. Murdock reaches to pull two additional bills from my hand. "Thank you," she whispers. She appears grateful; she may either cry, hug, or kiss me.

"Let me know when you need more. I'll go up and stake a claim on one of the bedrooms. Can you get a couple of bottles of white wine when you're at the store?"

"I sure can and thank you, Ms. Thompson, but Glen already put your suitcases in Miss Abigail's old bedroom, and I got it all ready for ya. I'll get Glen to take me to the store. We'll have a nice dinner tonight. Thank you and a great big welcome to your new home, Ms. Thompson!"

"Thank you very much, Mrs. Murdock."

*Is this my home now?*

"Supper is at six thirty. Hope that's okay? Glen won't be over ' til then, cause of the horses." Waving her hand, she adds, "Rosie, you leave Ms. Thompson alone, she don't need ya ta trip over."

"Six thirty is fine. May I call you Mona? And please, call me Miss Ellen. Rosie's no bother; we have a Sheltie back home."

As I head up the back staircase with Rosie, I notice in more detail the scratches and worn areas on the stair treads, realizing that this house does have potential. But do I have the energy to tackle such a project on my own? If my children are going to like their new home, there's a lot of work to do before they get here.

Flopping down on the bed suddenly drained of energy, I cover myself with the fresh-smelling comforter as Rosie jumps up, settling herself near the foot of the bed. Our Sassy was not allowed on the furniture. It's a small comfort, after all.

Lightning flashes and thunder rumbles as rain pelts the windows. According to the digital clock on the nightstand, it's nearly six o'clock. Although I slept, my brain didn't entirely shut down, and it's already working on a redesign of this room. The red case is on the floor next to the old dresser, so I reach inside for the stationery with the intention of writing down my thoughts. The leather books draw my attention. Is it time to see why the covers bulge?

Rosie woofs, jumping off the bed, reaching the closed bedroom door ahead of a knock. Pulling the door open, Mona puts a small package in my hands as a pleasant tang fills the room.

"This came today, Miss Ellen. Thought it might be important, so I brought it up. Come on, Rosie, Miss Ellen don't want ya botherin her."

"Thank you, but Rosie's no bother; I rather like her company. What is that delicious aroma?"

"That's supper! We're havin a roast tonight! It'll be ready directly. I'll buzz when it is." Mona smiles as she turns to walk softly away.

The small box is addressed to Mrs. Ellen D. Thompson and has no return address. Opening it carefully, a compressed wad of tissue paper contains my wedding rings, along with a stack of crisp one hundred dollar bills!

Since the FBI are the only ones that know my new identity, who else, besides Lenard and Gene could have sent this package? Were those two idiots part of the equation from the beginning? This thought makes me shudder.

Thinking there must be a safe place to put my newfound fortune, I take the large suitcase into the closet to remove the contents. It will be an excellent place to hide things until a better one comes along.

After putting most of my new clothes onto hangers, a faint voice announces that supper is ready. On close inspection, the source of the sound is coming from an old intercom on the wall next to the dresser. Wallpapered over several times, it's barely visible, except for two tiny buttons and a small black grill.

Rosie woofs, doing a little dance near the bedroom door. Following her down the back steps to the kitchen, the Murdock's are sitting at the table set for two.

Glen stands awkwardly. "You're supposed ta eat in the dining room, not in the kitchen with us help," he says dryly.

Motioning for him to sit, Rosie goes off to eat from her bowl near the back door. "Did Miss Abigail have rules that said you couldn't eat with her? I'm not eating in that big room alone."

*The Murdock's don't know what to make of me.*

"See, that's the thing. Tomorrow's bakin day, so the tables will all be full," Mona says quietly, looking flustered.

"Don't worry; we can eat wherever there's space. When my family comes, we'll all eat in the big dining room together; not you two in the kitchen by yourselves. Until Mr. Fancy-Pants and his guests show up, or we have a house full of people, we can eat here or in the Morning Room. I consider you family, and we will eat together as one. End of story."

Although they agree, it may take some getting used to, as after Miss Abigail died, they didn't think to go back to their Gate House for meals, as they have done things this way for the past thirty-some years.

Glen seems curious and asks, "Who's Mr. Fancy Pants?"

"He's one of the investors who purchased half the property with me. I don't suppose he'll show up any time soon, but if he does, you'll know who he is right away." As we become more relaxed with each other, Glen continues to stuff food into his mouth, as he rolls his eyes to heaven. "Do either of you know anything about these investors?"

"Mr. Lenard came by one day unannounced," he offers. "Said a woman bought half the place and you'd be comin first. There was a company or silent people or somethin that bought the other half of it. That's about it."

"Do you recall when that was?"

"About six weeks ago, maybe." Glen stuffs his mouth as if he hasn't eaten in a week, but it's more likely he hasn't seen beef in a while.

*The timetable doesn't seem right.*

"Did Lenard mention any specific names?"

"No, he never did say. Then Miss Gladys came by askin a bunch of questions." In between saying this, he packs more food into his mouth.

"What kind of questions did she ask? Dinner is delicious, Mona."

"Emmm, ya got that right, Missy," Glen moans happily, talking with his mouth full. "I sure have missed your cookin, Mona. She asked things like how much it cost to run the farm and what we pay for help.

But, I didn't know how ta answer other than what the horses eat and what we spend at the feed store," he says. "No one here 'cept Mona and me."

Mona looks up from her plate. "Gladys came inta the kitchen and asked me a bunch of questions, too, Miss Ellen."

"You mean about partners buying the place?" I inquire.

Mona shakes her head. "I could only tell her what the electric bill is. We have a well for water and septic, so there's no water bill. All the household stuff kind of got put on hold. We didn't buy nothin we didn't need, Miss Ellen."

"Since we're going to be working closely together, I want you to be completely honest with me, okay?" They both nod yes. "We have a lot to talk about. Did you notice anything odd about Gladys or Mr. Lenard?"

"Now that ya mention it," Glen mumbles, "they both made us swear we'd never tell anyone your business. We're ta keep our mouths shut no matter what we hear. Lenard made it sound very mysterious. No talkin ta the townspeople, even if they ask us questions about your family!"

Uneasy at first, we fall into an eye-opening conversation. I tell Mona and Glen the concocted background story Lenard instructed me to give, but leave out specific details, as they don't seem apropos. Then they talk about what it was like to run Ashwood Farms the years after Miss Abigail's brother died, but she didn't have a head for business. She trusted the Executor of the Ashwood Estate because she only cared about riding and entertaining her horsey friends.

The truth is, the Virginia Racing Commission wouldn't give her any license remotely related to racing, not for her Thoroughbreds, her trainers, jockeys, or drivers. Women had few rights back then, and no one stood up for her. It must have been a hard pill to swallow.

Glen says it was a darn shame because she had silks made for a Jockey named Dan. Without getting into the club down at the track, Dan felt it was impossible to compete as they flat out barred Ashwood. After a while, Abigail had no other choice, and that's when everyone drifted away from employment.

I'm acquainted with 'the club' and fully understand that they didn't want a woman in their inner sanctum, probably because of the obvious threat to their male egos. Chances are, she might have skewed the odds. Glen says that she was convinced her Thoroughbred, named

*Lexington's Jewel*, not only had a good trainer and a well-heeled jockey, but he was fast. He was so fast that he could take the Championship away from one of the golden boy jockeys.

"But you'll turn things around here, won't cha Ms. Thompson? I've got a very good feelin 'bout that!"

*Has Mona filled him with hope?*

"The old boys club has been around for a long time, Glen. I know how they operate; it's hard to get past them if they don't like you. Do you think we can outsmart them?"

Glen's eyes twinkle, and he stops chewing to smile at me. "Are ya fixin on farmin too?"

"I haven't got that far in my thinking yet, Glen. What's the buzz down at the feed store? What do people think about Ashwood? Did they say anything of interest?"

Daddy drummed many things into me. One was about the importance of gathering the proper information, and the other was about the subtler points of wagering. He said that during Seabiscuit's time, horseracing changed dramatically. It was a rough sport, and he continued to reiterate that it was no place for a woman.

"What do you know about the feed store?" Murdock asks in surprise.

"Don't tell me you girls don't do your share of gossip down there," I say laughing.

Murdock continues to stuff his mouth but eyes me cautiously. "We don't gossip. We talk about what's going on with everyone, that's all. Word gets around, Missy. I heard plenty from the guys down at the track when I used to go there, not so much now from the feed store," he says. "But I don't go there much anymore." Turning toward his wife, who has stopped eating, he adds, "I don't go there at all. I don't go there ever, Mona."

"I'm right, huh?"

Glen confirmed my suspicions that the old boys club is not only at the track, but it's also at the feed store. He doesn't see anything wrong with joining in with the crowd. It could work to our advantage in the future, should I want to plant information.

The bad news turns out to be the pile of unpaid bills that neither of them knows how to handle. Things were going along okay before the estate ran dry. It seems the banker, a Mr. Carl Yancy, along with the

Executor of the Estate, malinvested in an already downturned economy which led to the demise of the Ashwood Estate Fund.

It's nothing new that those with money vs. those without, tend to screw-over folks that don't pay attention and are trusting by nature. It's also my guess that Mona and Glen fall into this last category. They mention the only thing the bank would do to alleviate the debts, was to put the estate up for sale, but it has taken three long years.

They take turns explaining that during this time, they raised hens for eggs, and killed the chickens when they stopped laying eggs. A large garden supplied vegetables, and they ate plain hotdogs and are frankly quite sick of it. What little they received from boarding horses, and the baked goods sold in town kept them alive. With so little money coming in, there was barely enough to pay for the electricity or gas for the truck. My heart goes out to these hard working, loyal, and dependable people.

"Why didn't the bank step in with a solution? They could have sold some of the antiques. With all this acreage, they could have parceled it out to help you."

"That never came up," Glen says sadly. "You mean they coulda done that ta help us out?" Mona puts a loving hand on her husband's arm.

"Did you try to contact Miss Abagail's family?"

"Yancy said not ta bother 'em. Up 'til 'bout two months ago, we had no idea the bank found a buyer for this place. That's when Gladys showed up with Lenard the first time."

My brain is clicking away. "Are you sure that's the first time you met Lenard?"

"Yeah," Glen says ruefully. "That would be 'bout eight weeks ago. It was right after that heavy rain at the end of April. Two men tramped through the barn and said the bank should have a buyer pretty soon and ta sit tight."

Lenard did say that the investors were looking for someone to manage the farm, but the timeline doesn't correlate to my situation. "When did Lenard say a woman bought Ashwood?"

"When he first showed up, I told ya already," Glen says gruffly.

"You never met Gene before yesterday?"

"Yup," they both say.

Lenard's special teams might not have worked day and night on *my* plan. But they must have been working on a project to find buyers for this house for several months. Did they have this waiting in the wings to implement once they found the right sucker?

"Tell you what; I'm tired from the time changes from the last several days. Why don't we get started tomorrow? Gather all the receipts or whatever way you keep track of things, and we'll meet in the library around eight tomorrow morning. That way, I can start a spreadsheet."

"I got a simple way a keepin track of expenses, Missy. I don't need no spreadsheet," Glen says frowning.

*I'll bet he's wondering who's in charge now.*

"By the way, I didn't ask if you wanted to stay on here!"

Turning toward each other in bewilderment, Mona says, "We don't have nowhere else to go, Miss Ellen. It's been our home for so long our boys don't know any other than this."

"Good, then you'll stay. I have several ideas, but we can talk about that tomorrow. Good night to you. Thank you for a wonderful dinner, Mona."

Lenard must have been lying to me from day one! I'm trying to control my temper when a sweet scent greets me as I walk through the doorway of Abigail's bedroom. Temporarily distracted, the room appears almost too big for the existing furniture. I could sketch a small sitting room and kitchenette to take up half of the space. It might take three months to do it. Humm, three months is in the future. If my family isn't here within two, I'll crucify Lenard!

When the package showed up today, I meant to write down my thoughts. Digging out the paper and pen, I start to work on the list of items to go over with the Murdock's in the morning. Once my list is complete, I unpack the rest of the clothes and put my toiletries in the bathroom.

By now, it's nearly pitch black in the house. Curiosity takes me down the hallway to the clustered bedrooms on the right side of the house. Gladys said, it's in the same configuration as the left side. Light switches are not where I think they should be. When I find one and press the button, large furniture with washed out fabric and strikingly beautiful antiques are everywhere. All the bathrooms have old pedestal sinks, leaky toilets, and bathtubs with deep stains.

It will be a problematic renovation without the use of a computer, and the many contacts I had acquired throughout the years. Could this God-Awful nightmare be Ravi's fault? It's the most important interior design/renovation job of my life, and I have no money to buy anything!

*I'm suddenly very irritated with Ravi.*

Walking carefully down the front staircase to the library, I notice the beautiful square of the paneling in the hall as I pass. Trying to find the light switch, I turn on a floor lamp, where two bookcases are obstructing the view to the outside, blocking needed light. Strewn across a long, narrow pedestal wood table are the house plans, and I stop to linger there, thinking tomorrow will be a better time to view them.

Curious about AJ's office, and reaching in to feel the wall for a light switch, there isn't one. When I pull the chain on a green banker's lamp, it illuminates an old rotary telephone.

The top desk drawer contains a half-used eraser, a pen, a small flashlight (which I put in my back pocket), but little else. It has been cleaned out recently because there's a six-inch square void of dust. Pulling out the top drawer, I turn it over to find a key wedged into the side along with a tiny one stuck toward the back.

The larger key unlocks the top drawer, but someone jimmied the lock, and it's now useless. All the drawers are empty with no visible clue as to what the little key might unlock.

Back out in the library, I flop down on one of the sofas near the fireplace to make a quick assessment. All or most of the furniture will need to be cleaned and reupholstered. It was expensive fabric at one time, and the structures contain great bones. The tables only need a bit of furniture polish to return them to their former glory. That is, if I keep them, because they may be worth more if I sell them. And, if the investors don't come through with some money, that will be plan B.

Mrs. Ashwood's design ideas are utterly brilliant, mainly how the fireplaces are located on inside walls that are essentially open on both sides. The antique fire irons might fetch a good price along with some of the other items. Rosie pads softly into the room and settles near my feet to nuzzle my hand.

*I am suddenly homesick when I pat her head.*

Picking up a book from a dusty shelf, the memory of Abdul's fantastic library comes to mind. It contained some extraordinary books, but not this library. There's no classics here, except the outdated Funk & Wagnalls Dictionary, and the old Encyclopedia Britannica. If there were anything of value here, it's long gone.

As I walk, I take notes of the location of duplex receptacles, where the windows are, and the approximate size of each room. Passing through the arched alcove toward the billiard room, I hit the wood with a knuckle. To my surprise, it's hollow. Am I looking for a secret panel?

I shine the flashlight on either side where there's a small indentation in the wood on the left side about six feet up, which makes me laugh at the absurdity.

"This is insane," I whisper to myself. A déjà vu feeling washes over me as it slides away to reveal a dusty narrow staircase that's about three feet wide. Rosy isn't interested and waddles back to plop next to the fireplace in the library.

Judging from the settled dust on the treads, few know of the existence of this secret staircase. Moving cautiously up the ten or so feet, it reveals a sharp right turn at the top. When I shine the flashlight around, there's a passageway that crosses above the second-floor bedrooms then stops at a landing. Is this the attic?

At the top, there's a window covered with a black film that's peeling at the corners. The good news is that it hasn't been painted shut. Directly opposite this is a door, that when opened, accesses another staircase that drops down to another landing. Below this, an empty clothes pole hangs in front of a door that opens directly into Abigail's bedroom.

The whole thing is so smart that I almost can't contain my enthusiasm; however, my gut tells me that it needs to remain a closely guarded secret for now. Retracing my steps, I'm back in the alcove to touch the indentation, and the panel slides silently closed.

A two-piece lavatory under the secret staircase has access to both the library and billiard room via pocket doors. The sink has a dark brown stain, and neither faucets work when I turn the handles. The toilet has a matching ring inside the bowl and is quite disgusting.

In the billiard room, the pool table sports worn red felt with a square Tiffany-style leaded glass lamp that hangs over it. There is no sign of the balls. One wall contains a rack of bowed cue sticks, and a cube of blue chalk sits on the dusty wood floor under the table.

Out in the two-story hall, there's a modern powder room under the sweeping staircase. It has white wainscot around the lower half of the walls, wide baseboards, and upper walls painted in a delicate light blue. Back in the hallway, another door presumably leads to the dungeon of a basement that will remain unexplored until another time.

The paneled walls in the hall, are either mahogany or walnut. Small cracks are visible, but with some oil, a little diligence, and a lot of patience, they can be beautiful again. An enormous Grandfather clock majestically rests against the wall near the living room with the dial set at twelve ten, the large harp pendulum at rest.

The wood floors, worn around the once opulent area rugs, only need sanding and a coating of stain to bring them back to their original grandeur, although there isn't much that will help the holes in the rugs.

Drawn to light under the kitchen door, I expect to see Mona, but it's evident she's retired for the night and has left the little light on over the stove. The double switches near the doorway are yellow push-button type things from a by-gone era. One switch turns nothing on; the second switch turns on two large overhead fluorescent light fixtures that flicker and hum, then illuminate the sickly, green hue of the kitchen.

Rosy is beside me again, ambles over to her dish, giving it a push with her snout. Remembering that Sassy used to do the same thing when she wanted water, I fill her bowl from the spigot, suddenly lonely and overwhelmed. Thinking she needs to go out, I push the back door open, but she doesn't move, and I'm glad that she's chosen to stay with me tonight.

I gather a piece of pie and a glass of wine and Rosie follows me up the back stairs, where she makes herself at home at the foot of the bed again. Pipes somewhere deep within the house moan when I flush the toilet. That's the sound of money going down the drain pipe of home restoration. The faucets on the sink barely turn the water to a trickle, and I can't bring myself to take a bath in the old tub, and I'm in no mood to scrub it.

Curling up in the comforter, I wonder how I will ever make sense out of the chaos that is now my life. Will the ghosts of the past like the fact that there will be a new family living here? I wish with all my heart that Ravi were here, but then, we wouldn't be in this mess if he were. Or would we?

"Good night, Mrs. Ashwood. Good night Miss Abigail. And good night to you, dear little one who might have died in the dumbwaiter. I wish sweet dreams to you all. I don't mean to intrude, but can we all live here together in harmony?"

*Did someone sigh?*

On the first morning after my arrival, the sun tries to shine through angry-looking clouds. An acrid smell of rain permeates the air before large drops hit the window, which brings me fully awake.

After a quick breakfast, I delve into the box of bills and stacks of invoices left on the table by the Murdock's. I'm overwhelmed by the shear stack of unpaid bills. I'm sure that Glen is hoping I have a good idea on how to turn this place back into a productive horse farm, one that trains Thoroughbreds again, one we can all be proud of, especially one that's profitable. He wants to know how I intend to do this. I know where to start, but we need to set down some ground rules first.

The Murdock's and I are at the large table in the library. "First, I'm going to need a computer."

Glen snarls, "Whatcha need that for?"

"It's a great tool for searching the web, making spreadsheets, and gathering research, Glen."

Pointing to his ledger, pounding it with his finger, he says, "I got everthin ya need right here!"

"I know, but a spreadsheet can track what you've been doing. Then I'm going to research Ashwood Farms. If we're going to make this work, I need more information."

Glen seems a little annoyed. "Library in town has a place where they keep old records. Library lady must have 'em for this ole place, too. Don't see a need ta get one of them things. Been keepin books for thirty years, Missy. And they're accurate!"

His way is using an old calculator, but he mostly adds it up on paper. I want to ask him if he has an abacus, but then he may be offended, so I don't.

"I understand, Glen. You can keep doing that for another thirty if you want to. The way I see it, there's an immediate need for cash."

"We could take on more horses," he says thoughtfully. "There's plenty of room."

*Glen's used to doing things his way! May our struggle for power be brief.*

"Let me put it another way. You aren't making money the way you're going about it now. That part needs to change, Glen."

"Okay," he says thoughtfully. "We got five stalls with no horses in 'em. We could fix 'em up where the ole buggy is and make that stalls, too. Maybe we can use the old dairy part."

"What old buggy are you talking about, Glen? I didn't see one when we passed through there with Gladys. Can you possibly do any more work by yourself? Do you have extra money to hire someone to help you?"

Glen's face contorts slightly. "Miss Abigail said it might be worth somethin. If ya ask me, it's nothin but junk now anyways. Mice could a got hold of it by now. Maybe ya want ta work out in the barn with me?" he says with a wink. "There ain't no money left after givin the feed store most of it."

"You want me to help you muck out the stalls? Poop detail is not my favorite part of the barn. I've already been there and done that. If you thought the buggy was worth something, why didn't you sell it?"

"Wasn't ours to sell, Missy. Look, the bank gave us credit b'fore; they'll do it again now that you're here. Ya can ask b'cause you and those silent people own the whole shebang outright, don't ya?"

*He's stubborn; I'll give him that.*

"I'll talk to Mr. Yancy, but we need funds right now. What we need is an investor. We need; Oh my God, I can't believe I didn't think of this. We need a silent partner!" I excuse him so quickly that he storms out of the library as Mona suddenly remembers she has something cooking on the stove.

Since the old telephone is still working, I pick up the receiver and dial Lenard's number, but he says quite loudly, "Didn't you understand that all requests will go through me? You must never contact Mr. C or any one of the investors, EVER! You know the rules."

"Then you do it. Those men both said to let them know if I need anything, and I need something. You contact them for me and ask for money! We need financial assistance, pronto!"

Before hanging up on me, Lenard says, "Don't hold your breath. The purchase of the property strained all of their resources, including yours."

*That didn't go the way I planned it in my head!*

How will we turn this place around in three months if the silent partners/investor people won't help? Where will the money come from to pay off all these bills? From preliminary calculations, the debts amount to over $65,000 for the barn expenses alone. What can I do to generate money to live on in the meantime?

Clenching my teeth until my jaws hurt, I swivel in the chair to look out the old wavy glass window. On a hunch, I walk out to the southern paddock, strolling slowly over to the fence so *Lightning* won't spook. It's not long when he picks his head up, twitches his ears, then trots slowly toward me.

"Hello, *Lightning*. How are you at solving riddles?" As he nibbles contentedly on the carrots I snitched from the refrigerator, I softly talk to him. "Here's one for you. If a farm looks and smells like a horse farm, does that make it a horse farm?" He whinnies and shakes his big head up and down. "Okay, that's a good answer!" Looking into his big brown eye, I add, "That's what I thought. We'll have to work this out together."

As I walk back to the house, something occurs to me, and I wonder why I hadn't thought of it before. My parents didn't pay for my college education, and no one gave me money to start my business. I earned it myself. Deciding to find Glen to smooth things over, I head toward the barn to talk with him.

Cognizant of loud noises and sudden movements near large animals, I call out quietly, "Glen, are you here?" A shadowy movement catches my eye near the far end of the barn, which moves through the wall, disappearing. "That's odd; what's down there?"

Glen is standing a few feet away with an *I told-you-so* face. "I already told ya, Missy, there's not much in there except some old stuff, maybe the buggy."

"Didn't you see something down there?"

"You're dreamin," he says in an exasperated tone, turning to go back into his office.

"I thought I saw something go in here, rather melted through the wall. Do you have a ghost here, Glen? Something Gladys failed to mention in her disclosure of the property?"

Glen's ruddy features darken for a moment. "Nothin here, Missy, some old junk is all," he says.

"Then what's on the other side of the door?" I ask.

"Ya gonna tell me what throwin me outta your office was all about?"

"Glen, I'm sorry if I hurt your feelings, but I thought we could move forward a little faster if I called Lenard to see if he would get in touch with our silent partners."

*He wants to know he's still in charge, even though he isn't.*

"What'd he say?" Glen's manner softens a little; maybe he's a tad more hopeful now that I have come to apologize to him.

"Lenard said I'm not allowed to contact them. He'll try to do it for us. They're silent for a reason, so we must wait for them to contact me. Guess we'll need to be resourceful. No hard feelings, Glen?" Putting my hand out in a friendly gesture, he reluctantly takes it, holding onto it, which reminds me of Daddy's big hands.

"Maybe I'm used ta doin things my way for so long there ain't been nobody ta say otherwise. So, I guess I should be grateful ya came along when ya did ta buy this ole place and fix it up. Let's call it a draw, okay?"

"Are you a gambler, Glen?"

"Not for a long while, Missy."

"You and Mona are integral parts of the arrangement to get this place up and running. Any differences we might have, we have to resolve, because we're going to need each other's support."

As I walk toward the house, a plan begins to formulate. Mona is taking pans out of the old oven when I open the back door. "Mona, is there a car available, besides the old truck?"

"No," she says. "Why you askin?"

"I'd like to go into town to buy some things."

"I have ta make a delivery today, so I'll take you since you don't know your way 'round here. Be about thirty minutes or so."

"Give me a call when you're ready."

"Sure thing, Miss Ellen."

Pulling out the private stash, I'm both surprised and happy to count $5,000 in slightly used one hundred dollar bills that were in the box with my rings, which I add to the money Gene gave me.

After we get to town, Mona and I go our separate ways. Several hours later, I've managed to spend about half of the money. We now have a set of wireless phones, an answering machine, a laptop, a tablet, wireless printer, a calculator, and a set of walky-talkies. I also purchased four cellphones, drawing materials, a pair of sturdy boots, jeans, four plaid shirts, gloves, and a western hat. If I'm going to live here, I also need to look as if I belong.

While in town, I've also visited several establishments. A meeting has been set up for tomorrow morning at ten o'clock with the companies and vendors who own our outstanding invoices, along with a representative from the bank, the lawyer for the defunct Ashwood Estate, and the town's local antique dealer. The word *town* loosely describes Jasper, as its little more than a few brick buildings strung together, which reminds me of an old western town, minus the tumbleweed.

When we return, Mona goes off with her groceries while I empty the truck. I've rolled up the house plans to use the library table, and have set the boxes and equipment on it so that I can methodically open and put everything in place in old Mr. AJ's office.

Glen strolls in and looks around, and says, "Can I help ya, Missy? Ya got a mighty mess goin on here."

"You want to help *me* with my computer? This, from the man who operates a business with a hand calculator, pencil, and paper? No thanks, I can manage," I say laughing.

"Suit yourself, Missy, but ya gotta come and see what's b'hind that ole door in the barn," he says sheepishly.

"Can it wait, Glen. I'm in a pickle right now."

Reaching for my hand, he says with a wink, "Come and take a look."

"Okay."

The handle on the door looks like a loose piece of metal with a hook at the end. Glen pulls it up and slides the door open. Walking to an old tattered canvas, he yanks it off to reveal an elegant carriage.

"So there's nothing in here, huh?"

Glen starts to laugh. "It's a beauty, ain't it?" He reverently touches the beautiful black lacquered door with the hand-carved gold motif.

"We have a treasure that Mr. Tillman will most certainly be interested in seeing."

The cable company wired the new equipment, making it possible to connect to the world I have so desperately missed. It won't take long to do the research needed to bolster arguments that are sure to come when the meeting starts this morning.

Mona is in the library with her cart loaded with items to serve our guests. "They'll be here soon," she says, nervously punching our new throw pillows.

I warned them both at dinner last night that it will take their help to turn this farm around. Glen doesn't think we have a snowball's chance in hell and is skeptical by nature, as I'm quickly learning. The power struggles we experience are probably due to his stepped-on feelings when I show up out of thin air to take over.

*The new way of doing things is not easy for him to digest.*

The crunch of gravel draws my attention to the front window. As Glen ushers people into the library, I quickly gather my papers. Six men and two women are sitting on the sofas facing each other. Glen and I take the wing chairs.

"Good morning everyone. Thank you so much for coming on such short notice. My name is Ellen Thompson. I'm one of the owners of Ashwood Farms. I assume you came out of curiosity. Who would buy this rundown place and who's nuts enough to try and make it work, right?"

Several people laugh as they gaze at the goodies on the tray. I encourage them to help themselves to coffee and pastry and take about twenty minutes to lay out my plan, starting with our inherited debts. It addresses how we'll repay each vendor and what we want to see concerning running the horse farm.

One of the creditors speaks right up. "Gladys told us you're from Chicago. Know anythin about horses, Ms. Thompson?"

Another man inquires, "Got any experience runnin a farm?"

Judging from the hostility, I've decided to be as polite as possible. "You're aware of the fact that the original Mr. AJ Ashwood came from the Chicago area?"

"So what! That don't prove nothin," someone says, laughing.

"This farm owes us a lot of money!" another says in a terse tone.

Trying to maintain my composure, I say, "May I remind you that Mr. Ashwood didn't know anything about farming or the dairy business, but he managed to do all this!"

Observing how this group is chattering with one another as they take the pastry to stuff into their mouths, it reminds me of something that I witnessed a few weeks ago.

When Mr. Yancy clears his throat, Glen sets his cup down on his saucer with a clink. He is a rather robust man. In a clipped and rather loud voice he says, "You don't seem to have any credit history that we can verify, Mrs. Thompson. We can't take that great a risk on someone like that. You don't qualify to borrow money from my bank."

Turning to the Executor of the Ashwood Estate, I ask, "How did the Ashwood Estate fail, Mr. Allen? I would like to understand what happened to the money that Miss Abigail entrusted to your care." Mr.

Allen appears uncomfortable, shrugs his shoulders but offers no explanation. "As the Executor of the Ashwood Estate, would you allow me to look at the paperwork?"

Mr. Allen's face drains of color. "That won't be allowed b'cause we settled the estate a long time ago, Ms. Thompson. You don't have the right to ask for an investigation. You're not related to any of the Ashwood's, are you? B'sides, no heirs came fo'ward to claim anything!" he stammers.

"I find that a little perplexing, Mr. Allen. According to numerous sources, there should be several hundred thousand dollars left in the estate."

Glen sucks in his breath, as he was unaware of this information. It could have changed everything for them, as he and Mona practically ate dirt to stay alive these last few years.

Mr. Allen's face flushes a lovely shade of red. "Where did you get that kind of information?" he spews. "You can't prove that! I did nothing wrong. There were circumstances beyond our control. Tell 'em, Carl." He glances nervously at Mr. Yancy, who looks away quickly.

"I wonder what would turn up if the Attorney General launched an investigation into the missing funds, gentlemen."

Mr. Yancy spits when he talks. "The market tanked. We had no control over that as anyone here knows! We all lost our shirts during that time. You can't prove we did anything wrong!"

Mr. Allen nervously adds, "We had it on good authority that the money. . ."

"Shut up, you fool," Yancy hisses at Allen. "You can't prove anything, Mrs. Thompson. We did everything by the book. We all took a beating during that time, right everyone?"

Yancy stares at each person, and the room erupts in chatter. But, methinks Mr. Allen and Mr. Yancy protests too much. Now I'm sure that the estate funds were mishandled, and perhaps there are others. He is correct about one thing; I can't prove it, yet.

I'm clinking my cup with a spoon to get everyone's attention. "Thank you, Mr. Allen and Mr. Yancy, you don't have to say anymore, we all get it. So, let's move on. Now as far as the outstanding invoices…"

"Yeah, let's talk about that! You people owe me a considerable sum," one of the vendors shouts.

I knew this was coming. "Please consider giving us a little more time. If you could extend it out from thirty to sixty days, it will give us time to secure the funds from other sources since the bank has turned us down. We have been negotiating with our investors."

A man in a red plaid shirt raises his hand. "We need our money right now, Ms. Thompson. We need it ourselves to stay afloat."

"What kind of plan do you have in mind, Ms. Thompson?" another vendor asks.

"I know that you're all in need of your money now, but I'm asking for a little more time and a little more patience from you. I only became aware of these debts."

Yancy moves his bulk off the sofa and toward the door, saying, "We've spent enough time waiting as it is, Mrs. Thompson."

"Thanks for your hospitality," another vendor says, then stands to leave.

"Don't be too hasty," one of the women says. I recognize her from the antique shop as one of the owner's assistants. "I say we give her a chance."

"Sure, you would say that! She don't owe you money," plaid shirt says, as everyone starts to grumble.

"Yeah, we can't wait any longer," the feed store owner says.

"What would you have done if the investors and I hadn't come along?" I have held my tongue long enough. "You all seem ready to hang me. I inherited this debt; I did not cause it. I've simply asked for more time to pay you all back."

"You'd need to show more collateral and substantial credit history for any of us to trust you, Mrs. Thompson," Yancy adds. "This old rundown place isn't enough."

The antique shop owner, Mr. Tillman, speaks up saying, "But there is substantial collateral! We could sell the antiques. Wouldn't that help?"

No one takes him seriously as people drift toward the door.

Seeing the man's expression, I offer, "Would you like to look around, Mr. Tillman?" He thinks that's a good idea, as he's uncomfortable being in the same room with this bunch.

"We'll have to think about your proposal, Ms. Thompson," a vendor says, reaching for the last tart. "These are mighty good. I'll bet Ms. Murdock made these. Here's an idea for you, you should hire her out for parties. You could make a lot of money that way."

Mr. Yancy hovers near me and sticks his finger into my shoulder, saying, "I warned Abigail to do something about the situation before it all tumbled down around her head. She didn't put a penny into the upkeep of this house."

The other vendors say they won't extend further credit. They'll expect full payment within two weeks, or they'll file a lien against the property. Glen hangs back, giving me his *I told-you-so* face, walking out of the library with the last man.

Mr. Tillman is in the hallway conversing with the sweet woman who said to give us a chance along with another one of his assistants. They push me back into the library.

"Oh my, Mrs. Thompson, I don't know where to begin."

"Give it to me straight, Mr. Tillman. What do you think you can sell and what do you think it's all worth?"

They look from one to the other and grin. Mr. Tillman is a short, wiry man in a pinstriped suit. He sports light brown fuzz around an otherwise bald head. His glasses are too large for his face, but he's honest-looking and polite.

Mona returns to remove the dishes, brushing at invisible crumbs and I know she's listening to the conversation.

"It's hard to say without the proper research, but with an estate, there are protocols we follow, such as taking an inventory, and making lists for your approval. Then we take photos of everything and put a catalog together for the internet," Mr. Tillman says, all in a rush.

"So you'll take this on?" I ask.

Isabelle, one of Tillman's assistants, says with a big smile, "Oh, Ms. Thompson, we will indeed! We can't wait to get started!" She's a charming middle-aged woman with a round face, broad nose, and ruby red lips.

Tillman's other assistant adds, "We've wanted to come see this treasure trove for years."

"Oh my, yes," Tillman says. "We came by alright, but they wouldn't let us in. Judging from what we've seen so far, a quick calculation could bring in as much as a half a mill, wouldn't you say Isabelle? What about you Jenny?"

"Yes," they both say in agreement.

"Are you saying dollars, Mr. Tillman?"

"Yes, Mrs. Thompson, that would be in dollars."

*Bless my soul; ask and, ye shall receive!*

"That's only a quick assessment, of course, it's only the beginning." Mr. Tillman seems jittery, acting as if he's rushing to the prospector's office as he's fallen into a gold mine.

"You might want to see what we discovered in the barn," I tell the trio. "It's an old Brougham Carriage. I researched what type it is, and there may be more stuff up in the attic, provided it's in good shape."

"There's certainly no shortage of excellent pieces here, Ms. Thompson. Then there's the Wedgewood china, the silverware, the stemware, Royal Dalton's, along with other fine pieces of porcelain," Mr. Tillman says with wide eyes. "I b'lieve the vases over the mantle in the living room are genuine Rosewood."

"Imagine that," I say absently.

Mr. Tillman thanks me for allowing him to have first access to this most magnificent cache, being ever so grateful for the privilege of being part of this momentous occasion. He will come first thing tomorrow morning to get the ball rolling. Then he, Isabelle, and Jenny chatter away as they leave the library.

Mona is trying to hide her tears as she silently moves around the room. "I know you think that a stranger has made a terrible mistake, but this might be the only way to get the money we need to pay everyone back right away. Aren't you tired of living on a shoestring?

Mona considers this for a moment. Hugging me gently, she says, "I understand, honestly I do, Miss. Ellen, but it's that you're selling Miss Abigail's precious treasures. She wouldn't be happy if she knew we was sellin her stuff."

"If Miss Abigail were here, perhaps those two lunatics wouldn't have absconded with her money and left you with nothing. Look at it this way, we have no money right now. Any funds I had are gone. They went against my half of this property, and there's nothing left. The bank won't loan us a dime, because I haven't established credit."

Mona begins to shake her head as tears roll down her face. "I don't think it's right, Miss Ellen."

"Whether we think it's right or wrong, they're going to put a lien on the house in two weeks if we don't do something right now. The antiques are stuff. They aren't food, and they can't keep us warm in the winter unless we chop them up for firewood, so the best thing they can do for us--is we sell them. The money they generate will keep us fed and warm, and we can pay off the outstanding bills that have piled up. You have to trust me on this."

"Okay," she says, sniffing sadly. "I didn't know about all that." Mona goes back to her cleanup tasks, disappearing into the kitchen with the little push cart, as cups and saucers clink quietly. As her footsteps move beyond the kitchen door, it becomes eerily silent in the library.

Going over the morning's events, I mull over what we might be in for, as a gentle peace washes over me. Some hours later, I look up to see Glen standing in the doorway of my office. "Dinner's ready," he announces quietly.

How could the day have flown by so fast? Backing up the current information, I shut down my new password-protected computer. We spend the dinner hour discussing our various options, now that we have some. Glen has softened somewhat since Mona has filled him in on our little conversation in the library. Everything will be all right; we only need to give it a bit more time.

Am I quoting those idiots? Where, oh where, have my wits gone? They now need to trust me. My children need a stable environment, and I aim to give it to them.

"Mona, did you see who delivered that little box the other day?"

"No," she says. "The box was sittin by the back door when Glen and me came back from the market."

"What was in it," they both want to know.

"A little gift from a horse."

They think this is funny, and we all start to laugh.

Mr. Tillman arrives promptly at nine the next morning, along with his two assistants. They get to work quickly, chattering as they move from room to room. I've asked them to stay out of the upstairs right wing, as the antiques belong to the other investors. Then I turn my attention to the research that is now printing.

I marvel at the sheer efficiency of the wireless capabilities. What is so great, is that I can work from the comfort of my bedroom!

Something suddenly occurs to me. How did this slip my mind? Is my brain still muddled from the drugs, or is it a combination of things? I know how to place bets and make wise investments. That's how I paid for my college education.

Daddy took me to the racetrack when I was twelve. At first, it was a game, as the primary objective was to study horses and jockeys up close, which progressed to the tote board. After mastering that, it was on to the race card, then observation of the horses during races.

I had theories about how they moved, how they communicated, and what the odds were. It was our little secret, but eventually, I was able to put my finger on a horse and Daddy would place the bet.

Daddy called our winnings, *Ellen's Special Fund*. It not only paid for four years of college, my elaborate wedding and fantastic honeymoon, Ravi and I also used it to pay a sizeable down payment on our first home. It even set me up in an interior design business.

*Will this work again?*

We only need to do this long enough to get out from under this tremendous debt. A quick search reveals the closest racetrack is ten miles away. I don't know if my system still works, so I place several pretend bets online with the intention of checking back later.

It is past lunchtime when Mr. Tillman and his assistants assail me in the library. Handing me one of the clipboards, I'm stunned at the rows of items that are unbelievably detailed.

"What's the verdict? It doesn't look like you rejected much."

Tillman says enthusiastically, "It's only a preliminary list now, Mrs. Thompson. Cross off any pieces you don't want us to sell! "There are some wonderful pieces here."

Isabelle excitedly adds, "We'll return to catalog and photograph everything you approve. It'll be available online, distributed to select customers we know will appreciate the quality of the items."

I'm running calculations in my head. "Do you know how long that might take, Mr. Tillman?"

Rolling his eyes upward, he says, "It should take about three days to photograph. By the way, that old carriage in the barn is worth selling. I put feelers out, and someone put a bid in on it already! Are you okay with all this? You look a little concerned."

"I'm stunned with delight, Mr. Tillman!"

"We have to compare the items with analogous others, but we think that the value alone will bring people from all over the world," he says proudly.

Jenny asks candidly, "Do you know if there's any jewelry left from the Ashwood women? They were supposed to have a good-sized safe, but we didn't see one when we went through the house."

"I haven't looked everywhere yet myself. How big a safe are you talking?"

"It would be a good size, probably the size of a closet door maybe. Sure hope you find it," Isabelle says. "Antique jewelry usually draws people with money."

"What kind of timetable are we looking at, Mr. Tillman? And what might this auction cost?"

"Don't you worry about that, it's all included in our commission fee," Tillman muses. "We've done this before, Ms. Thompson, you're not to worry about a thing. Ah, you're worried about the creditors, aren't you? We can sell that carriage right away if that'll help you out?"

"Anything you sell now will help. How soon do you think we can generate seventy-five thousand?"

Tillman gasps, "That's how much you need right away?"

"Yes, I'm afraid it is. I inherited this mess. I'll figure a way around it for the short term."

"I'll not lie to you and say we can get this done quickly, because that's not how we do things," Tillman says.

"How soon might that take?"

"We'll want the best exposure so we'll need time to set up the appropriate accounts. It could take several months to get it to our liking."

"I understand and thank you. That's what I needed to know, exactly."

*"There are two primary choices in life,*

*to accept conditions as they exist,*

*or accept the responsibility for changing them."*

~ Dr. Denis Waitley

## Chapter Eight

## The Ancient Whisper

**S**ince Lenard hasn't responded to my request for money and the other investors did not attempt to make contact, it seems only fair that Mr. Tillman has access to the items on the other side of the house. He and his assistants are here to evaluate those antiques. I'll plead insanity when anyone asks where they are.

Tillman politely assails me in the hallway to give me the good news. "The combined value of the antiques in this house could exceed over a million dollars, Ms. Thompson!"

Isabelle is beaming, "It's going to be the biggest auction we've ever done. We can't wait to get started!"

Tillman cheerfully says, "It's a quick assessment, mind you. We'll be back in a couple of days when we can arrange for a photographer. It'll give you time to go over the lists b'cause I know you want to keep some of them."

The owner and employees of The Jasper Antique Emporium excitedly chat while they move toward the front door. As I glance at the clipboard, the items are arranged by category with the most valuable pieces near the top, followed by another list that needs repair or renovation.

Mrs. Ashwood's bedroom suite, the 4-poster bed on Mr. C's side of the house, the desks in both AJ's and Mrs. Ashwood's offices, the dining table, upholstered chairs, Grandfather clock, Wedgewood plates, crystal stemware, and silver are among the most valuable pieces. The real shocker is what the vintage chrome and vinyl fifties-style table and chairs are worth. Mr. Tillman thinks the set will bring in over $1,500 alone!

Laughing at the fact that all the Ashwood's were hoarders of the right order, I'm grateful *we* are the recipients of such good fortune. It's a puzzle why no one thought to take any of them when they left.

Crossing off AJ's desk and chair, making notations what furniture Mother will move here to replace some of the items, I'm figuring we can do with what we have until we can replace them. Each children's bedroom furniture and possessions will come to reside with them, but all of Ravi's and mine are forever gone.

Something suddenly occurs to me. Could the antiques possess an *ancient whisper* from the person who owned it? Could their spirit travel with the piece? Has the original Mrs. Ashwood or Miss Abigail been whispering to me since I walked through the front door? Is it their presence that roams the halls of this house? Could the little girl, who materializes upon occasion, be the one I sense the most?

It's a comfortable, non-threatening sensation that we are presided over by ancient spirits, who by nature are the very ones who loved this house. I'm humbled, grateful for Mrs. Ashwood's foresight and dedication to her convictions.

By bringing this beautiful old place back to its former glory, we can honor her memory. I can't do that without money. Only by selling the antiques will we be able to do that. May we all draw inspiration from the strong women who persevered and never gave up until there was no other choice

*The time is right to take a closer look at the house plans.*

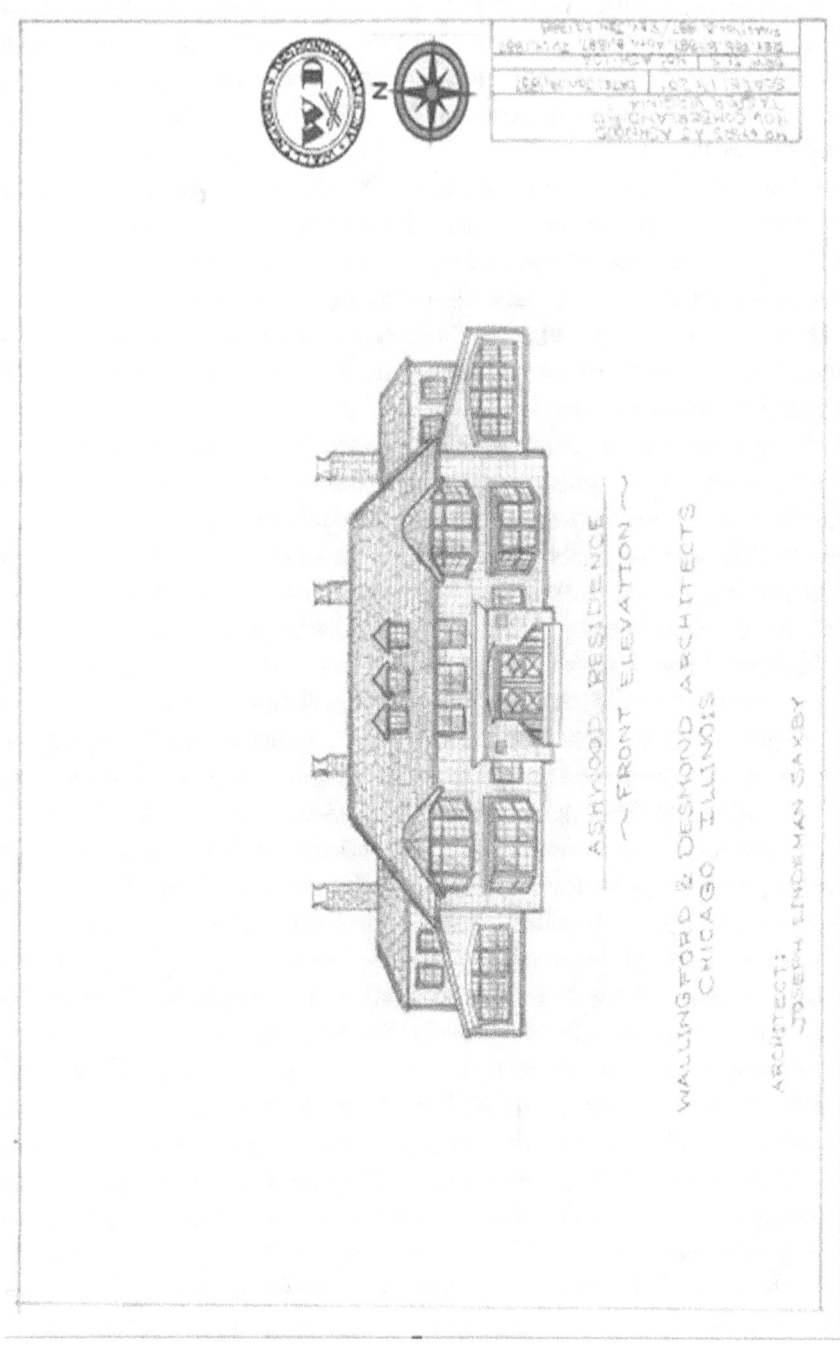

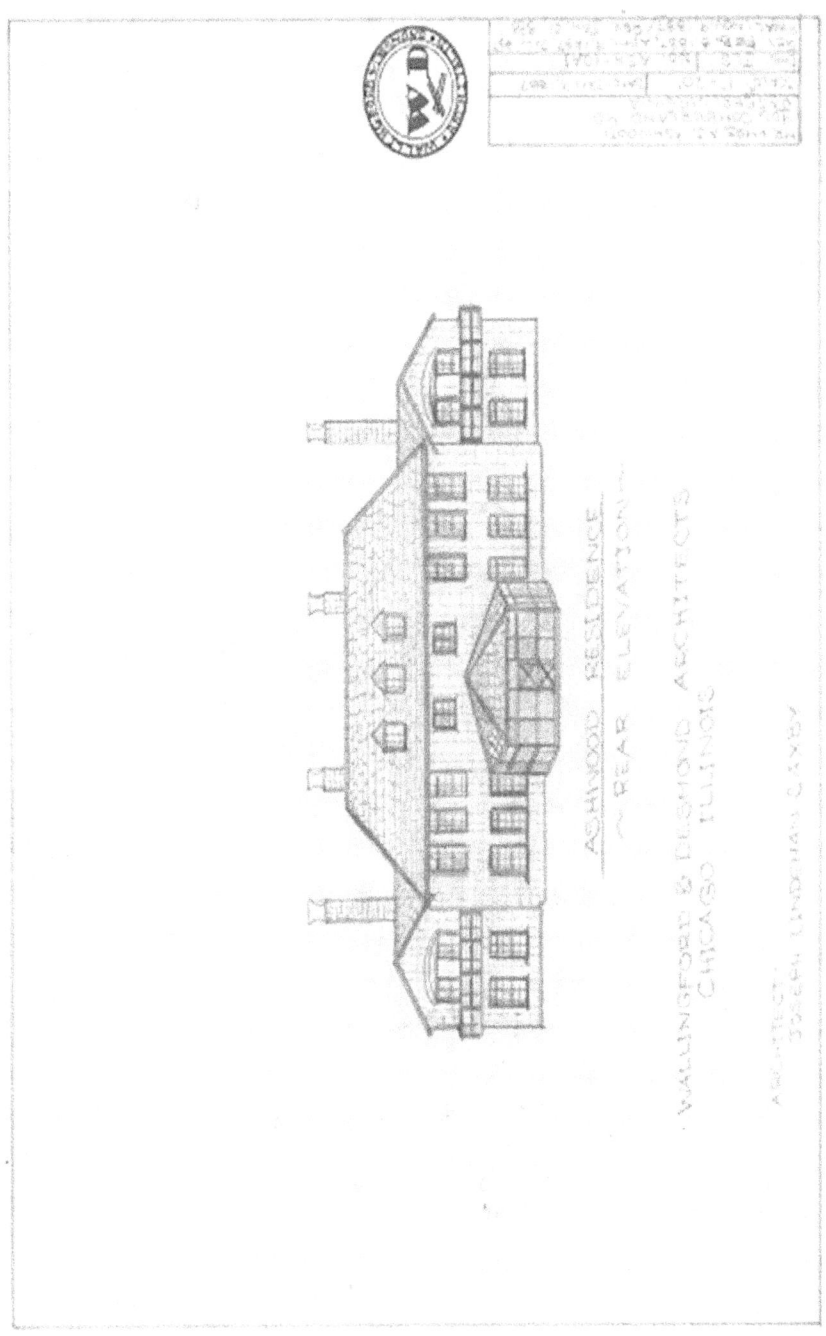

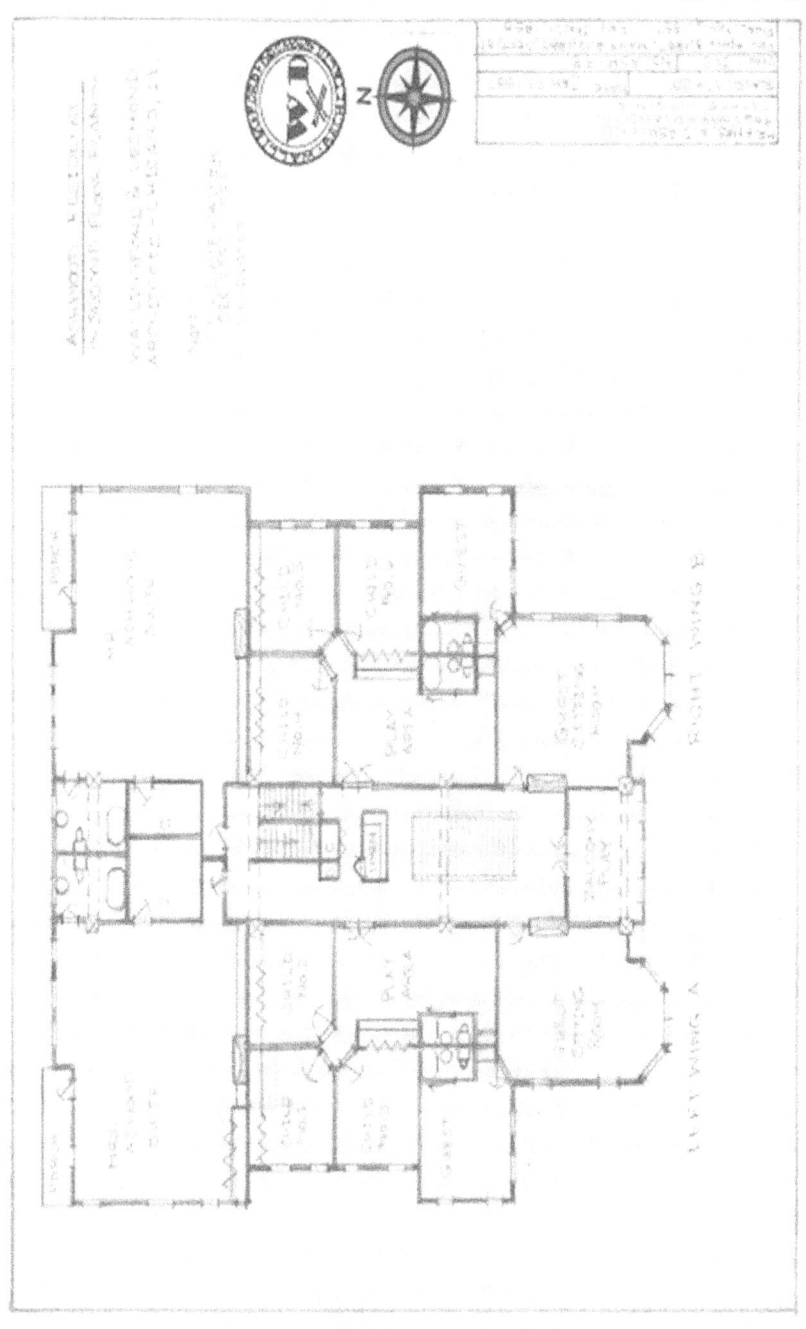

The rest of the week is spent preparing spreadsheets. The box of loose receipts and notes from Glen's ledger give a glimpse of how the Murdock's did the best they could under the circumstances. After Abigail died, and with no outside help, Glen singlehandedly took care of the barn and property. They lived frugally when the estate ran out of money and must have used whatever savings they had to exist.

Mr. Tillman took the kitchen table last week along with several loads of furniture. We are in the Morning Room having dinner, deciding collectively to call it that for lack of a better term.

"How did you find out there was no money left in the estate, Glen? Mr. Allen or Mr. Yancy must have known about your situation."

"I'll tell ya what he said, Missy. Mr. Yancy said ta mind my own business. If we didn't like the way things are done here, we could pack up and go live somewhere else. We don't have anywhere else ta go so we stayed put," Glen says, shrugging.

Mona says quietly, "Mr. Allen wouldn't take our calls. When we went ta see him, his secretary always said he was out. Our boys are married and have families of their own now. They don't want us showin up and askin ta live with 'em."

"Don't rightly know if I'd do that anyway. One boy lives in Idaho, and the other is in Arizona," Glen mutters.

I've propped a large tablet on an easel. "All I ask is that you hear me out before you make any decisions. We'll start with you, Mona. You will now have a budget for weekly groceries. It appears you were careful to keep expenses down."

"I tried, Miss Ellen," Mona says softly.

"From what I can determine, the household has accumulated about fifteen grand in debt. Have you kept track of how much money you put in from your savings?"

As Mona shakes her head from side to side, Glen answers, "We spent everythin we had ta survive, Miss Ellen. There ain't nothin left ta speak of."

Mona sniffs into her apron. "Miss Abigail used ta put an envelope on the counter every week for groceries and stuff. Then, after she died, there was a fund we could draw from at the bank."

"Then one day, it was closed," Glen adds.

"When we asked what happened, Yancy acted like we asked 'em for the moon. Told us there was nothin left in the account. We'd have to fend for ourselves or find another place ta live," Mona concludes.

"I'm sorry they mistreated you. I hope to repay you for whatever you spent. Mona, from now on, you'll receive a weekly salary. You can use the kitchen for your baking if you want to, but you must keep track of that separately. It can't mingle with the household funds. You can call that extra money, *Mona's Mad Money*."

"I've never had extra money b'fore!" Mona says laughing.

"You and Mother will share responsibility for the house and laundry if she comes with my children. You can hire help if you need to, and we can discuss additional things you might need." I place a batch of papers on the table in front of her, and she picks it up to flip through the pages. "Mother will assist you with menus, shopping, and help in the kitchen."

"Oh, that would be very nice if she can do that. She might not come?" Mona asks.

"We're not entirely sure about that, yet."

Mona seems pleased with the responsibility she will undertake. "*Mona's Mad Money,*" she says laughing, that's a great thing, Miss Ellen!"

"Glen, you are responsible for the feed, horses, grounds, and anything that has to do with the barn and property. Continue to have the pastures prepped, the lawn trimmed, etc. You will collect boarding fees according to the new schedule. You will also have a budget and a weekly salary."

Placing a batch of paper on the table in front of him; he turns it over without looking at it. "I've never had a budget to work with b'fore; guess you'll have ta teach me. I'm not much for learnin fast, but I'll give 'er a try. Why do ya need ta raise the fees?" he asks.

"Preliminary calculations put the barn expenses over what you take in with boarding fees. It comes to over $3,800 a month in debt times twelve for the time you had to do this without the estate's help. It comes to a whopping $45,600! We can and will train horses, give lessons, and turn this place around, but it will take time to do it."

"I didn't know it got that much," Glen grumbles, looking a little perplexed. "No wonder those men were angry. Beg pardon, Miss Ellen, but I don't know how this will work. The boarders might be angry if we raise the fees on 'em."

"They'll say; they got a good deal all these years."

"No, they won't," Glen says mournfully.

"I understand your concern, but hear the rest of it, okay? I'll oversee both budgets. I'll cut checks for all expenses, so receipts need to be on my desk each Saturday morning. And from now on, Ashwood Farms is going to be called Ashwood Stables; the name change is already in the works with a new website available sometime soon."

Glen looks confused, "What's a web?"

"I'll explain it to you later. We stand to make money when we sell the antiques."

As I say this, Mona dabs her face as Glen puts his arm around her shoulders. "It still bothers me we have ta do this, Miss Ellen."

"We can't avoid this. We need to wipe the slate clean, and with the sale of the antiques, it'll generate what we need. We can also establish medical plans and a decent pension to compensate for your many years of service here."

They both gasp at this because they don't have any medical coverage, pension plan, nor extra anything. "Sellin the antiques will surely help, then," Glen says in awe. "Right Mona?"

"With a weekly salary, you can't use it on anything other than yourselves. No using it for baking supplies, Mona, or feed for the barn, Glen. As you know, we have silent partners. They're so silent that we can't contact them, so I've made an executive decision to sell the antiques on their side. I'll deal with the fallout later. Do you have any questions?"

"You want us ta stay even after all the bills we ran up?" Glen asks.

"Of course, I want you to stay. I can't do this without you! This debt is not your fault. You held this place together with little more than spit."

"We told ya already; we don't have nowhere else ta go," Glen says.

"Then it's settled. Now that we'll have the funds to get out of debt let's go over the other half of my plan. This house needs a complete renovation, done in phases as we have funds. We will replace the furniture as needed. The kitchen will receive a much-needed transformation, and the entire house will be re-plumbed and rewired to bring it up to the twenty-first century, or at least up to code. Sometime down the road, we will reroof the entire structure. Mr. Yancy was correct about Miss Abigail putting very little into this house!"

The Murdock's quietly watch as I flip the pages on the tablet, going over each phase of the renovation until I'm almost hoarse from talking.

"We want the owners of our boarded horses to exercise their horses. We want them to see us train our champions, and get a sense of wonder again. The barn will have a new sign too, but I don't know what that will look like yet. Speaking of signs, the one near the street looks new, do you know anything about that, Glen?"

"Yeah. The old one fell over a few years ago. A few months ago, a new one appeared."

"That seems odd, okay, let's move on. Glen, did I hear you say that you haven't trained *Lightning* as a saddle horse?"

"Yeah, I said that," he says in bewilderment.

"Then you'll start by training *Lightning* to race at Billingsworth Racetrack."

Glen's eyes widen, trying to stifle a laugh, he says, "Sorry, please go on."

"Down the road, your Gate House will be renovated like the one here, it'll have a new kitchen."

"I don't know what to say, Miss Ellen. No one's paid us this much attention in years. You come along and . . ." Mona buries her face in her apron, turning to Glen for comfort.

"What Mona's tryin ta say, Missy, is that we're mighty grateful ya came along when ya did! We might not a got through the summer, and we was ready ta pack it in," Glen says mournfully.

"You don't have to do that now. When's the last time you were at the racetrack, Glen?"

He studies me for a moment, and then his rugged face changes expression into a big grin. "I told ya, Missy. I don't go there. Miss Abigail made me promise not ta go near that track, b'cause she was dead-set against gamblin."

"Were you a big gambler, Glen?"

Looking a bit guilty, he shakes his head no.

"Be ready in three days, okay? We're going on a little adventure."

"What should I be ready for, Missy?" he says laughing.

"We're going to the racetrack."

Glen looks worried. "And what are we gonna do there, Miss Ellen?"

"We're gonna win some money, Glen."

"Can't say as I ever won big when I went there b'fore. By the way, I forgot that ole buggy was in the barn. Guess Miss Abigail put the fear a God in me! Think you're gonna win some money, huh?"

"Be ready, okay?"

Glen lets out a hearty laugh. "You're ready all right. Ready ta lose some money, ya mean. I don't know what ya have in mind, but we don't have champions here either, Miss Ellen! And they don't come cheap if you're plannin on buyin one."

"Who says we have to buy one when we have one right here!"

"Ya did mention *Lightnin*. That's very funny, b'cause no one gets closer than tryin ta put a halter on that one, and ya sure don't know he's gonna like trainin either." Glen scratches his head, then laughs again. "Ya sure have some strange ideas, Missy."

"Don't you have any faith, Glen?"

Mona hugs me, leaning in to whisper that she has enough faith for all of us, and not to mind Glen. We have all had our share of going through the grist mill the last few weeks. We need something good to happen, so that we can move on to a better life.

I'm ready to go to the local track after studying the daily racing forms of the horses that participate in both harness and regular races. The racing forms haven't changed much since I used to do this, but it does take time to view the data of previous performances. The expected current performance of a runner is as important as the comments given by the racetrack.

All this information helps the handicapper decide where to place the wager. The fact that everything is now online makes it convenient. No need to scour a newspaper or go to the track before I'm ready.

The most significant change is what the track surface is composed of now. Racing surfaces changed when the risk of musculoskeletal injury was high. An article I read recently concludes that these injuries are the primary cause of death or retirement in expensive Thoroughbred racehorses.

Most of the dirt and turf tracks are made of synthetic materials because it might have the lowest values for most peak acceleration which is called all-weather racing, or AWR for short. It certainly cuts down on the mud that used to fling into the jockey's face when the track is less than dry, which also eliminates having to wear several sets of goggles, one on top of another when one or two pairs will do.

My search eventually gravitates to all things related to harness racing and handicapping. Another website calculates class ratings (CRs), speed ratings (SRs), and how they work together. If I'm going to be a handicapper again, what I'll need is an arsenal of ambitious information to fight the daily pari-mutuel mêlée.

It's a different game these days—high-powered and extremely competitive. It used to be so simple to me, or maybe I've been away from it so long it only looks difficult. My system of winning came easily, never questioning how much Daddy put away. When I found out, I was astounded!

Either way, I'm determined to get a handle on things again, and intensely study the televised races. Recharged and ready to move forward, I'm prepared to let go of the old life to embrace this new one. I have faith my plan will work.

We always took the rules Daddy taught me about betting very seriously, calling it RACING 101. Chuckling to think that he never told anyone that his first-born child was a natural gambler, I reacquaint myself with the rules.

---

### RACING 101
1. Make sure the horse you pick is consistent, that he races every one or two weeks
2. Who is the driver with the most win percentage? Is he racing your horse?
3. Who is my horse's competition?
4. How is my horse finishing in the final-quarter?
5. What has my horse's career been like so far?
6. Study the tote board and statistics as if it is your bible!

---

The house phone rings. Lenard is checking in to see how we're all getting along. He says he has purposely stayed away to give us a chance to settle into our new surroundings, along with the new identity, no doubt. No word yet when my family will come to Virginia, but Lenard assures me that it will be soon. Then I start to think about the ridiculous plan that was laid out for us mere weeks ago, which still doesn't quite make sense.

"Has Mother agreed to come with my children? I'm counting on you to get my family here as promised, including Mother. What about passports for all of them? Don't make me go over your head."

"Umm, those things take time, you know that, Ellen. All that is being worked out so stop worrying. And may I remind you, that you are not in a position to threaten me!"

"I'm not threatening you, Lenard, I'm making you a promise. You don't deliver; I promise to go over your head and straight to your boss. What have you found out about the investors? When are they going to send funds?"

"Ellen," Lenard's exasperated voice says. "Most of them are out of the country, and Mr. C has no cash to spare. I know he said to ask him if you need help with anything, but he cannot help you right now, so you will have to accept that."

"I do not have to accept that at all. The auction isn't for a while yet, and the creditors are breathing down my neck. I need money right now!"

Lenard snarls into the phone, "I am doing the best I can. What auction are you talking about?"

"Don't you remember? You told me how resourceful I am. You told me to sell some of the antiques, so that's what we're doing."

"Yes, now I remember; I knew you would think of something. If you are only selling a few items, why do you need an auction?"

"It's called survival, Lenard. Hold up your end of the bargain. Goodbye and remember my promise."

Today is also the day we have scheduled to go to the local racetrack. Once Glen gets the old truck started, we drive for about ten miles. He continually asks why we're doing this, but I tell him he's in for a surprise. The old feeling of excitement comes flooding back when the Billingsworth Racetrack sign comes into view. Then I get a flutter in my chest when I get a whiff of the pungent smell of manure that mingles with new-mown turf.

When Glen sees the sign, it reminds him of the two things Miss Abigail regaled upon him to stem the urge to gamble. "She used ta say, *'the Lord giveth and the Lord taketh away'* was one, and 'you can't beat the system, so don't spend all your wages at the track,' was the other."

As we get out of the truck, I notice that Glen didn't lock the doors. "You're not leaving the truck unlocked, are you, Glen?"

"Whoever wants it can take it. It ain't worth much, and whoever takes it would be doin us a favor if they did, Miss Ellen," he says chuckling. "Folks around here don't lock their stuff."

From my extensive research, Billingsworth uses a pari-mutuel wagering system of betting that utilizes an electronic machine. It totals all wagers, deducts all management charges, minuses taxes, which determines the final odds and payouts to the winners. If we win something today, it'll be the icing on the cake. We are here to have some fun, too.

Glen and I are in the grandstands after picking up a race card from the betting ring. While I'm c o n s i d e r i n g the information, he's studying the track with his binoculars.

"Who's your favorite, Missy? Who ya fixin on wagering on taday?"

Daddy said the same words every time we got into the stands, and it makes me smile. "Can't say yet, Glen, we haven't been here long enough to make that call."

"Come on, ya said ya got money burnin a hole in your pocket," he says, egging me on, clearly impatient. "Who ya figure's gonna win this one?"

"I'm not ready, Glen. Why don't you pick one?"

The familiar bugle sounds the *Call to the Post* signaling the race is about to begin, and I get goosebumps hearing it. It's like old times, I place a finger on the race card on a horse named *Just To Name A Few*.

Glen looks at my card and says, "You're mad as a hatter, Missy. That horse can't win if the jockey carried 'em over the finish line!"

"Where did you get that information, Glen? Have you been talking to the bookmaker downstairs? You shouldn't listen to him."

Glen comments negatively about the horse until the race is over and the horse wins. It'll take a few more winning races to convert him. He reminds me of Daddy, who was also impatient and complained until the third time we won.

"Let's ride it out a few more times, shall we?" I tell him.

Doing this with the race card a few more times, Glen's bewildered when the horse I pick wins again. "Ya coulda placed a bet on that one. What are ya waitin for?" Glen crosses his arms and sighs heavily, shaking his head from side to side. "Ya coulda won!" Then he squawks, "I coulda won!"

"Winning isn't everything. Half the fun is how you play the game! I'm still not ready, and I won't place a wager until then."

Meanwhile, Glen and I remain in the stands. Placing my finger on a horse called *Naturally Blonde*, I then hand Glen three crisp one hundred dollar bills.

Snatching them from my hand, he turns them over as his eyes widen. "Where did ya get these?"

"Across the board," I whisper. "You'll have to trust me that it's real money!"

Glen mutters under his breath, "Why come if you're gonna bet like a silly..." then he moves out of the stands to place the bet. He returns about ten minutes later with the betting slip, but I stuff it into his shirt pocket.

Changing the amounts incrementally during the day, each time, Glen continues to gripe that we shouldn't put that much on this horse, and then bellyaches about another race. When I ask him to cash in some of the tickets, and put a nickel on the next one, for a split-second, his eyes go wild. I wonder if he'll move, but then he starts grumbling something under his breath, leaving me to place the wager. When he returns, he complains about how we need to do this, and maybe we should try the daily double instead.

"Can you do any better at picking a winner, Glen?"

"No. But why don't we try a combination bet? It makes me nervous how ya keep wagerin the way ya do. Ya made me put five hundred dollars on that dumb horse."

"Do you want to hedge my bet? It looks like we're doing okay my way!"

"No, ya go ahead," he says stubbornly.

Glen doesn't understand my system and thinks I'm plumb out of my mind when I ask him to cash in some tickets and put three dimes on *Lucky Stevie*. The chances are he won't get it even if I explain because I've always wondered how it works.

By now, Glen has added up the winnings with the take removed, and he practically faints when I pick a horse named *Two To Tango* as our last winner of choice with odds of 20-1.

"Cash all the tickets and bet all of it, Glen, across the board this time."

His face drains of color and doesn't move to place the bet. "The guys downstairs won't like this, Miss Ellen," he whispers. "If ya win again, they won't like it at all."

"I don't care if they like it or not, bet it all. Are you going down there any time soon?"

"They think you're a chalk player and maybe you're cheatin or somethin anyway. I think we better knock it off for now. Take our winnins and skedaddle outta here," he says mournfully.

"Now why would they think I'm cheating? Have you been talking to the good old boys down there?"

"I was askin some questions, is all."

"I asked you not to speak to anyone except when you place a wager. They can't stop us from betting. Maybe they can. Are you going down to place the bet or do I have to go myself?"

"So, ya don't know nothin about racin horses. What are ya, a wise guy, Missy? I want ta know how ya know this stuff. What else don't I know?" he says glumly.

"Come on, Glen, a girl has to have some secrets. It would take too long to explain it to you. It's a gift, and we don't look a gift horse in the mouth, now do we?"

*He does not think this is funny.*

Glen is gone a very long time. When he returns, he seems preoccupied.

"Are you okay? Did you place the wager?"

Patting his pocket, I'm having doubts whether he placed the bet, but Glen nods yes, and we wait to see that the horse I choose wins, places and shows. The people in the grandstands stand in unison, as they yell, and wave their arms.

"Looks like other people bet on the same horse . . ."

Glen turns to me and says in disbelief, "How do ya do that, Miss Ellen?"

"I learned how to do it, that's all. Sometimes I'm wrong, you know."

"But, ya haven't been wrong once taday. And don't say it's a gift, ya know how ta bet! Ya better come downstairs with me. The guys were gettin suspicious b'fore, but they're not gonna like payin out this amount of money," Glen says forlornly. "Ya got a poke ta put it all in if they let ya take it?"

"You know they have to take taxes out of it so that it won't be that much. Don't worry; it'll all fit in my purse."

"It's more than ya think, Missy. It's way more than ya think."

To say the racetrack people are suspicious is an understatement! The men at the betting window are downright indignant we won so much today and have called the track manager. He asks us to step into his office for a little chat. He doesn't look happy, and he wants an explanation.

Trying to explain how I studied the tote board, the class and speed ratings, and all the other things that help me decide what horse to pick, the manager allows the winnings to go into my purse but emphasizes quite strongly that we are not to make a habit of winning too much again. When Daddy and I won, it wasn't this amount of money. We won a little at a time, over the course of several years.

*Is this a power struggle?*

Another option might be to place bets online, but I nix that, as it takes all the fun out of seeing Glen's face when we win. He also says he's never had so much fun or excitement in one day, except for when his boys were born.

Today, we have accomplished our primary objective for our immediate need for cash. Glen was correct; we won more than I thought we had. We have also established a pseudo-bond of silence where we will never, ever, speak of this again, not to anyone, either how I picked the winners or how much we won today. EVER!

With our winnings tucked into my bag, we head to the parking lot. "Glen, let's go add to your excitement. It's time to retire this old heap of metal, don't you think?"

Agreeing, we come away with a brand new truck for the farm and a nice sedan for my family. Glen knows I'm serious and he might even appreciate my talent that we can use a few more times before they won't let us wager at the track.

"So you know, if Lenard or Gene hears about this, they might be a little upset with me. I'm warning you that it might happen."

"I'll back ya up, Missy, don't ya worry about Ole Lenard, I can take him in a heartbeat."

Lenard thinks he's in charge. It is an ongoing power struggle.

Glen thinks he's in charge of the farm. Could this power struggle have been eliminated?

The money might bring on another power struggle when the bank deals with me now, or maybe the power struggle will be eliminated. What will Mr. C and the other investors say when they come to town and find out their antiques are missing?

I don't think they'll ultimately buy into the insanity thing.

*It is undoubtedly a power struggle in the making.*

Glen and I are returning from our latest trip to the track, being mindful of the manager's warning, and careful not to win too much. As we pass the Gate House, there is a black limousine sitting near the front door.

"Uh-oh, I'll bet Lenard got wind of our money situation," I say absently.

"How do ya know it's him? How could he know 'bout that?" Glen asks, clearly upset. "Maybe it's that silent guy ya said owns half of Ashwood."

"They have s p e c i a l ways of knowing things, Glen."

As I walk into the house, Glen hangs back at the garages in case I might need him. Lenard and Gene a r e waiting in the living room. Lenard stands abruptly, takes my arm, and roughly tries to pull me out into the hallway.

"Hello, Lenard, how are you? I'm fine, thanks for asking. Greetings, Gene, how are you? Nice of you to drop by after all these weeks!"

"Let's talk in a more private place, shall we?" Lenard spits. He looks angry; Gene's face is turning crimson.

"First, let go of my arm! And you don't have to be so rough, Lenard. What seems to be your problem today?"

"You, you are the problem today. Stay here," Lenard snaps at Gene. We're half-way into the library when he starts to yell. "Ellen, I am so disappointed with you right now! You know how important it is to keep a low profile! Your family's survival depends on it! Why did you go to that racetrack?"

Once we are in my office, he shuts the door and releases my arm. Then starts pacing back and forth in front of the windows.

"Why are you so upset? Our survival here at the farm was in jeopardy. The bank was going to put a lien on the property. We had no money to feed the horses! We had no money to feed ourselves! You certainly didn't help. It was our answer to how we could get money quickly."

"Why did you not sell some of the antiques as I suggested?" he wails.

"It takes time to sell that stuff. Mr. Tillman is working quickly, but it will be weeks, maybe months before the auction generates the money we need. We can't live on carrots, beans, and hard-boiled eggs until then."

"Oh, Ellen, you should not have done that, it spoiled everything." Lenard sits down on the sofa, then holds his head in his hands.

"What are you talking about?"

"You do not know what you unleashed by going to that racetrack! You must have won a lot of money."

"Aren't you being a little overly dramatic?"

"Ellen! There are eyes and ears everywhere. You cannot trust anyone!" he groans.

"You can't be trusted, either, Lenard."

Lenard looks wounded, "What do you mean by that? If you cannot trust us, how the bloody hell, do you think this was all put together?"

"I haven't exactly figured that out yet. How would you know about the racetrack and the money? You have spies at the track, don't you?"

Lenard's eyes grow wild for a second, then he starts to lick his lips. "I told you to keep a low profile. That is what will keep your family safe. Going to the racetrack and winning a lot of money is not keeping a low profile!"

"Don't be so theatrical. Did the track manager contact you? He was a little smug now that I think about it. Is he on your payroll? Is that what you mean by *eyes and ears*, Lenard?"

"Why, Ellen," Lenard stammers. "We do not have spies at the racetrack." When his phone rings, he pulls it out of his pocket, and says, "I am taking care of that right now, sir. Okay, yes, I am aware of that." Ending the call, he sticks his cellphone back into his pocket.

"You and your brilliant FBI team put me here with very little money and bills up the wazoo. You knew about the mess we were inheriting, yet you did nothing to help us. We had to do something before we starved to death. The debt was over sixty grand and rising. That smug banker in town wouldn't lend us a dime. The market wouldn't extend more credit. I have no credit cards because I don't have any money, because I'm a dead woman, remember? What were we supposed to live on?"

*If Lenard hasn't brought up the $5,000, maybe he isn't the one who sent it.*

Lenard looks dejected. "You did not give us enough time to take care of that. The investors will not be happy about this sudden turn of events," Lenard sputters, standing to pace the room.

"I don't see the connection. What do the investors have to do with the racetrack?"

"We would have helped you if you had been a little more patient," Lenard laments.

"We could have starved to death by then. You didn't help. There was no other recourse."

Lenard sits down on the sofa. "How many of the antiques will you sell?" He looks nervous, and a little more than annoyed now.

"As many as we need to, maybe all of them. It's up to me now; you put me in charge of this dump you call an estate. I intend to make it look like a real horse farm, not the rundown hunk of junk it is now."

Lenard's face contorts. "I suggested you sell *some* of the antiques. I did not say to sell *all of them!* What will I tell the investors about this? They will not be happy about it."

"Too late, Lenard, they're already gone. When will my family be here? May I remind you of our agreement? You better say they'll be here within the next few weeks, or I'm going over your head!"

After Lenard and Gene leave in a huff, I inform Mona and Glen that my family will be here in three weeks. Which reminds me that we have a lot to do before their furniture arrives.

Since accounts have been set up at various banks with our winnings, there will be no trouble paying for things. Word travels fast in a small town; Glen swears he didn't spill the beans, but Mr. Fancy-Yancy Banker, who denied a loan to us mere weeks ago, has contacted me three times to get me to open an account there.

It's amazing what a little money can do. The same people, who wouldn't extend time or credit, are now quite happy to give us as much as we need. The local feed store is more than delighted to make free deliveries each week. That's probably due more to Glen not wanting to get his new truck dirty than their generosity.

The bakery owners were afraid I wouldn't allow Mona to provide her melt-in-your-mouth pastries and loaves of bread. And after a lengthy conversation with them, they are more than willing to pay her for her services. They hadn't considered her costs. It makes for a happy Mrs. Murdock, with the stipulation that she can stop any time she chooses.

The townspeople of Jasper now wave when they see me as if I've been a part of this community for years. Having money changes everything!

Oh, ye of little faith, we managed to do this without any help from them! It indeed is a matter of Faith!

It is mid-July. Finalizing the sketches for each of the bedrooms and bathrooms that are in my wing of the house, I'm grateful Gladys left the original plans on the library table that first day. Taking breaks now and then to study the brittle blueprints, I chuckle because the hidden stairway is not on the plan. An odd space in the basement might hold another secret or two, but I'm not about to go down there, it's too spooky.

Using online stores to order linens and draperies, it'll alleviate the task of going out to stores and hauling everything back. Now that we have an appreciable credit balance, it gives me enormous pleasure to put these items on my shiny new credit card.

Knowing my family will be here soon, I wake each morning, exhilarated to get to work. As the weeks fly by, the upstairs transforms. My new bedroom furniture fits more into the ample space now, and the addition of a sofa-pit and TV on the wall makes it a bit cozier.

I purchased two wall safes that look like picture frames, mounting them between the studs of the exterior closet wall facing into my bedroom. Until we find that large safe Tillman's assistant asked about, it will suffice for small items. I have a strong feeling that it's in the basement, but I've no intention of going down there until it's necessary.

Oak Trees along the left and right sides of the house provide some relief from the heat of the summer, but we need more than that to reduce our impending discomfort when the heat index rises. The electrician installed overhead fans in each room, adding attic vents that make the second floor more comfortable.

We found more treasures in the attic; old baby carriages, a Victorian dollhouse, discarded toys, more antique furniture, and many knick-knacks that Tillman drooled over when he saw them! Jenny was ecstatic with the discovery of several trunks full of clothes until she opened them to find that most were moth-eaten and ruined beyond repair.

The wallpaper removal project in the middle children's bedroom revealed faded drawings most likely put there by Ashwood children through the centuries. I tucked them away for safekeeping.

The National Register of Historic Homes has specific criteria we must follow to stay within their guidelines when it comes to renovation. The windows are an odd size and will have to be custom-made. These will move down the list of must-haves while we give others priority.

Now all that's missing are the people who will occupy the rooms and the moving van full of furniture Lenard promised to be here tomorrow.

My family comes home today. Standing in the two-story hall near the staircase with Lenard and Gene, we're waiting for the sound of gravel that will signal their arrival. Since our episode in the library, Lenard has kept his distance. When I ask about how they broke the news that I'm alive to Mother, they take turns telling me about their encounter. They explained that she would have to make a choice. Gene says she was quiet when they asked if she wanted to come to Virginia with my children. She could leave and never see her other daughter and her family again, or stay in Evanston and let my children move without her.

Lenard made a point to say that she was not only irritated but wondered what my husband was into that caused this whole fiasco. Then she put her hand up, saying never mind, she didn't want to know. Gene then handed her my hand-printed list.

They both agreed that she understood that the precious items she could never part with will be here when she comes to Ashwood. The one piece in contention was her white baby grand piano. Once that was settled, she asked how soon the move would take place.

"We told her to convince the children to go to some camp so we could pack everything up and get it moved without their knowing anything," Lenard declares.

Gene leans toward me to whisper, "She said they would love the idea, and she would start on the plans right away. Sorry 'bout the dog."

"Ah, here they are. Get out of sight, Ellen. You will spoil the surprise." Lenard jerks his head toward the kitchen.

I have positioned myself near the closed connecting doors between the dining and living rooms where I peek through the opening. I can hear voices and things shuffling around and my first instinct is to run to them, but they need time for Lenard and Gene to explain a few things.

We don't know how they will react, but once everyone settles onto chairs or the sofa in the living room, Lenard and Gene commence with their rehearsed script. My eyes fill with tears at the sight of them. Have they all grown an inch or two?

At fifteen, Jason looks more like his father every day. His dark brown wavy hair is longer, sticking out the bottom of his baseball cap. Mel's thirteen-year-old facial expression is unreadable, as she looks shyly around the room. And my cherub little nine-year-old appears wholly lost.

When Jason notices the little chip near the foot pedal on the piano that only he and I are aware of, he must sense something is amiss. Looking around, he's on his feet within moments of Lenard saying I'm alive. Opening the door, he's in my arms so fast he nearly runs me down.

"I knew it. I knew it. I knew those men were wrong about you, Mom. They didn't have the caskets open so we couldn't see you or Dad. Oh, my God, Mom, you're here!" Picking me up, he twirls us both around. "Why didn't you call us? We were so worried about you. Where's Dad?"

Choking out words, "I have missed you all so . . ."

"They wouldn't let us see you or Dad. Is he here too?" Jason sees the look on my face. "Why didn't you call us? Grandma was very upset, we all were."

"I'm so sorry, sweetheart, there was nothing I could do about that. I'll explain all that later, okay?" Tears roll down his face. He's already three inches taller than I am and feels denser somehow, not the scrawny teenager I left a few months ago!

Mel suddenly shrieks, "Mom! I've missed you so much. It was awful without you and Daddy. I prayed and prayed it wasn't true. Why didn't you call us? We were all frantic! Oh, my God, you're here! You're here! Is Dad here too?"

Melanie's long dark hair is flying everywhere. She has put on a few pounds in all the right places. Then Curlie joins us, and she hangs on to my waist, wailing softly. I reach to tangle a free hand in her beautiful springy, reddish-brown hair.

"Where's my Daddy," she wails. "I want Daddy!"

Jason quietly shakes his head, which must mean something and she stops crying immediately.

We're all talking at once when I notice Mother standing in the doorway smiling. "Leave it to you to make life interesting. I don't know how I would have managed one more week without you, sweetheart."

I reach to pull her into our circle. "I don't know what to say to you, except, thank you for being there for them."

"No thanks are needed, Ellie. I did what any mother would do."

Mel's eyes are darting around the room. "You knew about this? Why didn't you tell us? Is it true, Mom? Are we gonna live here? Is this the dude ranch Grandma told us about? Hey, isn't that Grandma's hutch? How did it get here?"

"Hey, Mel, I told you it was the dude ranch. Didn't you see the horses outside? Geeze, you're so dense sometimes. How long have you known Mom was alive, Grandma? Never mind, I don't care, you're here now," Jason says, laughing in a deeper tone than I remember.

Curlie starts to squeal with excitement. "Is all our stuff here? My dolls and everything is in my new room? Oh, Mama, I missed you so much. I cried and cried."

Jason quietly says, "Sassy's dead, Mom. Hey, wait a minute! It's unbelievable! It's so awesome! Didn't you and Dad wanna buy a farm a few years ago? This house is so gigantic. I can play music all day and no one'll hear me, right? Do we have our own horse?"

*Who told them they each have a horse?*

"I don't know about that, but tell me what happened to our dog." They are all talking all at once now, coming in waves of jumbles of words and more tears.

"Please," one at a time, touching Jason on the shoulder, "You first."

"We found her in the kitchen when we came back to Grandma's house after your funeral. That seems so weird to say that because it's obvious you're not dead," Jason mumbles.

"There was nothing wrong with Sassy," Mel says, talking over Jason, trying to hold back her tears. "One minute she was fine, the next thing we know, she's dead."

"Yeah, she was dead, too, Mama. . . like you and Daddy." Curlie begins to wail again, and I hug her tightly. "I want my Daddy!"

Mother adds, "We don't understand it either, Ellie. She was fine before we left. The vet said it was something that happens to older dogs."

"I don't understand; she was only eight," I say a little surprised.

"She was lying on the floor next to her water bowl not moving," Jason says. As he says this, Rosie makes a beeline for him. "I was gonna ask about another dog, but hey, this one will do. Hello there, aren't you pretty?"

Mona and Glen have joined us in the dining room. "She's a border collie, Jason," Glen offers. "She helps me herd the horses. She's good 'bout it and takes her job real serious like."

All of the children are on the floor rubbing Rosie's tummy.

"Hello, Rosie. You look like our dog back home, only bigger, right Mom?" Mel asks.

I'm in awe of my family, who four short months ago were mourning their parents' deaths. With all they had to cope with during that time, it's as if we have not been apart. How they can bounce from their lives in Illinois to one in rural America is beyond me, but then there's that gift horse again.

"Mother, how are . . ."

Smiling and hugging me to her, she says, "How are they taking this so well? Because we roll with the punches; we are survivors, Ellie. They took everything in stride, and I must tell you how proud I am of them."

"Thank you for all you did, Mother. Remind me to tell you the story about an unbelievable vacation gone awry."

"I'll bet it's better than the one Lenard told me."

Glancing at Glen, he has a quizzical look on his face. "Speaking of the devils, where are Lenard and Gene?"

"They walked out the front door," Glen says, shrugging his shoulders. "Didn't say a word, left without so much as a goodbye. Come on Mona, let's get these folks a snack."

"Most of the house needs work as you can see, but your rooms are ready." As the children move ahead of us up the stairs to their respective rooms, we hear snippets of conversation as they run from room to room.

Mother whispers, "I have missed you something terrible, Ellie. Somehow, I didn't believe what Lenard told me before the funeral. He and Gene kept showing up telling me one thing, then another. After a while, it didn't add up. They passed themselves off as administrators of your estate. They went through both our houses tagging things. Then the blonde one told me my new name is Francesca L. Dillon."

"Wait a minute, Lenard specifically said he didn't contact you until six weeks ago. Could you have the timeline wrong?"

"I'm quite sure, Ellie. I love what I've seen so far," Mother says. "You've done a lot of work, it seems."

"We didn't have the time or money to redo the bathrooms yet. I wanted you to be comfortable for now."

Guiding Mother to the last room where the door remains shut, I open it to see her satisfied grin. Curlie appears to wrap herself around my waist again, moaning softly, "I didn't want you to go, Mama."

"Curlie, don't be such a cry-baby," Mel says. "Wow, Grandma, this is like a suite in a hotel or something. You have two rooms."

"I missed you so much! I miss Daddy too, but Grandma says he's not coming back, is he Mama. He went to heaven?" Curlie sniffs.

With tears in her eyes, Mother puts a hand over her mouth. "I'm sorry," she says softly.

"It's like you picked up Grandma's stuff and transplanted it right here," Mel says.

Snapping out of her mood, Curlie says, "I like it, Grandma. It looks like your old room at your old house. Mama, some woman bought our piano. It made me sad."

"Our rooms are great too. Come on Curlie don't hog Mom. Let her talk with Grandma." Mel takes Curlie's hand, not waiting for an answer.

"This is great!" Jason yells from down the hall. "Really rad, Mom, it's major mag!"

"We'll see how mag it is when he starts banging away on his drums."

The work crews did some extra work in Jason's room. They not only soundproofed the walls, but the ceiling, the floor, and every surface possible. That's so no one will hear him beat on his drums or play his guitar at all hours of the day or night.

Sitting on Mother's bed, she fills me in on how they coped after the accident. Since Jason and Melanie would have gone to new schools anyway, she knew they would adjust easier than Curlie. A shy child by nature, Curlie didn't have many friends, going to a new school won't be a problem for her. Her one request is that she wants to continue her piano lessons. Are we able to find her a new teacher?

My children are taking this dude ranch thing with no trouble. They thought it would be a great adventure. One by one they join us in Mother's room. After we tell them about Lenard's instructions, it doesn't seem to bother them in the least, as they think it's cool to be in the Federal Witness Protection Program. Of course, no one will ever know we're part of that program. And it slowly dawns on them that they'll never communicate with their friends or other members of our family, which elicits somewhat of a global moan.

"Unless we can get around it, that's the way it has to be. We have one more detail we need to discuss."

Mother hands them their new passports where they comment on their photos and new last name. After they hand them back, they start to ask the usual questions. When they're satisfied with the answers, they go off to investigate the other side of the second floor.

"That wasn't so bad," Mother says. Opening the suitcase Glen put near the end of her bed, she extracts a small package. Smiling sheepishly, she hands it to me. "I couldn't take the chance the movers wouldn't pack it. They disposed of so much of our things."

Memories flood back to the year 1982 as I touch the frame. We were at an equestrian event in Campbell Arena. My beautiful quarter horse, *Trinidad's Nephew,* won first place that day. A week later, I fell off *Trinidad* when he missed a jump during a vigorous practice and went down hard. The last thing I remember of that day was Daddy picking me up. If I close my eyes, I can still hear the shot that put *Trinidad* down. I broke my tailbone that day and haven't been on a horse since.

I thought that the picture was in Mother's attic amid boxes of other mementos, ribbons, trophies, and certificates. When I married Ravi, it didn't occur to me to take the memories with me. I thought Mother had cleaned out her attic and disposed of that stuff years ago.

Patting my hand, Mother says, "I watched the movers pack, Ellie. I took some of the items out of the boxes after they left because they were on your list! There are others; your wedding photo, Jason's Confirmation, my Fortieth Wedding Anniversary, and the kid's school pictures. This one is exceptional, and I knew you would want it."

"I don't know what to say, Mother! So many surprises today, so much emotion!"

"Ellie, you had a bad experience that doesn't mean you can't trust yourself. Look what's fallen into your lap! It's your second chance. Go for it. Brood a little if you must, but I see you out there with the horses. I see you doing whatever you set your mind on doing. If Daddy were here right now, he would be so very proud of you. I know I am."

"And because we own a horse farm, doesn't mean I'm going to ride one of them anytime soon." Wiping tears that somehow escape my eyes, the children come noisily back into the room to see if we're ready to go downstairs yet.

"Can we see the horses now, Mama?" Curlie asks with excitement.

"Yeah, let's go," Jason says, reaching to pull the photo out of my hands. "Hey, is this you, Mom? You look different." Jason fingers the frame, handing it off to Mel before she snatches it. "I didn't know you rode horses. Is that a trophy? What's the name of the horse?"

"Do you have a saddle and everything? How come you never told us about this?" Mel inquires.

Rolling easily into mother mode, "That was a very long time ago. I have nothing except that photo, and an old injury as a reminder. You need to change your clothes before we go downstairs. You all have shirts, jeans, and boots. Go ahead, we'll wait for you."

"I'm so glad this is over," Mother whispers as I hug her. "The photos are a reminder of days gone by, but they're also an inspiration for the future, our *new* future."

"I'm glad you and the children are finally here. I've been going nuts without you."

*It is not over. It's only the beginning.*

*"Happiness is not a station you arrive at,*

*but a manner of traveling."*

~ Margaret Lee Runbeck

# Chapter Nine

## A Matter of Faith

After my children consume their snack, Glen goes over the rules of the mudroom, telling them the importance of spraying their boots before trouping outside. Warning of horseflies, chiggers, and ticks, a horrific expression slowly slides across Mel's face for an instant, then fades away.

Glen proceeds to go over our barn rules. "Rule number one; no boots, no barn. Rule number two; there will be no shoutin in the barn. Turn off or silence your cellphones, so ya don't spook the horses. Ya don't want ta spook 'em b'cause they don't like that." Tickling Curlie on the arm, she squeals with delight. "No sirree, ya gotta be quiet like little church mice."

"What's rule number three?" Curlie asks innocently.

Glen says with a straight face, "Good question, little lady. Rule number three, if ya break rule number one and two, you're not allowed in the barn for a week."

"Oh," she says solemnly. "I'm gonna have ta remember them rules."

Jason reminds me of the father he will never see again and resentment surfaces for an instant, then doubt we would be here if he were alive. Nudging Jason as we walk, I ask, "Do you have your cellphone?"

"No. The limo driver confiscated them. He said it would interfere with the airline navigation equipment. Then we forgot about them," Jason says.

"It's okay; I have new ones for you."

Jason is suddenly serious. "I knew something was wrong when I tried to call you and Dad, and you didn't answer. I don't get it, what do our cellphones have to do with . . . Oh," he says as he gets the meaning behind it, making me chuckle that Jason questions everything as I do.

Mel turns around to ask, "Yeah, Mom, why did he take them? We could have got new phone numbers. All my friends' numbers are stored on it, and now I can't call . . . Oohh," Mel says softly when she also gets the meaning.

Curlie wiggles in-between them. "What are you talkin about you guys? How come you never tell me what's goin on? Mama, what are they talkin about?"

"Don't worry, sweetheart; they're talking teenage stuff."

My inquisitive children are now throwing questions at Glen. "How many horses do we have, Mr. Murdock?" Jason asks.

"We got six altogether, Jason," Glen chirps, then offers to take them around the property in the old golf cart after they say hello to the horses.

Mother and I settle ourselves at the old rickety picnic table on the back porch. As their appointed guardian, Mother is relieved that she doesn't have to raise the children by herself. My sister, Terre, offered to help, but she felt it was her duty alone. Mother likes Glen and Mona, grateful to have the busy work of menus to plan, shopping at the market, even looking forward to baking.

"Mother, there's something else you need to know. Please don't be upset with me, but I've had to resort to going to the racetrack. We didn't have money for food. It was our only way out."

With a twinkle in her eye, Mother smiles. "Ellen, you don't have to explain. Those two idiots didn't confiscate everything. I made one demand, besides the piano. When they sold our houses, your furniture vanished along with most of mine, except what was on your list. They went through our lock boxes at the bank. I was outraged when I found out that they took everything inside. Gene knew how upset losing your father's pension made me, so he pleaded with Lenard."

"I'm very sorry you had to go through that. Glen and I bet at the racetrack, and we won a lot of money. When Lenard found out, he was furious. How did you manage to get away with that and I didn't?"

"I said that if they didn't do it my way, none of us would move to Virginia," Mother says confidently.

"You called their bluff!" I'm amazed at her tenacity. "Good for you."

"They argued, hemmed, and hawed a bit, then finally gave in," Mother says, laughing. "I figured that if they didn't do what I asked, you'd be talking to their boss."

"I told Lenard several times that I'd go over his head and call his boss at the FBI and tattle on him. He knew I'd make a ruckus if you and the children didn't get here soon. How did you know they'd buy into that? You're not a gambler, Mother."

"I took a chance on your father, didn't I? I also have the children's college funds and what was in their bank accounts. I'll need to go to the bank to set them up," Mother says, hugging me tightly.

"I feel bad that you had to make the choice you did. I wasn't allowed to call you or Terre. I can't get over the fact we can never see or talk to them again." Tears are flowing down my face as Mother reaches to console me.

"Oh, but we can. We can communicate using the code your father devised many years ago. No one will ever suspect, not even Lenard."

"Ahh, I am so stupid! Why didn't I think of that? I could have gotten a note to you! The drugs are probably responsible for my addled brain!"

"First of all, Ellie, you're not stupid. What drugs are you talking about?" Mother asks.

"I'll tell you about it later."

"Can't wait to hear that part, Ellie. The code thing probably didn't occur to you. You must have had your hands full," Mother says patting my hand. "That code came in handy several times throughout the years, didn't it?"

"I remember that it was better than sending a telegram."

Mother sighs. "When I told Terre I was leaving with the children, she was naturally upset, but I told her not to worry, we'd keep in touch using the code."

"That makes me feel a little better. I'm curious, what did Lenard tell you when you first met him?"

"Lenard spread an incredible story the FBI cooked up that your children were going to live with their father's people in Montana because I could no longer care for them."

"Ravi does *not* have people in Montana. When Ravi and I first met, he explained that he had no close relatives and most of them were deceased. It made him unhappy to talk about it, so we didn't."

"Oh my," Mother says. "What have we gotten ourselves into?"

"Lenard has eyes and ears in places we don't even know about." I suddenly remember the manager at the racetrack. "I'm not at all sure we can trust them."

"They strike me as a bit devious, Ellie. I wanted to trust them at first, but after a while, something didn't seem quite right about them."

"Lenard and Gene are the ones who scare me. The people who are behind Ravi's death may still be out there. I haven't figured out why yet, but I will. We have to be very careful from now on about everything we say and do. Mona and Glen don't know the whole story. I'm not sure they should know yet."

Mother agrees that we share a concern that is ever-present, but we won't speak of it right now. "I can't wait to hear what happened to you."

"You're never going to believe it!"

As we walk into the barn, Glen whispers with the children as they sit on little stools absorbed in what he's saying. A closer look reveals that he's reading from a manual, apparently getting a jump on preparing them for riding lessons. When Jason sees us, he stands to stretch and moves toward the wall/door with no handle where we found the old carriage.

"What's in here? Got any bikes we can ride?"

Jason opens the door with ease, disappearing from view. It must be a mechanical thing men do to frustrate women because he figured it out so quickly.

"Not much ta see in there, son," Glen says in his direction. At that instant, a dull thump follows the sound of cracking wood. *Lightning* leaves the barn as plumes of dust filter out of the open doorway as some of the horses whinny and nicker.

"Jason, you okay?" Glen asks.

A coughing Jason says, "You guys should come and look at this! Geeze! Come here; I found something! Whoa, I didn't expect this!"

"More treasure, Glen?" I ask. "We have been here before and recently."

"Ain't we uncovered enough junk in here already? Nothin of value, son, 'cept some ole dairy equipment."

"Is that so, Mr. Murdock," I say, "May I remind you that those pieces of junk you refer to are keeping food in our bellies and a roof over our heads."

Jason sneezes several times as we move to the open doorway. A gaping hole is on the opposite wall where we found the old carriage. "I leaned against it, honest," Jason says in self-defense. "It just fell in. I swear."

Glen lets out a loud harrumph, and we move in unison toward a pile of rubble. Jason starts to pull at a threadbare tarp-like material that falls away to reveal an old car.

"You want to explain this, Mr. Murdock?"

"My God," Glen says in quiet reverence. "I didn't know this was here!"

The implication is of course, that if he knew, the bank could have sold it to add to the defunct estate, saving him and Mona much agony and despair.

The chassis is long and low. The dusty, dark red car has running boards that go up and over the large white wall tires that are flatter than a pancake. Two headlamps are protruding on either side of the large radiator as smaller lamps are clamped on to a bar near the front bumper.

"Miss Abigail has done it to you again, Glen," I whisper. "Must be worth a good penny if it's as old as some of the other antiques we gave Mr. Tillman to sell."

When the dust settles, and we all stop sneezing and coughing, we stroll around the car. Amazed at the spacious interior, Jason asks about the unusual-looking windshield and Mel notes the weird way the spare tire is sitting on the running board near the front of the car. Curlie asks about the big pipes that seem to float out from under the hood, wondering why cars don't look like this anymore.

Jason starts to cough again when he sits down behind the steering wheel as a puff bomb explodes under him. "Pahuff," he says, waving at the cloud surrounding him.

Glen seems bewildered by this discovery. "I don't remember this, Missy. And I sure as shootin don't remember there ever bein a room here."

"I wouldn't call it a room, Glen."

The room he refers to is approximately the size of two regular horse stalls. The only difference is that the construction looks as if it was supposed to be temporary. It's beyond comprehension how this car got in here. It must have been out of sight, and apparently out of mind for a very long time.

"I'll bet they built the wall around it after it was in here."

"Why didn't Abigail tell me about this?" Glen says, sighing heavily.

Touching Glen's arm, Mother says, "I'm guessing here, Mr. Murdock, but perhaps she didn't know it was here. The car could have been here before World War Two. Ellen's Daddy and I went to several antique car shows. Do you remember, Ellen? I believe that German brothers built this particular car, and Germany wasn't very popular then."

"Yes, I agree. Didn't Daddy want one of these?"

*I know what Jason's going to say next.*

"I can fix it up, Mom! I took a class this year. It wouldn't take much, would it? To fix up, I mean."

"Sorry sweetie, we probably will sell it."

"You mean we can't keep it?" Jason laments, "Why not? Why was it even here?"

"I'll tell you why, sweetie," trying to offer a quick explanation. "They probably didn't want anyone to know they had such an extravagant possession. Maybe they tried to sell it but had no buyers, so they built the wall to hide it. Let's get Mr. Tillman out to give us a professional assessment, and I'll do a little research to see what a restoration might cost."

"It would be so cool to drive this around. I'm almost ready for a driver's permit! Mom, you can't sell it! Let me fix it up, please, and then it won't cost you anything."

"I can tell you right now that it's worth a lot more to us if we sell it than if we keep it, Jason. I promise you, when you're ready, we'll get a proper car for you, but not right now."

Mel's rolling her eyes. "You don't even know how to drive, Jason. You want it to impress girls. And you don't know the first thing about fixing it up."

*What would Ravi say if he was standing here right now?*

Not one to sulk long, Jason goes back to open the glove compartment. "Mom, I was going to take Driver's Ed, can I still do that here?"

"I don't see why you can't. We'll make sure we add that to your schedule when we sign you up for school in the fall."

"It's an ole Duesenberg!" Glen whispers solemnly. "Look here at the emblem with the eagle and figure 8. It must be one of Mr. AJ's prized cars. I thought they was all gone." Fingering what remains of the convertible canopy, he pokes at the remnants of gnawed boxes on the disintegrating leather seats.

"If they were prominent people in the community, it would have been devastating for the farm and dairy to be cast in an unfavorable light during that time," Mother offers.

I put my hand on Glen's shoulder to comfort him. "Abigail was probably told by her family never to go snooping into the barn, and she repeated that story to you. She was a good, God-fearing person that obeyed her father until the end."

"Miss Abigail said I'm not ta go snoopin, so I didn't!" Glen sadly drops his head in resignation. Glancing at his watch, he declares, "The Missus wants us up at the house for supper. Why don't ya go on ahead?"

I hang back to talk with Glen. "Don't let it get to you. You were only honoring Miss Abigail's wishes. Let it go if you can. We know about it now."

"We could've saved the farm if we knew this car was here. We suffered for close ta two years b'fore ya came along. We ate vegetables till they came out our ears and very little meat. In the few months you've been here, you've managed ta, you've managed ta . . ."

"None of this is your fault, Glen. I'm glad we came along when we did because you would have had to vacate this place by the end of the year anyway. It seems none of the descendants cared about Ashwood. Everything would have been sold to satisfy the outstanding property taxes, or it would have gone into receivership."

"Ah, Missy, why didn't we know about it sooner?" Glen moans.

"It was meant to happen this way, Glen. See you at the house."

He needs a private moment to compose himself.

Mother's fully extended dining room table, the sixteen chairs that match it, her china hutch, and sideboard fits right into the room. During dinner, Mother converses easily with Mona, talking of favorite recipes while Glen laughs with the children. They are not only missing their father but their Grandfather. Maybe this is another reason why we're all together.

*I feel that we are so blessed.*

As Mel and Curlie clear the table, Glen says, "I got a question, Missy. Are you serious about racin *Lightnin*? Ya think we have another *Seabiscuit*? Ya plannin ta do some harness racin? Ya know he's not a Standard, don't ya? They won't let 'em race at Billingsworth."

"I have some news for you. I found out that he has forged papers. Someone pulled the wool over Miss Abigail's eyes. His real name is *Didgeridoo*. He is a Standardbred, and once we have the right papers, you can start training him."

"How'd ya find this out, Missy? Was it on that computer webby thingy ya got? *Lightnin* was foaled b'fore he came here. His dame came from a reputable breeder right down the road. He has the temperament of a Thoroughbred, and he acts like one, too."

Jason is trying to follow our conversation. "Mom, what's a standard mean? Are you gonna race horses? That would be awesome. Can I do that, too?"

Glen shakes his head, saying, "No, son, she's not gonna race horses. She ain't had no trainin."

"That's not entirely true, Mr. Murdock." Glen questions what has been, up to now, a stable relationship with his fellow horse people but he doesn't know what I dug up. "He's still a three-year-old so we can start training, and if he doesn't pan out, we'll get more Standardbreds and train them."

"You'll never get him ta trot."

"Then we'll get him to pace. Glen, you mentioned he wouldn't let you near him with a bridle, so we'll try a harness. He probably thought you were going to put a saddle on him. Horses are smarter than we think they are. Your breeders were not entirely truthful with you."

"And how would ya know all that, Missy?" Glen asks.

"It's what the old boys club does best. They'll sell a snowball and say it's a white rock. Gullible people buy that stuff all the time. You of all people should know that."

"Are ya callin me gullible, Missy?" Glen leans on his elbows, looking me straight in the face, but he also has a twinkle in his eye, so I know he's teasing.

"No, you silly goat, I'm saying that Miss Abigail was. She's the one who bought the mare, not you. There's documented proof of the length some owners and trainers will go for their horses to win."

Training is his thing, and he must feel I'm overstepping my bounds again.

"Mom, what's a standard mean?" Jason asks, "What are you two talking about? I wanna race too if you're gonna do that! Can I Mom?"

"Hang on a second, Jason. I guarantee that once we train *Didgeridoo*, he will not only win for us, but he might become our Champion."

Glen is now laughing heartily. "*Lightnin* a Champion! That's funny, Missy."

"Uppity owners want to win their way. They'll stop at nothing to achieve that. I know what I'm dealing with, Glen. We can talk about this another time."

Mother nods her head in silent agreement in a show of solidarity that surprises even me. Stopping near Glen, she says, "You need to know something about my daughter, Mr. Murdock. Trust her, because she knows a thing or two about horses. What she didn't learn on her own, her father taught her."

*No higher compliment has ever come my way!*

"I don't b'lieve it, Missy. I thought I knew horses," Glen says quietly.

"You probably know more about training than I do, Glen, but I do know about horses, and I do know how to bet to win."

"You go to the track to bet, Mom? Jason says quickly. "Wow, that's sure a surprise."

"I guess I don't know as much as I thought I did." Glen runs a calloused hand through his hair while reaching for his glass with the other.

"We'll beat them at their own game, Glen. I know horse temperament and such; you know about training horses, so you can teach me how to drive the race bike."

"Now you're gonna be the driver?" Glen asks in amazement.

"Mom, you're going to be a jockey? Can I do that too? We'd make a great team. How about it?"

"No, Jason, I don't want to be a jockey. What I intend to do is drive a race bike. You don't have to sit on the horse that way. It's a different way to race."

With that, Glen picks up his glass of wine, draining the contents.

"Glen, can we learn together? You train the horses and us, and we learn how to do it properly. Are you willing to teach both of us?"

Glen is now smiling, "Sure, Missy, why not?"

"Good. We'll need the truck tomorrow so we can pick up the new stuff that came in down at the train depot."

Glen nods his head because he knows when I say this, I'm serious. "Ya don't know the jargon, Missy. Ya need a jog cart and a race bike." Smirking, he leans over to rub Jason's head with his knuckles.

"And that's what we have you for, Mister Smarty Pants Trainer; we'll be picking up two of each tomorrow."

"Can you please tell me the difference between a Standard and a Thoroughbred?" Jason asks.

"Mr. Murdock will explain the difference, right Mr. Murdock?"

"I can't wait to start training!" Jason's urge to drive encompasses anything with two or four wheels; a tractor, a car, or a horse cart.

"Hold on a minute," Glen says, "You're too young ta race son; you'll wait a bit for that. Ya have lots a work b'fore they'll even consider a license."

"Is it a regular driver's license, like a car driver's license?" he asks.

"No son, it's a special license that ya get after ya pass rigorous trainin and stuff. I'd say it takes about three ta six months."

"Can't I at least start training with you before school starts?" Jason mumbles. Of course, the next obvious statement out of his mouth is; "I'll need a car to get around because we're so far out. I've been saving for a long time. Mom, can I have a car instead?"

"How did we get from training with a horse to a car?"

Glancing at Glen, there's a knowing look on his face. He'll keep quiet, as we don't want to undermine each other. Jason can train while he waits to turn the minimum age of sixteen, and he can be a licensed harness driver if he passes the stringent tests. That is if the Virginia Racing Commission approves his application. I haven't applied for one myself, so I'm uncertain of this process.

"Let it go for now, Jason. We'll talk about it later. You just got here."

When Glen excuses himself to go to the barn, Jason and Curlie beg to go with him. A stickler for rules about the barn, he repeats them again.

An email about the old Duesenberg car gets a response from Mr. Tillman almost immediately. He can't believe it was here the whole time and will come first thing tomorrow morning to look at it. In the meantime, he'll research the registration number Glen managed to locate.

Jumping out of bed with renewed energy, I'm determined to mend the chasm caused by Ravi's death. It's essential to connect the dots for the children and Mother. Once we air our concerns, the consensus is that we should move on with our new lives.

Mr. Tillman's appraisal of the car this morning made him leave in a breathless rush, saying he would be in touch with us very soon. Glen is in my office when he calls later that afternoon.

With the call on speakerphone, Tillman says, "The car will be the anchor piece of the entire estate sale, Ms. Thompson. The registration number identifies the car as a Model J made in the year 1930. It was Mr. AJ's car alright; made right here in America. They called it a Duesy for short. He didn't want to wait for a car, so he purchased a factory demonstrator during a trip to New York City with Ms. Ashwood. There are several other Model J's either on the market or held by private collectors, so it was easy to glean information. It's a Dual Cowl Phaeton J243. It's not as rare as it is collectible."

Glen asks candidly, "So ya think it's worth somethin?"

"I certainly do. Mr. AJ was the only owner, so that means low mileage, a big deal if it can be restored. Several celebrities own them now. Very few are in circulation. Say, you haven't run across a title, have you, Ms. Thompson?"

"No, we haven't found anything like that, Mr. Tillman. It's probably in that safe we haven't found yet. Do you think you can go back in time and find it? I only have the original house plans and very few papers to substantiate anything else. Mr. Yancy might help us there; he mentioned that I should come in sometime to get the deed for the house, so maybe he has more papers for the property. And by the way, how much will it take to restore it, money-wise?"

*Cha-ching goes the imaginary dollar signs floating past my eyes.*

"It'll take much more than the carriage, I'm sorry to say. I've already checked with a car enthusiast that works on foreign cars. He thinks it'll take about sixty grand or more if the engine needs to be replaced."

"Hum, that much?"

Tillman adds, "And I'll look into that title thing, but don't hold your breath on that. We might be able to get around it."

"That engine's no good bein out there all these years. The rest of it, b'sides the body, are in shreds," Glen says. "Can the mechanic get parts for it?"

"He has many sources for after-parts; it's what he does for a living, Glen. He figures the convertible top and leather seats will be easy to restore. If Mr. Ashwood put this car away, he also figures that the rest of the chrome is all in good condition."

"That's reassuring, Mr. Tillman, I think."

"I told him I saw the car and it's in remarkable shape. He needs to see it to give us a better idea of what it might cost to restore. Oh, it's worth about one mil, maybe more when it's restored," Tillman says finishing.

"Would that be dollars, Mr. Tillman?" I ask in amazement, as Glen's mouth drops open.

"Yes, Ms. Thompson, dollars. George says he's looking for a new project right now and can bring his flat-bed to get the car day after tomorrow. Is that satisfactory to you, Ms. Thompson?"

Glen pokes my arm. "Ain't ya gonna answer him, Missy?"

*How did we go from no money to wealthy in only a few months?*

Tillman asks again, "Ms. Thompson? Is that okay with you?"

"Certainly, Mr. Tillman. That will be perfectly fine."

Gerald, as Mr. Tillman insists I call him from now on, says money is coming in from the estate auction that continues to generate daily interest. The proceeds, minus commission, etc., are directly deposited into the account assigned explicitly to Auction Proceeds. A list of sold items, along with the winning bids, is also available for my perusal.

*It's beyond astounding!*

The restored and detailed Duesenberg Model J sold for a tidy sum as predicted. It took every bit of sixty grand to repair it because the engine block was indeed cracked. George, the eccentric foreign car mechanic, was able to locate needed parts and it purrs like a kitten now. An aficionado snatched it up quicker than a flea on a dog! (His words, not mine).

Our anticipated Phase One projects will commence shortly. We hashed and rehashed the need to bring the laundry to the second floor as no one wants to go down the basement to do it. It will go in what used to be the large linen closet, located near the back staircase where we might install a kitchenette.

Because Lenard saw fit to dispose of most of our possessions, we have nothing to store. New things are great as far as clothes go, but sentimental ornaments and little twinkle lights? What would have been the harm in keeping those?

Settling comfortably into a workable routine, everyone seems genuinely happy to be here. My children are taking on chores they would otherwise not have done back in Evanston. I find this strange, but Mother says to be happy about it, you know about that gift horse.

Where once Jason would have gone headlong into any situation, there is now an element of holding back, waiting as if he's thinking. He and I often sit at the rickety picnic table early in the morning to share our thoughts over cups of coffee. He then goes to help Glen in the barn before the rest of the household wakes up. It's a little unnerving that he looks so much like his father.

"Jason, did Dad ever talk to you about anything before he and I went to Kauai?"

Jason cocks his head to the side, as Ravi used to do. "You know, now that you mention it, he did act a little strange the day before you guys left. I didn't understand what he was trying to say. It was kind of confusing."

"What was strange and confusing about it, sweetie?"

"It wasn't what he said, as much as how he said it that made me irritated."

"What did he say, Jason?"

"He said I must be the man in the family if anything happened to him or you. That part didn't bother me, but then he said that I'd need to step up to the . . . Boy, now I can't remember the word he used.

"That's okay, sweetie, take your time."

"I'm to take care of my sisters if anything should happen. I asked him what he meant, but all he said was that he wanted me to know how important I'll be to the family if anything should happen to you or him."

"That's not so strange, Jason. I might have said the same thing to you if I'd thought of it. He probably wanted you to know he expected you to take his place if anything ever happened to one of us. And you did, didn't you?"

"That's not the part that annoyed me, Mom. He also said that I'd have unimagined responsibility someday. I might have to go far away from my family to be part of another one."

"Did you ask him to elaborate?"

"I tried to ask him, but he walked out of my room. I told you it was strange. It looked like he was crying. I've never seen Dad cry before. The more I thought about it, the more I didn't understand. Do you think he knew he was going to die? Can you explain that to me? What was he talking about?"

*What words can I possibly use to comfort him?*

"Maybe he meant that one day you'd get married and move out of our house to form another family."

"Oh," he says.

We don't talk about the funerals and the misery they caused. We do talk about our need to have a *fire drill* soon. When the time is right, we'll assemble the family, but for now, he's to watch his back, especially if he sees the slightest thing that looks off. Jason takes this in stride, something I've always admired about him.

Mel seems more mature to me and has blossomed into a teenager practically overnight. She helps both her Grandmother and Mona in the kitchen and appears happy to mix, fill, and bake. We haven't tackled the kitchen yet, and without a dishwasher, Mel wears long purple gloves to save her nail polish. She expresses a desire to help with the housekeeping, but flat-out refuses to go down into the dungeon to do laundry.

*I have yet to venture down there myself. I'm afraid of what I'll find.*

My little Curlie is shy, content to play quietly by herself. My sister and I would often discuss our children and attributed her aloofness as part of her personality, or it's because she's the youngest child. Curlie allows her older siblings to do things without her, channeling her passion into the piano, contentedly practicing for hours until someone interrupts her.

*I remember my obsession with horses at her age!*

Wanting a smooth enrollment into their respective new schools, I'm at my computer to verify the information Lenard and Gene gave me months ago. The envelope Mother brought with her contained their school transcripts, birth certificates, dental and medical records, and new social security cards.

Checking my emails for items that are still out for delivery, there's one from Mr. C that looks a little suspect. Is he contacting me because he wants to come to Ashwood? If he does, we'll be doing some scrambling.

**Coming to Virginia in week.**
**Will be there B4 Labor Day.**
**Have house ready. Bringing two guests. MC**
*Please do not reply to this email.*
*The information is intended only for the person or entity to*
*which it is addressed and may contain CONFIDENTIAL material.*

Lenard probably already knows about this. Taking a closer look at the date, it's from four days ago, which means that we only have a few days to get furniture, bedding, and linens for three rooms completed before Mr. C arrives.

Mona brings home magazines from her weekly shopping trip. Mr. C is always in the tabloids; kissing with this starlet, kibitzing with that celebrity, being ever the playboy. It could be my opportunity to confront him with his portion of the expenses. Then again, one of our silent partners may not be very quiet when he sees the invoices I'm going to prepare for him, and he takes a gander at the lack of antiques on his side of the house.

A day before Mr. C's arrival, Lenard calls our household together to debrief us about the upcoming visit. Gene is not with him. When we ask where he is, Lenard rudely says he's out on assignment.

Lenard emphasizes that we would be happier staying at the Dover Inn, but if we don't leave, we are to keep quiet and out of Mr. C's way. Explicitly directed at my children, they are, under no circumstances, allowed to talk to him or his guests. We are all to be polite, excusing ourselves quickly!

"Who is this guy, the President of the United States?" Jason mumbles under his breath.

Lenard snarls, "That will be obvious when you see him. Do not STARE at him! Do you understand? NO STARING is allowed! Don't go around blabbing that he's here, got it?"

Melanie's jaw drops, "WOW, he must be important."

After saying we agree, rolling our eyes, including Mother and Glen, Lenard leaves, satisfied we won't blow Mr. C's cover.

*One can only hope that Mr. C's visit is brief.*

We manage to furnish the bedrooms on Mr. C's side and patch up his bathrooms, although they look drab compared to our wing of the house because there was little time to do much else. We barely had time to apply a coat of sealer to the old, scratched wood floors before the big event. And since none of the investors saw fit to help us when we needed money, why should we accommodate them?

Mr. C and his guests arrive right on schedule in a white stretch limo during the hottest part of the day. My children are viewing the action from the large windows at the front of the second story sitting area overlooking the driveway, running to the side windows to get a better view. I'm sitting in my office, watching from the front windows.

Mona is at the front door to greet them as the chauffeur transfers the luggage to Glen's waiting hands. Trying to be invisible from the ensuing melodrama, I can hear Glen walking toward the staircase loaded with luggage, puffing his disapproval as he shuffles up the creaking staircase.

When he comes back down, I poke my head out of the library to mention that he should use the elevator in the hallway, then reminds me that he's not about to get into it.

"You don't have to, Glen. Put the luggage in it, press the button, and the guests can get their luggage out of it on the second floor all by themselves."

Shutting his eyes, he mumbles his thanks, as he didn't think about doing it that way, muttering that he hates that darn blasted thing. Sounds of laughter mingle with the clinking of aluminum, and it becomes eerily quiet until minutes later when chattering in the hallway follows the sound of people as they move up the staircase.

Not long after, I hear heavy footfalls coming down the staircase.

"Ellen Thompson, we need to talk!" Suddenly, my office door opens by an irate Mr. C. "Where is my antique four-poster bed? And where are all the other antiques that were on *my* side of the house? Where is that wonderful old Grandfather Clock in the hallway downstairs? Where are all my antiques!" he bellows.

"Hello, Mr. C. I'm so glad you could join us. Please, come in and sit down. They aren't all your antiques. Some of them were mine."

"Were? What have you done with them?" Sitting down on the sofa, he says, "I told everyone about all the wonderful antiques, and they were so impressed; they couldn't wait to see them. What's up there now looks very new."

"That's because all that stuff is new." I make a production out of moving papers around my desk.

He impatiently stands up to place his hands on the desk, saying, "I'm waiting!"

"I'm waiting too, for the money you said you'd send to help pay the expenses. While you were busy making headlines and partying, I was working like a dog here to pay off the debts we *both* inherited. Oh, will you sit down!"

"Alright, I'll sit, but I want an explanation," he huffs.

After he hears about our inherited debt, our accrued expenses, and the lack of cooperation from the fine citizens of Jasper, he is sincerely apologetic. Then I hand him a two-page invoice where he turns the page and looks up at me in surprise.

"Lenard said I couldn't, not under any circumstances, contact you. Or was I to bother any other investor," I say quietly.

"He said that?" he says, raising his eyebrows.

"Yes. I told you right from the beginning this place was in debt. You and Mr. A both agreed at that first meeting to share the expenses. I haven't seen one red cent from either of you. And, it was Lenard's idea to sell some of the antiques."

"Why would Lenard tell you that? It was one of the reasons that sold me on this place. They were so quaint and old. I thought things were under control here."

"Who said things were under control, Lenard? That's your share from the sale of the antiques minus what you owe for the replacement of the new furniture. Along with your portion of our accrued debt until the end of the year. Then I considered any profits from other sources, accounted for other items. What you see is what you owe me."

"I had no idea," he says.

As my way of getting in a smidge of revenge, I left off any profit from the carriage, the Duesenberg, and some other items, figuring what he doesn't know won't hurt.

"You are thorough, Ellen. I'll have my people look this over. I wasn't aware of the extent of the debts. Why would Lenard lead us to believe the estate was healthy financially when it wasn't?"

"Our friend Lenard strikes again. What exactly did he tell you?"

"He said it was a sound investment. The other investors agreed with it too," Mr. C says.

"How many investors are there? Maybe we can get them to help. It seems a little strange, but I'm aware of about five discrepancies Lenard told one of us that isn't true. I've asked him questions, and he conveniently doesn't answer any of them."

Mr. C appears confused. "Mr. A was the only investor that came to the meeting. Now that you mention it, Lenard dodged my questions and he never quite gave me a straight answer. Ellen, are you okay? You have a strange look on your face."

"Something is bothering me. Lenard has been out-of-sight lately. He showed up to lecture us about your visit, but Gene wasn't with him."

"What can I tell you?" Mr. C asks.

"I'm curious. When did you meet Lenard for the first time?"

"It was about a year ago. Lenard approached me and said there were some investors I should talk with."

"Did these investors have names?"

"No," he says. "I was told I must never know who they are. They knew about my little problem. I have gambling debts, Ellen. I'm not proud of it, but there it is."

"And that didn't seem strange to you? That he knew about your little problem?"

"No. I thought it was a great solution. I was in panic mode and had already put my Wyoming house up for sale to cover part of the debt. Lenard approached me at the open house. We got to talking, and I told him why I was selling the house. He said he knew someone who could help me. All I had to do was sign my name to some property they wanted to buy, but their identity had to remain a secret."

"They must have had this lined up waiting for the right opportunity to present itself. But you knew the man who was with you at the restaurant, didn't you?"

"I never met him before that day. Mr. A was already at the restaurant when I got there," he says. "That's why there was so much whispering going on. I was asked to leave right after I signed some papers."

"That's odd. I didn't think the FBI got involved with stuff like this. Lenard and Gene are Special FBI Agents, you know."

Mr. C begins to laugh so hard, that he has to wipe tears from his eyes. "Who told you they are Special FBI Agents?"

"He did! I saw his badge. They took care of everything for us. Put us in the--I'm probably not supposed to tell you this, but they put us in the Federal Witness Protection Program."

Seeing my serious expression, he stops laughing. "I'm sorry, Ellen. Did he tell you that? Lenard never told me he was FBI, but if he told you that, who am I to say otherwise. Just because he didn't show me his badge doesn't mean he isn't FBI."

"Look, I could use some help here. Please take this to your accountant as soon as you can, or I'll have to take drastic measures."

"I'll call them right away. I can't leave my guests for much longer, Ellen, but we'll work this out. I appreciate what you've done. I'll have this taken care of immediately, okay?"

"I would appreciate that."

We are no longer in need of financial assistance due to what we made at the track and what Gerald has sold for us, but I'm not about to disclose that information.

Smiling his trademark smile, Mr. C looks thoughtful for a moment. "Would you decorate my side of the house, too? That is if I send you the funds to do it?"

"I'll think about it." I've already thought about it. If he doesn't pay his half of the expenses, I might take the furniture out of his rooms and resell it. He can come back to empty rooms.

"Do you think Mrs. Murdock will be able to get what I've requested? I asked if she could get certain things for my guests and some wine."

"If you give her the money to do it, I'm sure she can accommodate you. What else do you need?"

Looking a little embarrassed, he says, "I'd like to entertain my guests without any of you . . . in the dining room."

"No problem there, I wouldn't dream of horning in on your little soirée. You and your guests can eat in the dining room, and we'll eat in the Morning Room. Will that suit you?"

"That would be fabulous, Ellen. I'll get back to my guests, then. Thanks so much," he says.

*Interesting that Lenard didn't tell him he was FBI. I had doubts before; now they may be valid.*

Mona has everything in hand, and there'll be no problem at all in taking care of Mr. C's entertaining requests. When Mel discovered who was here, she wanted to serve the entrées, but Jason flat out said he's not at all interested in doing any such thing. Could this be any more ridiculous?

But the truth of the matter is, that Grandma put her foot down; she'll serve. There will be no arguments, period, and end of discussion!

I love that she did that! I didn't like it when she did it to me when I was growing up, but I love that she did it to my children!

The information Mother brought will enable me to make the appropriate appointments at the medical center attached to the local hospital. I include myself because there might be lingering effects from the experimental drug.

During Curlie's appointment, we address her recurring nightmares, which the doctor attributes to the instability she must feel about the move from one state to another. The doctor sees nothing wrong if Curlie sleeps with me on occasion. Mother and I know it's more than that, but we have to keep that information to ourselves for now.

When I bring up the prominent ridges that cross the middles of each of my fingernails, the nurse asks if there has been a traumatic occurrence recently. Trying to explain the experimental drug without going into detail, she wonders if this could be the cause. No one can give a satisfactory answer without the name of the drug. She and Devon (Homeland Security in Kauai) share the same strange expression when she sees the faint pinpricks on the inside of both arms, saying she'll consult with the doctor.

Although the dental and medical records look authentic, we know how smart Lenard and his teams are with forgery. Is forgery still forgery when the government is involved? And how do they get away with this stuff! Was Lenard that sure I would go along with everything? Maybe it's not even our government! Why am I so doubtful all of a sudden? What is the nagging feeling at the peripheral edge of my consciousness?

*I must stop this imagining.*

The Metropolis, known as Stoneville, has major department stores to satisfy my fussy children. Trip number one is with Jason, who needs everything from jeans to underwear as he grew two inches since last Christmas and will be the easiest to please.

*Was that only six months ago?*

Trip number two is with Melanie, who hates everything in her closet. The dramatic Mel will die of embarrassment if she attends her new school and is not the fashion plate she things she is. Mel must have the latest and most magnificent tops and jeans that fit! Mel also pleads to have her hair streaked, perhaps a tasteful tattoo?

Trip number three is with Curlie, giving us time to be alone. Wandering from rack to rack, she's not too excited until she sees a little jewelry box. When she lifts the lid to hear a familiar tune, tears begin to roll down her face. I know what's making her sad; my little Curlie mourns the loss of her Daddy.

"I miss him, Mama."

"I know, sweetie, I do to." Grief shows up without warning. My little Curlie is the one most affected by the loss of her father, her childhood home, and all she knew to be right in her universe.

In the weeks before school starts, Glen takes the children on horse-trail rides, taking picnic lunches so that I can work at the house. They seem to enjoy this time together. Glen mentions his fondness for them, which means that mine most likely fill the void of not seeing his grandchildren.

School Bus No. 12 will pick all of them up at the end of our driveway each morning, precisely at 7:45 a.m. where it will take them to the Tri-County's school system. Nestled on a tree-lined, grassy area, it's not unlike a college or university campus. Accommodating classes from K-12: Jasper High School for Jason, Memorial Junior High for Melanie, and for Curlie, Washington Elementary School for Gifted Children.

Until they board the bus for home, there are after-school programs that provide a variety of options. Jason will practice with a small band in the music room, Mel will work with an apprentice in the art room throwing pottery, and Curlie will meet with a group of gifted children. Bus No. 12 will deposit them, along with a handful of neighbors, to their respective homes around 4:00 p.m.

A few weeks after school starts, Jason took me aside to say he thought the school bus might be under surveillance. Last week, he noticed a blue SUV that mostly followed for a little while, then turned off when the school bus made its final stop on the way to school. Yesterday, it followed the bus all the way to school, then parked in the teacher's area. No one got out, and it drove away when everyone was off the bus.

I'm a little frightened to think what this could mean. "Do you ever see the car after school?"

"Yeah, now that you mention it. It was in the parking lot last Thursday before we got on the bus to come home."

"Why did you wait until now to tell me?"

"I didn't connect the dots until now. It followed the bus until we came to our driveway. Then it drove past after the bus left. It looks like the same cars the FBI people use, Mom. The license plate was smeared with something, so I couldn't get a clear number."

"Jason, you have a sixth sense about things, as I do, so I'm going to give it to you straight. You must keep your eye on that car or any other vehicle that looks suspicious."

"What are you saying, Mom?"

"We might not be safe yet, Jason. I have a funny feeling about Lenard and Gene."

"Me too. I'll think about what we can do in case we have to do something quick. Don't worry, Dad left things in good hands; I'll take care of you and the girls." Leaning in to hug me, he kisses me on the cheek.

"I trust you, Jason. Be careful, okay?"

"I will, Mom. Don't worry about it. I got this," he says confidently.

Jason doesn't see the implications, but worry starts to creep in anyway. It's the *what ifs* that are contributing to my anxiety. The watchers may want to do my family harm. Is it someone we know? When I question Jason about his plan, he continually assures me that he has a sound one.

"They won't succeed. I'm on it, Mom. I'll take care of you and the girls, just like I promised Dad I would," he says positively.

When the calls come two days later, first from Principal Jenkins of Curlie's school, then Principal Lindale of Mel's school, and finally Principal Wilkins of Jason's school, I all but pass out from the shock, because none of them arrived today!

Telling myself repeatedly, Jason has a plan. Jason knows the drill. But, why doesn't he call? Oh, Dear God, please keep them safe! Please don't let anything happen to them, not now--not when we're reunited and things are going so well!

Assembling everyone in the kitchen, we put our heads together to figure out whether we should call the local police or Lenard. The discussion tends to lean toward the authorities, but Mother cautions about what Lenard drummed into us from day one: keep our mouths shut, and keep a low profile, because our very lives may depend on it. We never discussed a contingency plan if faced with this type of dilemma!

Temporarily forgetting that the Murdock's know little of our real situation, the look on Glen and Mona's faces are of pure shock. "There somethin ya forgot ta tell us, Missy?" Glen asks.

"Not now, Glen, it's too complicated. Can you go along with whatever we decide?"

"Suit yourself, but if ya was askin my opinion, I think we should call the Sheriff."

"I don't want to involve him yet, Glen. Let's wait for about thirty minutes. If we don't hear from Jason by then, we'll call Lenard." As I reach for my cellphone, it rings. Jason says they're all safe and back in their classrooms. They got off the bus, hiding in the bus garage until the SUV left.

"I had it totally under control," Jason says, "Nothing to worry about, okay? We'll see you at home tonight. Gotta get back, love ya."

"Call when you get on the bus to come home, alright?"

He says okay and hangs up, but the nagging sensation that this is not over has shaken me. Who are the people in the SUV? Are they involved with Ravi's death? My cellphone rings three more times, as principals of each school calls to say that my children are unharmed and back in their respective classrooms. Everything is back to normal.

*NORMAL!*

"Do you know who was following the bus in the SUV?" Are Lenard and Gene behind this? Why would they scare us like this?

"What SUV are you talking about, Mrs. Thompson?" Principal Wilkins asks. "Jason didn't mention a vehicle. Are you sure about that?"

Asking him to confer with the other principals, he says that the local police will keep an eye out, so this indeed doesn't happen again! When three-thirty rolls around, Jason calls to say that he, Mel, and Curlie are on the bus heading for home. He'll keep an eye out for suspicious activity, then adds, "Mom, don't worry. We'll see you around four."

Pacing back and forth, I'm at the end of the driveway waiting for the school bus. When Jason, Mel, and Curlie step down from the bus, I usher them down the driveway and into the house.

Jason lays out the plan that thwarted any would-be danger. He says it was so simple it was ridiculous. Mel and Curlie followed his instructions to the letter by staying on the bus. They hid on the floor until the driver took the bus into the garage. They waited, for what Jason thought was a reasonable amount of time, and when he deemed it safe, he escorted each of them back to their schools.

Of course, they had to explain what they did to avoid detention, but Jason said he was only doing what he thought was right. The principals dismissed them back to their classrooms with a warning; end of story.

Not for me it isn't! "Let's go into my office. I'm not mad at you, Jason so that you know, but I'm concerned. Why didn't you call or text me what was happening?"

"Mom, everything was under control," he says with confidence.

"You scared us half to death!" Taking a deep breath, I let it out slowly trying to calm myself.

"There was no immediate danger. It didn't occur to me to text you. As long as I was calm and made a game out of it, Mel and Curlie went along. If I looked scared or got heroic, they would've been worried, so I made it sound like a game. You have no idea how upset Curlie was when she found out about you and Dad. Grandma couldn't get her to stop sobbing for days. It was pretty bad."

"I didn't think of that angle, Jason. I'm sorry you were all put through that; if I could rewind time, I would."

"I know, Mom. Someday we'll find out what happened to Dad and why they took you," Jason says. "You have to trust me."

"Jason, this may not be an isolated incident. In fact, if you've seen that car more than once, it's a sure bet they'll reappear again. It may not be the same vehicle if they suspect you saw them today."

He's quiet for several moments, then reaches for my hand to give it a gentle squeeze. "Do you think it's the people who took you?"

"I've been trying to figure that out since your father died. There might be more to this than we can handle. We think that we need to call the police or get in touch with Lenard. What do you think we should do about this?"

Jason shrugs and then frowns. "I'll go along with whatever the rest of the adults think we should do. At this point, I'm clueless."

"Come on, Jason. You're holding back. You have an opinion, and I'd like to hear what it is."

"Aren't the FBI people supposed to protect us? You should let this Lenard character know what happened today. If it was him, then he'll be alerted to the fact we might be on to him."

"I see your point. When did you become so wise, sweetie? In the meantime, we better come up with a few scenarios, just in case."

"I've already got another one we can use the next time," Jason says assuredly.

*I pray there is no next time.*

*"In the midst of movement and chaos,*

*keep stillness inside of you."*

~ Deepak Chopra

# Chapter Ten

## Testing Theories

Lenard's cellphone goes straight to his voicemail. Leaving an abbreviated version of what happened to the children, I then wait for him to return my call. In the meantime, Jason will continually check the rear window every time they get on the school bus.

Several days later, he spots a red SUV with a smeared license plate as it attempts to pass across the double white line, but the bus driver is as adept at keeping the SUV at bay, as he is at keeping the kids in line on the bus. Jason texts me as this is happening.

The second call to Lenard also goes directly to his voicemail. Leaving another message, adding that I'm going to call his boss if he doesn't return my call today.

*What kind of protector is he?*

Another text comes in from Jason. They're at school now, nothing to worry about, as it was a real estate agent checking out the school system for a client who was merely late for his appointment. He'll text when they're on the way home.

Two hours later, Lenard calls. Roaring into my ear, he says, "Why did you leave such messages? I may not be able to answer my cellphone sometimes. I do have other projects, and I do have a life! What is the big emergency?"

"I thought you should be informed about the SUV that was following my children to school."

"There is nothing wrong with an SUV or limousine going to that school or following the bus, Ellen. After all, there are several wealthy children in that school district. Maybe the car picks some of them up and drops them off; did you think of that?"

"No," I say, letting out a long breath. "I didn't."

"Under no circumstances are you to contact the local police. Have you forgotten my warning? Go back and read the protocols to refresh your memory. I will get back to you when I can. In the future, do not leave threatening messages!"

Am I an over-reactive Mom? Is it my imagination, or is Lenard snippier than usual? Are we sitting ducks, waiting for the hunter to pop us one? It's a dreadful thought, one that is both disturbing and frightening, and it makes me cringe at the thought of *who* might be behind this.

Jason texts that he and his sisters are on their way home. I'm near the end of the driveway pacing back and forth, waiting for the school bus. Maybe he's not paying attention, because he hasn't answered my text.

"You're all twisted up, Missy," Glen says, waiting with me. "If ya don't trust Lenard, then we need ta contact the police. I know Sheriff Rocky, and he's a good man. He'll know what ta do."

"Thanks, Glen, I appreciate your concern. We may have to do that yet."

Glen notices the bus coming down the road, a puff of dirt is rolling under the tires as it stops at our driveway. They had to wait until the bus garage fixed their flat tire and they got a late start from the bus garage. Jason was distracted doing his homework and didn't see the need to bother me. Then next thing he knew, he was home.

After an uneventful week, I remain cautious as this is when people replace anxiety with complacency, letting their guard down. Jason's aware of my fear, nodding when he gets on the morning bus, but about twenty minutes later, he sends a text with **SOS red SUV**. It's our family code that equals: *help--no time to chat!* I almost run into Glen, who's standing near the garages.

"What's goin on, Missy?" he asks.

"Get the truck, Glen; we're going for a ride."

Mother must be watching from the doorway in the vestibule. She hands me my purse because she knows something's wrong. Glen's in the truck and presses down on the gas pedal as I slam the door.

"Ya wanna tell me what's goin on now, Missy? I got a shotgun b'hind the seat."

"Thanks, but I don't know how to shoot one of those. Head toward the school and go slow if you see a red SUV. He didn't explain, but Jason would never send a message like that unless there were no other choices."

Glen touches my arm, giving me a thumbs up. It is a gesture I have come to know as he is with me, no matter what. "Don't ya think we should call the Sheriff anyway? They know what ta do in these cases. What kind of message did the boy send? And I know how to use one; shotgun, I mean." Glen is going over the speed limit.

"I don't think we'll need that, but I'll file it away for future reference. Jason's message said we should be on the lookout for a red SUV."

As we round the crest of a hill on the double-lane highway, we see the SUV coming our way. The dark tint on the windows makes it impossible to see inside as it quickly passes. Both front and back license plates are unreadable. Jason texts: **the eagle has landed.** Then my cellphone rings with an automated message from the school that says they're experiencing a lock-down. Everything is under control, stay away from the campus pending an all-clear sign.

The next text from Jason: **Houston, we have a problem**.

"Oh, crap."

"What is it?" Glen asks.

"They're okay, but let's head to the school anyway. I'd like to know what happened and I'm not waiting until tonight to find out. The call was from the school, and they're all in lock-down mode. The text was from Jason, and there seems to be a problem."

"Ya got it, won't take but a minute. Hang on."

When we arrive at the campus, all of the children are outside on the grass areas sitting in small groups. Several police cars with their lights ablaze are parked near the high school. Also present is the local fire department, rescue squad, and a big grey truck with bright red letters that spell the words BOMB UNIT.

"What in the blazes . . ." Glen doesn't finish his sentence when a police officer waves us over. Lowering his window to speak to him, the officer honestly looks like Barney Fife from Mayberry.

"Glen, ain't seen you in a while, what ya doin here?"

"Howdy, Deputy Slim, this here's Ms. Thompson. She's the one who bought the Ashwood Farm. Her kids go here, one in each school. She got a text from her son that he was in trouble, so we came right on over."

Even though I cautioned Glen not to talk about us, so we don't draw unnecessary attention, he looks so proud after he says this, I let it go.

"Howdy, Ms. Thompson, we had a bomb scare a little bit ago and had ta go inta emergency lock-down mode." Sticking out his chest, he stops talking to pull up his pants. "The squad is still in the school checkin things out. Odd that nothin like this has ever happened here b'fore." Slim says, looking pleased with himself.

*Instinct is telling me that this is no bomb scare.*

"They're doin a right good job of keepin the kids from goin inta danger. You can park over yonder and wait if ya want. I'll signal when it's safe."

"Did ya see a red SUV near the high school, Slim?" Glen asks casually.

"No, by the time I got here, the only vehicles near the high school, was all the rescue squad people. Why, do ya think they have somethin ta do with this? Got a license plate I can run?"

"Don't know if they're involved. Don't have a plate for ya either, cause it was kinda smeared," Glen offers.

"Excuse me, Officer Slim? Glen and I saw a vehicle driving very fast away from the school, that's all. We don't know if it's related to this, but you might want to check it out."

Slim pops a small notebook from his shirt pocket. "That's Deputy Slim, Ma'am. Did you get the license plate? Oh, wait, ya said that already. Any marks on the vehicle that ya noticed?"

"No, Slim, the windows were so dark we couldn't see who was drivin, but they were speedin," Glen says.

"That's not much ta go on, but we'll check it out. You're welcome ta wait over in the visitor's lot until we give the all clear sign." Slim touches the brim of his hat in a polite gesture, and says, "Ma'am, nice ta meet ya and have a nice day. See ya later, Glen."

Glen pulls into a parking space as I text back and forth with Jason. From where we're parked, Mel is sitting with her class, and Glen spots Curlie's red hair, so we know she's safe. About an hour later, some of the vehicles near the high school begin to move away as the groups of children line up.

Deputy Slim saunters over to say that the school board says that all of the students can take the rest of the day off. He begins by saying that the threat is narrowed down to the high school. They don't want to take any chances, so with everyone gone, the authorities can finish their investigation.

I don't want my children to get on their bus, so I text Jason first. As the school buses line up, we can see Jason walking toward Curlie and Mel to inform them we're here to pick them up. Once they're all safely in the truck with us, we head toward home. On the way back, Jason makes jokes about the bomb scare. The buzz is that it's the most exciting thing that's happened to the school campus in its short history.

After dinner, as the girls are clearing the table and Glen has gone off toward the barn, Jason signals for us to go outside to our 'safe zone' near the southern paddock.

"Mom, there was no bomb. I had to invent something, so I . . ."

"Oh My God, Jason, you are responsible for this? Do you know it's a crime to call the police on a false incident? Do you know how much money it costs the county to bring in the bomb squad *and* the fire department?"

"I had to do something to throw the guy off. Can't we send them money and not tell them it's from us? I did what I had to!" Jason seems rattled. "Listen, okay? I had a good reason for doing it."

"Okay, spill it!"

"The red SUV not only followed the bus, but it also came onto the campus. It did this yesterday. I didn't tell you, because I didn't want to alarm you. They waited behind the bus. When it started up again, it stopped when the bus did, too. It looked too suspicious to me, so I told Mel and Curlie to put their extra clothes on over their other clothes."

"That was clever, Jason. The girls were in disguise. If you got off the bus in disguise, then they should have driven away."

"That's just it, Mom. I didn't change my clothes. I wanted to see if it was my imagination."

"You deliberately put yourself into harms' way? What were you thinking?"

"I had a good reason. This time a man came right up to me and tried to pull me away. Right in front of the school, in broad daylight, Mom!"

"He was right there by the front door of the school?"

"I figured he'd let go if I yelled there was a bomb somewhere inside, so that's what I did. As soon as I yelled, he let go of me and ran back to the SUV, and it took off. The Principal must have called the Sheriff, and that's what happened."

Hugging my son, he genuinely looks troubled by what he did. "I'm so sorry that we seem to be caught up in some mystery, Jason. I don't know that this is related to what happened to Dad, but it might. Perhaps the nightmare hasn't been resolved yet."

"I had to do it, Mom. There was no other choice."

"I know, sweetie. You did what I would've expected you to do. You took charge of the situation and, okay, so you maybe could have yelled something else, but it's done and over for now. We'll send an anonymous check around Christmas to cover their costs. I'm grateful all of you are safe."

"There's something else. The guy looked familiar."

"How familiar?"

"He might have been wearing a wig or something. He had a fake beard and mustache, I could see the glue. He called me by name, so he knew who I was."

My invisible *Mom radar* goes off at the mere mention of a mustache. "I've had enough of this. I'm taking all of you to school and picking all of you up until we find out who's behind this."

Jason says okay, then gives me a hug, and apologizes again. I'm relieved for now, but we must remain vigilant, nonetheless. Lenard should know about this latest incident. Unfortunately, his cellphone goes straight to voicemail.

This time his message says, "You have reached Special Agent Lenard Casings. I am temporarily out of the country and unavailable for the next two weeks. If you need to leave a message, I will be checking them daily. Have a nice day."

I'm keeping track of how often I call Lenard, and how often he doesn't return my calls. Glen says I worry too much; Mother says I'm not worried enough. What is the happy medium?

Either Glen or I drive the children back and forth to school for the better part of a week until Deputy Slim shows up in our driveway one morning ahead of the school bus. He says the kids are safe again and to please allow them to ride the bus.

Since the school complex is a feeder school system, meaning children come from other communities to fill the seats, the Tri-County School Boards banded together to protect them. Slim assures us that the best of the best is on duty and not to worry, as he will follow the bus every morning and every afternoon.

Barney Fife's face shows up as Deputy Slim touches the brim of his hat, saying, "Have a nice day, Ma'am."

Jason, Mel, and Curlie dutifully get out of our car and onto the bus when it comes down the street to stop at our driveway. Has a new theory presented itself? Whoever is responsible is probably not happy their little plan didn't work. The betting woman in me knows they will return to try again.

Mr. C and his guests were so preoccupied with their activities and such that they were unaware of the drama that played out during their visit. He came to thank me for allowing his guests to rest and rejuvenate, in the peaceful surroundings that I worked so hard to create. He even stayed two extra days. He suggests we install a swimming pool, maybe a pool house, also reminding me about his wine cellar request. Would I give this extra attention, as he's planning to bring some vintage bottles with him the next time he's here?

I've given his ideas some thought all right. "I'm still waiting for your part of the expenses. If and when that's taken care of; I'll consider your other requests. Is that fair, Mr. C?"

"Yes, yes, Ellen, we can talk about this later," he says, continuing his elaborate expression of thanks. Asking the Murdock's into the library to thank them for everything, he presents Mona with a box of expensive chocolate truffles while Glen and I receive a handshake.

Mr. C was uncharacteristically nice to my children when they accidentally met in the hallway or out in the barn, saying how well-mannered they are and I should be very proud of them. He seems genuine, and then I remember that he's an actor!

Although *Didgeridoo* stayed away from all of them, he did poke his head around the barn when Mr. C and his guests went to spend the day on a trail ride and picnic somewhere on the property.

Glen's still amused at this, and I remind him again that the horse is probably smarter than we are.

It reminds me of the theories I want to test about other things concerning horses. If a new parent wants to know about child development, there's Dr. Spock. Theories abound about human development, reference Darwin's Theory of Evolution, and if you ask Mona, her theory is about what kind of flour is used to make 'the best darn pastry' in America.

One of my theories has to do with Einstein's Theory of Relativity and the whole space-time continuum thing as it relates to racing horses. Daddy would tease me whenever he caught me reading *Relativity: The Special and the General Theory.*

Einstein's book is the study of how two events if run simultaneous for one observer, might not be simultaneous for the other observer-- if both observers are moving, that is. He argued that maximum speed is finite; that no physical object, field line, or message can travel faster than the speed of light in a vacuum.

Daddy and I were frequent visitors to the farms that trained Thoroughbreds, and often went to the racetrack to see them in action. In the years we went to the track, I learned to observe many things.

While my sister, Terre, concentrated on dancing and the legendary career she would have as a prima ballerina, I focused on horses. It was my little secret, much as Zorro's secret of living two lives, and no one would suspect that I was destined to be the first female jockey to win the Triple Crown! (It was my secret dream.) It never came true, but a girl can dream, can't she?

Writing everything down in a little notebook, this became valuable information. To my twelve-year-old mind, I thought owners were giving specific signals to trainers, and then the trainers would signal to the jockeys, and back to the owners again. Daddy said it's probably like the signals a baseball coach gives his players out on the field during a game.

I considered my annotations as scientific observations, looking for the horse that ran on the inside of the track, as it appeared to move faster than the one on the outside. Illusion or not, it was the best place to be in to win. After diligent studying, I developed a system that was uniquely mine. It only failed when I didn't pay close attention, was distracted, or didn't gather enough information before the race.

My real dream, of course, was to be on the winning horse! I wanted to become a jockey. When I shared my intention with Mother and Daddy, they strictly forbade me to consider such a career. It was too dangerous; it was no place for their daughter; period and end of discussion! So I kept my scientific observations to myself after that.

Then one day, when Daddy and I were at the racetrack, he kiddingly asked which horse I favored to win that day. He saw me place my finger on a horse and when I picked three winners in a row, I knew when he left me in the stands--he was going to place a bet. We waited for the horse I chose to win, and the rest, as they say, is history.

Long before I named a horse to win, much study came before it; the tote board, horse's owner, jockey, and all known statistics. If I followed my theory, we didn't often lose. Should that happen, I figured that the owner, jockey, or driver manipulated or skewed the data somehow. Daddy would laugh and say not to worry, "You win some, you lose some; don't lose more than you win, and don't tell Mother we were at the track!"

Then, of course, there's that little something Mr. Murdock mentions about the *club* down at the track. It is one theory I want to test; will the members of this club allow a relative unknown into their midst without some confrontation? Can Ashwood Stables become prosperous again?

Several women throughout history have made significant inroads into the racing world. I dearly want to challenge my theory about racing. That being; a woman can train, race, and win at the racetrack as well, if not better than a man if given enough information and training.

If I throw a monkey wrench into this male domain, will they rebel? Or will they come to terms with the fact that they can't control the odds anymore?

*It will probably cause quite a stir, but that's my intention.*

My family is being affected by Ravi's absence, and as upset as I've been with him, I miss him, too. The time may be right to bring up a contingency plan. When I married Ravi, he came up with the secret code and the term fire drill. Ravi was the one who insisted we carry walkie-talkies whenever we went camping or out for a walk, and adamant we took self-defense classes, instilling in us that being careful might save our life one day.

*Has he always looked over his shoulder?*

It came as no surprise when Jason says, "Mom, we need a fire drill."

"I meant to do that! Thanks for reminding me."

Jason is thinking of the red SUV incident and doesn't want a repeat. Even if they do the disguise thing again, will it thwart the deed next time? After dinner, with chores completed, Mother and I are in my room when Jason, Mel, and Curlie drift in to settle onto the sofa pit.

"What's up, Mom?" Mel asks. "Jay says we're having a family meeting. Why are you so secretive, Jay?"

"You'll see. Did you check the house for bugs, Mom?" he asks quietly.

Curlie screams, "Bugs! What kind of bugs?"

"It's not that kind of bug, sweetie. I thought we did that already. Have you found something?"

"I think so." Jason opens his hand to show us a tiny squashed metal piece the size of a pea. "I wasn't even looking. Mr. Murdock sent me into his office to get something on a shelf, and there it was. I didn't want him to think I was snooping, so I squashed it and put it in my pocket."

I place the little thing inside an extra button bag that came on a blouse I purchased recently. Then Mel proceeds to somberly remind us how our code came in handy when Jason fell off his trail bike and rolled down a ravine when we were on vacation two years ago.

"I don't remember that," Curlie says, wrinkling her face.

Mother touches her head, lovingly saying, "You were probably too young, honey."

"Yeah, Mom, remember when that man took Curlie when we were at that amusement park in North Carolina?" Mel says, jarring me back to the present.

Curlie wails, "Somebody took me?" Mother reaches to hug her, saying soothing words to comfort her. "I don't remember that either."

"You weren't gone very long," Mel says. "Some guard found you right away."

Jason nods his head. "You and Dad were upset when the police caught up with the guy trying to leave the park with her. They let the man go because he had a photo of his daughter, that looked a lot like Curlie."

Trying to stifle the terrifying memory, it suddenly reminds me how fragile life is. Mother notices and steers us back to our list. I'm hoping we never have to use the last one.

I remind them again of the importance of listening, keeping our mouths shut, because someone is no doubt watching. It isn't clear about who that might be, but I have a theory about this.

Could it be the other half of our investor team named Mr. A? He was gruff during that meeting in the restaurant. Or could it be the far-reaching hand of Abdul and his compatriots? Perhaps it's the people who made the plane explode that killed Ravi and all those people.

---

Fire Drill = we need a contingency plan.
Houston we have a problem = there is a situation
Eagle has landed = we are safe and ok
Horse has left the barn = our target is leaving
Target = someone identified as a threat to us
HOT = FIRE
STAT = get help I'm in trouble
OOG = out of gas
SOS = help--no time to chat
FOG = full of gas
ER = I'm hurt bad
Free popcorn, anything free = lie
CODE BLUE = get everyone to safety.

---

"Mom, what happened to you when you were gone so long?" Jason asks, "I'd like to know."

"I can't go into that right now, Jason. Someday soon I will, I promise."

We talk about our options during situations that might arise, implementing our signal system, then go over the use of the walky-talkies. I again stress the importance of using our codes if we have to say something in front of others, going over broadcasting texts. We should have no trouble doing this, except for Curlie, as it comes so natural to the rest of us.

"Remember, if you see anything suspicious, like a car that's following the bus to school, or the same car follows you home, a limo or SUV, you need to let us know about it right away by broadcasting it to us."

"Mama, I'm scared!" Curlie already has nightmares.

"I know, sweetie," I say trying to soothe her. I don't mean to add to her stress, but what we've discussed may keep her safe.

Jason, kneeling in front of her to take her small hands in his, says, "It's okay Curlie; Mel and I will be with you. Nothing's going to happen on my watch." Jason takes her other hand, places it on top of his as Mel adds her hand to the pile.

"See, like the Three Musketeers," Mel says confidently.

Jason glances at me, and he smiles self-assuredly. "It'll be okay Curlie, I promise."

*Shoes come in pairs, when will the other one drop?*

When we mention the small bug Jason found in his office; Glen agrees to purchase surveillance equipment with motion detectors. He will travel to Maryland to a company Gerald Tillman recommends, as he installed several cameras in his antique shop last year. Gerald also says we might want to keep a closer eye on the property now that we are semi-wealthy.

"Is it Ole Miss Abigail's ghost ya think's roamin the house?" Glen asks with a chuckle, "And ya want ta catch her?"

"Maybe," I say. "And maybe we can catch the little leprechaun that scared you so silly you won't get into Abigail's elevator?"

Glen screws up his face. "I didn't say it was a leprechaun, Missy."

"Then what was it?"

"Can't say for sure," he grumbles. "Don't want to talk about it."

"I'm not comfortable sharing information with you yet. If we get anything on tape, then maybe we can discuss it. Right now, it's a feeling that someone is watching. None of us planted that metal thingy in your office. It's better to be safe than sorry, wouldn't you agree?"

"Humph," he says. "S'pose you'll tell me what this is about when you're ready."

"By the way, Glen, do you own a handgun? If you do, can you get another one? I know you have a shotgun, but do you also have a CWP?"

Glen says yes, yes, and yes, then looks concerned, but doesn't ask questions. He accepts there must be a need for it. I don't want to learn how to shoot a shotgun, but a handgun's a different story altogether.

With the household mostly back to our *new normal,* Glen and I will concentrate on testing my theory about *Didgeridoo,* as we now have his papers to prove his lineage. However, since Glen is doing all the work while Jason's in school, it leaves little time.

I've stepped in to assist him, but I can't throw the hay into the loft or shovel out the stalls as quickly as he can. It's far more laborious and more tiring than I remember. I've said on more than one occasion that it's not rocket science, but Glen reminds me it's because I'm a woman.

"You're doin that all wrong, Missy," Glen sputters at me. "Ya gotta lift and throw more than that or you'll be here all day. That hay shoulda been in the loft by now. Ya make a terrible ranch hand, Missy!"

"You're right. I do make a terrible ranch hand. How the heck did you do this all by yourself, old man?"

After he stops laughing, we agree he needs to hire help. We discover other things about each other, often discussing topics we find interesting. We've come to rely on each other, and I trust the Murdock's with my family's very lives. Glen still questions my methods most of the time regarding the barn, but pays close attention when we discuss matters of the house, property, and finances.

Sitting at the old picnic table sipping my morning coffee, I notice the crisp smell of autumn that's permeating the air. October is glorious here in Virginia. A distant hum of a tractor off in a field somewhere is mingling with brays and sounds coming from our barn. The sky is bright with cumulous clouds rolling by. The line of large Oak Trees is majestically changing their leaves from green to a soft yellow and orange. Everything seems right and pleasant in my little corner of the world.

Terre's latest coded letter says Chicago is changing seasons too. I wish with all my heart we could be together for Christmas, but she doesn't want to jeopardize our welfare right now. We've put our plans of getting together on hold for the time being.

Christmas was always a magical time of the year for us, and I wonder what it will be like in our new home. Without our ornaments and treasured Christmas items, it will be difficult to get through.

Lenard and Gene pop into my mind, as they oversaw the removal of those treasured items. What are they up to and why have they been so unnervingly absent? Are they doing anything about my abduction and Ravi's death, or have they told me they would and have dropped the ball on that?

Glen's whistle brings me abruptly back to the present. Waving his walkie-talkie in the air, he puts it to his ear. After I turn it on, he says "get a move on; the company's a-callin.'" He's interviewing potential ranch hands today. A green pickup truck with a Virginia license plate has pulled into the parking area near the barn. The owner stands when he sees me, tips his hat off his head, and waits for Glen's introduction.

"This here's the owner of Ashwood," Glen says. "This is Hank Mitchell, Miss Ellen; he's from Stoneville, and he's interested in working here with us, coffee?" Then he proceeds to pour from the bottomless pot of coffee that always seems to emit a pungent odor.

"Nice to meet you, Ma'am," Hank says in a lazy drawl. Sticking his hand out to shake mine, he offers me the chair. Motioning for him to sit, he takes the mug Glen hands him.

"I'll stand, thanks."

"Says here ya worked for Lambert Stables over in Orwell? Eight years. Want ta tell us what ya did there?" Glen asks.

Remaining quiet as instructed, Glen nudges me as I stifle a laugh, shaking my head slightly when Hank tells us his experience with horses. He then thanks Hank for coming and we watch him get into his truck.

"What do ya think of Hank?" Glen asks.

"Do you honestly want my opinion?"

Glen ponders this for a moment, then says, "Yes, Missy, I want your opinion. I think he'll do."

"I don't."

"Miss Ellen, if we don't give 'em a try, how will ya know?" Glen growls.

"His hands aren't rough, and it looks like he stepped into those clothes out of a suit. Hank isn't what he appears to be, if that's even his real name."

"You're kiddin!" Glen says. "Okay. Steve's comin' in about thirty minutes. Let's give him a crack at this."

For the next two days, we interview a string of men named Darren, Sam, Donny, Elwood, Travis, Dean, Tommy, Chad, Billy-Bob, Charlie, and Blackie. They all turn out to be lacking true horse sense. And generally too green to have been on a farm when Glen and I grill them about simple tasks. When we call the phone numbers on their reference letters, we aren't surprised to find that none of these men worked at or near where they said they did.

"Where did you say you got these guys, Glen?"

"I called the number off the card Lenard gave me. He said if I need any help ta give this agency a call."

"That explains it!"

Glen looks dejected. "Explains what?"

"Lenard's keeping busy all right. We'll find help another way, okay? Why don't you go down to the track sometime this week and look at the work-wanted board? There's always someone looking for work around there. We'll screen them and run our own background checks."

Glen's a trusting soul that doesn't like the fact I get things quicker than he does. I reassure him that we'll bypass Lenard's attempt to have eyes and ears planted on our property for the intention of keeping a pulse on things.

Lenard's motives are not simple or innocent. Daddy taught me to watch my back. All those times we went to the track together, he would say how devious some owners are. He'd say, "Its mum's the word; keep it to yourself for now."

Glen doesn't have to know I learned early to trust my instincts. Daddy said it came natural and Jason has this ability to watch, listen, and make an assessment all within a split second. Daddy also said horseracing is like that. "You have a gift, use it wisely, and don't let your Mother know we go to the track."

After the children get on the school bus, I ask Glen to monitor our first session of training with *Didgeridoo*.

"I know you're the trainer, Glen, but would you indulge me a little? I have a theory about something and want the chance to prove it. Let *Didge* in when I'm a few feet away." I'm walking around inside the paddock, as our new practice track isn't ready yet.

"Okay, Missy let's give 'er a try."

My unorthodox methods amuse Glen, but I've been around horses long enough to know there are different ways to train them. It isn't long when *Didge* sidles up to walk beside me. He may bolt at any time, so I murmur to him while Glen and Rosie stand outside the fence to watch.

Glen's still amazed *Didge* allows me to put a halter on him. When I reach up to click the lead rope, we continue in a gentle arc until a cellphone rings. He jerks the line out of my hand and gallops away.

The cellphone is mine! I forgot one of our cardinal barn rules to turn our cellphones off or put it on vibrate. By this time, *Didge* is at the far end of the pasture with his rump facing me. It's his way of saying that he doesn't like the noise, go away and leave me alone. Glen is laughing, saying that will get me kicked out of the barn.

The following week, we're out on our new mile-long practice track composed of crushed limestone, as *Didge* doesn't wear shoes. The Farrier had argued this point with Miss Abigail when the former horse named *Lightning* was old enough to run around the fenced-in property. She maintained it was unnecessary to shoe her horses and stuck to her guns until she died. It is also a cause of disagreement with Glen as he figures I'll find out when my horse doesn't win. Which brings up another point, when we do race, we'll have to declare that our horse is unshod.

Glen harps on and on that we didn't need to put that kind of money into such a long practice track, as a shorter one would have done. But my theory is that our horses should practice and train on the same length of tracks they'll run on when they race. He maintains it will make no difference, but I contend they will.

Then he starts in on the use of hopples, saying we must use them as we train, but I would like to see *Didge* perform without them.

Rosie is herding *Didge* to the open gate. It isn't long when he's walking next to me; he has no halter on today, so we'll dispense with the lead rope. We go around one time and then head back to the barn.

"That's it? Glen says laughing. "Is that how ya think you're goin ta train him? I don't think you'll get him ta trot that way. Why don't ya let me at him?" Glen runs a hand over his face, past his wiry mustache, stopping to rest his hand on his chin.

"You had the better part of three years to do that, Glen. Why didn't you work with him then? Besides, he's getting used to me."

*I know how he hates to be wrong.*

"How much time do ya need, Missy? Do I have time ta go on vacation with my wife?"

"As much time as it takes, Mister Negative."

Every afternoon we repeat this, picking up the pace, jogging, then I try running as fast as I can. *Didge is* moving both legs on the same side forward in unison in a natural gait. Tiring faster than *Didge,* I stop halfway around the track with a pain in my right side.

Glen comes running out of the barn waving a white flag!

*Now it's my turn to laugh.*

"I'm sorry I ever doubted ya, Missy," he says in a breathless rush. Sticking the flag in his back pocket, he says, "Come here! Ya have ta see the photo I took. He's a natural, Missy! Look at his legs! I can't b'lieve it! How'd ya know?"

"I told you he was a Standardbred horse."

By this time, *Didge* has moved away and lost interest. As Glen and I study the picture, he zooms it in and out until we hear the familiar sound of the school bus brakes stutter to a stop near the end of the driveway.

"Your ranch hand's home."

Always wanting to get the last word in, he leans in to say, "I still think we should use them hopples on *Didge.*"

"We'll do that if we need to. *Didge* needs to get used to us first."

My theory about Didge is now fact. He can run as a pacer, not a trotter. As a pacer, he'll be faster and more critical to the betters at the track. The driver's job is to keep the horse even so that he can't break stride. Glen then argues why we need to use them. We get into discussions about what he contends is the correct term for the straps that are put on the horse's legs for that purpose.

"Tomato, to mat o, potato, pa tat o, hobbles, hopples, what is the difference?"

He thinks he's right, and maybe he is. All of the training videos show them on all of the harness racing pacer's legs, not necessarily on the trotters'. However, I'm adamant we don't use these yet.

We can now move on to my plans. Plan A involves *Didge* and how he reacts when we hook him up to a jog cart with no driver, allowing him to walk around the track. My theory for this is, although he won't like it, he'll get used to it quickly.

Plan B is to add another horse and jog cart, again with no driver. If this works, then maybe *Didge* will let me go to Plan C, which is to add a driver to his cart.

All this has to wait as other things take precedence, namely our quest for ranch help. Glen took several cards from the work board down at the track, but so far, he's received few return calls. He went again yesterday and ran into someone he says will stop by to meet us today.

Our first impression of Mr. Kurtis Anderson, II, is that he knows horses. He looks and walks the part of the horse/farm/ranch hand type we're looking for, and he is ruggedly handsome, tall, and muscular. His red pickup truck has Idaho vanity plates (WNBCB085) with a horse motif. When I start to laugh, Glen wants to know what the joke is.

"It's his license plate. I'm sure you'll figure it out," I say chuckling.

Glen and I agree we'll give Kurtis a chance once we know his background checks out. Of course, his papers could be forged like mine, but Glen needs help in the barn because I'm not up to mucking the stalls and throwing the bales around anymore, especially with him looking over my shoulder making snide remarks.

Kurtis Anderson starts tomorrow. He has no place to live and wonders if he can bunk over the garages? Since it has neither heat, air conditioning, nor running water, we agree that he can bunk in one of the small rooms off the kitchen, which are currently unoccupied.

We observe that Kurtis is on his cellphone every once in a while, and Glen and I wonder who might be on the other end. After a few weeks, his demeanor doesn't fit his description of the rodeo cowboy persona he gave us the first day. I'm not a suspicious person by nature, but I get a strange vibe from Kurtis when he looks my way. It isn't exactly creepy, but it's unsettling somewhat.

*Glen remarks that he must be sweet on me.*

During a routine check of our new surveillance disks, it captures a shadow coming into my office. Watching closely as the person tries to pry open the new lock on the bottom drawer of my desk, he gives up when it doesn't open. Then he starts to rummage through any drawer that will open, messes with the papers on the desktop, then moves to the bookcases, looking directly into our hidden camera.

"Gotcha! I'll bet I know who you're working for, Mr. Kurtis."

Copying the tape to a disk, I put it into a sleeve and place it into the secret compartment that I discovered in the paneling behind my desk. It's another one of Mrs. Ashwood's clever additions.

As anyone who lives near the Great Lakes can attest, we know what lake effect snow is like during the winter. We Chicagoans go into *winter mode* when temperatures drop into the 50s and snuggle up in our electric blankets and warm sleepwear.

Here in Virginia, we're uncertain that the old furnace, deep in the bowels of the basement, will keep us warm in this draughty old house. It belches black soot from time to time, and we find it on nearly everything. The local HVAC dealer said we should seriously think about a modern replacement that includes a cooling system. It would only cost a mere ten to twelve thousand dollars, and that's to start.

Until we can address the furnace issue, we have opened and cleaned the fireplaces, laying in several cords of wood, thanks to Kurtis. Glen says we're in a valley, and it doesn't get that cold here anyway, a little frost, maybe a little snow in December. He doesn't know how cold it gets in the main house at night as he goes off to his warm little cottage by the driveway or he sits in his stinky office with a quartz heater.

We wake to a light frost on the inside of the windows, which reminds me of our need to replace them. It moved down on the renovation list when other things took precedence. As I look out my bedroom window, the fields are dusted white in places with little sticks jutting out of the ground like the resistant weeds they are.

Thanksgiving is around the corner. Mr. C sent an email saying to expect five people this time. He wants a traditional turkey dinner with all the trimmings. Then he asks if I redecorated his rooms yet. Can he send wine ahead for his new cellar? Again, there is a *do not reply to this email message.*

Lenard's cellphone goes straight to his voicemail. When he calls two days later, I explain that I cannot reply to Mr. C's email request, and ask where he has been. Why does it take so long for him to get back to me?

"Why would you need to reply to his email?" Lenard asks gruffly. "Get the house ready as he asked you. And I don't have to report to you, Ellen. Don't you have enough to keep you busy without sticking your nose into my affairs!"

"What are you so huffed up about, Lenard? Give me access to him, and I won't bother you again. I need to discuss farm matters with him."

"Whatever you have to say to him, you can tell me. What is it, Ellen? You cannot have access to him. You know the rules."

"Tell him that he's welcome to spend Thanksgiving here at Ashwood, but he hasn't paid for his half of the expenses from the invoice I gave him during his last visit. It's only fair to inform him that he has to buy and prepare his own food. He'll also have to chop wood for the fireplace, do his laundry, and wash his flippin dishes."

"That is a little harsh, Ellen. I will not send him a message like that."

"Do I need to go over your head, Lenard?"

"Do not threaten me! I will do it this time but do not expect me to do it again. I am involved with other projects, and I am a very busy man!"

"Also tell him that I won't redecorate or put in a wine cellar until I see some money. But, please, do send some wine so we can enjoy it!"

"I will not send a message like that," Lenard snaps. "He will think we're..."

"Send it Lenard!"

Mr. C's return reply is speedy. He's had a change of plans and will be spending Thanksgiving in California after all. He's sorry for the oversight, but he'll send a check post haste. His sincerest apologies, and he hopes there is no ill will.

Although the children are disappointed that Mr. C is not coming, they let it drop after a few days. Since we have nothing except memories from our past celebrations, I surprise everyone with boxes of new ornaments and tiny twinkle lights. Mel takes the opportunity to share what she's been doing after school by opening a box containing twenty-four delicate hand-painted ornaments, each tied with red ribbon. None of us knew she had this talent.

During the weekend before their winter break, Jason, Mel, and Curlie are in the loft making a ruckus. I'm almost to the top of the ladder when Jason throws a bale of hay over my head. I duck trying to grab it, but it throws me off balance. Skipping several rungs on the ladder, I land like a lump on the barn floor. I'm judging from the pain in my left arm, that it's broken.

Mel screams, "Jay, Mom fell!"

Jason comes thumping down the ladder, and I can feel his hot breath near my face as he tenderly touches my cheek. "Mom? Can you hear me? Your arm looks funny. I didn't know you were on the ladder or I wouldn't have thrown that bale. You're not okay, are you?"

"ER," I manage to say. The pain allows for only a whisper.

"I understand," he says, turning toward Glen, who has come out of his office. "Get the truck, Mr. Murdock. Mom needs a doctor."

"Got it," he says.

"Mel, go get ice and tell Grandma what happened," Jason says, taking command. Curlie softly cries until Mel takes her by the hand to assure her that it was only an accident. "Curlie, go get the blanket off Mr. Murdock's chair," Jason asks her gently.

Rosie, who has entered the barn with Kurtis, is now whimpering and trying to lick my face while Jason is pulling her back by the collar. Kurtis then picks me up to carry me to the waiting truck. Mel returns with both the ice and Mother, who settles a towel under my arm.

Kurtis says not to worry about anything; he'll take care of chores tonight, but as Glen backs the truck up, Kurtis is visible in the passenger side mirror. He is talking on his cellphone.

Glen drives us to the nearest medical facility where they x-ray my arm, and I'm given something for the pain. It doesn't require surgery, but I'll have to come back in a few days when the swelling goes down so that they can cast it. Three hours later, we arrive back home in time for dinner.

Mother says she thought Jason would be the one to break something first. Mona baked me an entire pie, and Glen feels to blame for my clumsiness, but I assure him that it's entirely my fault for not paying attention. Kurtis is making a new ladder as several rungs completely broke during my way down to the barn floor.

After the children are tucked in their rooms for the night, I sneak into my office to contemplate our next move. The doctor said it would take about six weeks for my arm to heal properly. He gave strict orders that I can't go near the barn, or get on the practice cart until my arm heals. It presents the opportunity to concentrate on building permits for the next phase of the renovation plan, so it feels more like home, our home. I'm at my desk when Kurtis knocks on the doorjamb.

"How are you doing, Miss Ellen?"

"Okay, for someone with a broken wing!"

"I came to check on you. Do you need anything before I turn in?" Kurtis sits down on the sofa, even though I haven't invited him to do so.

I'm in modest pain and semi-snarky mood. "I know how you're checking, Kurtis. You can tell Lenard I said hello. Get your things and get the hell out of here."

Kurtis looks at me in surprise. "How did you know?" he asks.

"It's more like, when did I know. I had my suspicions the first day you came here. I saw you make a call on your cellphone when we left today."

"That doesn't prove anything. You don't know who I was talking to," Kurtis says defensively.

"Oh? The fall didn't break the cellphone in my pocket. It's the oddest thing because Lenard called while we were in x-ray, said how sorry he was I was injured. I've left message after message for that man, and he doesn't call back for days, yet he called today."

"That still doesn't prove anything," Kurtis mutters.

"But you don't deny knowing him. You can take your eyes and ears off this property when you leave. And don't let the door hit you in the ass on your way out!"

*He is unaware that his image was on the tape.*

"You could use my help now, Ellen. Why don't you let me stay until your arm heals? I won't tell anyone what you're doing here. Let me stay, okay?" Kurtis asks.

"Goodbye, Kurtis. We'll miss your help, but not your connection to Lenard. It was a sneaky thing for both of you to do. If you're not out of here in thirty minutes, I'm calling Sheriff Rocky. And tell Mr. Lenard I'm going over his head and calling his boss if he doesn't stop this insidious snooping!"

A short time later, the back screen door slams shut, and Kurtis' truck leaves the driveway spewing gravel. Five minutes later, Glen comes running into my office. He wants to know why Kurtis lit '*outta here like lipstick on a pig.*'

"What does that mean, Glen?"

"It's an expression," he says, "means slippery or somethin."

Trying to explain that Kurtis is one of Lenard's spies, Glen expresses concern, realizing the ramifications of his departure. We need to do the whole interview thing again. Maybe we'll get lucky this time, and someone will fall into our midst, someone we can trust completely, and someone who doesn't know Lenard or Gene. Someone who wants an honest job on an unpretentious horse farm.

*A girl can dream, can't she?*

On a whim, I contact Gerald as he mentioned he knew someone who was on a ranch out west and might be coming back this way. He says he spoke with his family in North Carolina and it seems Gerald's

Aunt Brenda has an old friend who has a son who's looking for a job. He also has experience with horses and may be what we need.

The man's name is Reed Devlin. He holds a Bachelor of Equine Studies and Therapeutic Horsemanship from the University of Wyoming, which sounds too good to be true. I'm skeptical until the head of the University says that Reed Devlin is indeed who he says he is. He taught at the university for several years, then went to work for a local ranch. He's a nice fellow, a good student when he studied there, mentioning that he often saw his name in the newspaper, something to do with disabled children out at Diablo's Dude Ranch.

Gerald knows what we went through interviewing the last time, although I left out parts about why Kurtis is no longer with us, he assures me we won't be disappointed. Reed will be here day after tomorrow. Gerald also mentions that we are sure to like him.

Glen offers his opinion by mumbling under his breath that we might as well try it because things can't get much worse. After Kurtis left, Glen bribed several men down at the track, which mostly showed up when they said they would, but mostly didn't do much when they did.

*In my opinion, Reed is getting here right in the nick of time!*

*"Hope springs eternal."*

~ Alexander Pope

# *Chapter Eleven*

## Trial and Error

**A** construction crew is here to replace the old copper tubing in the bathrooms. Our architect also located a reputable manufacturer who makes double-glazed replacement windows that the National Register approves. They assure us they will fit right into the odd sized frames perfectly.

*Has anything fit perfectly here?*

The next construction crew will check the attic ceiling, walls, and flooring. They will then spray insulation where there is none, making sure the roof is sound. We have doubts about it, as there are numerous patches to suggest otherwise. It comes as no surprise when the roofer presents a hefty bill to replace it. No one questions why there's a wall above my bedroom and buys my explanation that it's a closet to store wool clothes.

The third construction crew is wrecking the kitchen. After we devoted countless hours to the design, consulting with all the women of the house, we've come up with a new configuration. It will allow for better access to all rooms coming into and out of this central hub. No one can use it right now, because it's bare from ceiling to floor, including all lathwork and plaster.

The joists under the sagging kitchen floor have been replaced, including the back porch. It was necessary to dig along the foundation and lay perforated pipe to wick away water that had been seeping into the basement. Then new gutters and downspouts were tied into a system that now drains out into the yard away from the house, which should take care of the damp dungeon odor in the basement.

The kitchen countertops are approximately seven to ten days out from being delivered. The timetable puts the completion for this at another week, maybe two, which means our choices are to cater our meals, go out to eat, or use Mona's new kitchen.

We used the restaurant option a few times but Mother and Mona complained about the unimaginative chef who puts mushrooms in nearly every dish! Frankly, we're a little sick of pizza, Chinese take-out, tacos, and are extremely anxious to get this done. Either way, we're spending our first Christmas together in our new house with our new family, with or without our new kitchen.

Every day, a truck or two delivers boxes of every size that contain cabinets, appliances, fixtures, handles, tile, and flooring that go into the unused Billiard Room we now call THE STORE. Mother's in charge, making sure things are available for the contractors. Workers have to sign in for what they need for the day; then Mother locks it up at night to keep things from going missing. The alcove has been temporarily boarded up, also to help prevent this from happening.

The Gate House kitchen renovation moved up a notch and Mona is happy to abandon the mess at the Manor House in favor of her own. She's doing her usual baking in her shiny new stainless steel 9.2 cubic foot double ovens installed yesterday. We all laugh when Mona tells us she has another theory about baked goods that taste better, baked in new ovens.

The engineer sent a report that explains in painful detail that the barn structures need stabilization, as they can no longer take the load off the loft and roof sections. If we don't do this, the barn will collapse and kill all within. It will take a hoist and crane-type piece of equipment to right it.

The engineer suggests we think about doing this soon before snow accumulates and it falls in on itself this winter. The bill for this work is as staggering an amount as the one presented for the new roof for the Manor House. It will take a team of workers to install reinforced steel beams. But, before they perform any work, the county engineers have to review the proposal, which needs approval before securing the necessary and costly permits.

When will we see the conclusion to the never-ending projects that require urgent attention here? The words *money pit* and *black hole* hardly come close to what I want to call it!

We are pleasantly surprised how comfy the house is now. When moths flutter amidst the flames or things crawl out of the woodpiles, it doesn't bother Jason, but it freaks Mel out when something scurries across the floor. The big hairy spider Jason caught yesterday went to school so his Science class could study it. Mel and Curlie refused to sit with him on the bus.

Commotion is going on all over the house as crews come in and out. Mother has taken charge of directing traffic. With her trusty clipboard in hand, she makes sure the workers are where they're supposed to be, not snooping in and around where they don't belong.

The Maryland Company that supplied us with the surveillance equipment is here to install a state-of-the-art alarm system because I'm not sure our little drama is over. They were asked to use unmarked vehicles and no-name shirts, so that they can blend in with other workers.

The plumbing contractor ran into difficulties in some of the bathrooms, which will halt work for now until the first of the year. He's apologetic for the disappointment, but there isn't a lot he can do about it. When you're dealing with a house this old, it's very unpredictable.

We all breathe a collective sigh of relief when Mr. C sends an elegant Christmas card with *Best Wishes and Good Cheer for a Happy & Healthy New Year*. He's going skiing somewhere in the Alps, having his Christmas Holiday on the Italian Riviera.

*There is no check with the card, only glitter.*

It reminds me of Lenard's silence, as he hasn't returned my call from last week. Leaving him another message, I again ask him to request funds from the other investors. I'm starting to get angry when Glen buzzes the walkie-talkie.

"Reed's here, better get a move on, Missy, if you want ta meet him."

"Please, God," I pray. "Let this be our Prince, so we don't have to kiss any more frogs! At the thought of Prince, my mind wanders to a faraway land. Why has Abdul popped into my head?

*Go away! I don't have time for you today!*

Reed's background check came back with sterling results, but we need to meet him in person to make our final evaluation! As I get to the barn, Glen is busy filling his cup from his never-ending pot of stale coffee, then offers some to Reed, but he declines. I like him already.

"This is Ms. Thompson, Reed, owner of Ashwood."

"It's nice to meet you, Mrs. Thompson," he says in a smooth, clear voice. Extending a calloused hand, my quick assessment of Reed is a favorable one judging from his easy smile and general politeness. We saw none of this when we interviewed the dirty dozen Lenard sent our way.

"Hello, Reed, please sit down and tell us a little about yourself."

"Gerald Tillman said you needed someone to help with the horses. I know horses, so here I am. I was sorely looking for a job," Reed says quietly.

Reed looks like an honest to goodness cowboy. He talks like one and sounds like one, too. Glen's serious face gradually softens to a kind of amazement as Reed starts describing how he went out west after he fell off his horse playing polo. His moment of glory dashed with the broken leg that kept him out of the '92 Olympics.

Someone mentioned a school for therapeutic horsemanship, and he knew he had to pursue it after his recovery. Once he graduated, he stayed at the University of Wyoming to teach. He left after a few years to work at a nearby ranch.

The owner had a great program that he let Reed manage. It is where he met, married, and divorced his wife of nine years. She abandoned Reed when he started to devote too many hours to the disabled children who flocked to his lessons. She couldn't handle it, apparently needing more attention than he could give her.

When the Diablo Dude Ranch went belly-up, Reed wasn't prepared to purchase it. The new owner told him they would no longer run a babysitting service and practically shut it down overnight. Reed is 32 years old; he's ready and willing, no job is too small or too big.

"If you want me to give riding lessons or some training, a fence mended or put in; I can do that. If you want the stalls mucked out, wood chopped, stacked and feed hauled in, whatever you need me to do. Is that what you needed to know?" he says finishing with a grin.

Glen and I can spot a liar at ten paces. When we conducted all the interviews that netted us that bunch of misfits that called themselves cowboys, we immediately saw through their ruse.

"Good so far, Reed. Do you know a Lenard Casings?" I ask.

"No, can't say as I know anyone by that name," Reed responds.

"Do you know a Gene Thornburg?"

"No, don't know anyone by that name either, Miss Ellen," Reed says, scratching his head, wrinkling his forehead.

"How many bales of hay can ya handle at once?" Glen asks.

"Interesting question, one under each arm with a bag of feed on my head," Reed answers.

"Can you be trusted to run the stables by yourself if Glen has to be away?" I hadn't told Glen I would ask this, and by his expression, he is a bit confused.

"Am I going somewhere, Missy?" Glen asks, then I tap him on the arm and he says, "Oh."

"I've had a lot of experience managing stables if that's what you're asking. I put a plan together for Diablo Dude Ranch. The man who bought it didn't want to run it that way anymore and chucked the whole thing out, including me. I brought the material if you want to see it," he concludes."

"Yes, I'd like to go over it with you. So, you've never heard of Lenard or Gene, hum?"

"No, never heard of either one of them. Should I know these people? Are they important to the stables?"

He seems so sincere that I want to throw him a curve ball. "Do you know a Ravenalt Andress?"

Glen and Reed both say, "Who?" at the same time.

"Never mind, I wanted to see if you knew him either."

"Know anything about breakin a horse?" Glen asks.

Reed shrugs his broad shoulders and nods, "Oh yeah. I did a little rodeo stint awhile back."

"Tell us a little about the lessons for the children."

"Sure. The children are special and need to feel like they're normal, that they don't have handicaps, and the horses made them feel good.

We do simple things at first and progress from there. The horses are trained to be gentle, and you can hang your hat on their smiles, the children's smile, not the horses, I think they chuckle though."

"You have a sense of humor, that's good. What do you know about harness racing?"

Reed scratches his head again, "Miss Ellen, I have to be honest with you. I don't know anything about harness racing. But I do know how to train horses and how to care and feed them." His words are what we want to hear, exactly. "I can also make websites and brochures, and know a little marketing and what I don't know, I can sure learn."

Glen and I glance at each other and then at Reed. "You're hired," we say together.

Is this a déjà vu moment left over from a Lenard and Gene routine? I get a cold chill at the thought. Glen leans forward to shake Reed's hand and then I do the same.

"Welcome aboard, Reed. Come to the house when you've seen everything Glen wants to show you. We can fill out the stack of forms I know you're anxious to get to."

"Sure thing, Miss Ellen, and thank you," Reed says, grinning. His laugh is natural and relaxed.

"Oh, we didn't mention salary . . ."

"That's okay. We can talk about it later. I know you'll be fair. You look like honest folks to me. And thanks for giving me a chance."

Glen and I exchange glances, he smiles broadly, nodding his head and I know that he's as pleased with Reed as I am.

"Don't thank us yet, Reed. You need to give it three months. If either one of us doesn't like the arrangement, we part as friends, okay?" Didn't Mr. C and Lenard say those same words to me, not six months ago?

"That seems fair to me, Miss Ellen."

"I have to warn you; I have three children who will make your life miserable if you screw anything up!" Pointing my finger at him, Glen sucks in his breath.

Reed's smile turns into easy laughter. "I know kids, Miss Ellen, almost as well as I know horses."

As I study this teddy bear of a man, it gives me comfort. "They're going to like you, Mr. Reed; they're going to like you very much."

Reed will stay in an upstairs bedroom until his room and bathroom are ready on the ground floor off the kitchen. The servant's quarters over the garages may or may never be livable again, and it's off the radar as far as renovations go.

The surveillance equipment and motion detectors, strategically placed within the house, are now operational. Items installed in the barn give us additional peace of mind.

Since Glen refused to vacate his space in the barn, Reed will make himself at home in Mrs. Ashwood's office off the Morning room. The built-in bookshelves await his unpacked boxes that are stacked along one wall.

He wanted to put his old, battered, flea-infested sofa in there, but I made him take it to the dump. He's quite all right with the leather one taking its place. He's a big man who dwarfs the chair he's sitting on at the desk he brought with him. The astounding thing is that he looks comfortable. It's as if Mrs. Ashwood had this room built for him.

As I begin to recall our past Thanksgivings, we'd talk about our annual Holiday Surprise Day after consuming our dinner. Each family member would put a suggestion into a paper bag and Mother would select someone to pull it out. All twelve of us loved doing this on the second Sunday in December. It was a magical time of the year for us. We walked about town oohing and ahhing over colorful window displays before attending the local ballet when they performed the Nutcracker. We had many an excellent dinner in lakefront restaurants during this time.

*How will we do this with so many family members not present?*

When no one mentions the Holiday Surprise Day, Mother says we're going to start a new tradition. Reed came up with a perfect replacement called the *Magic of Christmas*. Glen and Reed purchased a pair of draft horses and a wagon at auction a few days ago. It will be used to take people around the property for five dollars a person. It follows the old horse trails into the woods and around the little creek on our property.

The pine and spruce trees line most of the paths, and it's picturesque any time of the year, but it becomes a whimsical place at dusk because Reed hung large lighted ornaments along the trail. Once the ride is over, our guests are invited into the living room of the Manor House to warm themselves by the ever-present fire, and of course treated to Mona's decorated cookies and steaming mugs of hot chocolate.

The amazing part is that people will come from as close as the bustling town of Stoneville, and as far away as Washington D. C. The *Magic of Christmas* is Reed's project, his sole responsibility, and will collect and distribute the funds to a children's charity of his choice. Reed not only made a brochure for the *Magic of Christmas* but one for Ashwood Stables, complete with websites and photos.

"It'll be trial and error at first," Reed says. "You have to try something to see if it works, and if it does, then it can become a success with a little work. You know all about that, Miss Ellen. Glen said you turned this place around right quick. He showed me the old photos."

"Did he? Yes, it sure was trial and error, and we marvel at all we did. I'm very grateful for what we have, because in a way, that too, is a magical gift."

One thing stands out about Reed. He's not a braggart and beams when he says the *Magic of Christmas* is booked solid until the end of February, which means that the charity he chose will have their coffers filled to the brim for the upcoming holidays.

In the two weeks since Reed is with us, he ingratiates himself with Curlie when he figures out her real name of Cuthbertina. She's delighted as no one else has ever known what it is except her family!

The barn stabilization went so well we can go into it without the threat of it falling in on us. Glen and Reed then decorated it with garland strung with L.E.D. lights, then did the same thing along the fence at the entrance to the driveway. We purchased enough faux wreaths and red bows for every forward-facing window, including the Gate House and garages. Mona says they hadn't been able to do that type of thing since Miss Abigail was around.

"This is how it's supposed ta look," Mona says in quiet reverence. "It's like a picture postcard!"

*At night, it is truly magical!*

New-fallen snow covers the ground, and our new windows have frost on the outside instead of the inside. Glen says that's funny because it doesn't usually snow here. Could he be wrong about this?

"Can't remember," he says, chuckling.

The furnace continues to belch black soot, but the house is warm and comfortable. The visible cracks in the outside brick and chimneys are nonexistent, thanks to the repointing, the many tubes of caulking, and bags of mortar. All gutters, downspouts, and splash guards function properly, and we are *snug as a bug in a rug*, as Glen seems pleased to say.

Our first Christmas in our new house promises to be memorable, but it isn't complete until Glen, Reed, and the children traipse out to the back forty to dig up a five or six-foot spruce tree. After Christmas, we'll plant it near the Manor House in remembrance of this auspicious occasion. It's sitting in a big tub filled with water, waiting for Mel's unique ornaments and the boxes of items I squirreled away that will now become our new memories.

Lenard and Gene sent a colossal tower of goodies along with a note that their offices have moved. They'll also be out of the country on assignment, have a wonderful holiday, and don't worry about Mr. C, as he'll be okay.

It doesn't feel right as there's no return address on the package. As long as we have no immediate threat, as there were a few months ago, we don't need them snooping around anyway. Mona says she hasn't seen anything in the tabloids even related to Mr. C, nothing connected with movies or otherwise. Then I remember that he mentioned some gambling debts. Could this be what Lenard means?

Sitting in my office, I absently stick a pencil in the opening of the cast that remains on my arm. Maybe I can coerce Reed to saw it off because it itches so terribly.

With tears in her eyes, Mother wraps on the doorjamb. "Houston, we have a problem!"

"What is it, Mother? Have you heard from Terre?"

"Yes, it's Danny. He's had an accident. I want to go to Terre, but I know I'm not supposed to leave. I don't want to let either of you down. What should we do, Ellie?"

"What happened to Danny?" Has the long arm of our troubles found my sister and her family?

"There was a freak accident, and Danny needs surgery," Mother sniffs.

"What kind of freak accident was it?"

"Terre said they left Danny home alone. They're trying to carry on our tradition of doing Holiday Surprise Day," Mother says, dabbing her face.

"He's seventeen; they often leave him alone. It's more like he doesn't want to see the Nutcracker again, Mother. Are you sure?"

"Danny said he had a headache. They asked him to check in every hour or so. When he didn't, Terre and Dennis got worried and went home. That's when they found him in the kitchen, lying on the floor with an arrow through his shoulder. The police think it's someone hunting near their house. It went right through the back door window right into Danny!"

"Terre has a contingency plan that she and her husband taught their children as we instructed ours, but this doesn't seem logical. I don't want you going anywhere. Let me think about this, and we'll come up with something, okay? When is the surgery scheduled?"

*A sense of foreboding washes over me.*

"It's in a few hours. I can't get there that fast anyway. Oh, Ellie, I know that look, you don't think it's an accident do you?"

"I don't know, but you can't go. How good of an actress are you? You have to act like nothing's wrong, or Mel and Curlie will know something's up. I know Jason can handle this and I'll tell him later."

Mother is understandably concerned. Someone is up to something, I'm sure of it. Is this the second shoe to drop? Who is trying to scare us? I don't feel comfortable involving Lenard. I need to formulate a plan.

Taking Reed outside to discuss a detour from his holiday plans, he readily agrees to do something for me, saying he'll get in and out without anyone asking questions. I'm so grateful that I hug him, surprised when he hugs me back. His aftershave lingers on my cheek, which then reminds me of Ravi. A peacefulness about him makes me contented. It's at this point that my gut tells me that Reed can be trusted implicitly.

The next morning, Reed announces he's going home for Christmas and will be gone about three days. Glen and Jason will handle the chores and with the *Magic of Christmas* suspended for a few days; the workload is less. Mother's eyes reflect trepidation. If she suspects anything, she's keeping it to herself.

Rummaging around in my closet, I pull out the suitcase stuffed with presents that were secreted away and suddenly remember the three leather books. Removing them from the wall safe, I sit in the middle of the closet floor. What could possibly make them bulge?

Using a metal nail file, I carefully loosen the leather from the inside cover of *Moby Dick*. Exerting slight pressure, I slip it along the edge where it doesn't match. When it breaks free, the leather cover comes away stiffly. Thin plastic covers two flat folded bundles that are on top of the front of the book.

I wouldn't put smuggling drugs past Abdul or Jam-ale, except it isn't what I think it is. On the back of the book are three piles of flattened, discolored one thousand dollar bills, the face being someone distinguished like one of our U.S. Presidents, but he doesn't look familiar.

*Are the bills counterfeit?*

During college and summer months, I worked at a bank, but I don't remember seeing bills of this denomination. It will be difficult to count as its fragile and stuck together. Struck by the implications of what this might mean, I carefully peel the plastic off the folded papers, realizing I can't decipher the writing. It appears to be the same type of script as the notes Abdul wrote me, but they aren't in English and I can't read them.

Comparing the note Abdul put in *For Whom The Bell Tolls;* it's evident another hand wrote these a long time ago. A small ink smudge near the bottom looks familiar. It's the same design tattooed on Jamaile's neck and arm.

Curious about the other two books, I repeat the process to find the same thing under each of the other covers. The documents are not the same but have comparable writing with additional piles of flattened bills. The last book contains a tiny object that looks similar in size to a computer chip.

Footsteps in the hallway indicate someone is walking toward my room. "I'm wrapping Christmas presents, do not come in here!"

"Okay, Mom, only checking on you," Jason says as Rosie woofs.

Using my laptop, I search a website about U.S. Treasury Currency. It turns out that Grover Cleveland is the one who graces the front. The discolored bill on the monitor looks like the one in my hand, right down to the serial numbers and seal. The backs of the money are all green, and they look like monopoly money compared to our currency today.

My research finds that limited amounts of $500, $1,000, and $5,000 bills were printed at one time, along with a $10,000 bill. The money in my possession is dated 1934A Federal Reserve Notes and are for Government use only, but are still considered legal tender. They don't exactly look real to me, because the ink seems faded and the green looks different, but they must be worth a small fortune in the hands of a collector.

What are the odds of finding something of this magnitude? It smacks of intrigue to me, but I don't dare take the money to the bank, especially to that blowhard Yancy. Since the little chip thing is unexplainable, it will wait until an expert can determine what it is.

Gathering up the piles, I take the bundles and little chip to the safes to put with the tiny key and the bug Jason found. Why did Abdul entrust this to my keeping? What did he expect me to do with all this? Was I supposed to turn the books over to Lenard? Why didn't he warn me about it?

Curious about the value of the books, I run a search on each of them, shocked beyond words to find a First Edition *Moby Dick* is worth upwards of $40,000! This *Moby Dick* is not the same one I sacrilegiously defaced, but it has no doubt decreased its worth, too.

The Italian book is currently worth about $17,000. Since I didn't touch that one, it's most likely why Abdul kept it. The rest of the search is discouraging as the other books are not first editions.

*On a hunch, I call Lenard's cellphone. It is disconnected.*

Locating the FBI website, it states that their offices are closed due to the Christmas Holidays, but will reopen on January third. If this is an emergency, call 911 or your local police department.

At the contact prompt, I leave my name and phone number, but no message other than I want to speak to someone in authority about an issue with a few of their agents.

The coziness of our living room, the smell of pine boughs permeating the air, and the crackle of wood in the fireplace make us feel truly blessed to spend this holiday together. But it comes and goes all too fast.

We paused to recall that a few months ago; we were living completely different lives. We didn't know what the future held for us then, but we are content in the knowledge that we have one now.

Reed returns saying he has news. Rosie takes the opportunity to accompany us outside. He not only did what I asked him to do, but he was also able to spend a day with his parents on the way back to Ashwood.

"What did you find out?" I ask anxiously.

"I went to the hospital and met your sister and her husband like you asked me to and gave them your letter. And I have to tell you, Miss Ellen, they're scared right now."

"I know she appreciated that you went there. Did the police find anything?"

"The police gave them a doozy of a story about a hunter who was in the woods. It's such a bogus story it isn't funny, Miss Ellen. They live in a nice neighborhood. To have a hunter with that kind of bow and arrow is highly unlikely. I couldn't ask the local police about it, so I left it at that."

In the back of my mind, this story didn't wash anyway, and now Reed is confirming my fears. "Thank you, Reed. How's Danny doing?"

"The boy's going to be alright, Miss Ellen. It was a clean wound. It was a big shock for him, though."

"You gave up your Christmas to do this for us."

"I was happy to do it." Reed smiles, "You know I have a soft spot for kids in trouble. And I spent yesterday with my family, so it's all good."

"I don't know how to thank you, Reed."

"No thanks are needed. You're good to me, letting me stay here, giving me a job when you did."

"What did you tell my sister?"

"I told them exactly what you told me and gave them your envelope. Then your sister wrote this for you." Handing me a folded piece of paper, I open it to read, then put it into my pocket with the intention of sharing it with Mother later.

"At least Terre and her family will be safe for a while, Reed. Um, did you also get that little package I asked you to get?"

"I'll bring it to your office later, Miss Ellen. It's in my suitcase."

I asked Reed to get a small Glock pistol as he has a CWP. Both Daddy and Ravi insisted Jason and I learn how to use one as they were away on business so often. Lenard thought I shouldn't have mine because the one in my bedroom nightstand never made it to

Virginia. My license isn't valid anyway, so I'll have to reapply sometime down the road.

Reed will eventually get two more pistols, maybe a shotgun for hunting. Glen meant to honor my request, but with one thing or another, we both forgot about it. Jason is a proficient shot, and we'll practice together, as soon as things settle down again.

"I was wondering how you learned to shoot a thing like that, Miss Ellen. Why you would even need one?"

"It's for security. I lost my husband a few months ago. I'll feel more secure having it."

"Glen mentioned that. From what I've gathered, you must've lived an unusual life before you all came here. You and your family must be wrapped up in the most intriguing story I've ever had the pleasure of being a part of," Reed says thoughtfully. "Are you running from the MOB by any chance?"

I'm trying to be nonchalant, repeating the concocted story that we were to tell people if they asked why we moved here. "Don't be silly, Reed. Up until a few months ago, our lives were rather mundane and normal. I had to get away after my husband died. We decided to come to Virginia to raise horses."

"Either way, you can count me in, cause so far, my life hasn't been all that exciting. I have your back, Miss Ellen; no matter what, you can count on me."

After dinner, I share my sister's letter with Reed and Mother, cautioning Reed that there may be things in it I can't explain right now. He looks bewildered, and it must take considerable effort to keep his mouth shut, but he goes along with the request.

Mother takes the letter. She reads it, then looks up to say, "Thank you, Reed, it means a lot to all of us to know that Terre and her family are okay for the time being. I hope it doesn't come to . . ." She lets her sentence hang in the air and walks away.

"I know you have questions, Reed, but let this rest for now."

Reed shakes his head in understanding. Reaching into his pocket for the little pistol, he hesitates before handing it over. "Take your time, Miss Ellen. I'm not going anywhere unless you decide I don't fit in here."

"Honestly, it's quite a quagmire. I'm not sure I believe it myself. Someday we'll talk about it, but not now. If it doesn't make sense to me, how can it make sense to you? Besides, I think you fit very nicely into our eclectic family."

*Dear Ellie and Mother,*

*Your man, Reed came right when we needed him. The doctor said Danny should be okay. He'll have a little scar, but he's young and healthy and doing well. It's lucky that they are all on vacation, so no one knows at his school.*

*After Dennis and I talked it over, we will do what you ask. We will remain here for the time being and take the necessary precautions.*

*Please stay safe, and we will let Mother know if there is anything out of the ordinary or if anything strange happens, we will contact her in the usual way.*

*Until we meet at the prearranged place on the date you designated, we will be on our guard. Take care of yourselves. I can't imagine what you've been through, but I hope we'll be able to sit down one day to talk about it. That's what I miss most about you!*

*Much Love and Thoughts, Terre and family*

"Fair enough, Miss Ellen. I'll take your word for it and reckon you'll tell me when you're ready. Good night, and thanks for everything."

"Oh, no, Reed, it's my family who thanks you. You were the only one we trusted to pull this off for us."

"Happy to do it and let me know if there is anything else I can do for you."

"There is one more thing, Reed."

"What's that?" he says laughing, raising his eyebrows.

"Can you saw this thing off my arm; it's driving me crazy!"

"Sure, I'll go get a saw."

We finally have someone we can trust. Although Reed is missing information about my family, he will be someone who Glen and I can talk with about our ideas for the farm. Until then, we are going to enjoy the start of the New Year. And the removal of this incongruous, itchy cast!

On the fourth day of January, a Mr. Evan Taylor calls from the FBI Special Agent Unit Office. He begins by asking what my purpose was for calling their office and then starts to give me the third degree. Without going into too much detail, I request the supervisor for Lenard Casings, Gene Thornburg, and Andrea Simmons, mentioning their appalling behavior and mishandling of my case.

Mr. Taylor puts me on hold, and after several minutes he informs me that there are no people with those names operating out of their office as agents. "They don't show up anywhere else within the FBI spectrum for that matter, either, Ma'am. Could you be mistaken about what office they said they represent? Could they be with the CIA?"

"I'm quite certain their badges said FBI, Special Agents."

"I'm sorry to inform you, Ma'am, but we have no one by those names. I suggest you contact the CIA."

Mr. Taylor says the CIA's Office of Intelligence & Analysis might be able to help me. He kindly gives me their number and wishes me luck. A Mr. Hopkins puts me on hold, returning a few minutes later to inform me that there is no record of any agents with those names. He also checked with the U.S. Department of Justice who administers the Federal Witness Protection Program, and there is no record of us, either.

*Why didn't I deal with it when my gut first told me to call the FBI?*

Mr. Hopkins then transfers me to a Mr. Adrian Sellers who is from the Daily Operations Office. He sounds sympathetic when I tell him why I've called.

"What's this all about, Mrs. Thompson? How can I help you?"

I'm still reeling from the news that neither office has ever heard of any of us. When I don't answer, Mr. Sellers asks if I would care to come into their office to discuss the matter. Agreeing, I then make an appointment for the following week. As I share this news with the family, they are not surprised at this development.

Jason says, "It explains so much, yet it doesn't."

"What kind of convoluted situation are you people in?" Glen wants to know.

But I don't have those answers. Ravi and I are responsible for this fiasco! We've involved everyone we love! Why wasn't I more in-tune with my instincts? It is bizarre! How could I have been this bamboozled by Lenard and Gene? They were so convincing! What will we uncover, once I tell my story to yet another group of people? Will they believe me?

*It's a disturbing development I should have anticipated.*

I have typed, recorded, copied and burned CDs, including all of my original notes and sketches, asking my family for patience as this situation unravels. They have given me their unending support with their promise to remain cautious while I'm gone. Jason offers to come with me to meet Mr. Sellers, but I decline his invitation knowing that he has an English exam tomorrow.

The trip north along Route 95 is uneventful until I try to navigate from McLean to Langley and miss the exit. When the GPS squawks to get off, I listen to it this time.

The CIA structure is a one-story building with glass windows across the front. A large, menacing-looking guard greets me. He takes my passport, looks at my face and hands it back. Sticking a VISITOR pass on the inside of my windshield, he says that the visitor's parking lot is straight ahead.

The young woman at the reception desk reaches for my passport and driver's license. Smiling, she says a Mr. Sellers, from the Office of IA, is expecting me. As she hands back my items, she nods to a uniformed guard standing off to the side of an elaborate security screening machine. With light blue gloves, this guard runs a wand through my purse and bag, then places them onto a conveyor belt.

Another guard escorts me into a small room where she points to an X on the floor, asking me to stand in front of a white screen. Moments later, she hands me a photo badge with my name in big bold letters. I must sign out at the front desk, where the badge is turned in. I must sign back in to retrieve my name badge whenever I return.

*What makes her think I'm coming back?*

A young woman in a colorful dress escorts me to a large room. The furnishings are like any ordinary conference room with two large nondescript paintings of gently sloping hillsides and colonial type houses on one wall, with a large white board with markers on another.

At the room's center is a large table with several rolling chairs. A window overlooks a small pond where geese and ducks are wandering past. I sit down as the door opens, and a man with a toothy grin walks in ahead of a much taller man.

"Mrs. Thompson? Thanks for coming in today," says the shorter man. He takes my outstretched hand, holding it gently, saying, "I'm Agent Adrian Sellers, and this is Agent Lawrence Desmond. We're from the Office of Intelligence & Analysis. We're so glad you came in to meet with us today. Can we get you something to drink?"

Mr. Desmond pulls a chair out and sits down, asking politely, "Did you have a nice Holiday, Mrs. Thompson?"

"Let's cut the crap, shall we? I have a horrendous story, and frankly, I'm a little crazy because of it. And yes, it was a nice Holiday, thanks. May I see your identification please?"

"Sure," Mr. Sellers says with a grin. He unclips a badge from his belt and lays it on the table, pushing it toward me. Lawrence reaches for his badge and then tosses it on the table, where it lands with a clunk. "You realize you are in the official CIA building, don't you?"

They're not in folded cases like the ones Lenard and Gene flashed at me. They seem to be the genuine article, but then what do I know? Studying Mr. Sellers for a moment, he has neatly trimmed brown hair and eyes to match. He's pleasant but not too friendly, and appears to be the senior of the duo.

Mr. Desmond towers over Adrian. He must have left his jacket in another room. His holster hangs over one shoulder, and he nonchalantly dislodges it when I look at him, laying it on the table.

"Mrs. Thompson, you got me thinking so I ran those names you gave me through our system again, legal and illegal . . ." The men laugh at some inside joke. "Those people are nowhere in our system."

"Why doesn't that surprise me? Are you people for real? Almost everyone I've met in the last six months is not who they say they are!"

In a gentle tone, Mr. Sellers says, "We're real, Mrs. Thompson. Would you like to tell us what this is all about? Maybe we can help you."

"How much time do you have?"

"All the time you need, Ma'am," Mr. Desmond says.

"Those fake idiot FBI people confiscated everything and gave us new identities. I have all the papers they gave us, the one the bank gave me for the property, all our passports, and social security cards. Can you check to see if these are real?"

"It might take a few days to verify," Mr. Sellers says, reaching for the packet. "There is a possibility they might not be real."

"I figured as much."

Mr. Desmond nods his head. "Do you mind if we record this?"

"I don't know if you need to. I've gone ahead and put it all on CDs and printed copies for you." I pull out a bundle of papers that took the better part of last week to compile. "I made two copies in the event more people need to see them today. It will help you understand what happened. I wanted it down on paper as the official report."

Mr. Sellers picks up one of the copies, handing his partner the other one. "Can I write on this?" he asks politely.

"Yes, they're yours now."

Pushing the CDs toward them, I add, "It's a backup of the same information, Mr. Sellers."

"Please call me Adrian. May I call you Ellen?" he asks politely.

"And call me Lawrence, Ma'am, we don't need to be so formal."

"Sure," I manage to say.

The agents sit close together, glancing up occasionally, pointing to something on a page, as they continue to read. About an hour later, Adrian stands to stretch. He walks over to the phone to request coffee. A short time later, the door opens, and the young woman who brought me into this room sets a tray on the table.

"What, no candy bar today, Sara?" Lawrence says, teasing the woman.

"Not today, buster, your wife told me you're on a diet," she retorts with a snort. "She means it this time."

Lawrence looks puppy dog sad. "What could one little candy bar hurt?"

"Not falling for that again, Larry. She said no sugar, and she means no candy bars!"

Sara turns to ask if I want anything. We could walk to a cafeteria; Adrian and Lawrence might need more time to go over my information. Adrian stops scribbling in the margin and says I should do that. Sara talks about the building as we walk.

Out of curiosity, I ask her what it's like to work in this environment. She laughs, saying she's a gofer waiting to complete her studies until she can apply for one of the specialty services.

Since it isn't lunchtime, there are few people in the cafeteria now. As I gravitate to yogurt and fresh fruit, Sara goes off to talk with a young man who waved to her when we walked in. She then escorts me back to Interview Room 4 where another man is sitting at the head of the table.

The man stands to greet me, firmly shaking my hand, saying. "Hello Mrs. Thompson, please sit down."

"Ellen, Levi Johnson represents the National Clandestine Service Office," Adrian says. "We feel there are possible international overtones in your information. He's our immediate superior and is here to verify facts from your report."

"That was wise of you to draw their faces; it will go a long way in helping us to identify them when we run them through our databases," Mr. Johnson explains.

Adrian asks, "And that symbol you drew; any idea what that is?"

"No, I drew it the way I saw it. It reminds me of the Greek Mythology symbol for Gemini, but I could be wrong! I'm giving you my best guess for the tattoo that was on Jam-ale's neck and arm."

Mr. Johnson looks up from his keyboard. "I can't fathom what this is all about yet, Mrs. Thompson. It's beyond peculiar. What is your real maiden name?"

"My real maiden name is Peters, Mr. Johnson. Does that sound familiar to you?"

He blinks, and politely says, "I can't say yet, but all the people you name here, including Andrea Simmons, don't operate within the United States spectrum of agencies. And please call me Levi."

"I had already come to that conclusion."

Adrian asks, "Would you be willing to spend the night, either in a hotel or perhaps with Sara? You will be perfectly safe with her. We might be at this for quite a while."

"We want to be sure how to proceed. Your report is quite extraordinary but mostly incredible," Laurence adds.

"Sure," I say. "On a hunch, I threw a change of clothes in a bag."

Speaking in a concerned kind of way, Adrian says, "Do you always play your hunches? I agree that this is the most unusual report we've ever run across. Is this everything?"

"You have it all right there." I'm telling a little white lie, as I don't know who to trust at this point.

Lawrence looks up from his notes. "You nailed the make and model, but did you by any chance get a license plate on any of the limos?"

"No, they were positioned sideways, so I didn't get a direct look at them."

My report contains everything from my abduction at the Kauai Airport, to finding the three leather books in my red case on the way to Virginia. I described in painful detail the information Lenard and Gene swore me to uphold and the way I found out that they are phony FBI agents.

I've held back the information about the documents, currency, the tiny piece that looks like a computer chip, and the little bug Jason found. I do mention our dog Sassy, the incident at the schools, the odd accident that left my nephew Danny with a hole in his shoulder, and our suspicions that someone is trying to scare us. I also describe the trouble we got into with the manager at the racetrack when we won so much money.

Adrian is curious about why the amount of money we won would attract the attention of the track manager, but Levi brings him back to my report.

"Mrs. Thompson, we need to run this through our data banks, get our teams on it, consult with Interpol, that kind of thing." Levi says.

Adrian glances at the scribbles he made along a page, asking, "Did this Lenard tell you what your husband's real name was?"

"If he did, I don't remember."

Lawrence leans forward, asking, "When was the last time you had contact with Lenard or Gene?"

"It was before Christmas. They sent boxes of goodies with no return address. The note that came with it is on page 25, I believe. They were moving to new offices, but they didn't say where."

Adrian flips to that page, then converses with Lawrence and Levi. "Do you remember the name of the restaurant where you met the foreign person? Were there others in the booth beside Mr. C and Mr. A? Did you get a good look at him?"

"No, the restaurant looked closed. There was a blue tarp over the sign. It was dark inside the whole time. Mr. C doesn't even know who he is."

*They aren't surprised at Mr. C's real identity.*

"I thought I'd heard everything, but this is the most atypical story I've ever heard. How about you boys?" Levi asks.

"None of our agents would conduct themselves in this manner," Lawrence says. "We'll have to do some work, Ma'am. Special Agents, CIA, U.S. Marshals, or FBI, don't act this way, I assure you."

"Do you feel your family is in danger?" Levi asks.

Before I answer, Adrian also asks, "Would you like protection?"

When I start to laugh, they all seem concerned. "That's pretty funny because I thought, silly me, that the FBI *was* protecting us, but yes, I feel like we're sitting ducks waiting for the next scary event. Then you believe me? You believe this cockamamie story?"

"It's too unbelievable for you to have made it up," Levi says.

Adrian concurs by adding, "I assure you, Mrs. Thompson, we will find the underlying cause of this, one way or another."

"We have to gather information and run it through our foreign office to see if there's a connection," Levi adds. "It's triggering something I saw recently in a field report."

"What kind of connection are you talking about?"

Levi stands to walk toward me. "We can't say what that is yet, not until we run this information through our databases. May I see your cellphone?"

Handing it to him, he slides the back off and takes it apart. Removing the battery, he turns it over, then checks the inside. When he's satisfied, he puts it all back together. I chuckle as Jason did this to all of our devices, including the walkie-talkies, only last week.

"I suppose you're wondering why I trusted Lenard and Gene."

Adrian raises his eyebrows. "Why did you trust them?"

"They made it sound as if the bad guys were still out there and if they knew I was still alive, they'd go on the hunt to kill my family if I didn't cooperate. What would you have done?"

Lawrence seems sympathetic. "I would probably have done the same thing."

"I agree. No one can fault you for that," Adrian says checking his watch. "Why don't we break for lunch."

Levi agrees. "Why don't you go home with Sara and we'll get going on our research. We'll call you if we find anything."

Sara is waiting outside to take me to her condominium a few miles away. After putting me in her spare bedroom, she says to try and relax while she makes us some lunch. Calling Mother to report what's happening here, she says things are uneventful there; rest while I can, everyone is okay.

Sara takes her job seriously, even if it's to babysit me. We talk easily about family but stay away from my situation. After a light dinner, with no news from CIA Headquarters, I go to bed early, as I'm fatigued from getting up to make the drive to Langley this morning.

Now that the real CIA is involved, perhaps we'll have closure to our mystery. Unfortunately, sleep doesn't come quickly, and I toss and turn for a long time.

It's nearly seven o'clock the next morning when my cellphone rings. It's Adrian Sellers asking when I can get back to their office. They have news about what their teams discovered last night but want to say it in person, not over the phone.

Sara and I arrive at CIA Headquarters, where I wait in the same Interview Room 4. She brings in a carafe of coffee and a tray of pastries, whispering that she hopes everything works out for my family. Should I dread what the CIA people are about to tell me? On the other hand, should I be relieved that they believe me?

Mr. Levi comes in a short time later followed by Adrian, Lawrence, and several others.

"Good morning Mrs. Thompson," Levi says. "These good people stayed up most of the night to dig through the mound of material your report generated. By that I mean, when we put both Ellen and Ravenalt Andress into the database, some attention-grabbing information came out. What caught us off guard are the sketches you made."

"We're glad you did that, Mrs. Thompson," says the head nerd of the bunch, named Jewels. "When we ran the pictures we made from your sketches, it ejected some additional information; we hit the jackpot!"

"It seems these good folks had to come and meet you in person," Levi says thoughtfully. "Nothing of this magnitude has ever happened to our agency before."

"You've been on quite an adventure, haven't you?" Adrian says.

"Now you have some idea of what it was like for me," I manage to say.

Everyone suddenly begins to talk at once. Someone grabs my hand to shake it while another squeezes my shoulder. A woman says what a great job I did in capturing the essence of my ordeal.

They never thought this would happen as Homeland Security is so tight these days. They wonder how I slipped through the cracks and they hope my situation comes to a swift conclusion. The office in

Kauai is beyond surprised by the CIA's involvement, given the experience of their highly trained individuals.

I'm flabbergasted. "You believe me?"

When I say this, everyone in the room stops talking, and then they all talk at once again. Some laugh as others reach out to me. The facts checked out, all of them.

Homeland Security confirmed the employment of Jennifer Holmes and Devon Michaels. They were out of town for the Christmas Holidays and didn't get back to the office until yesterday.

Questioned at length, they certainly remember me, the woman named Andrea Simmons, and the three men who identified themselves as Special Agents of the FBI. It seems that no one questioned their authenticity. Their credentials looked to be in order, and they all acted their parts so convincingly, they were never suspect.

Lenard and Andrea told Homeland they were part of a team sent to investigate the crash of Flight 1703 that inexplicably exploded shortly after takeoff on March 17th. Homeland Security's Holmes and Michael's had instructions that came straight from the FBI (or so they were told) to detain a woman claiming to be Ellen Andress. They were to contact Special Agent Lenard Casings immediately, which they did.

Levi questioned the delay between the time they found me and when Lenard and Gene showed up, then attributed this to my absence of identification and their lack of communication within their office. Homeland Security assumed the FBI took care of things after they watched me leave with them, going about their business, forgetting about it until Levi contacted them last night.

Both Airport and Homeland Security express embarrassment about being duped by people pretending to be from the FBI. That's the good news. The bad news is that no one knows the whereabouts of Andrea, Lenard, Gene, or the agent named Tom.

"They will likely try to get in touch with you again, Mrs. Thompson, but we'll be ready for them," Adrian says with a chuckle.

"What? I don't understand. What happens if those crazy people try to contact us? Who made the plane explode? What about that?"

Adrian reaches to take my hand as people slowly file out of the conference room. "We don't have all the answers yet, Ellen. There are some other things that we need to look into, and we'll explain it to you when we have more information, but if these characters went to so much trouble to settle you into a program, then they want something in return."

"Why don't you go home to your family until we get this settled?" Levi says kindly.

I am suddenly afraid. "How can I go home and tell my family we're sitting ducks? What if these nutty people show up unexpectedly, can I blast them off my property? I own a handgun."

Levi shakes his head and starts to laugh. "I don't think you'll need to resort to using your handgun. I think they're laying low for now. If they've been watching, then they know you're here. It's my guess they want something from you, and they're waiting for the right moment."

"That doesn't make me feel any better. I think I'll stick with my first thought of blasting the crazy people."

Adrian hands me a dangling metal black and silver square on a slim silver chain. "We're going to provide you and your family with protection. Levi has given direct authority for Larry and me to come to Ashwood when we get things arranged. In the meantime, if you need us for *any* emergency, press the black button. It's a device that triggers a signal right into our office."

"What do you have to arrange? Why do you have to come to my house? Are we all in that much danger? Can't you tell me what's going on? I'm scared to think Lenard and Gene are out there and no one knows where they are."

"You're going to have to trust us, Ellen," Adrian says.

"If I had a dollar every time I heard that the last six months, I'd be rich!"

Lawrence adds, "We're the good guys, Mrs. Thompson, we're here to help you."

"I heard that line too!"

Levi smiles. "My advice is to try to carry on with your life and not let all this get to you. Thanks for coming in and bringing this to our attention. We'll do the best we can to get it resolved for you, the quickest way possible."

Adrian walks me to my car. He says I did the right thing by coming in to talk with them, and I should try not to worry.

Heading home, I'm less concerned about our situation, but more than a little curious about the information they uncovered. Levi said to carry on as best we can, and carry on we shall!

*"An obstacle is often a stepping stone."*

~ Prescott

# Chapter Twelve

## Things Are Not Always What They Seem

**W**hile we wait to hear from Adrian Sellers, we delve into what work remains at the Manor House. Our phase one didn't go as planned as the new roof and windows took priority. Glen's office desperately cried out for an overhaul, and we needed a proper tack room.

Once completed, we'll move the crews back to the Manor House to finish whatever remains before spring training starts. The rest will wait for the final phase, where we'll complete whatever needs attention if there is such a thing.

"Let's face it," Mother announces one day, "this is a mansion. The sheer depth and breadth of a house this size is what makes it so expensive."

*How much more will we have to sink into it?*

Our Landscape Designer submitted an excellent plan for the main house and grounds. That part will commence as soon as the ground is workable. Then the painters can conclude their contracted assignments.

Not only is the new track too wet to train, but it's also so dreary that no one has come out to ride their horses in over a week. The wood around the paddocks is green with mold. Glen says Jason and Mel can give the fence a *'lick and a promise'* with a can of white paint if it ever stops raining.

Spring is God's way of renewal. It reminds me of crocus that break through the snow and blooming daffodils that pop up like wild tiger lilies along backroads. I recall cutting Queen Ann's' lace near ditches and mailboxes, sticking them into jars of colored water and it makes me a little homesick.

I'm suddenly homesick for Evanston and think of Ravi.

"Don't think *Didge* is gonna work out, Missy." Glen narrows his eyes at me. "Why don't we keep our eyes out for one or more Standardbreds?"

Glen, Reed, and I are in my office to go over the latest receipts, making generalities about what we want to accomplish this spring. Reed seems amiable to most things, but Glen's skepticism must be rubbing off on him.

"Maybe Glen's right, Miss Ellen. Maybe we should let it go until next year."

"Glen's been talking to you about this, has he?" Reed lowers his head, as Glen rolls his eyes. "He doesn't think that the owner of Ashwood Stables knows enough about racing to consider, well, racing. I've given this a lot of thought. If this doesn't work out, we can do it your way, but until that happens, I would like to know that you two are behind me two hundred percent."

"Do ya know what it takes ta get all the licenses and permits, Missy?"

"Yes, Glen, I do."

"Not ta mention all the other fees and whatnot that you'll be required ta get? Ya do know they'll fingerprint all of us and run checks on us," Glen mumbles.

Rosie suddenly leaves the room, and we figure she's in need of water or something. She can open the back door with her snout, so we go back to our discussion.

"I do know about the fees and whatnot the Racing Commission needs to accept our application. Do you have something to hide, I don't. Is there something in your background you don't want me to know? How about you Reed, do you have any skeletons in your closet?"

"I was thinkin about your former life," Glen says with a serious face.

"Oh, that; I've been told that it won't be a problem."

Reed's eyes widen, saying, "What are you two talking about?"

"Let's not discuss that. It's not my first rodeo, boys!"

We discuss our options for nearly an hour trying my best to convince Glen and Reed that I know what I'm doing, saying they should trust me when the silent alarm goes off. We stare at each other, momentarily frozen in place. It's two thirty in the afternoon and I mentally note where everyone should be right now.

Glen yells, "It's the barn!" Reed and I follow, but when we get to the barn door, he says, "This was open when we went inta the house for our meetin."

An eerie quiet greets us as Glen slowly pushes the door open. Rosie is lying on the floor, motionless. Glen and Reed cautiously move forward, then Reed waves for me to stay back while he pulls his Glock from an inside pocket.

Luckily, I grabbed my cellphone, and I'm texting Jason a quick message. He responds that everyone is okay, then wants to know what's going on. I text him to sit tight; we'll get back to him soon.

*Frick* and *Frack*, the nicknames we gave the Clydesdale horses that comprise the team for the *Magic of Christmas*, are munching happily at a stack of hay near their feet.

"*Didge* must be in his stall as he's not outside," Reed says. "I'll go check on him."

Glen kneels beside Rosie to feel her pulse. "Rosie's breathin, it looks like she's asleep."

"Why would she be asleep in the middle of the barn floor?"

"*Didge* is down, Miss Ellen."

"What?" Glen and I say together.

Reed crouches beside the still horse with his hand under his neck. When he pulls his hand away, there's a large blob of blood on it. "He won't be racing any time soon I'm afraid, he's dead."

"That can't be!" I say in disbelief.

As I kneel beside him, he puts a big arm around my shoulder, saying nothing for a while, as tears flow down my face. Glen is solemn, and then moves toward his office, saying, "I'm callin Rocky."

*We must involve the authorities now as there's no way around it.*

Reed whispers, "What have you got yourself into, Miss Ellen? Maybe you should tell me about it?"

I meant to tell him months ago. "It's very complicated, Reed. I should have told you a while ago so when things happen to us, you'd understand."

"How about starting at the beginning?" Reed surprises me with his compassion and concern. "I have great listening skills."

*It is times such as this that I miss Ravi the most.*

"We'll talk when this little drama's over. What happened to Rosie? Who would want to harm her? How is this possible? *Didge* was healthy and strong. How did someone get in here to do this, Reed?"

"Rocky's on his way," Glen says, handing Reed a wet towel to wipe the blood off his hands.

"Rosie's awake," Glen says, moving to her.

Rosie has her eyes open now, but remains prone, as if she's frozen. Reed runs his hands over her fur, remarking there are no bumps or lumps.

Kneeling beside her, I sniff near her snout. "Reed, what do you smell? It's familiar to me, and I want to gag, but I can't place it."

Reed frowns. "I don't know what it is. It smells like cleaning solution."

Glen murmurs, "We don't keep anythin like that in the barn! We have linseed oil for saddles and stuff, but that's all locked up."

"Would you check, Glen?" He nods and ambles off toward his supply cupboard.

Holding Rosie's snout gently in his hands, Reed leans in to sniff again. "Can't say what it is. Something strange going on here, Miss Ellen."

"Why don't you take a look around outside. See if there are any footprints in the mud."

Reed nods as he stands, "Got your pistol?"

"No. Mine's locked in my top desk drawer." I've given it little thought since acquiring my CWP. Maybe I should carry it on my person as Reed does with his.

"I'll snoop around until the posse shows up." He puts a hand on my shoulder, giving it a little squeeze, adding, "I don't know what this is all about, but I'm here for you, okay? Are you sure you weren't married to the MOB?"

"No. But it looks like it, doesn't it?"

"I can't wait to hear all about it," Reed says moving silently away.

While he looks for clues outside, I look around inside. When I come out of the last stall, Glen is standing near his office holding his old white coffee mug.

"Sheriff Rocky called the Vet, too. Told us not ta touch nothin and he'll be here quick as he can. It don't add up, Missy. Somethin mighty strange goin on here."

Reed comes around the front of the barn to say there's no indication of foul play. No sign anyone was outside, and I wonder if they came down from the sky, like *Mission Impossible* episodes where people dropped on fine wire. Glancing up, I wonder if there are traces of mud on the insides of the new cupola.

"You don't suppose they could have come through there, do you? A slim, agile person might be able to fit through it."

"You're not thinking they came in that way." Reed looks up in amazement. "No, that's impossible!"

"Did you find any footprints outside that aren't ours? If there aren't any, then that's the logical way they got in here. I told you and Glen that anything is possible with these people."

Although there are no sirens, the gravel crunches on the driveway to signal an approaching vehicle. Glen goes to greet our guest and comes back with a man he introduces as Sheriff Rockford. It instantly reminds me of an old TV series called The Rockford Files, but unlike the TV character, this Rocky is a tall, broad-shouldered man with a neatly trimmed goatee and mustache.

"Dr. Crocket said she'll be here soon as she delivers the breech calf down the road," he says. "Sorry to meet you under these circumstances, Ma'am. I'm Sheriff Rocky."

Rocky looks into the stall to confirm that our horse is dead and then takes each of us aside to ask questions, noting this in a small flip-style notebook.

The local veterinarian arrives as Rocky concludes his questioning. Dr. Jessica Crocket is a tall exotic-looking woman in a clean white lab coat over jeans and a t-shirt; her long, thick brown hair is tied into a ponytail, accentuating her high cheekbones. When Glen introduces Dr. Crocket to Reed, she temporarily loses her chain of thought when they shake hands. Recovering quickly, she goes into doctor mode, bending to examine the mark on *Didge's* neck.

"I'll need to run tests. I'll call in the medical examiner for you Sheriff," Dr. Crocket says, swabbing the area. "I'll send this to the lab. It might take a week or two for the results."

Reed takes her elbow, saying, "Could you take a look at our dog, too?"

"Sure, what's wrong with Rosie?"

"We don't know," Reed says.

Rosie is now sitting up. Dr. Crocket pulls the dog's eyelids up, then down, then she squeezes her paws. "It looks like Rosie was drugged," she says. "Did she get into someone's pills?"

"How long have you lived here, Mrs. Thompson?" Sheriff Rocky asks me, "You ruffle someone's feathers that you know of?"

Not wanting to disclose sensitive information, I ask, "Would you like to come inside so we can discuss this further, Sheriff?"

"Yes, Ma'am. Got any coffee to offer an ole Sheriff?" He says this in a kindly sort of way, but I'm guessing he's fishing for one of Mona's cookies.

"I'm sure we can find one for you."

I'm hoping that our new surveillance equipment might show what transpired in the barn today. As we walk back to the Manor House, I alert Mother, inquiring about coffee and goodies.

When we walk into the house, Sheriff Rocky smacks his lips as delicious aromas greet us. Mother and Mona are baking Wednesday's items for the bakery. Settling into my office, Mother arrives to ask what the commotion is all about, eyeing the officer warily.

Rocky removes his hat, then gently takes Mother's hand. He tells her that our horse is dead, but a thorough investigation will be conducted, and not to worry. Although she's composed, there's obvious concern in her eyes.

"We'll talk later; we need to review the camera footage. I'll tell the children when they come home. We might have some answers by then. Are you able to get the good Sheriff here a cup of coffee?"

"And a cookie or two, if you don't mind, Ma'am," Rocky says politely.

Texting Jason that everything is under control, we cram around my desk to review the surveillance tape. When a smudge appears across the lens of the camera rotating to the left, the Sheriff nudges closer to the computer screen, commenting, "That's mighty odd, Ms. Thompson. See there, what's that up in the corner?"

Several things stand out; the camera is moving, or the recording device is skipping. Replaying the tape again, we see a shadow knocking the camera to the side. All that's visible is the inside of an empty stall and the barn floor.

"Perhaps my theory about people dropping from the sky isn't that far-fetched!"

Sheriff Rocky runs a hand through his nonexistent hair. "Don't rightly know what that is, but it could be your attacker."

"Miss Ellen, it could be our ghost, you know," Glen says with a straight face as Reed nudges him with his elbow. "Maybe someone's playin a prank on us."

Rocky narrows his eyes at Glen. "Some prank! What do you mean? You sayin you have a ghost up here? You think a ghost did this?"

*Is he serious?*

"What I mean is, there's been some strange stuff happnin lately." Glen turns toward me, and I mentally tell him to be quiet, shaking my head slightly. "We thought it might be the kid's havin a little fun is all."

Reed turns to Glen. "Or it could be one of the workers trying to be funny."

Now it's my turn to ask questions. "Do you think Jason or one of the workers we hired to do the work here is responsible, gentlemen?"

"We're not sayin that, but maybe they wanted ta scare Ms. Thompson, you know, a little prank or somethin but nothin like what happened ta *Didge*, though," Glen says. "Never thought they'd go that far."

Rocky glares at him. "What are you talkin about, Glen? And who is Jason?"

"Why didn't you say anything about pranks before this? Jason is my son, Sheriff. He wouldn't play tricks on us like this. What *are* you trying to say, Glen?"

Glen tries to explain. "Okay, I don't think this has anythin ta do with Jason. I never thought they meant what they said!"

I'm slowly losing my patience. "Who do you mean by *they* Glen?"

"They told me ta stay away from the track and ta tell ya . . ." Glen hesitates, turning his head away.

"What he's trying to say is," Reed offers, "it could be someone else."

I'm tapping my foot in annoyance.

"What *are* you tryin ta say, son?" the Sheriff asks Reed.

Glen shakes his head, saying, "Somebody don't want Ms. Thompson at the track. They made it clear they don't want her anywhere near the place, not ta bet, but ta race either."

"I might understand why someone wouldn't want us to bet, Glen, but how would they know we're planning to race?" I ask.

Sheriff Rocky is taking all this in, making notes in his little book.

Glen seems distraught. "I coulda let it slip when I was down at the feed store, Missy."

"You two didn't rehearse this enough. I thought I asked you not to spread things around with what we're doing here!"

"I didn't mean for it ta come out. Christ, we weren't even trainin *Didge* yet. I guess I was shootin off my mouth," Glen laments. "I'm proud of what we're doin ta get the farm back its former glory. Don't even know who was there when I said it."

"They didn't have to kill our horse to get their point across, did they?

*Has my paranoia rubbed off on them and they're trying to protect me?*

Sheriff Rocky puts his hand up. "I'll ask the questions here if you don't mind, Ms. Thompson. Do you know who these men are?"

"Not really," Glen says mournfully.

"Tell me about the strange things then," the Sheriff asks.

"Reed and I both thought we closed and locked the barn doors, but several morning's we found them unlocked."

"Anything of value go missin that you know of?" Rocky inquires, raising his pen in anticipation.

"We looked around, and nothin' seems ta be missin except that old saddle we kept on a hook ta remind us of the old days, but we thought one of the workers took it as a souvenir," Glen mumbles.

Rocky turns toward me. "How much money did you win at the track, Ms. Thompson? Enough they'd want to kill your horse to prevent you from winnin more?" He pours himself a cup of coffee and snatches two cookies from the tea cart Mother left near the door of my office.

"It was certainly not enough for anyone to do this! Why didn't you tell me about this, gentlemen?"

"I'll ask the questions if you don't mind, Ms. Thompson." Turning to face Glen and Reed, he says. "Why *didn't* you tell her about this, boys?" Rocky waits for them to answer, nibbling on his cookie when the apparatus on his shoulder crackles. "Excuse me, Ma'am, I have ta take this."

Rocky walks into the library where we can't hear him. A few minutes later, he comes back to inform us he has to take care of another matter. Downing the last of his coffee, he takes two more cookies, and says, "Do not move or touch anything until the forensic team has time to look at the dead horse. Sorry Ma'am, didn't mean for it to sound that way. I'll send a truck as they'll want to run tests. Thanks for the coffee and the cookies."

Glen and Reed move toward the doorway. "Hold it right there you two. Come back in here. What else didn't you tell him that you'd like to share with me?"

Reed glances at Glen, and something passes between them—that triggers a déjà vu sensation of Abdul and Jam-ale, *and* Lenard and Gene. It's the way they looked at each other, didn't say a word, intentionally leaving me out.

"Do sit down. I'm waiting, gentlemen."

"Promise ya won't get mad, Missy? We didn't want ta say much in front of the Sheriff. We didn't know it would come to this."

"How bad is it? Give it to me straight, guys."

Reed pleads, "First, promise you won't get mad."

"I'll try not to be mad, but you two look like partners in crime. I'm not a fragile doll, so tell me, and don't leave anything out."

"Ya know when I went ta look for some help b'fore Reed even got here? Some men got in my face and told me ta tell ya ta stay away from the track. And the last time I went with Reed ta see if anyone was willin ta work a few days a week, some guys pushed us up against a wall."

"They didn't hurt us, but they were rough looking guys that I recognize from hanging around the betting window," Reed adds.

"So you and Glen go to the track to bet?"

"No, it's not like that. Glen wanted to try to do what you do. It didn't work anyway. We didn't win anything."

"After all that's happened to us in the last few months, you didn't think you should tell me about this?"

Reed looks a little guilty. "They didn't punch us, or anything, roughed us up a little is all. I did dig into the history of the place and put two and two together from what Glen told me what this place used to do, it was natural for me to do some snooping."

"Is that all you did?"

"I guess I asked too many questions. They got in my face and said to stop it. Maybe someone got wind of what we're fixing to do. That's what I think, I don't think they're related," Reed sighs heavily. "Maybe they are. Yes, that's pretty much all of it."

"Got anything to add, Glen?"

"No," he says. "I'm sorry, Missy. When ya got involved with the big house, I thought ya'd forget about racin. I never thought these people could do somethin like killin one of our horses."

"Oh, they're capable of it alright and a whole lot more. We don't know who *they* are yet, but I bet my last dollar this is not the end of it. Someone doesn't want us to race, and someone wants to scare the crap out of us. So, take your pick because it isn't over yet, boys, not by a long shot. Do you still think I'm nuts for involving the CIA?"

"We're sorry, Missy, maybe we shoulda called the Sheriff sooner like I told ya to do. Like we talked about after the SUV and bomb scare incident last fall," Glen thunders.

"Bomb scare? What *are* you people into?" Reed starts to laugh. "You gotta tell me about that one!"

"Listen to me, both of you. It's not your first rodeo either. It's a little setback, a reminder that we need to watch our backs. There are dangerous people out there, and one or more of them may want to harm us. The bomb scare thing is another story for another time. It looks like they got in a sneak attack. We'll fight back."

*Are Lenard's words coming back to haunt me?*

"What are you planning to do, Miss Ellen?"

"For starters, until further notice, all trips to the track are suspended. We'll cease training until we are sure there won't be any more incidents. Reed, you can still set up riding lessons and do what you planned with *Frick and Frack*. Do we agree on this, gentlemen?"

"Yes," they both say.

When the children hear about our horse, they don't say anything for a few minutes. Then Jason says that he had a feeling something was about to happen but didn't say anything as he's sometimes wrong. Next time, he won't hesitate.

I didn't press the square on the chain around my neck, as it didn't occur to me. In retrospect, perhaps that would have been a good idea. I'll bet Mr. Sellers is going to be slightly upset when he finds out.

It can't be an isolated incident, but I don't want to alarm the family, so I research neighboring farms; specifically, those that are racing horses at Billingsworth Racetrack. Who's out to nip our little enterprise in the bud? We must never let our guard down as the next time; it may be something other than a horse that gets hurt.

Once the surveillance equipment is operational again, we add hidden cameras that include a photosensitive eye that snaps a photo of all who pass through the barn. Then we add a not-so-silent alarm, a new recording device, additional lights with motion detectors positioned at the front and rear of the barn, and along the main house on each end.

No one questions the device the workers install in the cupola in the barn, or the tiny little detectors placed inside. Reed points out that it won't stop anyone from dropping from the sky, but it may prove how the culprits got into the barn.

A new gate is now across the driveway which Glen says seems a little ridiculous, as the fence around the pastures isn't secure in any way either by an electric current or cameras. And why exactly do we need all this stuff?

He thought I was paranoid before, and most certainly thinks I have lost control of my wits. He may be right, except for the fact we have a dead horse! The other fact remains; the old boys club is alive and the ringleader might live down the road from us.

Agent Sellers calls to say he and his partner found the Dover Inn where he says the owner will give them an excellent weekly rate. It doesn't seem right given all the rooms we have here, so I ask if they might want to stay on the property with us. Sounds like a good plan, but he'll have to clear it with Levi first.

I proceed to fill Adrian in on our latest incident. He expresses concern, wanting to know why I didn't press the black button to send a signal. I think he's bought my lame answer of, *"I forgot to do that,"* until he says we'll talk when he gets here.

A few days later, Agent Sellers rolls into our driveway in a dark blue convertible as Agent Desmond arrives in a full-size grey sedan. We settle them into one of the bedrooms with twin beds set up on Mr. C's side of the house, as we figure he won't be gracing us with his presence any time soon.

Agent Sellers doesn't hesitate to inform me that he and Agent Desmond will now deal with any or all issues. Is he upset with me because I didn't alert the CIA?

"A little," he says. "We'll want to talk with everyone involved."

After our guests settle in, they come to the barn dressed in work clothes and cowboy boots. When I present them as our new ranch hands that we borrowed from the CIA, Glen and Reed chuckle. They can laugh all they want; they will remain with us until we are free of threats. Our dead horse is proof enough to suggest this protection. It's their promise to me, and I'm holding them to it.

Levi's team is working on the information I provided. They are following many leads, and it's only a matter of time before something turns up. When they sent my sketches to Interpol, it generated a worldwide search, flagging several places around the globe that coincide with the explosion of the plane Ravi was on and another operation.

In keeping with his word, Levi's weekly calls will continually inform me about how his group will keep their ear to the ground. By the way, Mr. C is under investigation due to a nasty tax issue, and it's ninety-nine percent probable he'll serve jail time.

*I've barred him from setting foot on this property as we've not seen a red cent toward his enormous debt to us!*

When the rain and slop subside, allowing the ground to dry for a few days, the horses are set free to roam in the pastures on the newly sprouted grass.

Agents Adrian and Larry fit right in here. Glen and Reed help them adjust to the toil and sweat that comes with running a stable and have asked us to call them by their first names. Adrian seems to like it here, but Larry misses his family, so he goes back every weekend leaving Adrian with us. It's during this down time that we take our little pistols to the target range.

"You're a decent shot there, Miss Ellen," Adrian quips. "You're pretty good too, Jason. Both of you are almost as good as I am at hitting the target. Where did you say you learned to do this?"

"My husband taught us. He thought a woman should be armed."

"And dangerous?" he says laughing.

"Funny, Mr. Sellers. Come on Jason; it's your turn. Can you teach Jason how to use a shotgun?"

Jason takes the little Glock, takes aim, and hits the target a little off-center. "Mom, that's a great idea. Can I go hunting with it?"

"That's not a bad idea," Adrian muses. "Are you the responsible type, Jason? Can I trust you not to abuse the privilege, son? What do you want to hunt, squirrels and chipmunks?"

"Now you sound like my father, Adrian," Jason says soberly.

"You may call him Mr. Adrian. Remember our rule about adults? But yes, Jason is trustworthy, aren't you?" I don't elaborate on why I think my son is ready to learn how to shoot a shotgun, but I figure Adrian will garner that information soon enough for himself.

"Yes I am, Mr. Adrian, and I am ready and willing."

Adrian smiles his silly grin and makes a little salute. "We can start next weekend. I assume you have a suitable weapon in mind?"

"Glen has them locked up in the barn."

"Then, we can start next week."

"Woo Hoo," Jason says, jumping up and down.

We've decided that Glen and Reed will choose two Standardbred racehorses from a reputable farm in Kentucky. We were going to get another one anyway, as Jason and I can't use the same horse for training. They didn't want to hear my suggestions as to preferences, so it's up to them to choose wisely. The owner and I agreed that if Reed and Glen like what they see, they'll let me know and I'll transfer the money.

Glen is reluctant to do this, after what happened a few weeks ago, but I assure him it will be okay. It could flush out the villains, or it could cause more trouble, but we can't sit back and take this lying down!

A few days later, Reed calls to say they have two promising horses named *Raindrop Dew* and *Lester's Best*. They will be home after papers are in order and the money transfers. Mr. Gravely, the owner, seems impressed with my questions and general knowledge of horses. He mentions that they are fine specimens from a long line of winners.

When Glen and Reed get back with the new horses, Adrian and Jason are on hand to offload them. Mel, Curlie, Mother, and I watch by the fence as they lead them into the pasture to stretch their legs.

They look splendid; sleek and full of energy, all Mr. Gravely said they would be and then some.

Dr. Crocket will be here tomorrow to give our new horses a once over, and we can then get down to their training, including our own. We won't advertise we're doing this, to be on the safe side. She also has some news about the sample sent to the lab and wants to talk to us about it before she says anything to Sheriff Rocky.

Reed invites her to join us for dinner, and she readily accepts. When we introduce Agents Adrian and Lawrence from the CIA, she smiles curiously at them, but we then tell her they are here for some R & R. After dinner, we assemble in the library where Dr. Crocket asks us to call her Dr. Jessica, or plain Jess.

Mel and Curlie are reluctantly helping Mother and Mona in the kitchen as Dr. Jess tells us about the lab results. Her preliminary report indicates that *Didge* received a massive dose of some experimental drug.

I freeze at the mention of this word. "Did you say experimental drug?"

"Yes, Mrs. Thompson. First indications are that he must have put up a fight to sustain that kind of laceration on his neck. He died quickly, so he didn't suffer long."

Jason is sitting on the arm of my chair, leaning in, he whispers, "Geeze, Mom, is that what they gave you?"

"Who knows, Jason?" Dr. Jessica stops to stare at us. "Please go on."

She then explains there's no substance like that in her database. Larry opens his laptop, asking her to send him the report and sample so he can forward it to CIA Headquarters for their teams to have a go at it.

"I thought you were on R & R?" Dr. Jessica asks Larry.

"We are, but if while we're here Mrs. Thompson can benefit from our expertise, why not use it?" he answers politely.

"That's the cause of immediate death, anyway," she continues. "A lethal drug overdose. But, it isn't uncommon for trainers to administer drugs to their horses to enhance their performance." Dr. Jessica looks at the incredulous expression on Glen's face.

Glen growls, "Are ya sayin I had somethin ta do with this?"

"I'm not saying that you were involved or that you could have done this, Mr. Murdock. What I am saying is that trainers, in general, do this. They give their horse a substance called *First Time Lasix*."

"I've heard of this bein used, but nobody owns up to it," Glen says sadly. "And I wouldn't use it even if Ms. Thompson ordered me to!"

"Beg your pardon, Dr. Jess, why do trainers use it?" Reed asks.

Dr. Jessica smiles thoughtfully. "It's used in the treatment of high blood pressure and given to the horse about an hour before a race. It's supposed to control bleeding through the nose during a race."

"Aren't there controls put in place to help prevent this sort of thing?" Reed questions.

"The answer to that is yes and no. The Racing Commission has strict guidelines and rules governing the use of illegal drugs. With so many pharmacist shops available, anyone can get these drugs. It's difficult to regulate them, and offenders go unprosecuted until it repeatedly happens to the same stables."

"I don't get it. Whatever happened to honesty?" Reed sighs heavily.

Glen says absently, "What's that old sayin about no honor among thieves?"

"Maybe the *club* employs that as their motto," I add sarcastically.

Adrian has a quizzical expression on his face although he continues to listen.

"What is it you always say, Mom? That these people will do anything to gain the advantage?" Jason adds.

Glen declares, "It's a horrible thing ta do ta an innocent animal."

Dr. Jessica sighs. "I agree with you, and it makes me angry to think that they get away with it. Other pain drugs are used for that purpose, and if given in higher doses, it masks injury. It is difficult to detect during prerace examinations; I can't detect them anyway."

Larry adds, "It's ridiculous to think this goes on and no one can stop it."

"And you can't do anything about it?" Adrian asks.

"You have to understand that the horse may not feel the pain of an existing injury, so that it may run harder. It's impossible to catch someone in the act of administering the drug," she says, "even when there is surveillance equipment. If they gave the animal these drugs, it puts excess stress on an existing injury. I've seen this time and time again, and I'm utterly helpless." Dr. Jessica looks disturbed by this, glancing at Reed, she says, "I wish I could do more."

Glen is shaking his head. "We may never know what they did ta *Didge*! What about Rosie, what'd they do ta her?"

"As for Rosie, it's fairly certain that she was given chloroform. It was enough to knock her out. It's mostly harmless when given in small doses. There shouldn't be lingering effects. I'm sorry I couldn't give you better news, but the pathologist will continue to run tests."

*Chloroform. Could this be what I remember as the foul taste in my mouth after I woke in captivity?*

I'm a little curious. "Dr. Jessica, may I ask a question?"

"Sure, if it's quick, I have to attend to some livestock before I go home."

"Could the chloroform be given in conjunction with another drug, say the experimental drug? Hypothetically speaking, could this be administered to humans? Would the results of going to sleep have the same results?"

"Mrs. Thompson, that's a good question. I can't answer that. I'll ask around at the lab the next time I'm there. By the way, I don't buy your R & R story. Why is the CIA involved in this?"

"We're not at liberty to discuss that with you," Adrian says, sipping his wine.

Dr. Jessica studies Adrian's face for several awkward seconds, and then finally says, "Thank you for a wonderful dinner, Mrs. Thompson, everyone, if you will excuse me."

We thank Dr. Jessica for coming to deliver her news. Adrian, Larry, and Reed walk out with her while Glen, Jason, and I remain in the library where we stare at the unlit fireplace. Where each of us has gone is anyone's guess.

Mother walks in and asks, "Did Dr. Crocket hypnotize you?"

Glen excuses himself to go to the barn as Mother sits down near me. "I'm glad Adrian and Lawrence are here, Ellie."

"Me too," Jason says. "I wonder what's coming next?"

"Things are not always what they seem, Jason. We have no concrete answers for many things right now."

*I hope that someday soon, we'll figure it all out.*

Adrian informs me that the documents Lenard gave me for the Ashwood properties are authentic. As it turns out, our passports, social security cards, including birth certificates are all real! I'm surprised at this news. The U.S. Department of Justice certified them and advised that I stop worrying.

Moving our efforts back to training, the information according to the State of Virginia Code on Harness Racing says the responsibility for the eligibility of a horse for a race rests with the trainer, not with the owner, as I wrongly assumed. It doesn't change anything other than Glen thinks he has the upper hand. My only request is that Glen and Reed trust me. They express how worried they are if we continue down the racing path, but I have an ace up my sleeve.

Jason and I are ready to transition to the jog carts, and he has no trouble sitting on the hard bench, but it's so painful for me, that after the first time around the track I want to scream! My first thought is that my brilliant idea won't work now. Adrian suggests I abandon the idea altogether. Then we get into a discussion about what is suitable women's roles.

"You think I should be in the kitchen with Mother and Mona and not out here trying to race, don't you?"

"No, I think that if I were your husband, I'd be trying to talk you out of it," he says walking away.

"If you were my husband, you would be encouraging me to go after my dream."

Adrian turns around. "You don't have to take my advice, Mrs. Thompson. I don't want anything to happen to you on my watch. It would reflect negatively on my performance record."

"Thanks, Mr. Sellers; I'll take that under advisement."

"Are you being sarcastic, Mrs. Thompson?"

"Why no, Mr. Sellers, but that was sweet of you to take an interest in my safety."

Glen storms into the barn mumbling under his breath, "You looked miserable out there. How are ya goin ta focus? I can't get a time with you squirmin around on that bench! Want me ta get some paddin or something for your b'hind?"

"It's an old injury that's come back to haunt me that's all. You know, that's a good idea. Let's see if padding will help."

The pain has everything to do with the placement of my feet as they are angled to reach the footrest. It throws me back when *Lester* moves to pace as the cart jerks forward. When this happens, there's no comfortable position to shift into when trying to juggle things.

The crop is in one hand while the reins are in the other, and I'm trying to balance on that damn bench while *Lester's* tail brushes my face! If I can sit in a donut, it may lessen the pressure on my tailbone.

*I can take a little pain . . . I did have three children!*

As I pour over the Virginia Fact Book provided by The Jockey Club and peruse the license criteria, nothing untoward jumps out that might prevent Ashwood Stables from moving forward. We'll reregister our new racing colors, as the mice didn't leave much to identify the old ones. We found an old faded photo on a bookshelf, but it's difficult to see the pattern, let alone colors.

Jason is helping with the tedious process, visiting the local library that has limited archives about Ashwood Farms. He did research connected with the dairy business, harness racing archives, etc. He hasn't turned anything up except the fact red, grey, and black were the colors used.

Using one of the sample designs from the book that registers silks and stables, we can modify one to look as close to what once graced the jackets and saddlecloths of the horses who raced here. It needs to be a simple, yet distinct pattern, something that will allow us to pick out our horse and driver quickly when they go around the track. Lingering on the design page to compare the photo with the designs, Jason and I eventually settle on one that looks like a close match.

Next, we choose a new jacket that is eligible for registration. The pattern for the jacket has a three-inch cluster of black stars that are on a bright red background with a grey collar and cuffs. After placing a call to The Jockey Club, we'll have to wait until we get word that they accept or reject our choice.

Several hours later, the call comes that says we are a go for our silk design. Moving from that set of papers, we proceed to fill out all the necessary forms to order four pairs of silks in our colors; two for Jason, because he might yet grow an inch or two, and two for me.

The rules have changed over the years, and all drivers are required to wear safety helmets. Choosing a matching Snap-On red topper with three black stars, the registration goes into Ellen D. Thompson's name. Jason gets bored, nagging that he isn't needed and leaves so I can attack the mound of forms for the Virginia Racing Commission. I'm about to go cross-eyed when Adrian strolls into my office.

Adrian has become an unexpected confidant; his demeanor is relaxed and non-threatening, and I enjoy his company. Talking with someone who understands helps me cope with things. He and Larry know our entire story, and we're grateful that Adrian likes working with the horses. He has no wife to pull him back to Langley as Larry does; no children for whom he needs to coach baseball, no hobby to de-stress on, and he likes to muck out the stalls, often riding the boarded horses when they need exercise.

It allows Reed more time with his new girlfriend, Dr. Jessica. I laugh every time he says this because it reminds me of that gift horse thing.

"How's it coming with the applications?" Adrian has a contagious smile and is downright adorable.

I didn't understand why Larry and Adrian's superiors allowed them to stay here, but the longer they're here, the more he tells of what they have uncovered. He also mentions that he might have to withhold information until his superiors are satisfied it won't jeopardize our safety.

"Jason got so bored he left a while ago. I'm up to my eyebrows in this stuff, but I can take a break. Have you heard anything new from your fearless leader and his sidekick Jewels?"

Levi works tirelessly on our behalf to find the underlying cause of our ridiculous escapades. Adrian or Larry check in with him and his group every day as his teams of experts continue their efforts to tie together incidents, as they are sure we're involved in an ongoing scheme that includes many people and several countries. Perhaps it's global.

It's only a matter of time before headquarters identifies my abductors. The odd thing is that the trail went cold on Lenard, Gene, their bouncer comrade Tom, and Andrea. They have people waiting for them to surface.

"How does all this work, once it gets going, I mean?" he asks.

"Here's the skinny on that. The racing secretary writes up something about our horses called a condition. Jason and I will be newbies, and it'll be our maiden race, which means we're green. We're not the crème de la crème, and I don't intend to imply that we are. I do want to be at the top of the pyramid someday. Eventually running stakes and handicap races."

"May I ask how you know all this stuff, Ellie?"

"It's a long story, Adrian; it would bore you to death."

"I'd like to hear it. It's probably more interesting than mucking out the stalls."

"Here, all this time I thought you liked doing that, Mr. CIA man."

Adrian grins, saying, "I do. Can you take a break from all this?"

"Sure, this can wait. What's up?" Pushing the pile of papers to the left side of the desk, thinking there is news from Levi he wants to share. "Did Levi and his team of geniuses uncover a plot to overthrow a foreign government?"

He laughs. "No, nothing like that. I thought you might be feeling a little stuck here since Larry and I came. He gets to go back to Langley every weekend. You know that old saying about how all work and no play makes a person dull?" Stopping to give this more thought, he says, "Or is it about a man named Jack and if he doesn't take a break it makes him cranky and dull? Would you like to go out to dinner tonight or something?"

"Jason mentioned an Italian place in town that makes a delicious chicken parmesan. Mona and Mother started dinner by now, but I'll see if they can postpone it until tomorrow."

As I reach for the walkie-talkie, Adrian grabs it off the desk. Flashing his toothy grin at me, he says, "I thought that it would only be you and me."

"Oh."

"It's only dinner, Ellie. Can you tear yourself away? This whole thing wasn't set up to make you feel like a prisoner!" Adrian sees the look on my face, and the déjà vu sensation threatens to overtake me. "I'm sorry, that wasn't the right thing to say, was it?"

I don't know how long I sit there not talking. I've been there and done that so many times, it suddenly occurs to me that Ravi's death means I'm a widow. I hadn't felt like one until now. No one's even used that term in front of me, not even Mother.

Adrian cocks his head to the side, "Ellie. Are you okay?"

"Yes, Adrian, that sounds wonderful. I'll go change."

Adrian is scrolling through his cellphone, "The place I have in mind won't let you in if you wear jeans . . ."

"Got it. Let me tell Mona we won't be joining them for dinner tonight. I'll meet you in the living room in about twenty minutes, okay?"

The family won't miss us, as Dr. Jessica will be joining them this evening, entertaining them no doubt with the craziness that is her animal life, something that never gets old.

Adrian and I will travel out of Jasper for our dinner. It is lovely and relaxing, and I genuinely enjoy it. I try to remember the last time I went out to dinner then recall that it was Kauai, and I was with Ravi.

Lingering over dessert, Adrian jokes about his family, talking on about how he came to be with the CIA, and then asks about Chicago.

"Something occurred to me today, Adrian. It's not how I planned my life, but we're making the most of what has come our way. But I can't share my life with anyone until we resolve this *thing* that hangs around us like the plague. I feel like my head is in a noose and someone is tightening it little by little."

Reaching for my hand, Adrian squeezes it lightly. "I understand, Ellie. It's hard to trust people after what you and your family have been through, so why don't we work on being friends and colleagues?"

"I'd like that. Thanks for understanding."

When we return home, Glen beeps the walkie-talkie for us to come to the barn as Dr. Jessica has the results of the other test the lab ran on *Didge's* blood sample. We find them huddled into Glen's expanded office.

Dr. Jessica's tablet is open in front of her and bluntly says, "I already told you what some trainers inject their horses with on race day. To be clear, they are illegal. That was a massive dose of corticosteroids in that sample besides the experimental drug that has no name."

"What's corta what?" Glen asks.

"Corticosteroids," she corrects. "It's called the race day med." She matter-of-factly says this, but I know she has a disdain for anyone who wants to injure or harm innocent animals.

Adrian interrupts. "At least we know what, now we need to know why. I'll call Levi and tell him the news. Will you email the report to me?"

"Sure," she says. "Who is Levi?"

Adrian grins. "You don't need to know that."

Dr. Jessica adds, "Need anything else, Mr. Sellers?"

"No. Thanks for your cooperation, Dr. Jessica," he says, walking away.

Reed asks, "Do we know who might have done this yet?"

"That's Sheriff Rocky's department. I can only tell you what they used. The sample that I took indicates that delivery was quick. I can tell you with some certainty that although it was violent, your horse did not suffer very long."

"Oh, that makes me feel a whole lot better."

By the end of May, I am a licensed harness driver. And thanks to custom-made seat cushions, I'm now able to sit comfortably on both the jog cart and race bike benches. The pain is now tolerable, yet anyone who sees either benches thinks it's hilarious!

Jason's trained as a driver, but not licensed as one. The rules have changed since the manuals were printed and he must be eighteen to apply now. He's understandably angry at this turn of events. It blows my plan out of the water, as I had intended to have Jason do the bulk of the racing. He was my ACE in the hole!

Thanks to a very patient Reed and the Driver's Education Department at his school, Jason has a Virginia Driver's License. He continually pesters me about a car, and if he had such a vehicle of his own, he could take the girls wherever they needed to go.

At the beginning of June, our silks arrive, and Jason steps up his bombardment about getting a car. The hassle now is what kind and how much I will give toward its purchase. Then racing becomes the topic of discussion. I'm out in the barn after a short ride around the trails with Adrian. (I walked, he rode)

"Why do you feel you have to do this, Ellie?" Adrian asks as he brushes a boarders' horse.

Glen is hooking up the race bike, glances up as we talk and doesn't say anything as he passes.

"It's not the kitchen thing again, is it?"

"I don't think you belong in the kitchen, Ellie. I've done some checking, and it's not safe for a woman to be racing. These people can be brutal," he mutters.

"Where did you hear that? Was it from a little old man with a mustache?"

Laughing, he says, "I know how to do research too, you know."

Glen pokes his head over the stall, "Ya don't know Miss Ellen like I do, Mr. Adrian. She *will* find a way ta do it, once she makes up her mind she wants ta do somethin."

"Give it a rest, you two. I need my team to be with me, including you, Adrian. It's all about winning the purse."

Adrian screws up his face, "If it's a purse full of money you want, can't you do that thing you do when you pick a winner?"

Glen is chuckling as he walks away.

"How do you know about that? I distinctly remember that didn't go into my report, Mr. Sellers."

Adrian blinks. "You told me," then he looks down at the ground. "No, I stand corrected, you won at the track, and the track manager told you not to come back. I asked you how much money you won, but you never said."

"Nice save, Adrian."

Adrian makes me laugh, and I like that about him. Ravi was solemn, but I attributed that to his personality. Adrian has an adorable side and often jokes his way out of situations. I wonder if he misses Langley and his friends.

"Okay! Glen and I were discussing how to get you to quit this nonsense. If you feel you have to do this, then we'll help you any way we can, right Glen?"

In the meantime, Glen is nowhere in sight.

"I think Elvis has left the building."

Adrian leans in to whisper, "I'm sorry, Ellie, was that out of line?"

"No Adrian, it wasn't out of line."

"Good afternoon to you, Mrs. Thompson," he says, whistling softly. "I'll see you back at the house for dinner."

"Mom, the mail's here!" Jason says running into the barn.

"It must be important for you to get all worked up about it. Might it be from the racing commission?"

"Yes," he urges. "Open it!"

We had anticipated some problems as nothing related to horseracing has been easy thus far, and when I tear open the envelope and begin to read to myself, Jason becomes impatient, saying, "What does it say, Mom?"

"It says that the National Racing Compact determined that our eligibility has not been met and refers to us consorting with, why don't I just read it. '*Consorting with, or has an ownership, partnership, or*

279

*other commercial interest with or business ties to any person who is or has been involved with or has any jurisdiction at any time pleaded guilty or nolo contendare to or was found guilty or been convicted of '*, yikes, someone look up the word nolo contendare. What is all this gobbledygook?"

"Keep reading," Adrian says, pressing numbers on his cellphone.

"Where was I? Yatta, yatta, yatta," I'm reading ahead when Glen clears his throat. "Sorry. *'any person who has been found guilty or been convicted of forfeited bail or been fined for, or currently has a criminal indictment or complaint pending for illegal gambling, extortion racketeering involving organized crime, fraud, race-fixing or any other effort to predetermine the outcome of a race, bookmaking, touting, pool-setting, bet solicitation, or other similar conduct, or its equivalent, in any jurisdiction."*

"Mom, what the heck does that mean?" Jason asks.

"Not sure, sweetie. Maybe Mr. Sellers is finding out what it means." I tear open the second envelope. "This one's from the State of Virginia, Harness Racing License Department. It refers to a big number part B: Consideration of Application."

"What's that all about?" Jason asks.

"It seems that the commission feels that we should not have a license. It's not in the public interest, as my integrity comes into scrutiny. To add insult to injury, they don't feel that I qualify. Oh, now I get what's going on." Clenching my teeth, it dawns on me how serious this is.

*We are all stunned.*

Glen sputters, "What the hell does all that mean?"

"It means we can't race at Billingsworth," Reed sighs.

Shaking my head, "And from this day forth, there will be no license issued due to the commission's review."

Jason mumbles, "They can't do that; can they, Mom?" He's genuinely upset. "Mom, does that mean we can never race?"

"I don't know, Jason. I understand rules change, but it might have something to do with Mr. C since his name is on the deed. They somehow found a loophole."

"Didn't Lenard say not to worry about 'em in his Christmas card?" Glen mumbles, "Maybe we shoulda worried about 'em."

Adrian nods, "Levi mentioned an on-going investigation for your Mr. C that has to do with an income tax issue."

"He has to be at the root of this," I mutter under my breath. "Son of a gun, we were so close to getting our license."

Glen asks pointedly, "How did they know about his connection with our stables? He wasn't the only one who bought it. Didn't ya say private investors or a corporation bought parts of it?"

Adrian gently takes the papers out of my hands and walks away. "Don't worry we'll get it straightened out."

"Thanks." This latest development seems like an insurmountable challenge. Will it take a leap of faith to overcome this latest obstacle?

"I sure hope Mr. Adrian can fix this," J a s o n says sadly. "I know how you were looking forward to racing. Can we talk about that car now?"

"Nice try, Ace." Reed grabs Jason around the neck, putting him in a headlock. S q u i r m i n g  o u t  o f  h i s  g r a s p, he keeps asking about a car.

When Adrian returns, he says, "Ellie, will you walk with me, please?" We walk toward the southern pasture and c l i m b  u p  o n  the fence. "I have some  disturbing news I couldn't say in front of the others."

"Go ahead, Adrian. It can't be as bad as what I just read."

"Yes it can," he says.

"What is it? Y o u  l o o k  v e r y  s e r i o u s ."

"I gave Levi the information about what the racing people did. It seems that Mr. C is indeed involved. Although he signed his name to the mortgage, the corporation or silent partners did not. They don't exist."

*He lets this sink in for a moment.*

"Oh, boy, why am I not surprised at that? If Lenard and Gene are not FBI agents, what makes me think that they were remotely telling the truth about anything else? Give it to me straight, I'm wearing my big girl pants."

"Levi and his group received data that might be a little disturbing. I'm not at liberty to tell you all of it. His team ran the composites through the databases again, and Lenard and Gene were already in Kauai when you got there."

"That's not too surprising. Did Lenard and Gene kill all the real FBI agents and take their place? It's not news, and it's hardly shocking."

"Shall I continue?" he says raising his eyebrows.

"Yes, what else is there?"

"All remaining pieces of the aircraft were moved to a hanger after the accident and placed under guard because they thought that whoever did it would return for something," he says quietly. "They thought the FBI Special Ops Team left in April."

"But they didn't."

"They did, yes, but, look Ellen; I don't want to compound what's going on right now, but you need to know something."

"Then, please continue."

"Homeland Security did a thorough investigation. Lenard, Gene, Tom, and Andrea, were passing themselves off as Special Agents for more than six months. Now, if you remember, no one bothered to check their credentials, they waltzed in and passed out their cards. After the accident, they came to the airport and said to let them know if a person named Ellen Andress showed up."

"Interesting, go on, Adrian."

"They didn't happen to be there, Ellie. They were there *before* the plane exploded. They were waiting for you, only you disappeared."

"Mother and I worked that part out already. We started mistrusting them a while ago. Do you think they're responsible for the explosion?"

"We don't know that yet, Ellie."

"I have two regrets, Adrian. One is that we didn't investigate who they were and the second one is that we didn't come to the CIA sooner."

Adrian has an adorable expression on his face. "I can't go into detail, but Levi had you and Ravi on his radar. He thought something was going to happen, even told Larry and me to expect it, but he didn't know what it was."

"So you think we met because of kismet?"

"Who is that? No, I think it was meant to happen." He sees the mirth in my eyes. "Wait a minute, is that an oxymoron?"

Laughing so hard, I almost fall off the fence. "I'll bet you kept your friends laughing when you were growing up, didn't you?"

"Thanks. I kinda like you, too."

*"A quitter never wins and a winner never quits."*

~ Napoleon Hill

# Chapter Thirteen

## Triumphs, Transitions, & Distractions

Gazing up at the sky, it somehow reminds me of the discovery of vast numbers of galaxies that are out there not visible to the naked eye. It also reminds me just how fragile life is. It can change in mere seconds.

"That's not the worst of it," Adrian says soberly. "Lenard Casings seems to have fallen off the face of the earth, and they found Gene Thornburg floating in the Potomac River last night."

"Can't say this comes as any great surprise, Adrian."

"There was no identification on him, but Levi's team recognized him through the sketch you made. He said he's someone who could have been hired by a country to either - I'm not sure I can tell you."

"Adrian, are you trying to say he was a mercenary; someone who kills for hire?"

"How do you know about this stuff?" he asks.

"I read a lot."

"Levi and his group are convinced Lenard and Andrea are going to surface because they want something."

I'm not ready to tell Adrian about the items that I put into my safe just yet, and instead, say, "My family has a secret code that we need to share with everyone. We can do this at dinner tonight, alright?"

"Is it Morse code or the kind the ER people use?"

"It's more like a contingency plan."

Adrian seems thoughtful. "You mean like a fire drill, so everyone knows how to get out of the house in case there's a fire? That's an excellent idea."

"Yes, a fire drill, like that, exactly."

"Aren't you affected by what I told you?" he asks.

"I'm affected, but you told us to carry on, didn't you? That is what we're doing, precisely. We keep them guessing. What do they think I have? A million dollars? Is it the goose that lays golden eggs?"

"How can you make jokes like that?" he frowns.

"Because Adrian, that's the one thing they can't take away from me!" I say laughing.

"Don't forget your dignity; they can't take that away either. Isn't there a song about that?" he muses.

"There you go, we have to keep our humor or else we'll go stark raving mad."

"I suppose you're right. Levi doesn't know what they want, but I'm curious about something. Did Abdul and his giant friend give you anything besides grief?"

"Only the three books. Will this ever make sense to us?"

"It will, eventually. We always get our man. Or is that the Canadian Royal Mounted Police. I'm pretty sure it's us, too. Oh, I see now what you mean about humor," he says, letting out a hearty laugh. Adrian has a gentleness about him, and it goes a long way to bolster my feeling that he is the genuine article. "Ellie," he says finally. "It occurs to me that we might have a mole in our midst."

I'm trying to stifle a chuckle. "Who could slip past our radar? What makes you think we have a mole?"

Adrian sighs. "Maybe someone tampered with the equipment, or maybe it's one of those men who came by looking for work."

"They'd never get past Glen the Gatekeeper. Wait a minute; the mole has to be you or Larry. You were the last to join us."

Watching his reaction, he looks as if I have just shot him straight through the heart. I want to see how he explains it away.

"We're the good guys. Larry, me, we would never hurt you. I swore to uphold the law, and I'm the one who pleaded with Levi to let us come here. Oh, I see how you would think . . ." Running his hand over his face, he takes a breath and looks away.

Rosie runs out of the barn as I jump down from the fence. She woofs softly and nuzzles Adrian's hand. Here's the second thing to give me hope. The dog accepts unconditionally the man who fits into our family as comfortable as a leather glove conforms to your hand.

"Was that a test, Ellie? Please tell me you believe me? You came to us, remember?"

"Of course I believe you, Adrian, but we have been fooled before by some fairly crafty people. You will have to forgive me if I'm a little skeptical from time to time."

"Whew," he says, hugging me. "You nearly gave me heart failure." When I try to pull away, he whispers, "I like being at Ashwood, but I do hope your case comes to a swift and good conclusion."

"We're grateful you and Larry have been with us, Mr. CIA man. I'm going to be sad when you leave."

"Are you? Why Mrs. Thompson, I'd need a very good reason to give up my career. What, what was that, Mrs. Thompson? Did you say don't go?"

"You're such a clown. I'd never tell you to give up your career for us."

"You wouldn't?" he says sweetly.

"No, I wouldn't, and you shouldn't try to talk me out of racing, either."

"After all we've been through, you wound me, Ma'am."

"That's what I like about you, Adrian, you don't mince words."

"I almost forgot. Levi also discovered that Mr. A is a known criminal. Sorry for all the bad news." Leaning toward me, he kisses me lightly on the lips. "When this is all over, Ellie, when this is behind us..." stepping back, he adds, "that was unprofessional of me. I'm sorry, it won't happen again."

"That's okay; I won't tell anyone."

At dinner, I present our secret code. Adrian and Larry think this is an outstanding way to let everyone know of the potential for danger. As I discussed with my children a few months ago, each person will need to commit them to memory. Mother and the children are the only ones who know about the secret stairway. I'm going with my instincts here, in case I'm wrong.

"We might move forward with the plans for the new swimming pool, because we can't do much else right now," I announce.

Everyone cheers at this news as the heat index has risen to an uncomfortable level. I also rented a four-bedroom oceanfront house in picturesque Cape Cod where we'll have three glorious weeks that will give us a much-needed diversion and distraction.

Mother feels safer having Adrian along for protection, hinting that maybe he'll never leave, even if our case concludes. It's agreed that Reed and the Murdock's will stay behind and Larry will alert us if something needs immediate attention. Dr. Jessica will also stay at the Manor House while we're away, giving her a break, leaving her burgeoning practice at night to two interns who look promising.

Our flight to Barnstable Municipal Airport in Massachusetts is uneventful, arriving right on schedule. About thirty minutes after we load our luggage into our rented van, everyone cheers when the ocean comes into view. As we turn into the driveway of our rented house, someone waves from the top deck of the house next door. Urging Mother to go and introduce herself, she looks at me as if I've lost my mind and won't go unless I give her a little hint.

"Go on; you'll be pleasantly surprised who our neighbors are."

Jason's head pops up, "Is that...? How did you do this?" Dropping his case, he moves to stand next to his Grandmother, who is being welcomed into the neighbor's house by a woman I've known all my life, my sister Terre. Terre pulls Mother inside, then reaches for Jason. Mel and Curlie notice the commotion and ask what's going on, but they're already moving toward the door.

Adrian grins. "Looks like this was a good idea, Ellie."

If all goes as planned back home and our enemies allow us this needed vacation, it will be. It's well over a year since our family's journey began. Terre and I chose these beach houses for the express purpose of visiting with each other. Each home has three bedrooms on the street level and one sizeable dormitory-style room on the lower level. Terre and Dennis arrived a few days ago and settled into their house, but Adrian is anything but casual about our safety, going room to room with a little device that can detect electronic bugs.

Ginny and Lindy are my nieces who are celebrating their twelfth birthday tomorrow. We've planned a sumptuous feast for the occasion, complete with cake, balloons, party favors, and prizes. The adults realize this is silly, but we also know that the time spent away from our families has been hardest on the children. They need a little fun and distraction.

Most any afternoon, our chefs, Dennis and Adrian, take turns grilling our dinner, kiddingly argue as to who makes the better margarita.

Someone declares that it can't get any better than this! The ocean is right outside our doors, and our family is right next door. Mother is understandably happy. She's even more so when we share the plan to bring Terre and her family to Virginia, once we resolve our situation. She and Dennis naturally have many questions, but Adrian asks that we stick to generalities for now. At some point in the future, we'll discuss it, but for now, we're here to relax and enjoy our time together!

When Terre and I are alone, I explain that Mr. Levi mentioned that until the bad guys are apprehended, we must be patient. She understood, acknowledging that it might take a while for this to happen.

The separation has been hardest on the children, as they used to be together often. Making up for lost time, the girls are down at the beach, while Jason and Danny are in their *man cave*. It's not long when Jason and Danny get restless, suggesting they take one of the vans into town to check out some 'stuff.'

Adrian is naturally reluctant. "It's not a good idea, fellas."

After a brief conversation with Levi, Adrian confirmed that his instinct was correct, saying that Lenard surfaced yesterday. We must be cautious and stay close to the houses. If we do go out, we all go. For added protection, Levi assigned extra security and apologized for the inconvenience, then said we'll like who the CIA sends to be with us.

A married couple named Kellie and Drew McGuire will stay at Ashwood and pretend to be Reed's family. Larry can then go home the last week we're gone, to be with his wife and two children.

Two days later, we hear laughter as Adrian and the new security team talks in the driveway. When they come around the house, the men look like beach bums, because of their crazy Hawaiian shirts, dark tans, and sun-bleached hair. Leaning their surfboards against the house, they wave up at us. They're old friends of Adrian's, named Josh Heyburn and Jake Evans, who've been partners for nine years. Josh makes Adrian belly laugh, something we haven't seen since he came to Ashwood.

The agents quickly came up with plans; Josh and Jake will stay in the large room at Terre's house, each taking 12-hour shifts. Josh will accompany anyone going into town for supplies while Jake will accompany those going out during the evening, with the curfew set for ten p.m. The only ones who complain are Danny and Jason.

From the top deck of our house, Adrian can often be found scanning the ocean area behind our homes using high-powered binoculars. One day, Curlie questioned what he was doing. "I'm checking the ocean for jumping fish; want me to tell you when I spot one? Hey, I think I saw a whale."

Curlie accepted his explanation, but I know he's on the case. She thinks the seagulls are saying *ow* when they try to fly into the wind, and he says they're squawking because no one left a morsel of food on the beach.

It's a balmy summer night, and I'm on the upper deck trying to absorb the sound of the ocean, hoping to commit it to memory. Most of the adults have crashed after a superb meal of lobster and homemade ice cream.

Adrian appears with two glasses of wine. Keeping his voice soft, he hands one to me saying, "Are you thinking of what's going on back home, or are you wondering if we'll have some drama here. Am I close?"

"That's very observant of you. I'm trying to memorize the sound of the ocean, so when I'm stressed, I can replay it in my mind. What should I be thinking, Mr. CIA man?"

"It's my job to be observant, Mrs. Thompson. I thought I heard the wheels of your mind cranking away."

"Will there ever be a time when we don't have to look over our shoulder, Adrian? Are we safe from Lenard? Do they know who this Abdul person is and why they took me? Have they figured out what he has to do with Ravi and the plane exploding?"

Adrian chuckles. "It's interesting how your brain works. It's an intriguing technique you have there, Mrs. Thompson."

"It's something I've always done, probably annoys people now that you mention it."

"You have a marvelous mind," Adrian says quietly. "You ought to consider working for the CIA."

I'm studying him in the moonlight. "You must be joking. I don't mean to say them out loud. It helps me work things out; sorry if it bothers you."

"It doesn't bother me. I think it's fascinating how your mind works. You come up with good questions. Honestly, you'd make a good agent, Ellie."

"Okay, now you're making fun of me."

"No," he begins. Taking my hand, he holds it close to his chest. "I'm not going to lie to you. We all want this to be over, but we also want a good outcome."

"We all want that, Adrian."

Soft music is coming from the direction of the open doors on the ocean side of Terre's house, where most of the children are watching a movie.

"I read and reread your report you gave us that first day," he says.

"You carry the report with you?"

"No, well yes, it's on my laptop. Larry and I refer to it often. Ellie, I'm very concerned that if you go to the racetrack, it's going to open up some sort of . . ."

"I know you're worried, and I'm a little worried myself, but, I'm a big girl."

"I'm not exactly worried . . ." There's obvious concern in his voice. "We don't know who we're dealing with yet and there may be more to this whole thing than meets the eye."

"I know you can't share that with me. I've given this a lot of thought, and the more I think about it, the more I'm convinced that it could flush the vermin out."

He tilts his head, saying, "What do you mean?"

"If someone doesn't want me to race and it turns out to be the organized group I think it is, you'll get them when they show up, right?"

"I'm sure I never said we were investigating organized groups," Adrian says.

"I assumed that you were. It looked like mob type stuff going on at that restaurant with no name. They must be on the CIA's radar. Why else would you and Larry physically come to live with us?"

Shaking his head, Adrian takes a sip from his glass, then says, "You have a pulse on the situation, Ellen."

"Haven't you been investigating the people at the racetrack? And aren't you going to be with us every step of the way?"

A gentle breeze blows hair into my face. In a tender moment, Adrian reaches forward to brush the strand behind my ear, pulling back when he realizes he might have overstepped his bounds. He's here, after all, to protect us, not to socialize with us.

"Adrian, I'm not fragile. I know how to take care of myself, and I want you to do your job, but frankly, Dad, you're a tad overprotective."

"They're a rough bunch, Ellie," he sighs.

"You're singing to the choir, Mr. CIA man."

"Levi told me that the racetrack people are a force to be reckoned with and he mentioned other unexplained incidents not unlike what happened to your horse. I think they're sending you a message. Don't race, they might harm *you* next time."

"I've known about people like that since I was ten years old. I wanted to be a jockey until my parents said I couldn't. So, I found something else to occupy myself. I only bet on a sure thing, and I'm putting my money on you, Adrian Sellers. You're who I pick to win."

He suddenly hugs me until I say I can't breathe. "I'm sorry, Ellie, but I've grown fond of your family. You have no idea how difficult this makes things. They would take me off the case if they knew I crossed the line. It could jeopardize everything."

"I don't see where you crossed the line. Aren't we supposed to look like a couple? Are you able to do your job without getting involved?"

Looking over the rim of his glass, saying, "You're going to make it difficult, but yes, Ellie, I'll be able to do my job. I want to see it through and make sure all the bad guys are apprehended."

"Then let's put our feelings aside until this is all over and concentrate on what we have to do to finish this thing. Look, I've been thinking . . ."

It's time to share the contents of my safe because I'm tired of shouldering it. Adrian is honest and can be trusted with our lives and our secrets. May God help me if I'm wrong, but he's growing on me along with his adorable toothy grin.

"Let's go inside," he says, taking my hand. "Did you say let's put *our* feelings aside?"

"Adrian, I have something to tell you. I've kept this from you to make sure I can trust you. Oh, don't look at me like that."

"Please go on," he says. "I'm used to people withholding information."

"You know what we've been through and frankly it isn't easy to trust people. After all, someone killed my husband, then took everything we valued."

"I understand. Let me have it. I'm wearing my big boy pants, and it's not my first rodeo, so go ahead," he mumbles.

"Do you recall the books Abdul sent home with me? I found a bunch of documents under the covers with the same type of tattoo on each one, but they aren't in English, so I couldn't read them."

Adrian frowns. "Okay, anything else?"

"There's a substantial pile of U. S. Currency, dating from the year 1934. It's real, I already checked."

"Old money, that's not so unusual, Ellie, they still haven't found all the loot that was taken during the heists of the 1930s. You know, Al Capone, Bonnie and Clyde, and those gangster types? There's a lot still not accounted for."

"Besides that, there's a tiny little chip of some kind, and it's all hidden away at my house."

Waiting for him to react in a negative way, he shocks me when he doesn't. "Ellie, I guess you're full of little surprises. How do you know what kind of currency it is?"

"I researched it, but I can't decipher the documents or know what the little chip is without help."

Adrian seems lost in thought for several minutes. Is he coming up with the same hypothesis as I have? "This could be the stuff Lenard and Gene were after. It may be why they tried so hard to deceive you. I don't know what the little chip is for unless it's to pass information. Why don't we let Levi and his group decide what course of action to pursue when we get back to Virginia? Or, I could call him now, if you like."

I'm relieved that he didn't ask where I hid the documents or suggest that the couple at our house look for them, which makes me trust him even more. "This might be tied together, but why did Abdul give me the books with all that stuff in them?"

Adrian looks pensive. "This raises more questions. Lenard and Gene knew you had the books, but didn't take them. What if Abdul's people didn't know what was under the book covers?"

"I'm pretty sure he knew because the books I took from Abdul's library are not the ones I have now. I believe that the books' alteration happened during the time between leaving his palace and when I found them in the tent."

"Okay, he knew what was under the book covers. Could Abdul's enemies have hired Lenard and Gene, and you were the go-between?"

"Go between for what? It doesn't sound right. Then Lenard or Gene could have taken the books at any time, but they didn't. I do know that Abdul's people were at the Kauai Airport the same time Lenard and Gene were, but what's the connection? Were the books what they were looking for under their noses all the time and they didn't know it? Is this the golden egg?"

"That's what we have to find out, Ellie."

We sit for several minutes, each quiet with our thoughts. "What's the common denominator? Could this be where Ravi came in? What could he possibly have to do with this?"

"I don't know, but Lenard and Gene both told you that he wasn't truthful with you and it wasn't his real name. Think back, Ellie, when did you first meet Ravi?"

"It was on my college campus about a month before I graduated. A student was walking past my dorm one day; he asked if I could tell him where the Administration Office was located, and then asked if I wanted to grab a cup of coffee."

"That was his pickup line?" Adrian asks. "Let's grab a cup of coffee?"

"Yes. Ravi's new employer was sending him to another state for an assignment, but his diploma had not come in the mail, so he came to pick it up."

"Had you ever seen Ravi before that day? Did he say he was graduating that year?" Adrian looks like he's on to something.

"I assumed that he did. We went for coffee, got to talking, now that I think about it, we never went to the Administration Office."

"And you said Ravi's parents were dead and there are no other living relatives?"

"Let me think. I didn't question Ravi about that because we were falling in love then, and he was so exotic to me, beautiful almost. Why would he lie to me?"

"And Ravi happened to be walking past your dorm when you ran into him. What's the name of the college you attended?"

Adrian calls Levi, asking him to check the college records. There's a lump in my throat the size of a golf ball, and it's difficult to swallow. Could the man I knew for over twenty years have lied to me from day one? In the back of my mind, the possibility existed, but we had children together!

Adrian is writing something in his field book. "Thanks, Levi, I'll tell her." Laying his cellphone on the coffee table, he pours the last of the wine into our glasses. Talking in almost a whisper, he says, "Ellie, Ravenalt Andress never went to nor did he graduate from any college in these United States, or anywhere else for that matter. Lenard was right about one thing, that isn't his real name."

"What is his real name?"

"His real name is . . ." checking the little notebook, he quietly says, "His name was Crown Prince Bas im Dhul Fa riq O bag ur. He came into this country in 1986 by way of Canada. Your parents came to America through Canada, didn't they?"

I can only shake my head yes.

"He came in by way of Canada, but his country of origin is Saudi Arabia," he adds.

"I don't understand, Adrian. My father never knew Ravi before I met him, not that I know of anyway. Did you say, Saudi Arabia?"

"Are you sure your father didn't know him?" Adrian asks.

"I'm not sure of anything anymore. What did you say Ravi's real name was?"

Adrian glances at his notes, "Crown Prince Basim Dhul Fariq Obagur. Does that ring a bell?"

"The prince part does, but nothing after that. Did you find out what Abdul's name is?"

Adrian consults his notes, flipping back a few pages. "Yes, here it is, Crown Prince Akdemir Halim Abdul Obagur."

The thought hits us both at the same time, and we say together, **"They're brothers!"**

As the realization of what this means sinks in, blood starts to drain from my head, and dizziness takes over. Adrian shakes me lightly.

"Ellen! Snap out of it; you're scaring me! Here, lie down. I'm going to get your Mother."

"No, don't get her." I close my eyes. "Abdul said he made a promise and he had to honor that promise. He made a promise to Ravi, Adrian. Why did Ravi lie to me and say his family was gone?"

All the questions that were unanswered before I met Adrian are suddenly beginning to make sense. Moments later, the sliding door opens as Adrian tells Jake that everything's alright. Jake's walking the perimeter on his way through and thought something was wrong, so he stopped by to check.

"We'll get everything cleared up, Ellie. Levi will continue to dig at the information, and his teams will decipher the documents. It's hard to say if it all fits together. What was this promise all about that Abdul mentioned? You didn't put that part in your report."

"It didn't seem important at the time. Abdul was yammering on about stuff. He did say it had something to do with me, but he wouldn't come right out and say." A feeling of betrayal is rising as memories of my captivity surface. "It does explain why Abdul looked familiar, but not about keeping me a prisoner. At some time in the future, he said he might discuss it with me. They were brothers! That explains so much."

"Certainly looks that way. We'll get this sorted out, Ellie, that's my promise to you."

"Adrian, do you think they grabbed the wrong person at the airport, and the woman took my place? Was Ravi supposed to travel with the books and not me? Did they cook this up after things went so wrong and did Abdul take me instead of the other woman? How in the hell could I have been so blind?"

Sitting next to me on the sofa, Adrian hugs me, whispering that the answers are out there. "I'm sure it's important, but let's not allow it to spoil our holiday, okay?"

"Why didn't Abdul tell me he was Ravi's brother? He was trying to keep me safe, but from what? It still doesn't explain why he locked me in that damn room and made me feel like a prisoner! How will I ever explain this to my children? Jason's going to be so angry and disappointed; he'll feel betrayed, as I do."

"Try to put it out of your mind for now. We don't have all the answers, and I'll help you explain it to them."

"I'm glad you're here with us."

Touching his head to mine, he says, "Time will heal that for you. I don't know how long that will take, but I'm here for you."

The shadow of a man is visible through the sliding doors, and Adrian gives the signal everything is OK as Jake moves away to walk the perimeters of both houses again.

Adrian turns off the light, "Come here," he whispers.

After the initial shock that Ravi is Abdul's brother, I resign to one day meet up with him to iron everything out.

*That is, of course, if I don't strangle him and his giant sidekick first!*

How could three weeks fly by so fast? Josh and Jake are now off duty, working on their tans, but they're careful observers, cautious, being mindful of potential trouble.

Adrian reports that Larry and the McGuire's say that everything is hunky-dory at the stables in Virginia and we shouldn't be suspicious of every car that drives by, or boats that float past, as they are looking at the great beach houses. He ever-scans the horizon while keeping his eyes on the children, insisting that we should not lower our guard one iota.

Our new concern is why and how Abdul is involved, especially since Ravi never mentioned him. Had there been a serious misunderstanding between the brothers? Adrian keeps assuring me that Levi's teams will uncover the mystery in due time.

TIME; it's what we're out of now, as we part company after having spent such a beautiful and relaxing time together. Josh and Jake are dismissed from duty in Cape Cod but then assigned to Terre's family. They will accompany them home and will bunk at their residence until Levi deems that the situation is free of threat.

Our trip home is uneventful. Upon our arrival, Mona informed us that she planned a sumptuous lunch for us. Kellie and Drew McGuire thoroughly enjoyed their time at Ashwood. They rode the trails and picnicked as they watched the house and grounds. They reported that all surveillance equipment is working correctly and everything is in order. They'll leave shortly to return to Langley; Larry will be back sometime tonight.

At dinner, we take turns telling the Murdock's and Reed what a great time we had knowing there was nothing to worry about back at the ranch. Reed mentions that he and Dr. Jessica went out several times, and he seems smitten with her. Do we hear wedding bells? Not so fast, he says, he's been down that bumpy road before and not anxious for history to repeat itself. They're taking things slow, getting to know each other.

Somehow, we're all tired from our restful vacation. One by one, the children gravitate to their rooms as the adults retire to the library.

"We had no trouble here whatsoever," Reed says laughing. "We had a good time with my new family, Kellie and Drew."

"A course, we didn't go ta the track or do anythin ta cause a stir, either," Glen adds, making a face. "That McGuire couple checked this place, sometimes twice a day. They never left here ta go nowhere and I'm mighty grateful there was no monkey business like the *Didge* thing."

"We had several new kids come for riding lessons; someone suggested we do a camp next year. A woman by the name of Patricia Baldwin used to board her horse here years ago, remembers Miss Abigail. Says she wants to give us one of her horses. I told her I'd talk with you, Miss Ellen," Reed adds.

"I think that would be excellent, Reed, what do you need to get that going?"

"That stuff is in my office; we can talk about it later," he says.

"We kept our noses clean, like you asked, Missy," Glen says proudly.

"Have you heard from Sheriff Rocky? Did Dr. Jess or the lab find anything else?"

"Rocky did call a week or so ago. Said the autopsy showed something, but I don't remember what he said," Reed says skewing his face trying to remember. "Sorry, I forgot to write it down." He looks a bit embarrassed. "Jessie was here, and we got involved."

"Yeah, ya forgot, ya mean." Glen lets out a hoot.

"Sheriff Rocky said he was sending you a copy of something and it should be in that pile of mail on your desk," Reed says. "Come on, Glen, let's go finish up in the barn and call it a night. Glad you're all home. Good night everyone."

"If we didn't have such good help here, we couldn't have gone away. Thanks, you two."

Stacks of mail and catalogs litter the top of my desk. As I begin to separate them, there are several letters from the State of Virginia Racing Commission, one from Dr. Jessica, and two official-looking ones from Sheriff Rockford. Which one will be good news, which one will be bad?

Choosing to open one from Sheriff Rocky, it states that their investigation into who killed our horse uncovered illegal practices. Horse owners are indeed using the race day medications at the local racetrack. It's not something they can prove. For the time being, they are suspending the investigation, until more evidence presents itself.

*He doesn't fool me; he's dropping this like a hot potato!*

Dr. Jessica's letter gets right to the point about the drug used to euthanize our *Didgeridoo*. The preliminary reports from the animal coroner and pathologist say, "*although the race day medicine called FTL is what was administered to the horse in question in a large dose; it's not what killed him.*" They think it's another drug; however, the laboratory is unable to isolate it.

Sheriff Rocky's second letter mentions a theory they are kicking around; that someone is out to warn Ashwood Stables that the new kid in town is not welcome.

*Honestly, that's no surprise!*

I think that we should have a whiteboard like the police use. Detectives put all the evidence on it, along with arrows and lines that connect to the scene of the crime. We all agree that a crime has been committed, not only against an innocent animal but a crime against our family. But the pièce de résistance is the letter from the Virginia Racing Commission. They have not only refused our stable license; they have barred us from stepping hoof or boot onto the Billingsworth Race Track!

Sauntering into my office, Adrian notices my expression and holds out his hand. Reading the letter while pressing buttons on his cellphone, he says, "We need your help." He's about to go into detail, then stops when a car pulls into the driveway.

Adrian heads down the hallway to greet Larry as I move up the staircase. It's an opportunity to retrieve the items from my little safes. Putting the documents and other things into a plain manila envelope, I take it to the open door where Larry and Adrian recline on their twin beds.

"Sorry to disturb you, fellas. Here's the stuff we talked about, Adrian."

He strolls toward me as Larry remains on his bed, saying with his eyes closed, "Hey there Miss Ellen, did you have a good vacation with your family?"

"Yes, we did, thanks to you, Adrian, and the McGuire's. Did you have a nice time with yours?" He nods that he did. "Mrs. Murdock is fixing your favorite for dinner tomorrow."

"That's nice, Miss Ellen," Larry says quietly.

Handing the package to Adrian, he tosses it on his bed and pushes me into the hallway. "Thank you, Mrs. Thompson, I'll share this with Larry when he recovers from his vacation."

By giving the CIA this information, we have nothing to lose. My only wish is for this drama to end, so we can get back to the business of living our lives without threat.

"You look a little tired, Mrs. Thompson. Is there anything I can do for you?" Adrian rolls his eyes in a mirthful way, then grins comically.

"Not unless you can get the racing commission to take another look at our application and get the process going for our license. Maybe we aren't done with all this if we can still race."

"Got a call into Levi. I read him the letter and reminded him of what you and your family gave up in the line of duty for your country," Adrian says quietly.

"We don't qualify for anything like that. What is it that you think I did for my country?"

"Nothing, my mistake. Levi and his teams will come up with something to help you. You and Jason will get your chance to race, even though I think it's too dangerous."

Adrian looks left and then right. Reaching to pull me into a bear hug, he whispers in my ear, "I don't want you to get hurt." He then kisses my cheek tenderly.

"I hope you and your cronies can work miracles. It's going to take one to get through that hogwash." Giving him a little squeeze, I say, "Good Night, Adrian."

"Sleep tight," he says absently. "Don't let the bedbugs bite."

The next day, Adrian takes the envelope back to Langley in an attempt to decipher the documents, investigate the currency, and have their crack team put the little chip and bug under scrutiny. I had to promise to keep my chin up and not get hurt while he's gone. Even though we can't race, nothing is stopping us from training.

Work crews are completing the swimming pool, the chain-link fence surrounding it, and the Guest House. The sandstone patio is sealed, the barbeque area is now functional, and our new patio furniture makes it look like a tropical oasis. We could have enjoyed this when the temperatures were high this summer, but the spa will feel good, especially after a long day of training.

Our government knows how to work miracles, or at least Levi does! A day after Adrian's departure, a registered letter arrives. We should expect to receive our licenses shortly. Unfortunately, there is a condition attached to it. All of us, trainers and drivers included, will be scrutinized and should we meander once over the line, we're out!

That's the good news. The bad news is that the commission was so sure they could stop us, they shredded all the permits and applications, including the checks!

Glen shakes his head at this news, and says, "Did ya think it would be easy, Missy? Why do ya try so hard ta get inta that club, when they don't want us there!"

"I never said it would be easy, Glen, nothing that is worth it, ever is. After all, if it were easy, everyone would do it."

"Ah ha, sure thing, Missy."

About a week later, the notice arrives that the commission wants to move forward with having our fingerprints done along with a bar-coded picture badge worn at all times when we're at the track. Adrian doesn't want to blow his cover, so he'll remain out of the barn and stable area for the time being so that he can blend into the crowd.

Our first race is less than ten days away. Jason and I are by all accounts, considered amateurs, and the racing secretary will place us as such. The intention is to move up in class, but we can only do that if we have a few races under our belts, or if we place or win.

Jason and I are on the practice track. "Come on back 'round, Missy. Reed, are ya set? Keep a sharp eye out if *Raindrop* or *Lester* swerves when ya come alongside each other. Give hand signals if ya get inta trouble. You don't want ta be third on the rail," Glen hollers.

Even though the commission has given the go-ahead, my enthusiasm wanes these last few days. I don't look forward to this as once I had. Can I get through the race without a complete meltdown?

*Maybe it's pre-race day jitters.*

Reed and Glen continually instruct us, as there are strict guidelines to follow. Glen cautions us repeatedly about the aggression of other drivers and the potential for getting into trouble. My head hurts thinking of all the things we must remember, but Jason seems undaunted.

"I'd like to time you guys today." Reed moves next to Glen, checking his stopwatch. "Signal when you're ready. Okay, on my mark...ready...go!" Reed lowers a flag to signal that we should tap our horses' rump (never, ever more than that) using the crop to get them moving.

*Lester* paces in his usual spunky style today. Turning my head slightly to see Jason, he's sporting a big grin as *Raindrop* falls into place alongside us. We're training to watch our horses interact with others, mindful of those drivers who are on either side of us, who might be in front or behind. As long as we remain in control of our horse, we can peek at each other.

Race bikes can suddenly veer in different directions, throwing you and your horse off the pace. Drivers must move off to either the outside or inside of the track, rejoining the others when the horse regains the proper gait. It's wise to take it easy at first and be patient and make our move when we're sure it's safe.

"Let's try it again," Reed says.

Giving the signal to accelerate on his mark, Jason and I are neck and neck as we pass Reed. Surprisingly, *Lester* catches up to *Raindrop*. A beat later, *Raindrop* moves past *Lester*. They keep doing this until Reed goes by in a blur, slowing when Glen gives us the signal to stop.

Jason jumps off his bench to pat *Raindrop*. "Mom, we did it! Wasn't that amazing? We're ready to race at the track!"

"Ya both did a furlong in fifteen seconds," Glen says proudly. "Now aren't ya glad we put them ole hopples on 'em right from the start?"

"There must be something wrong with your stopwatch, old man. We weren't going that fast."

"Yes, you were," Reed says, laughing. "We both timed you!"

"Hear that Mom?" Jason says, nearly out of breath from jumping up and down.

"That's right," Glen says, patting me on the back. "Looks real promisin, Missy. Let's do it again."

For the next hour or so, our horses go around the track as if they are competing with each other, but I can't wait until this ends as my legs and back hurt and my bum are sore.

Glen waves for us to come in. "Let's get these horses a good rub down and a shower, maybe a little extra feed for the job they did."

While Jason jumps off his cart, Reed clips a lead rope on *Raindrop* as Glen takes *Lester*, who says a bit sheepishly, "Guess you're gonna get your wish. I hope ya know what you're up against, Missy. Are ya sure ya can stand sittin on that bench? It ain't too late ta pull out, ya know."

"We're newbie's, Glen. We'll stay away from the bad people, and maybe I can find something to numb my butt by then."

"Even if they accept ya in the stables, they don't have ta be nice," he cautions.

"We're no threat to them. It's not as if we can go the distance. I'll probably be dead last for most of the race anyway."

"Ya be real careful out there, okay? Stick close ta me, or Reed. Your Mama will be mad at me if I let anythin happen ta ya."

It's evident that Glen worries about what will happen once we get to the track on race day, and frankly, so am I. "I will be extra careful, okay Glen?"

"But, if ya even think ya have a chance, don't blow it! Move inta the chute and inta the pocket like I taught ya ta do and watch your back, front, sides, and everywhere else, Missy," Glen says as he gives my shoulder a little squeeze.

Adrian calls to say he has some good and bad news. It seems the CIA dissected and analyzed the contents of the envelope, and it yielded some startling information, but he's hesitant to tell me.

"Oh, let me have it, Adrian. I'm wearing . . ."

"Your big girl pants, I know. It seems that you were right, the Prince and his brother Basim were trying to smuggle documents into the United States, but not for the reasons we thought."

"Is that the good news or the bad news?"

"That's the good news. I'll tell you more when I get there."

"What's the bad news?"

"The bad news is that little chip might be an electronic device the team can't readily decipher yet; Jewels can't anyway. They'll work on that until they're able to determine what it is."

"It stumped Jewels, the electronics genius?"

"Yes, hard to do, but that bug Jason found can be purchased anywhere. It pretty much lost its charm when he smashed it. No word on who purchased it or who put it in Glen's office."

"Is there more bad news?"

"No, there's more good news. The currency is worth a small fortune. The teams don't know if the documents and the money are tied together, but you can expect a finder's fee."

"What kind of finder's fee are we talking about, Mr. CIA man?"

"They think it'll be close to $500,000. You'll have enough in your purse so you won't have to race."

"What does the CIA consider a small fortune, Adrian?"

"Levi thinks it might be worth billions," he says.

"Oh, that is a small fortune. I have to give this horseracing thing a try. I need to do this, perhaps for all the wrong reasons, but I have to try it at least one season."

"I figured that's what you'd say. I'll be there in time for dinner."

"Good, travel safe, Adrian."

"I will do my best, Mrs. Thompson."

Today is race day. I'm more than a little nervous because it's unclear how much the racing community will react to our presence. Will they ignore us, or will they allow us to race without incident? Jason seems undeterred, excited that we're finally getting our wish.

As Jason helps Reed and Glen load the horses into the trailer, Adrian is backing up the new truck and enclosed trailer we purchased last week. He reluctantly agrees to observe and keep his eye on things, leaving all the betting to me.

Mother stands beside me. She hasn't said much since Adrian informed her of the contents of the envelope he took to Langley. I'm not sure if she's upset with me, because I didn't share that with her, or that I told Adrian instead of her. I also haven't shared the news about Ravi and Abdul as it hasn't been the right time to disclose that connection.

"Ellie, please be careful out there today," Mother says thoughtfully.

"Why don't you come with us? Then you can see for yourself how careful we are."

Tears fill her eyes. "I'll stay here. Ellen, you need to be extremely careful. You think you know everything there is to know about horseracing, but promise me to be on guard."

"What are you trying to say, Mother?"

"Daddy told me what you and he were doing. I didn't approve at first, but then he told me how much he put away for you."

"Then, what's the big deal?"

"I have a funny feeling about today, that's all. Like those déjà vu things you get. I have them too, on occasion."

"I promise we'll be very cautious and very watchful. So that you know, I don't plan on making this a career."

"That's a relief," she sighs.

Hugging her, saying, "Jason is much stronger and younger, he's the one who should be racing. I need to know what it's like out there. Do you understand that?"

"Yes sweetheart, I'm a silly old mom. I love you, Ellie. You and your sister are my whole world. I don't think I can lose you a second time and survive."

"We'll be back before you know it. I love you, too. I'll call when we're on the way home, okay?"

Adrian and I are in the new truck, while Glen, Reed, and Jason haul the horses as Larry volunteered to stay behind. Once the guard clears us at the entrance gate at Billingsworth Racetrack, we drive toward the staging area where our trucks and trailers will remain. Glen mutters to himself that they put us in the farthest stalls in the most distant barn.

"How bad can it be, Glen? So it's a little hike, we can all use a little exercise."

Grumbling, he says, "No problem, Missy, but don't expect a barn warmin party either."

Most owners stable their horses here for the duration of the racing season, but it's not obligatory. In an unprecedented show of solidarity, the men agreed with me that we transport our horses and not let them stable here.

During their pre-race day lecture, Glen and Reed's instructions were decisive and direct. Adrian then took over what he expects of us. It's imperative that each team stays together, whether we're in the stables or the enclosure waiting to go out to our race.

Our cellphones must be turned off or put on vibrate in the barn area, per the racetrack rules. Should we need to send a message, we're to use the group texting that we programmed into our phones.

Adrian cautions us to be mindful that our race bikes or gear are vulnerable to sabotage, so be vigilant. If one of us has to leave the other, we are to alert everyone to where we are, even if it's to go to the restroom. Once the race begins, the drivers will be on their own out there on the track.

Wanting to see if our hunch is correct, Adrian cleverly installed an ingenious device that detects movement on the outside of both trailers and trucks. If anyone so much as touches the metal, it will send a signal to his smartphone, then the alarm will beep ten times.

It reminds me of a funny story that Daddy told about an owner who had a signal worked out with his trainer. If he used his handkerchief to wipe his forehead, that meant the trainer should get to the betting window to place a wager on a particular horse they agreed upon previously. Unfortunately, it was a sweltering day, and the owner took out his handkerchief and began to wipe his face, forgetting about the signal, but by then it was too late.

While Glen and Reed settle the horses into their stalls, Adrian walks to the other side of the track to observe, because he doesn't have a badge that will admit him to our barn.

I attempt to calm myself by meditating as the prearranged time nears to discuss the rules with the track official. It is the meeting that all drivers and jockeys must attend that takes place before the first race of the day. The chief steward will discuss the rules and all the generalities that may or may not happen during each race, then checks that our helmets are the approved variety.

"Some folks might not take kindly to a woman with no experience that wants to join the inner sanctum here at the racetrack, Mrs. Thompson. May I remind you both that you're here under *trial* conditions?" Sounding strangely like Glen with his doomsday warning, he then softens his tone. "The likelihood of being confronted (he avoids naming anyone in particular), is very high. You should be mindful of that."

"Our trainers covered every contingency, but thank you for the warning, sir."

Putting a hand on Jason's shoulder, he says, "You be careful out there, son. This warning's for you, too. I'd hate to think this is your first and last day here."

"I understand, sir," Jason says.

"We've trained long and hard to do this," I say. "All we need is a chance to prove it." Then the chief steward dismisses us and wishes us luck on the track today, handing me a paper with his signature.

"Wonder where they placed you, Mom. Mr. Adrian is looking at the board right now. He's supposed to text me. Wait, here it is."

**MOM up for race board place 6.**

"Better show Glen."

When Jason shows Glen the message, he's not happy as he thinks the racing secretary has it in for us, as we're somewhere toward the end of the mechanical arm at the outside.

"It's the name of the game, Glen. We weren't expecting a party, remember?"

In the barn, there's a hubbub of activity as jockeys and trainers walk past our stalls, either leading horses in or out. Some of them talk with one another, all while ignoring us as if there's an invisible shield over our stalls.

Proudly wearing my new silks and tall leather boots, I adjust the goggles attached to the front of my helmet, then wait for Glen's signal. Taking several deep breaths to gain my center, I'm startled when he says, "You're up, Missy. Ya can still withdraw. Jess is in the stands, and we can call her back ta verify your withdrawal."

"We're merely getting our feet wet, Glen. I'm going to make you proud today, you will see."

It's a little like Christopher Columbus on his Maiden Voyage, because this is, after all, our maiden race. With my lucky No.14 attached to *Lester's* headpiece, and saddle towel, how can we go wrong?

Glen takes this opportunity to badger me a little. "Ya gotta look relaxed and natural. Then move up when ya think it's time. Ya don't have ta be more than a nose away for a photo finish."

"*Lester's* green. I'm green, and they all know that. They don't think we'll even place, look where they put us in the lineup. We don't have a snowball's chance in hell of getting to the inside today."

That's okay with me, as we're in a non-graded stakes race. The racing secretary's race-day book put us with the same kind of conditions as most of the other horses running today, except for those who have had more races and are not doing so great.

*What's the big deal?*

I'm grateful we aren't running coupled today or Jason and I would have to compete with each other. And we don't know how our horses will react when we line up for the first time behind the mechanical arm.

I'm praying that *Lester* will like running next to other horses as he does at home. I'm not so worried about the horses we'll be racing against today--it's the other drivers that will be the real threat as they have so much more experience.

At this point, I want to get this over with and out of my system.

*"It's not whether you get knocked down,*

*it's whether you get up."*

~Vince Lombardi

# Chapter Fourteen

## Déjà vu Again

The bugle sounds the *Call to the Post* that signals racers have five to ten minutes to get into position before the scheduled start time. Glen leads *Lester's Best* to the enclosure to wait for the parade that will take us onto the track. So far so good as we follow No. 4, settling to the right of him behind the mechanical arm.

When all drivers are in position, the starter truck moves forward as we pick up speed behind it. As the arms fold forward, we begin to pass the truck.

The other drivers may know it's my first time today and at this terrifying thought, something unusual begins to happen. I have little control over my body shaking. It's as if someone wound me up with an invisible key. Is this intimidation trepidation? I certainly hope this doesn't happen every time. No one can probably see the jerking, but it will not stop.

Lester begins to inch closer to the other horses. We aren't dead last, but we are far from the favorite, who looks like he won't relinquish the lead to anyone. I don't dare try to find Glen or Adrian in the crowd for fear of breaking my concentration.

Reed and Glen drummed their do's and don'ts rules into Jason and me to the point of distraction. Do check left and right, don't hold the reins too tight or too loose, don't reach up to adjust the goggles once the race begins, do keep our horses pacing correctly, and finally, do try to smile and don't fall off your seat!

Of course, we must also keep in mind the other things such as; don't beat our horses on the rump, do gently tap, don't pull too hard to either side, so our horse knows everything is okay, and most importantly, don't forget to breathe. Am I in over my head? I won't give Glen the satisfaction that I'm having the least bit of trouble.

*Lester* effortlessly moves forward to keep pace with the other horses. I don't dare take him to the rail yet as the other drivers will box me in. For now, we move merrily along until someone from behind comes into my peripheral vision to the right. We're three abreast when *Lester* takes this as a challenge, picking up the pace without any encouragement.

*Lester* passes him, moving ahead to pass two other bikes while I struggle to hold things together. Heeding Glen's warning; that if *Lester* wants to run faster than I'm comfortable, gently pull back, but not too hard or too quick as he's likely to break stride. Where will we be then, out of the race altogether? Or overturned face down on the track?

When the race is over, the TrackMaster motions us off, and Glen's smiling face pushes through the crowd to greet us. He's as proud as a peacock as he holds up four fingers.

"Good job! That was some cracklin pace ya two were doin," he declares, clicking the lead rope onto *Lester's* halter.

"Let me get off of this blasted seat first." Trying not to let on about the pain, Glen notices, giving me his *I told you so* face.

"Not enough paddin, huh? Are ya ready ta quit yet?" he says shaking his head, laughing.

"Give it a rest, Glen." I'm in no mood to word wrestle with him right now.

Jason and Reed are standing near the stalls. Jason mouths 'good for you' as Reed says the scuttlebutt is that *Lester's* a sleeper and if word gets around, the boys may double their efforts to keep me from placing again. They could knock me right out of the game if I'm not careful.

Reed and Jason go into *Raindrop's* stall to prepare him for racing later today. As I brush *Lester* down, a shadow falls across the mesh gate. *Lester* seems jittery, shakes his head, and stomps a hoof while I brush him down.

"Hey, you there. Are you from Ashwood?" a man says gruffly.

Turning, a large man wearing an obnoxious plaid jacket that cannot disguise his protruding stomach is standing in the doorway. His squat-looking cap sits on top of his shocking-white hair, which sticks out at the sides. He looks so comical that I start to laugh.

As I continue to brush *Lester*, I try to ignore him, then say, "Yes. What's it to you?"

"You had a good first time out there on the track taday, girlie. Don't suppose you know the rules about first-timers, do ya?"

*Maybe he'll go away if I don't say anything.*

"Are you playing dumb with me? I make or break all the jockeys and drivers here. You don't stand a chance without my help."

I turn slowly to face him. "Is that so? And you would be Mr.?"

"You enjoy your day here taday, little lady because it's gonna be your last one." The big man turns to walk away.

My Daddy didn't raise any fools. Unclipping the mesh gate, I move into the barn and say loud enough for him to hear, "Excuse me? To be clear, did I hear you correctly?"

The big man turns around. "You heard me. Don't make me repeat it," he snarls.

"Did you tell me that I can't race here? Mind telling me what your rules are?"

Glen is walking into the barn as Reed and Jason poke their heads around the corner of *Raindrop's* stall. Reed puts his arm out to stop Jason who's attempting to come to my rescue. I can hear him say, "Stay put, son, your Mama has this well in hand."

"I got way more friends around here than you do, girlie. You don't belong here," he says, turning away.

"What you're saying is that I can't join your little reindeer games, because you don't approve. Who died and made you the boss?"

Several others are now crowding around Reed, Jason, and Glen. The man turns around to face me. Wrinkling his face, he says, "That's right, I don't approve, and I say you can't join, so you can't race here!" When he turns to leave, a crowd has gathered, but no one will get out of his way.

"Maybe I don't want to join your little club."

The man turns toward me again, but this time, his face is now a deep red. Could it pop like a balloon? "You don't want to mess with me, girlie. I'll make it simple for ya. Finish your day here, but you're not welcome to return. I know people that'll back me up!"

"You can threaten all you want. You don't have the right to push me around. Not now, *not ever!*"

The man turns on his heel, saying, "Get outta my way." Pushing through the crowd, he stomps out of the barn. I start to laugh at the soft applause as a driver comes forward to shake my hand. Others then slowly move in around us, patting me on the back.

A tall man pushes out of the crowd, to say, "I'm Emil Lassiter, owner of Lassiter Stables. I can't b'lieve you stood up to that man! No one has ever done that b'fore. We've all paid the price to race here, so I welcome you. You and your horse passed up one of Mr. Jenkins,' and I'll wager you'll beat him someday."

"After today, I'm not sure there will be a next time. The Racing Commission gave us a special condition."

Mr. Lassiter hands me one of his business cards. Glancing at it quickly; I know who he is and where he lives. He's as full of baloney as Jenkins.

Emil smiles. "I know the history of Ashwood Farms, and we're all proud to have you. When you have some time, I wouldn't mind sittin down with you and your trainers to maybe help you with what I know, so you don't make the mistakes I've seen this bunch make."

"Thank you, Mr. Lassiter, I'll think about it."

"Pleasure to meet you, Ma'am. Have a nice day." Lassiter waves to one of the jockeys and they walk out of the barn.

A jockey waves to the group who gathered behind Jenkins, and then approaches to introduce himself. "I'm called Jockey Jerry. We were told you'd be here today, Ms. Thompson. Jenkins sent his boys in to tell us we weren't to talk to you or make you feel welcome in any way. Sorry, we did that to you. It's a real pleasure to meet you and have the famous Ashwood's back racing here again."

"Thanks, Jerry. I'd like you to meet our teams."

Others come forward to shake our hands and talk with Glen, Reed, and Jason. Jerry says the favorites are not in this barn as they are stabled where the Jenkins', Lassiter's, McDermott's, and the Claremont's have free reign.

"Lassiter don't belong in here with the likes of us, Ms. Thompson. He came through to see what you look like up close. His horses are with the others. You let us know if you need anything, alright?"

"Same goes, Jerry. I appreciate that. We'll be careful. Thanks for the warning."

"Guess ya got your little welcome party after all," Glen chides. "Better get a move on, Missy. Jason's up in thirty minutes."

Mr. Jenkins is a blowhard, but Mr. Lassiter is the owner that lives down the road from us. Which one will have us thrown off the track first? Or which one got the Racing Commission to revoke our license? Could either of them be responsible for *Didge's* demise?

My brain slowly recalls something that Mr. A said about things not always being what they seem. Who is the enemy here? Who is blowing smoke? We'll take this with a grain of salt, and keep alert because we don't know whom to trust.

My cellphone vibrates as Adrian texts: **Good job. U R best!** Adrian doesn't want us separated, but Glen says Jason needs first-day information from me, sending me to the enclosure while he stays with *Lester*.

Jason is excited; the mere fact he isn't nervous means he's ready. As we talk about what to expect, *Raindrop's* ears twitch. I'm about to capture this momentous occasion when something triggers the hairs on the back of my neck. As I ready my cellphone to take a photo, there's someone in the background that wasn't there a second ago. Zooming in, I take additional pictures acting like a doting mother.

After giving Jason my blessing to have fun on his maiden voyage, I excuse myself to go to the restroom. Flipping through the pictures, I wonder if it could be Lenard in disguise. To be safe, I text Adrian and the others: **TARGET hat-jeans-beard-glasses-wht-T-shrt-Cud B LENARD!** Oh, crap! Does he have to do this now? A moment later, Adrian texts back: **ON IT.**

The bugle sounds the familiar get into position tune as we watch Jason line up for the parade going onto the track. Jason turns back, giving a thumbs up when he sees me, and then we move to the outside fence to observe.

"He'll be alright, Miss Ellen," Reed says. "He's strong and focused."

"Jason's not the one I'm worried about, Reed."

"The racing secretary put him in a good position. Too bad he didn't do that for you."

"Did you get my text? Do you understand what it means?" As the pace truck's arms fold up and the horses move forward, Reed takes his phone out of his pocket and nods.

Jason is not too close to the leader, but somewhere in the middle. It's odd how things look at track level. It's also different when you're viewing this action up in the grandstands. It's quite another story when you're the driver.

When the driver to Jason's left edges in front of *Raindrop*, Jason must anticipate this move and pulls back on the reins. It allows the horse to move without upsetting the other drivers and horses around him. *Raindrop* then moves into the position the horse displaced so effortlessly; it looks as if he's gliding on pudding.

"Did that happen when I raced?" I ask Reed.

"Yes, but you were probably too focused on what you were doing to see it. Jason's doing good, for a first-timer, Miss Ellen. You should be very proud of him. We're proud of you too!" he says, patting my shoulder.

The favorite's in the chute and moves ahead at a good clip when Jason sees an opportunity to get into the pocket. Reed sucks in a breath, and whispers, "Stay where you are, Jason. Stay where you are! You're in a good place. Don't do anything stupid! Good boy, now stay b'hind him and let him be!"

A text comes from Adrian: **horse left barn. safe now. hungry. good race.** Lenard, (or whoever it is), must be gone. The word hungry is our signal to meet at the cooler as he can't come into the barn or parade area without a name badge.

After Jason places third, our new friends congratulate him. He stays behind with Reed to brush *Raindrop* while I pass around the photo I took earlier. Most shake their heads no, except one. Could he know something? Perhaps he's one of Mr. Lassiter's spies or one of Mr. Jenkins' boys.

When I get to the truck, Adrian has the cooler open. "Why are you alone, Mrs. Thompson?"

"New rules. I forgot, Mr. CIA man."

"Okay, I'll let this pass, this one time, Ellie, but there's a reason you need to follow the rules." Changing to a higher pitched voice, he says, "Hey there Ms. Thompson, lookie here at what Ms. Mona packed for us taday! Don't you look sexy in them pants! And I love your boots! Where, oh where did you get them?"

"Adrian, be serious. You need to see this picture I took."

As I try to find the photo of Lenard, he plunges his hand into the cooler, bobs his head up and down, then takes a lid off of a container and pretends to eat.

"Want some?" he says with a pretend mouthful.

"Adrian, do you think the racetrack manager contacted Lenard after he found out we registered to race today? How else would he know we'd be here?"

"At this point, we don't know for sure if it is Lenard. I don't know how he knew you were here, but that's a possibility. If that was Lenard, he spotted me, and he's either gone or hiding out somewhere. I alerted Larry, so he's keeping an eye out for him at Ashwood."

"Okay. FYI, we're going to try this again next week. Glen said we might come to the track on Wednesday and Saturday if we want, so I'll go and help them pack up the gear."

"I'll just…" Adrian begins to stuff his mouth, waving a chicken leg in the air. "I'll text Glen that you're on your way back. Just be careful."

When Mother told me about her *funny feeling* this morning, was it about Lenard or racing?

On our second foray into the harness racing world, we come to Billingsworth prepared for confrontation. After the formalities with the chief steward are over, I'm relieved there's no lecture from him today.

*Lester* and I try to avoid other drivers, but it seems they have it in for us, as we're immediately boxed in. As my frustration level hits the roof, I vow not to give up when a hole suddenly opens, and *Lester* moves into it, but we are immediately boxed in again.

That's okay; I'll take the third place, thank you very much. I shouldn't count my chickens before they hatch, as this may not be how we finish the race. The drivers will be accelerating in the later part of the race that could change everything.

Suddenly, *Lester* twitches his ears as the crop from the driver on our right crosses over into our space, narrowly missing *Lester's* rump. The Harness Racing Rules flash past my eyes. I'll remember the ones I'm going to recite to the Racing Commission once this race is over.

This little incident set in motion several things. When the offending driver moved forward, the driver directly in front of us came in contact with his wheel, and it naturally outraged the driver. It threw his horse off the pace, where it must have panicked and tried to gallop, so the driver had to remove him from the race, but by then, the race was over.

What the offending driver did is immediate grounds for removal. The racing rules we studied forward, backward, and upside down, clearly state what is acceptable and what are apparent infractions. Serious injury can happen if these rules are not followed.

Exhausted and sore, I can't wait to get off the race bike seat. Jason is with Glen and waves. "Mom, I thought that driver was going to cut you off, but his horse did something funny. You came in third!" Jason says beaming.

Guess my hero got a well-deserved second spot for helping me today. I will thank him later.

We are driving to Billingsworth Racetrack on our third trek in our quest to win a first. With our horses settled into their stalls, Jason and I meet with the chief steward to have our usual little chat.

Once we return to the barn, Glen, Reed, and Jason stay behind to take care of things. Adrian stands near the gate and walks with me to our truck to get lunch for everyone.

"I have a feeling that person will show up today, Adrian."

"How do you know that for sure?" he asks.

"I can't explain it, but I can bet with utmost certainty that it's Lenard. He must be desperate to get his hands on the documents and currency. What I don't understand is why they're important to him. He can't be working for Abdul, so it must be Mr. A. The person who sent him knows I have the items. If Lenard doesn't deliver them, will they come to Ashwood? Did they kill our *Didge* to send us a message?"

"We got that covered. Levi is sending a team by helicopter as we speak."

"My, how intriguing, Mr. CIA man. How is this team getting here? Are they dropping an SUV from the sky? Are they parachuting in?"

"Mrs. Thompson, I love how your mind works. What's with you and people dropping from the sky? No, they'll touch down on the back forty, so they don't scare the horses. See, I do pay attention to what you say."

"I never said you didn't pay attention."

Adrian gives me his best grin. "Ellie, this isn't Mission Impossible, it's only a mission." He laughs and stuffs food into his mouth at the same time. "You do think of the most unusual things. Sheriff Rocky and his squad are on their way in unmarked vehicles."

"I'm on deck in an hour. You know, Adrian, we do make a good team; all except that food you consume, I gain weight looking at it, but you eat and eat and never gain a pound. How do you do that?"

"Would you take this back with you? Glen's on his way to meet you. Be on guard, because I don't want anything to happen to you or your family. Text me when you get to the barn."

"You're letting me go by myself? What if I encounter Lenard on the way?"

"Do you honestly think Lenard is dumb enough to show his face in broad daylight? Glen's probably near the gate by now, go." Pointing his finger at me, it reminds me of Jam-ale—and a déjà vu sensation comes over me as a chill runs up my spine. "You'll be fine. Text when you get there, okay? I can watch you from here."

Adrian loads my arms with a small cooler and a grocery bag filled with food. I'm close to the barn door, but there's no sign of Glen. When several rough-looking individuals start to surround me, I nearly drop the food.

This time, it reminds me of Jam-ale's army. They take turns saying things such as I don't belong here, I should pack up and never come back, no one wants a woman in the barn to spoil things, and I should go home and bake a pie. Then someone smacks his hand with a riding crop, as another says I'm not welcome here and never will be.

"Missy, are ya okay?" Glen's voice calls from outside the circle.

"You need some help, Ms. Thompson?" A familiar voice asks.

The men move off as if choreographed like a scene from *West Side Story* and the altercation ends. Standing near Glen are all my unlikely heroes, including Jerry and the drivers from our barn.

"Thank you, fellas, that was mighty kind of you," I say gratefully.

"Here, let me take that for ya." Glen reaches to take the cooler.

"I thought you were going to meet me, Glen?"

"Sorry, I kinda got sidetracked," he says sheepishly. "Ya sure know how to rub folks the wrong way. Some fella came in right after ya left saying how ya owed him somethin and he's here ta collect it. Said he'd be back."

"That must have been Lenard. I'm not thinking nice thoughts about him right now." I'm flipping to the images I captured last week. "Does this look like the person you saw?"

Glen looks surprised. "Yeah, the guy looked like that, but nothin like Lenard, Missy. He had a scruffy beard, dirty t-shirt, black eyeglasses, dirty jeans."

"He was in disguise."

"Oh, good grief," Glen says shaking his head. "How come I didn't know that?"

"Because, he was in disguise, Glen. Adrian's already called in support, and they should be here soon. Stay close to the horses and watch your back. I don't think he's harmless."

"Me neither, Missy."

I'm texting Adrian we're back in the barn. He texts back: **Eagle landed. Stay safe.**

With the horses cared for and everyone else watered and fed, I sneak into *Lester's* stall to relax before my race. A small bench is attached to the inside of the stall wall that is long and wide enough for me to stretch out. I'll be awake immediately if anyone comes near here.

Using a roll of paper towels as a neck support, I close my eyes. Sometime later, something moves next to me, which brings me awake. Poised with a government issue firearm, Adrian crouches beside me, where he puts a finger to his lips. He backs silently into the corner as *Lester* munches contentedly on some hay.

A few moments later, I stand on the bench and flatten myself against the inside wall as a gloved hand appears to unhook the mesh gate. Poking my head up, I say, "Hey there Mr. Lenard, where have you been? It's about time you showed your ugly face."

The man looks startled and stops dead in his tracks. The baseball cap hides his hair, but his beard and glasses only add to his comical appearance, and I nearly fall off the bench laughing.

"Shut up! I have been waiting to talk to you, Ellen," Lenard snarls, licking his lips in that annoying habit of his.

"A master of disguise, I see. You look ridiculous. Guess your partner had a falling out with some bad guys. Know anything about that?"

"Keep your voice down."

"You know; I've learned a lot about you since you went away. I don't know whether to feel sorry for you or laugh at you."

"You have been nothing but trouble since we picked you up in Kauai. If you hand over the documents and currency, there will be no trouble."

As I try to keep the monologue going, his shaking hand is leveling a small pistol at my chest.

"What is it you think I have, Lenard?"

"Cut the crap, Ellen! You have important papers and money that belongs to my boss, and he wants it back." Lenard licks his lips again, as his eyes dart from left to right.

"Why is that stuff so important, Lenard? And what makes you think I still have it?"

Spitting as he talks, "Stop it! You probably have it back at the house, so come along quietly, and we can take care of it now. Besides, you owe it to us, after what we did for you."

"I owe you nothing, Lenard. After you dumped me at Ashwood and took everything I hold near and dear to me! I should shoot *you* where you stand, you dirty rat!"

"What are you going to shoot me with, hum, your finger? If you do not fork it over . . ." Lenard's face distorts into an ugly grimace.

"Excuse me, pork face; you have mistaken me for someone who gives a damn!"

Adrian steps into view pointing his pistol directly at Lenard's head. In his best Clint Eastwood imitation, he says, "Go ahead, punk, make my day. You'll be dead before you pull the trigger."

*There's no doubt that Adrian will shoot him if he so much as sneezes.*

Sheriff Rocky strolls into the barn as three men in army fatigues move noiselessly behind Lenard to push his face down onto the floor. While one cuffs him, the second one takes the pistol out of his hand, as the third man reads him his rights. As he tries to squirm away from the men, Lenard howls obscenities in a foreign language.

"I've always wanted to say that," Adrian says, blowing invisible smoke from the end of his pistol, which he twirls and pockets into his holster in one smooth move.

317

"I'm not sure Dirty Harry used those exact words, but you're still *my* hero." Stepping down from the bench to hug him, he doesn't seem to mind when I wrap my arms around his neck to kiss him. "Thanks, Adrian, you saved my life!"

Grabbing both my arms, he says, "What were you thinking, taking a nap when Lenard was on the prowl?"

"I'm exhausted. My body hurts, and my nerves are a jangled mess. I'm a light sleeper; I woke up when you came in, didn't I?"

"You're not a light sleeper. I was sitting on the floor thirty minutes before I woke you up. My legs were so cramped I didn't think I could stand up."

"But you unwound yourself to save the day!"

Glen steps into *Lester's* stall, saying, "I saw the Sheriff and a bunch of army people haulin someone away. Please tell me it was Lenard."

"Yes, my good man, it was indeed Lenard," Adrian says proudly.

"I'm glad ya caught 'em. Say, how long ya two gonna keep this a secret?"

Adrian and I are standing very close together with our arms entwined. Pulling away, he mutters, "Don't know what you're talking about Mr. Murdock. Must keep our country safe. Have a good race, Mrs. Thompson."

"Come on Missy, let's get a move on, it's time ta get ta the parade," Glen says, waving his hand in the air.

Once our races are over, we pack up our gear and head home. As we hash over what happened today, Adrian and I discuss the consequences of alerting the Virginia Commission about what happened during my harrowing race last week.

He says to let it go for now because we have bigger fish to fry. Sometime down the road, there will be an opportunity to bring this incident to the Racing Commission's attention, but not now.

Jason and I held our own on the track today. And, we are incredibly proud that at least one criminal is off the streets and apprehended. Now, if only we can round up the rest of the crazy cast of characters as easily!

*Once we figure out who they are, that is.*

Larry is with a crack CIA team and the U.S. Marshals who assisted in Lenard's capture today. He says a SWAT team took Lenard to a maximum security facility, where he lawyered up. Funny thing about that, as no one can locate this attorney.

Soaking my aching body in our new spa attached to the swimming pool, Adrian comes to join me. He carries a tray with cups that slosh when he walks and lowers it for me to take one. "May I offer you a refreshment, Mrs. Thompson?"

"Are you allowed to fraternize with your clients, Mr. CIA man?"

"I assure you this is strictly business, Mrs. Thompson. I came to inform you that Levi and his highly evolved group of nerds, headed by one unusual person named Jewels, found out something of interest about the documents and other items you gave him to investigate. If you don't want to hear it, I can go to the Guest House and leave you alone."

"Come on, Adrian, I'm too tired to debate with you."

Flashing his irresistible grin, he says, "If this is too much for you, why don't you hang up your helmet? You proved yourself at the track, what's there left to accomplish?"

"Please stop trying to talk me out of it. What did the illustrious Levi and his lovely bunch of coconuts find out this time?"

"Good thing you're sitting down. The documents are in Arabic; the old script doesn't describe it properly. They're ancient, as you thought, Ellie, and they are considered precious."

"If they're so valuable, why did Abdul give them to me?"

"They have everything to do with the Palace of the King of Obagur. That is one Basim Abdul Fariq Obagur."

"So what?"

"Ellie, that's Prince Basim's and Prince Akdimmer's father."

"I'm so glad you learned how to pronounce their names, but I'm too tired to think. Can't you give me the skinny version?"

"Alright, the documents have so far revealed that your husband, Basim slash Ravi, Prince Number One and his brother, Abdul, Prince Number Two, inherited a vast fortune from their very dead father. They also state that they're the rightful owners of that palace you were probably at and it's a deed. Others are for other properties and other pieces of wealth. They may be old, but they are genuine."

"What does that have to do with us now, Adrian?"

"We think we know how this is all tied together, but it has everything to do with lineage, much like you establish for your horses. Levi has a theory. Because the father, King Basim, is dead and Abdul has no heir, they may come after your son."

"They wouldn't dare."

"Oh, yes, they dare and can, and they most likely will, Ellie. You must prepare your family for this possibility."

"Abdul can't take Jason; he's not old enough! I will not let them take my son!"

"We don't intend to let them, Ellie. It's our job to make sure it doesn't happen. We aim to keep you and your family safe."

My body starts to shake with rage. "Abdul can't take him out of the country, can he? What about the little chip?"

"I'll get to that, but first, you have to hear about why Basim slash Ravi left the palace in the first place. It isn't what we thought at all."

Closing my eyes to let the warm water penetrate my sore muscles, I'm hoping it'll wash away his words. "I don't want to hear anymore."

"You need to hear this. Basim's father sent him out of the country; he didn't have a falling out with him as we originally thought. When the King died, his first son, Prince Basim, was supposed to take over, but he died. The King's number two son, Prince Akdim was reluctant to take on the responsibility, knowing his brother was alive."

"This isn't making sense, Adrian. Abdul said the King and Queen were out of the country. He explained away their absence, but you mean to tell me he's been dead for many years? And there's no queen either?"

"It looks like the parents have been out of the picture for quite a long time. I realize that the facts are a little odd, but from what we can gather, Basim was supposed to have died years ago, and Abdul kept this a secret all these years. We don't know how, but we think you were a pawn. Abdul probably knew where his brother was all along."

"Don't these people have many wives? Can't one of their sons take over so they won't come after Jason?"

"I don't know how that works. Maybe Levi knows. Ellen, Basim didn't happen to be here in this country, he asked for asylum, or rather his father asked for asylum on his behalf. There was much turmoil in his country back then."

"Please get to the point, Adrian."

"Here's the hard part, Ellie, your father sponsored Basim."

"What do you mean by sponsored?"

Taking a sip from his glass, he says, "That means someone vouches for another and in this case, the company who gave your father his first job in Chicago sponsored Basim."

"Daddy was involved!"

"Yes. The company is called the National Clandestine Branch of the CIA; it's Levi's Branch."

"What! Are you saying that my Daddy worked for the CIA? I thought Lenard cooked up a good story, but this tops it! It does explain some things if it's true. Does my Mother know any of this? Did she also know about Ravi slash Basim?"

"I don't know what your Mother knows. Your father knew of Basim's dilemma. There was a hit out on him. If he returned, he was as good as dead. He didn't want any part of the palace or the fortune."

"This news sucks, Adrian."

"When Basim was training, you were away at college. He underwent plastic surgery to change his appearance and had his family tattoo removed."

"This is incredible! Daddy and Ravi both lied to Mother and me."

"We think that either Basim or Abdul hid the documents in the books. Levi isn't sure about that except that the little chip is a homing device. It was tracking you from the moment you left Saudi until you gave it to us. He knows where you are."

We sit in silence for some time as Adrian allows time for this information to be absorbed. "It explains why Daddy and Ravi were away at the same time," I say finally.

"They often traveled together as a team," Adrian says, taking a swig from his glass.

"Oh crap! The nightmare is not over, then."

"We assume that Abdul intends to take Jason back to the Royal Palace, making him a Crown Prince, to install him as the rightful heir."

"That will happen over my dead body! I don't want Jason to go with Abdul, its halfway around the world. I can't bear this Adrian; my head hurts from all this nonsense."

As I cling to Adrian, he whispers encouraging words. "We'll do everything within our power to make sure that doesn't happen, but Jason needs to know what we uncovered."

I want to scream that this most offensive thing will never take place! "Oh, Sweet Jesus, when he's twenty-one, he can do whatever he wants."

"But for right now, we need to tell him the truth," he murmurs.

It isn't clear if Basim/Ravi kept in touch with Abdul all these years, but my gut says he did. The information is appalling. The promise Abdul alluded to and the documents in Levi's possession are vital clues.

"Why didn't we sit down when I was there to hash things out?"

"My guess is, he felt you weren't ready to hear all of it. You had lost your husband, and you didn't want to stay there."

What is the purpose of all this secrecy and trickery? What is the connection to Lenard and his need to retrieve the documents and currency for his boss?

Adrian gathers Mother, Jason, and I to apprise us of what the CIA has uncovered, leaving the girls out of it for now. Mother and I share the feeling of betrayal, and don't understand how we could have spent that many years with Daddy and Ravi, and not know them at all!

Jason is quiet when Adrian tells him he's a potential target and why, saying that some things are predestined, and we don't always have control over them. Predestined to become King by Decree, Basim/Ravi fled his country when he rejected that role, leaving everything to his younger brother, Akdemir.

Jason wrestles with this information. "Is this Abdul the guy that took you and brought you back, Mom? Was Dad a Muslim? Would I have to convert to that?"

"I don't remember discussing this with you. And I have no idea about any of that."

"I hear stuff you guys talk about when you think we aren't around," Jason says. "Why didn't Dad tell me? I would have understood."

"I don't know why he didn't share that part of his life with us, sweetie. I thought I knew him and it turns out that I didn't. You understand Abdul is your uncle?"

"Yeah, I got that."

"Do you understand about being in danger and what might be in store for you?"

"No, I don't know what that means, but I'd like to know."

We begin our explanation by saying that by the very definition of the word predestined, it means that a decision has already been made.

It's in advance to something that will happen in the future. In this case, Jason's future is already determined by fate or divine decree.

Jason shakes his head that he gets it and then says, "This is wrong. It does make sense, but why didn't Dad say anything?"

"I'm sorry, sweetie, this might be what Dad was trying to tell you the day before we left for Kauai. It must have bothered him so much that he came to talk to you."

Although he looks distraught, I know he'll think about and assimilate this information, and will ask questions when he's ready. We do not inform Mel and Curlie that they may be Princesses in a land far away, requesting Jason not to discuss it with them. We also agree that he'll be part of all future discussions about our family, as he's an integral player.

Several days later we're gathered to go over our new plans as there's a special event at Billingsworth Race Track over the Labor Day weekend which might tie into an attempted abduction. Adrian says we must appear to be going on about our usual routine. He then lays out the first plan that we're to follow when we race. We add text signals to our secret codes in case Abdul or Jam-ale is spotted, so that we can alert people quickly.

Levi sent recent photos of them, which elicits comments when we pass them around. The picture of Jam-ale doesn't do him justice. He looks almost normal, not the seven-foot giant and menacing person I know him to be!

Larry lays out the second plan that involves us at Ashwood Stables, both day and night contingencies. It's a lot to understand and comprehend and Curlie clings to me, as she's understandably scared.

Following this, the agents go over the nighttime plan. If the family receives the signal to do so, we will lock ourselves into the designated place of safety. It turns out to be the space in the basement that had me baffled for so long.

Adrian and I ventured down to check it out one day. It was initially a root cellar for seasonal fruits, vegetables, and canned goods. Its construction suggests that the build date is around the 1960s and is a bomb shelter. A walk-in wine cellar disguises it.

*Surprise, there was one here all along!*

At the far wall of this wine cellar, we knocked, pulled, and generally wondered how we'd get into the room without using a stick of dynamite. Purely by accident, Adrian shoved, then pulled at the heavy wine shelves in the middle of the wall. Behind it was a steel door. Once the door was opened, it revealed a large cement room with walls about three feet thick; there are no windows.

Then the wine shelves go back against the wall once the steel door closes. Someone from inside the shelter can operate the ingenuous block and tackle assembly, closing the door, pulling the wine shelves together.

We laughed about the vault in a corner, putting curiosity aside until we can return to open it. Then we began the arduous task of removing old moldy cots and expired food left rusting on storage shelves. A no-frills bathroom, complete with shower, comprise the rest of the space.

Then we tackled the problem of a proper source of air-type conditioning/filtration system should the occupants need to remain inside for long periods of time. Modeled after the Biosphere Two in Arizona, it will scrub inside air for habitation.

If Adrian is correct in assuming that Abdul and his henchmen are already aware of where we are, then we must fortify our grounds to meet him headlong. Whichever way, we are prepared. I have a plan of my own and will share it with my immediate family later tonight.

A week before Labor Day, Adrian informed us that Levi's team discovered that a new investor is in the process of buying out all the other investors portions of this property, including Mr. C's.

"How can this be done without our knowledge? Can we sue Mr. Yancy for this underhanded deception? Can't we ask Levi and his group to investigate this?"

*Could this new investor be Abdul? Why didn't we see this coming?*

"I don't think we can ask the CIA to get involved with this one."

"Why not? What's to stop Abdul from opening the front door? He can waltz right in anytime he wants. He can say, 'Hi honey, I'm home!' And we can't stop him?"

*I'm suddenly sick to my stomach.*

"Whoever it is, they have every right to come onto the property, Ellie. Barring anything out-of-the-ordinary, you need to trust us to keep you safe," Adrian says confidently.

Two U.S. Marshals are positioned near the house, guns at the ready, tapping their earpieces much as in the movies I don't want Jason to watch, but he does anyway.

After dinner one night, a drawn-out debate ensues between the adults as we share our concerns. Then we get into a discussion about the most mundane subjects, which makes us all laugh. As we turn in for the night, Adrian reaches for my hand when we get to the top of the stairs.

Kissing my forehead, he says, "Try to get some sleep, Mrs. Thompson."

"I'll try, Mr. CIA man. Sleep good yourself."

It's nearly twelve a.m. when I wake with a start. Whispering **CODE BLUE** to Mother and the children, they comply immediately, each of them so trained they don't hesitate.

I remind them to stuff their beds to make it appear as if they are asleep, then grab their spare pillow, and follow me. Texting Adrian that we're heading toward the shelter in the basement, he says he'll alert the others.

A short time later, a sleepy Mona, a grumpy Glen, and a wide-eyed Reed are giving the password we worked out that allows them entry through the steel door. As everyone sleeps, Reed and I remain awake.

Surveillance equipment is set up on a desk with four monitors. On monitor No.1, we watch in silence as a shadowy hand opens the rear screen door. On monitor No. 2, the perimeter surveillance lights wink out, while monitors No. 3 and 4 remain motionless. Reed surmises that they're either disabled or nonfunctional.

Unable to text or use our cellphones while we're in the shelter, we have to wait until Adrian lets us know that the coast is clear. About forty-five minutes later, he sticks a handwritten note in front of camera monitor No.1.

*All secure. Stay there tonight. See U in morning.*

We repeat this for the next five nights, but nothing else happens.

Labor Day weekend arrives. We remind Mother, Mona, and the girls to go directly to the shelter in the basement should they hear anything off-kilter while we're at the racetrack. They have explicit instructions not to leave the property for any reason whatsoever. They must remain in the house, not even if they receive a call we've met with an accident, because it could be a deception.

On the way to Billingsworth Racetrack, there are signs along the highway advertising the Arabian Horse Show called the Blue & Silver Ensemble that will take place this afternoon. It's the county's biggest event, and the grand display is of mounted riders dressed in elaborate blue and silver costumes. Headscarves cover all but the rider's eyes.

I'm betting the largest one is Jam-ale. How will anyone be able to tell who is who? It comes as no surprise to Adrian, except it threatens to unnerve me.

"Wow!" Jason says excitedly, "They are massive horses! Look at their costumes." Turning toward me, he realizes what this might mean. "Are they here, Mom?"

"Probably. You should be very careful. Remember what we rehearsed and stay out of sight when Adrian gives the signal, your life may depend on it, sweetie."

I hug him to reassure both of us how much we wish for his safety. Am I overreacting? If what Adrian has told me is true, then we must not let our guard down, not now when the threat is so real.

After our meeting with the chief steward, Adrian and I go to the owner's box as Jason and Reed wait in the enclosure for the parade to begin.

My silks are underneath my street clothes because Adrian advises keeping out of sight until his fellow agents have thoroughly checked the area. He's confident that Abdul won't try anything funny until after the horse show begins.

"Are you nervous? "Adrian asks. Putting a hand on my shoulder, he says, "Everything is under control, Mrs. Thompson."

"I'm beyond nervous. Here is where that trust in God comes in. I must let go and trust," I say, choking on my words as tears leak from my eyes.

"We won't let anything happen, Ellie, I promise."

The bugle sounds the signal as Jason and *Raindrop* move into place on the track behind the pace truck. Reed texts: **OK to race.** Glen is back with *Lester*, along with a woman named Lena, who is in a set of our silks. Lena texts: **OK in barn.**

Using my binoculars, I begin to scan the stands and the track. *Raindrop* seems out of sorts today, so Jason gently drops him back and to the right, away from the other drivers. He recovers quickly but has lost valuable time and momentum, ending in the eighth position. I know he'll blame himself for the poor showing.

Adrian comes and goes as he pleases now, because of the special badge he wears. We are taking a stroll to look at the Arabian Stallion that's on display. Adrian texts: **A and E to check Arab Horse.**

A U. S. Marshal guards a tethered rider-less Arabian Stallion, and people are milling around it to view the elaborate costume up close. Crystal and cobalt blue stones with silver trim runs along the headband, the odd-shaped saddlecloth, and across the neckpiece. Tiny silver bells dangle from silver tassels that jingle when the horse moves. The tinkling bells remind me of that last night before Jam-ale returned me to the Kauai airport restroom.

"Better get back," Adrian whispers, taking my arm as we walk away. Tapping his earpiece, he says, "Copy that. Steady as she goes, Mrs. Thompson. Stay out of trouble out there, okay?"

Glen waits near our barn with *Lester*. I've removed my street clothes and given them to Adrian as we wait for the parade to begin.

"I double-checked the tack for ya," Glen says. "You're placed good taday, so don't blow it." When everything looks to be in order, he mouths OK, gives me a thumbs-up signal as the race bikes ahead of us move forward.

*Lester* and I move quickly into position behind the retractable arms of the starter truck. It's an excellent place to be in until the race starts and my body starts to shake. I tell myself that the pressure on my bum is secondary to keeping it all together.

From the start of the race, I realize there's no way to avoid being trapped between race bikes, unless *Lester* stumbles, or the driver next to us moves over. The driver to my right is not one of our barn mates, so I glower at him with my worst face. How do I overcome this in the future?

*Maybe there is no future.*

Then, by the Grace of God, a hole opens up as the driver to the left breaks stride and falls back. *Lester* responds in a surprising display of power. He is pacing great today, and I don't want to jeopardize or compromise what might be a move up the chain of class for him, so I refrain from pulling on the reins.

A flash of some kind catches my eye as we come down the home stretch, but I ignore it hearing Glen's words echo in my head to get into the chute, then realize we're already in it. Two drivers are ahead of us; we can't move to the right or left to pass, so this is where we'll remain.

Glen holds up three fingers when we get close to him. He snaps on *Lester*'s lead rope whispering to him as I jump down from the seat as gingerly as possible. My bum has not adjusted to the rigors of sitting in the donut of a seat on the race bike, and no amount of padding will help that.

"Had enough yet, Missy?" Glen asks.

"Not yet, Old Man."

There's a flash off to the right in my peripheral edge of vision again, but it's the lone Arabian Stallion's costume, as it twinkles in the sunlight. My cellphone vibrates, glancing at the screen, Adrian texts: **good job.**

Adrian waits for me near our stalls. I quickly throw my street clothes over my silks, and then he escorts me to the owner's box again where we sit with Dr. Jess and Reed. Jason is now with two undercover agents somewhere in the grandstands (I think) while Glen and Lena stay with our horses. Lena is roughly the same size as Jason, so no one will be able to distinguish her from him from a distance.

While the other CIA agents and U.S. Marshals move around the racetrack to observe, I use small binoculars to scan the crowd. When I spot a familiar face, my heart starts to pound. Nudging Adrian, I text Jason: **AB stands/L side.** As I wait patiently for a response, the next time I look up again, he's gone.

Adrian says, "Stay here, all of you."

He's gone perhaps five minutes when I text: **Any Luck?**

Adrian texts: **No sign of AB.**

Text to Adrian: **Going to barn.**

Adrian texts: **OK – be careful!**

The barn door is shut when I get there. Jockeys and owners are standing around outside asking each other what happened and why can't we get inside? Speculating on what might be happening for several moments, there's a distant sound of a siren that grows louder. Then it stops at the far end of our barn.

Text to Glen: **Where are you?** He doesn't respond.

Text to Adrian: **Our barn closed. Something wrong. Glen is not responding.**

I'm about to panic when the door slides open, and Glen walks out. "There's been an accident, Missy," Glen whispers. "It's Lena. The emergency people are takin her ta the hospital."

"What happened?"

Taking my arm, he pulls me away from the others. "It happened so fast I couldn't react. One minute Miss Lena was standin there brushin *Raindrop*, the next minute she was on the ground! I didn't see or hear anythin, Missy. I turned my back for one second! It's some bunch of hooligans ya got mixed up with."

"I'm sorry about all this, Glen."

He seems shaken. "It was sure right of us ta remove Jason when we did."

"I agree." Text to Adrian: **L down, the ambulance taking her - don't know what happened.**

Adrian texts: **Meet me, hungry.**

We will discuss plan changes. When I get to our truck, Adrian's already chomping on a chicken leg. "L's going to be okay," he says. "I spoke with our agent who went with her to the hospital. She took a blow to the head, but the paramedics are hopeful there's no damage. The security guard says someone told him the horse pushed her off the stool when she was grooming him."

"*Raindrop* would never do that."

"The doctor says she has a concussion. They can't be sure if she fell, or someone hit her on the back of the head, but they're keeping her overnight for observation. Our agent will stay with her to make sure no one comes looking for her."

"Have you heard from J?"

"He's fine. A couple of our finest is with him. Larry already checked in, and nothing's happening back at the ranch. Good call about switching J with L. Want some, it's delicious."

"Is there any left?"

"Of course there is," he says grinning. "We're not exactly sure who's responsible for L's accident, Ellie. I know you think it's Abdul and his giant friend, but it could be someone working with Lenard, too."

"Did they think they could take him in broad daylight?"

"I don't know," Adrian says.

We talk about the morning's events and wonder when Abdul will make his move. I guess they can't take Jason if they can't find him. "Adrian, do you think L's accident is a diversion? Jam-ale might be lurking around here somewhere. Do you think the racetrack people will suspend the horse show if you ask them?"

"Mrs. Thompson, are you sure you wouldn't like to make the CIA your next career instead of racing? You ask a lot of outstanding questions."

"No thanks, Mr. Sellers, that's your shtick, not mine."

"Then brace yourself; the racetrack will likely go on with the horse show. The track owners paid a lot of money to have these people come, and they probably don't want to issue a refund or reschedule it. Short of an explosion, nothing is going to stop it."

"Can you arrange one, Mr. Sellers?"

"Are you serious, Mrs. Thompson?"

"Quite serious."

"Sorry, I'm not into demolition. My specialty is clandestine missions, secret handshakes, and ghost stories," Adrian grins.

*"Happiness is when what you think, what you say,*

*and what you do are in harmony."*

~ Mahatma Gandhi

# *Chapter Fifteen*

## Predestined Decree

For nearly an hour, Adrian and I wander around waiting for the entertainment to begin. In that time, we haven't seen either Jam-ale or Abdul. Our trainers stay close to the barn with several agents as we head over to the grandstands.

At precisely three o'clock, the announcer's booming voice asks for our attention at the far end of the track as exotic music plays over the sound system. The music sounds vaguely familiar, like the chanting I heard during my captivity—and I stiffen.

The Arabian Stallions and their riders prance into the middle grassy area in full regalia as thousands of tiny bells tinkle. The twenty-five horses and riders make an impressive display as they line up twelve to a side, while one hangs back. The riders are wearing dark blue headscarves that hide most of their features, except for their eyes.

A creepy feeling begins to seep into the pit of my stomach. Although I was blindfolded most of the time, these men could be the ones who escorted me on my journey that last night. Could the lone rider giving hand signals be Jam-ale?

Nudging Adrian and pointing at my text: **Jam-ale giving signals**. He nods in understanding, touching his earpiece, saying, "Look alive. Big man giving signals to riders could be Abdul's sidekick."

We watch as the group goes through their extraordinary performance, as riders charge at each other so close they almost touch, then veer off at the last second. It reminds me of the Lipizzaner Stallions of Vienna, because the horses do fancy tricks, crisscrossing in front of each other, perhaps reenacting what appears as a battle. The crowd responds with thunderous applause when the show is over.

We leave the grandstands quickly to meet up with Glen and Reed near the barn. With our gear in tow, we head toward our trucks and trailers with *Lester* and *Raindrop*. Several people are milling around our vehicles, but I laugh at the stranger who is sitting behind the wheel of Glen's truck. Jason is wearing a blond wig, mustache, and sunglasses! He's relieved now that this day is finally over and there were no altercations, but I warn him that the danger is very much with us.

When we turn into our driveway, Ashwood Stables looks as if a party's in full swing. Adrian explains that a group of trainees came out of the woods to reconnoiter with the CIA agents and will camp here tonight.

Mother and the others are in the living room to greet us. "I would like to speak to this Abdul person," she expresses. "I would like to give him a piece of my mind. He has scared us all half to death!"

"Me too," Curlie chimes in, whimpering, "I don't like this stuff, Mama. I want them to go away!"

Adrian puts a hand over hers and in a gentle gesture that makes her turn toward him, he says, "Please don't worry, Curlie. We won't let anything happen to you or your family."

"You promise?" she asks, struggling not to cry.

"I promise," Adrian says. "The troops will melt into the scenery, and you won't even know they're here."

"I promise, too, Curlie," Larry says. "We know what to do, and we'll take care of the bad guys."

Mel's forlorn voice borders on a whine. "How long is this group gonna stay here? My friends already think we're weird, but this is unbelievable!"

Jason is uncharacteristically quiet, glancing at me, he nods his head in agreement, because he knows that promises only go so far, which makes him a little skeptical.

After a quiet dinner, everyone begins to scatter to the four corners of the Manor House while I go into my office to catch up on some paperwork.

Adrian raps on the doorjamb. "I'm checking in on you before I go out to the Guest House. Want to join me in the spa later, Mrs. Thompson? It might work the kinks out of your body."

"Not tonight, Mr. Sellers, I'm too wired from the excitement of today. I'll soak in my tub tonight if that's okay with you."

"Is your radar telling you that Abdul's going to show up tonight?"

"Yes. What do your sources say about how long Abdul and his horse people will be here? Since he must have a visa or something, what point of entry did they use to get their horses here? He must have a private jet waiting on the tarmac for a quick getaway."

Adrian sighs. "You would make a great agent with all the questions you ask. I'll even bet you'd get through the training in half the time with your brains and ability!"

"I know how you bet, Mr. CIA man. I know he's here, so why hasn't he tried to contact us, hum?"

"Try to stop driving yourself crazy. How could his men gain access? We have people out in the field, next to the house, and out in the barn. I think he has a sense that we're prepared and not to try anything funny."

"Okay, Mr. CIA man, but they could drop from the sky or walk in the front door."

"Give it a rest with the people in the sky already, Ellie, and go to bed," Adrian says sweetly. "Good Night, Irene."

"Good Night, John Boy. Laughing, he walks off toward the kitchen.

After a good soak in my jetted tub, I put on clothes instead of my pajamas. My gut says something *will* happen tonight and I can't shake it.

Texting a message, I glance at the clock to note it's nearly ten o'clock, then tiptoe down the hall. **CODE BLUE**, I whisper to Mel, Curlie, Jason, and Mother. Instantly awake, they move into position, not in the shelter in the basement, but into the secret staircase.

The only complaint comes from Mother, who says if she has to be in a bent position for any length of time, she might be so stiff in the morning we might find her dead. Feeling guilty, I ask her to come and sleep with me.

Since the outside temperature has dropped, I switch on the little fan in the window at the top of the secret staircase to ensure it remains cool. Then I open my bedroom windows. Falling asleep, I wake when there's a loud noise outside. A few minutes later, I hear Adrian calling my name from my bedroom door.

Adrian talks quietly as he approaches, "I think we're going to get some company." He closes the door quietly, but in the moonlight, I can see that he's fully clothed and is wearing glow-in-the-dark neon green and blue sneakers that look comically out of place. He grins when he sees Mother asleep on the other side of my bed, then chuckles at my hunting vest, jeans, sneakers, and the Glock I'm holding.

When I nudge Mother awake, the expression on her weary face tells me she doesn't like this drama one bit. Her instructions are to go into the bathroom, then join the children on the stairs if I leave the bedroom. As she begins to move toward the bathroom, there's a sound near the back screened-in porch. Mother turns to come back, but Adrian waves for her to keep going.

Seconds later, we hear the squeak of the back door that Glen wanted to oil yesterday. Now I'm grateful that he forgot to do it. As the back stairs creak, Adrian motions for me to join Mother, but I'm not about to budge. Although my bedroom is in semi-darkness, there is no mistaking the massive body that fills the doorframe when the door suddenly opens.

"Stay where you are," Adrian says in a deep voice, moving to shield me. "How the hell did you get in here?" He must be touching his earpiece because he then says, "Respond!"

"His Royal Highness wishes to speak to you, Ma'dame," Jam-ale says in quiet gruffness.

Adrian takes one hand off his gun to cup my thigh, saying, "Stay behind me, Ellie. We don't know what he might do."

Sounds of muffled footsteps patter up and down the hallway as doors are opened and closed. A figure, dressed entirely in black, moves in to converse with Jam-ale and then runs silently away. It looks a lot like Jam-ale's band of merry army men are also here.

"Brought your ninja's I see, big guy. You couldn't come through the front door like everyone else?"

"Come," Jam-ale says, motioning with his hand. "No harm will come to you."

"You had to come in the dead of night to scare my family? What the hell is wrong with you people?" Undaunted, he moves forward with his hand out.

"Not gonna happen, big guy," Adrian says, moving his gun to aim at the menacing man's big head.

Ignoring this, Jam-ale motions to me again, "Come. We wish no harm."

"She's not going anywhere with you, pal."

I let out a little chuckle when Adrian says this as it seems a bit comical for him to be calling Jam-ale *pal*. He takes one hand off his pistol to tap his earpiece again, then turns to me, blinking three times, which is the signal to press the silver piece on my necklace, so I comply.

Jam-ale motions to me again, sighs loudly, making that annoying 'tsk' sound saying, "We talk, only talk, no weapons. We put all weapons down. His Highness waits downstairs. Come, Ma'dame."

"Abdul is downstairs? Did you bring him here? Hey Adrian, what do we have to lose by talking to the man? Let's go down and see what his Royal Highness Prince pain-in-the-ass has to say."

Jam-ale puts his hands out to his side. "He wants to see only you, Ma'dame," he says.

Adrian grabs my arm, and I see the terror in his eyes. "No, Ellie, it could be a trap! Don't go."

"I promise no harm. I am person of the word, you know this," Jam-ale says. Coming closer, he says, "Put the gun away, we only talk."

"Either he comes, or I don't go," I insist.

"No one's responding," Adrian mutters. "Where is everyone?"

Jam-ale seems a little impatient. "He may come, Ma'dame. Let us go."

As we all walk toward the front staircase, I whisper to Adrian. "Did you hear that loud noise? It sounded like an explosion."

"I was getting out of the spa when I saw you open your windows. Is everyone else with the others?"

I don't want to give anything away, so I don't answer his question. "How did you know they were here, Adrian?"

"I heard the noise too. I came in to make sure you were okay. Good thing you aren't wearing a sexy nightgown!"

"Sorry to disappoint you, but I don't wear sexy nightgowns. Good thing you're not wearing your PJs!"

Two men dressed entirely in black are in the downstairs hallway, one stands near the vestibule doors, while the other opens the French doors to the living room.

Abdul is standing near the fireplace holding my wedding photo. As he puts the frame back on the mantle, his blue ring glistens in the light as he turns toward us.

"Good evening, my dearest Ellen. Thank you Jamaile. I hope you don't mind the lateness of the hour. We have unfinished business to attend to, my dear."

As if he's now noticing Adrian, he glances at him briefly but doesn't question why he's here. He acts as if he owns the place, and then I remember that he does.

"Are you serious? It's the wee hours of the morning, Abdul. What do you want at this ridiculous hour?" I'm not precisely snarky, but not warm and fuzzy either.

He smiles, and says, "I was looking forward to seeing you. I wanted to meet your family today. Do you enjoy racing, Ellen?"

"Cut the crap, Abdul. Why are you here?"

"We have unfinished business which we need to take care of quickly, without prying eyes," he says quietly. "I am also here to set the record straight. I doubt others know a complete truth."

"I think I know what your unfinished business is, and quite frankly, who do you think these *others* are, Abdul? From what I've determined, you lied to me from the day I met you."

Jam-ale shifts slightly, clearing his throat. Adrian fidgets with his shoelace, then taps his earpiece again. Glancing up, he shakes his head from side to side.

"I have not lied to you, my dearest Ellen. Everything I have told you has been the truth, as near as it can be said. It is important that you understand what I am about to tell you."

Abdul begins to walk around the room touching objects, which reminds me of when he did this at his palace during my incarceration there. "You have ten minutes to explain before the Feds get here." I don't know if this is correct, Adrian only said that if I press the middle of the necklace, a signal is sent, and so far, his fellow agents and U.S. Marshals haven't so much as said *boo*. "Isn't that right, Mr. Sellers?"

"That's right, Mrs. Thompson," he says soberly. "You had ten minutes; now it's nine."

Abdul glances at Jam-ale, and I get annoyed when he does this. Turning toward me, he says, "It began many years ago. There were two brothers; the elder one wanted to experience the world. He wanted to escape his destiny while the younger one remained loyal to his family. One day, the older brother vanished. His family searched for many years, and it was much later when they discovered he was living an alternative life."

"You're talking about you and my husband, Ravi, aren't you?"

"Yes. Basim is the man you called Ravi. We tried to reason with him. We tried to show him how important he was to our family; however, he refused to return. Basim met a man who treated him as a son, not the object of scrutiny. He was happy living in the United States with his family where he could then go whenever or wherever he wanted; not subjected to the prying eyes of the palace, or having to justify his every move."

"Imagine that. Was this older brother locked into his room, too?"

Abdul continues, ignoring my comment. "Basim was willing to give up everything to stay with you, Ellen. When he did that, he took with him the hope of an heir. It was after Basim left that I contracted a disease which rendered me unable to produce one. You can see how important Jason is to me."

"Back the train up a minute, Mr. Abdul, I met Ravi after he left your country. Don't blame me for keeping him from his kingly duties. He made that decision himself. I had nothing to do with it."

"I am not placing blame upon you, Ellen. It is not the point of the story. My promise to Basim was to take you as my wife if anything happened to him. It is a common practice in my country. I will take care of you and your family for as long as I live."

"You must be joking! I wouldn't consent to marry you in a thousand years. Why didn't you tell me you were my brother-in-law? Why did you lock me in that room? I'm supposed to be grateful, bow down to you, and give you my son? It's not going to happen, Abdul! In my book, Ravi lied to me. You may *not* think you lied, but you did–by omission!"

"Ellen, listen to me. Can you not see that I not only want to install Jason as the rightful heir to our fortune, but I also want all of you to be my family?"

I glance at Adrian, but he doesn't say anything. He must be waiting for me to say something witty. "This is your big speech, Abdul? Nothing about why you held me prisoner for all those weeks? Nothing about why you sent those books home with me? Why did you use me in such a despicable arrangement? Did you and Basim/ Ravi have this all planned and something went wrong?"

"I told you several times that I could not discuss matters of State with you. Some things cannot be said now. Believe me when I say that my brother loved you and his children very much. He loved you so much he gave up his fortune and his throne for all of you."

"Why should I believe you? You and Jam-ale broke into my house in the middle of the night to bring me this news? It suggests that you are a selfish man even to think I would go along with this ridiculous scheme of yours."

"The books with the documents inside them are for Jason. They are his future. They belong to my people and my country, and they are now for him. May I have the books so that I may prove this to you?"

"This is unbelievable! Why didn't you share this information while I was there with you? Couldn't you have waited until morning to discuss this? You could have at least let me know you were in town."

"We thought it best to do it this way," he says, glancing at his sidekick, who stands stoically near Abdul.

"You know, in this country, we call it breaking and entering. It's a felony if I'm not mistaken, isn't that right Agent Sellers? Add harassment and brandishing of weapons . . ."

Adrian leans close to me and says, "It's a felony. You are correct, Mrs. Thompson, that makes it a federal offense." He blinks three times, giving me the signal to press the black button again. Then he adds, "He does own part of the house, so it's not technically breaking and entering."

Whispering to him, I chuckle, saying, "Yeah, I'll bet you a hundred bucks that Jam-ale here has some weapon hidden on his person and won't hesitate to use it. That's harassment and brandishing, as I understand it. Would you like to place a small wager on that Mr. Sellers?"

"You're on, Mrs. Thompson," Adrian says as we shake hands.

It elicits something of a growl from Jam-ale, and he steps closer to Abdul.

"Ellen, may I have the books now? I can prove all of this to you."

"The funny thing about that, Mr. Prince, is that we don't have that stuff. I sent the books out for restoration. They were a little damaged, you see. You aren't welcome here so GET OUT."

Abdul's voice cracks. "Where are they? I must have them!" He looks shaken at this news. He and Jam-ale shift closer together, speaking for a moment or two. "They are essential, Ellen. What do you mean they were damaged? When may I have them?"

"Don't get your knickers in a twist. The books had to be glued back together after I unsealed everything. They're in a very safe place. My government has them. You know, the s a m e government you said wouldn't help me? I t's the same government you said didn't want to get involved. They're now involved."

Abdul now looks as if he's about to panic. "You did not destroy the documents when you unsealed them, did you? We must have them; they are extremely important, both to Jason and to me!"

*He caused me anguish. Now it's his turn to squirm.*

"How did you get in here undetected?" Adrian questions. "The perimeter is surrounded!"

"It was necessary to do this while we had our little talk. Ellen, you must retrieve those documents."

"Okay, we talked, it's late, and I'm tired." Standing to stretch, I yawn as Jam-ale shifts to block the Prince.

Pushing the big man aside with the back of his hand, Abdul says, "It is alright Jamaile, Ellen will not harm me."

"Not today anyway. I suggest we postpone discussions until you have an invitation. In the meantime, I will request the return of the documents, but we need time to get them here." The mantle clock chimes two thirty. "Where are the guards, Mr. Sellers?"

He shakes his head, mouthing words, 'I don't know.'

"They will be all right in a few hours," Abdul volunteers. "No need to be concerned."

"Then negotiations are over for tonight. Do come back when you have a proper invitation, Mr. Prince. Lock up when you leave, okay?"

I grab Adrian's arm to pull him with me as Abdul's hand lands on Jam-ale's arm, apparently to keep him from following us. By the time we reach the top of the stairs, I'm shaking so badly, Adrian has to hold me up.

"You did great! Don't fall apart now, Super Girl," he whispers.

Minutes later, we hear the familiar squeak of the back door, as it slams shut and we surmise that the Prince and his henchmen have left the building--or roof.

"I can't believe his unmitigated gall at walking into this house at this hour!"

Mother comes to my room and says to keep our voices down. "The children are back in their beds. No need to sleep in that contorted position any longer than necessary." As Mother leaves, she turns to say, "Thank you, Adrian. We are glad you are here."

"What does she mean by contorted position?" he asks. "I thought the shelter was comfortable. Weren't they in the shelter with the others?"

"It's a little fail-safe thing we devised, that's all. Why didn't anyone respond to you?"

"I don't know. Maybe Abdul's men had a jamming device. I thought we had that covered. I'll try to raise them again." Tapping his earpiece, he says, "Perimeter 1, report, over."

"Perimeter 1, an explosion in the field, sir, over."

Tapping his earpiece, he says, "Perimeter 2, report, over."

"Perimeter 2, an explosion in the field sir, over."

Tapping his earpiece, he says "Perimeter 3, report, over."

"Perimeter 3, an explosion in the field, sir, over."

"This sounds strange. What happened to the men in the barn? Where are they? Okay, search anyway. Suspects were in the house, and no one stopped them! And check the roof. L24, are you there?"

"Check the roof, that's funny Adrian. Larry is down in the shelter with all the others. Did your office get the signal from my necklace?"

Adrian shakes his head as his cellphone rings. Answering it he says, "Thanks, you did get the message, what happened? Okay, I'll call when I have more information."

"What did they say?"

"Levi's team was alerted when the signal was received. By then, our men were back in position. He doesn't understand the delay."

"Go to bed, Mr. Sellers. You look like you could use some sleep."

"No, I have to check on the others . . ."

"They're okay. I texted the adults hours ago, and they're all tucked nice and neat in the shelter with Larry. Why don't we let them sleep down there tonight? They're getting used to this routine anyway."

"Guess you were right about your feeling that they would come here tonight."

"Go get some sleep and thank you for keeping us safe, yet once again, Mr. CIA man."

"I'm sleeping downstairs," Adrian says. "if that's okay with you?"

I have no objection to that as long as he gets some answers for me in the morning. We will be eternally grateful for Mrs. Ashwood's foresight and battles she had with her architect. Specifically, the little secret places she designed into this beautiful old house that kept my family safe tonight.

After the children leave for school, Adrian and Larry tell us what the investigation turned up. The commotion came from a helicopter that exploded when it hit the ground a short distance from where the agents were camped. When they all received the same signal, they naturally went to investigate, and to assist with the rescue.

While they attempted to put the fire out, a smoke-like cloud drifted out, and everyone fell asleep. When the agents woke, there were no bodies near the wreckage, which then led them to the conclusion that the helicopter was remote-controlled. By that time, the drama in the house was over.

"We're dealing with professionals here," Adrian cautions. "The two guards posted at the front and rear of the house by the Sheriff's Department were asleep."

*None of us buys into this; we know how drugs work.*

"What do we do now Adrian?"

"We wait for The Great Abdul to contact you again."

"You might ask Mr. Levi to return Abdul's precious documents."

"Sure, I'll have Levi overnight them here," Larry says.

"You know, if they're that important, maybe we can use them to keep Jason with us, for a while anyway."

Adrian has a quizzical expression on his face. "What do you have in mind?"

"I'll tell you later, okay?"

"Thank you, Adrian and Larry, for being here with us," Mother says. "We're very grateful. I don't mind telling you that it nearly gave me a heart attack."

"You're welcome, Francesca. Levi is a bit worried how Abdul and what's-his-bigness got in here without detection," Larry says.

"And I have to agree with him; it's more than bizarre," Adrian adds.

"That's not exactly what I'm thinking. Bizarre isn't the right word to use, Adrian. It's more like peculiar. Why didn't he call and ask to meet with us?"

"Maybe they planned to hightail it out of here during the night?" Larry speculates.

"I don't like what they did," Mother adds. "I agree with you, Ellie. Why did he have to do that hocus pocus stuff and scare us half to death?"

"Love how your minds work, ladies," Adrian laughs. "I'll try to find out for you."

Abdul calls the next day to discuss the documents. I inform him that we need at least five additional days. Although the papers came intact four days ago, it gives us more time to work out how we'll proceed. Then we formally invite His Royal Painness and his 'party' to join us for lunch.

The next day, protocols arrive by registered mail which includes etiquette for accepting royalty, a strict dietary regimen, the times of arrival, departure, etc. that we must adhere to during the royal visit.

To add insult to injury, from now on, we must address Abdul as either His Royal Highness (befitting his status) or by his first name of Prince Akdemir. It's as difficult to pronounce as Jam-ale's name. I'll have to get around it by practicing.

I'm doing a slow burn at the prospect of confronting Ak-dim-er and his party. Jason is also anxious to ask his uncle about his father and the country he left behind. Mona and Mother are busy trying to follow their protocols, while the children study the proper etiquette.

When the day arrives, Ak-dim-er returns with his entourage that includes several limos, (shiny and black; which makes me shiver at the sight of them) along with a horse trailer all decked out in blue and silver.

Adrian remarks that this is not how he and his midnight cowboys came here the last time. I wonder if they were involved with the school incident last year. Or was it Lenard as we suspect? Why are we entertaining the person who kept me captive? Adrian says to go along with this as it might lead us to the solution to our problems.

All security teams, both U.S. Marshals and CIA, are in place, stationed around the perimeter of the house and barn, and along the driveway. The rest of the household braces for what we hope will be the first and last time we have to entertain His Most Royal Highness Prince Ak-dim-er (pain-in-the-ass).

We are following the protocols to the letter and are in the vestibule to greet our royal guests. The Prince seems happy. Is it because my family is in attendance? Or is it the fact that no one is wearing jeans?

Their protocols can take a flying leap. I'm not about to bow or curtsey to him. As the designated head of household here, I greet the Prince first and then respond to the Ambassadors of Goodwill. They are two of the men who were in the library at the palace the day I lost it and demanded to go home. They regard me pleasantly enough but are a bit standoffish. Jam-ale is conspicuously absent. I can see him through the open doors moving around their horse trailer.

After practicing for days trying to pronounce his name, I can finally introduce Crown Prince Ak-dim-er to each family member. He, in turn, introduces his people, who follow us as we move quickly down the line, where he shakes each family member's hand.

Cordialities and formalities aside, Ak-dim-er seems charming. He talks to Mother when I make introductions, then lingers when he comes to Jason, taking both of his hands in his. He makes some remark to Mel, and of course, when he gets to Curlie, she curtsies!

It's as if we're at the royal court and they greet other royalty. How did we fall through this black hole? Catching Adrian's eye, he smiles, because he must be thinking the same thing.

When I poke my head around the guests, there's some type of commotion near the barn. Glen stands alongside the elaborate horse trailer talking with Jam-ale. I interrupt to ask what's going on, but Prince Ak-dim-er assures me that it's a surprise, and would I wait until later?

After lunch, the Prince asks if he might speak to Jason alone in the library. "You may join us, if that is suitable to you, Ellen?"

"Under the circumstances, I will join you."

Adrian and I exchange a glance, and this means he will remain close. We move to the library where Ak-dim-er stands near the fireplace. Adrian's legs are visible through the fireplace screen as he paces back and forth in the hallway.

"Jason, I want you to know that your father was proud of you. The times we met, he shared many things about all of you. One of them is that he loved you so much that he could not leave you to return to our country. I tried many times to change his mind."

"I'd like to know about your country. From what I've read, the money from your oil has made you lots of enemies," Jason says.

"That money has helped our country go from trading to one of the world's largest oil producing regions," Ak-dim-er says proudly. "We have educated our leaders and have much to offer the world."

Jason watches his uncle for a moment. "We studied the Ottoman Empire last year. I know how history is sometimes written the wrong way; take the American Indians for example. Cowboys and Indians were glorified, and it wasn't like that at all."

*I had no idea Jason felt this way.*

The door opens, and Jam-ale strolls in pushing Mona's tea cart. It looks so comical to me that I chuckle. He then walks over to whisper something in Ak-dim-er's ear. An astonished expression crosses Jason's face because the sheer size of the man is intimidating. The painting above the mantle is precisely seven feet from the floor to the bottom of the frame; Jam-ale's big head is a few inches below it.

Jason slowly shakes his head. "I won't go back with you. I don't care what you have to say. I won't go back with you!"

"Hear me out, Jason; you may not have the correct information about my country." Prince Ak-dim-er studies my face for several seconds, then continues. "Many years ago, there were two kingdoms, the Hejaz, and the Nejd. They were united to form the Kingdom of Saudi Arabia. Did you study that? It is truly a wondrous place, full of history, exotic foods, massive structures, billowing deserts, and rich in culture and art."

"That's what the history books say, but what I wanna know about is the Saudi Arabia that my father came from. If he loved it so much, why did he leave to come here? Why didn't he tell us about that, and you?"

"Jason, there are many reasons why he could not share that part of his life with you. There were circumstances, almost beyond his control." Akdemir tilts his head, blinking at Jam-ale.

"I'd like to know why my husband left Saudi, too. I feel as if the last twenty years of our lives together was a complete lie."

"Ellen, I am sure that was not Basim's intention. Come with me, Jason. See for yourself. You will not be disappointed. Come back with me now, and train to take your rightful place as heir. You will have everything you ever wanted and more. You will have the finest education, the fastest car. You will lack for nothing."

I know that Jason wants to see the world because we've talked about it many times. What stresses me about this conversation is that Mr. Prince is trying to flaunt his wealth. I hope he's retained my lectures about this.

Jason ponders this for several moments and in a clear, unfaltering voice says, "I will not go with you. My place is here with my family."

"Perhaps I did not make myself clear," the Prince says quietly.

"You put my Mother through hell, and I can't forgive you for that. Actually, you put the rest of us through hell, too. Did you have anything to do with my father's death?"

I'm relieved to know that he isn't falling prey to what Abdul's wealth could mean to him. "I didn't tell you what happened, Jason, how do you know about that?"

"Mr. Adrian told me. I won't go with him, Mom. I belong here with you, and the rest of the family. I don't want anything to do with you!" Jason looks at his uncle and folds his arms over his chest. "You can't make me go with you."

Ak-dim-er sits down on the sofa next to Jason. "Perhaps I did not correctly say this. You do not have a choice, Jason. Royal blood runs through your veins. You belong with me. The documents decree this."

"Excuse me, Mr. Prince, but experts deciphered them, and there's nothing to support your theory that Jason has to go with you."

"I will decide that, Ellen. May I have the documents now?"

"Sure. They're in my office. I'll be right back."

When I return to the library, Mr. Prince has his hand open. The notes Jewels wrote on a separate sheet are still in my secret cubby hole, so I give him only what he asked for, the documents. He opens the first delicate page, studies it, then refolds it, doing the same to the rest of them. His excitement quickly turns to frustration. "Are these all of the documents?" he asks in surprise.

"As far as I know, this is what was under the covers of the books you gave me."

"I do not understand! They are valuable documents, yes, but they are not the documents I refer to specifically." He looks perplexed, glances at Jam-ale then back to me. "Where are the rest of the documents that were in the books, Ellen?"

"You hold everything right there. There are no others."

"These are not the traditional documents handed down from generation to generation with explicit instructions of how to conduct the business of our households. My father brought me into his chambers one day. I remember reading them. I remember reading these, but these are not the ones I need."

"Guess you came all this way for nothing. You should have phoned, and I would have told you about them. I could have saved you the trip and the drama."

"These are deeds for properties that will be passed on, but there must be others. Where can they possibly be? Basim would never deceive me!" He has a faraway look in his eyes, then closes them. "Without them, others will attempt to . . . we must find them, and quickly!"

Jam-ale begins to pour something from the teapot and crosses the room to hand him a cup.

"What makes them so important?" I inquire.

"They establish the rights of the heirs. Without the documents, Fariq will assume that he is the next heir, not me! That would be very bad for our kingdom. Basim would have known what to do."

"Who is Faa . . . rick?" Jason asks.

It's evident that Ak-dim-er is shaken by this news. "Fariq is a son from one of my father's other wives. Basim and I are from our father's first wife. Most of the other children are female. The other three males are too young to challenge the decree. Fariq is next in line if we cannot produce the documents."

"That settles it; Jason goes nowhere. Thanks for coming all this way. So glad you could join us for lunch."

Ak-dim-er's face drains of color. "How could I have been so deceived by my father? I don't understand. Basim said the documents in the books are truly the ones that will provide the right of succession. Was Basim also deceived?"

"I didn't know about my father either," Jason says sadly. "He never said anything about him being a prince. Mom, he never told me anything like that! He sure didn't say anything about you, Mr. Abdul!"

I can feel my blood pressure rise. "Look, my father didn't tell me things either. Nothing ever is what it seems, Jason. It appears that all of our fathers lied to us. By the way, what was the currency doing in the books?"

"What currency? Only the documents and the little chip were inside the books."

"No, you're wrong about that, Mr. Prince. There were also stacks of old money."

"I know nothing of this old money. It simply cannot be," he says quietly. He begins to talk about his father and what he thought was a privileged upbringing and the fact that Basim had some dark secret, which he will never reveal. The part he wants to make clear to us is that he tried to save his brother and he meant only to protect me.

"Perhaps this Fariq person has the documents in question, and maybe you should seek asylum in another country, say Canada, for example. You can't stay here; he might find you. If you knew where I was all this time, he might know where you are, too."

"It must be Fariq who got to them first. He is part of a ruthless group. When I discovered Basim left the books at the palace the last time Jamaile smuggled him in, I was determined to return them as they must at all costs be with the person who takes over the throne, meaning Basim or Jason."

"You expect us to believe this crap? You mean that your people were at the Kauai airport to give Ravi back the books? Maybe he wanted you to have them. Aren't you next in line?"

"Ellen, I cannot tell you everything. I know nothing about the currency and the chip was Basim's idea. We always knew where he was, based upon where the chip went. We left it in the book to help us find you. We never meant any harm." He seems more than a little sad.

"We have all been duped by our fathers. Yours, Jason's, and mine." I stand up ready to end this.

"We must find the other documents before it is too late."

"And where do you think we're going to find them? As long as we're asking for things, can I ask my questions now? You told me you would answer them one day."

"Yes, Ellen. I will answer your questions as best as I am able. Do you want to do this while Jason is present?"

"Yup. Did you abduct me and take me to Arabia?"

"I did not abduct you, my dear Ellen, you were taken to safety, and it is called the Kingdom of Saudi Arabia."

"Who is responsible for exploding the plane Ravi was on?"

"We believe it is our enemies who want to control the flow of oil and the extreme wealth it creates."

"Then we can assume it's your step-brother Fariq who is the enemy until we can prove otherwise?"

"Yes," Akdemir says.

"Who was the woman who took my place?"

Jason has a strange expression on his face but says nothing.

"We do not know her identity. Basim is the only one who can answer that question."

"Seeing as he isn't here right now, why did you buy out Mr. C's part of the property and the other investor's? How did you even know about them?" He looks confused. "Are you kidding? He's part of what's wrong with this whole thing!"

"Allow me to explain, Ellen."

"I can't wait to hear you explain this one."

He seems slightly embarrassed. "When we pinpointed the chip in the book, we sent someone to gather information about the property. We discovered multiple people and companies listed on the deed."

Jason wants to jump in, but I shake my head at him. "Wait, okay?"

"But Mom, I have some questions of my own," he says.

"It occurred to us that to keep you and your family safe, we also had to rid the investors of their hold on this property."

"Yeah, that makes no sense," Jason says.

"Who did Lenard and Gene work for, and why did they lie so convincingly and set up this elaborate ruse to leave me hanging here? And I need clarification of other issues you failed to provide while I was, um, kept in luxury at your palace."

"I know nothing of these people named Lenard and Gene." Akdemir and Jamale glance at each other; he shrugs and shakes his big head. "It was a rational move to purchase their portions of this property, Ellen. It was going out for bid. Did you not know this? Your banker was most informative when we contacted him about the purchase."

"Yes, about the banker. How much money did he receive for commission for selling it to you? And how did you know it was up for bid? You must have a global network of spies."

"The banker received the going rate for the transaction. If that is what you want to call the people who are involved with your protection, then they are spies. They have been instructed to help you, not hinder you in any way."

"The banker had no right to sell you this house. The CIA certified that I owned this place. What about the currency?"

"Again, I know nothing about that. Basim must have kept it with the documents for a reason. Perhaps your father knew why it was with the books."

"What do you know about my father?"

"I am not at liberty to discuss this right now, Ellen."

"Why were my notes removed from my red case?" Turning to confront the giant in the room, "Did you have anything to do with that? I trusted you both, and you made a fool out of me!"

"Yeah, why did you do that to my Mom? Wasn't it bad enough our Dad was killed?" Jason says, coming to my rescue. "You aren't welcome here. You need to leave."

"Thanks, sweetie. Look, I fully expected repercussions with the authorities, but you could have given back my passport and wallet! Do you have any idea how awful it was for me?"

Ak-dim-er seems pensive. "If my government knew of your presence, there would be dire consequences. I did tell you that, Ellen. We had no choice other than to do it that way."

"You find the right documents to prove who you are and Jason stays with us until he's twenty-one. If everything is in order, he can make up his mind to stay here with us, or go to Saudi with you."

"Mom, I already told him I won't go with him, not now, not ever!" Jason says passionately.

"Jason, let him at least look for them. When and if he's able to show us, then you can decide to stay with us here in Virginia or go to Saudi Arabia. Does that sound fair to you, because I'm not willing to allow you to take him!"

Pulling the large silver and blue ring off his finger, he hands it to Jason. "I want you to have this. It belonged to my father, and his father before him. Your father wore it briefly, giving it to me before he left. I am certain he would want you to have it. It rightfully belongs to you. Will you accept it in good faith?"

"Okay, hold it right there, pal. There's no homing device built into it, is there? I'm going to have it tested, and it won't look good if I find that it's bugged."

"My dearest Ellen, you can trust me when I say there is no bug in it." Akdemir stands as does Jason, and I think this is over when he turns to me. "I am in your debt, my dearest Ellen. I never meant for any hostility between us. Except for all of you, my family is all dead. That is why it is important that we are together." He turns to Jason and places both hands on his shoulders. "I will ask again if you will come with me today, Jason, to fight for your rightful place as lawful heir to the Kingdom of Saudi Arabia."

"I still have questions." Moving closer to them, Jam-ale moves closer to the Prince. "Don't worry Jam-ale; I won't hurt him." I'm probably not pronouncing his name correctly, but at this stage of the game, I don't care.

"Ah, yes, your questions, you always have questions, do you not?" the Prince says with a laugh.

"What made Basim/Ravi so unhappy that he didn't want to live there?"

"That is something I cannot share with you." Akdemir looks embarrassed when he says this. "I do have one more item to discuss with you both. Jason cannot race at the track any longer. It is forbidden."

"Whoa there Mr. Abdul, you can't tell me what to do, you're not my father. We have a few rules of our own, right Mom?" Jason says flatly.

"It is too dangerous for the future heir to do this dangerous thing. Moreover, yes, I can, Jason. According to the real documents, all of you belong to my kingdom. You shall do as I say as head of this household."

"That's interesting, Ak-dim-er. Until you can produce those documents, I'm head of household here, and Jason stays put until he's twenty-one."

"Jason, you are my only hope," he says, turning to plead with him.

Jason stands his ground and shakes his head. "NO! I will not go with you. No friggin way!" he says adamantly, then moves to stand near me.

"Perhaps you will change your mind when you are older. We will find the documents, and you will see." Jam-ale nods his head toward the Prince. "Ah, yes, Jamaile, it is time. My dearest Ellen, if you and your family will come to your barn, there is something that has been long in coming."

Adrian joins us in the hallway when we come out of the library, then notices the ring on Jason's finger. Jam-ale steps into the living room to ask the others to join us outside.

We gather at the barn where Akdemir presents us with two magnificent Arabian Stallions named *Abbas*, (Arabic for lion), and

*Husayn,* (meaning Good, The founder), along with their papers. It is an unexpected show of generosity in the face of Jason's defiant turndown of his offer.

"I give these to you for a very belated wedding gift. I could not contact Basim at that time and hope you will accept them and cherish them as he cherished you."

"I don't know what to say. It's a very generous gift, Ak-dim-er."

Taking the lead ropes from Jam-ale, he puts them in my hands, saying, "I thank you for your hospitality. I wish you well with much happiness. May I return to spend some time with you and your family?"

"Of course, this is your home, too, apparently. But I want to get something straight. You are not to take Jason or threaten him or us in any way, is that understood?"

"Yes, Ellen, you have my word on this," the Prince answers softly.

"If either one of you or anyone you know set foot on this property again without our knowledge, I will personally put a bullet in their head. Is that understood? I must have your word, and Jam-ale's or I will fight you tooth and nail. And then I'll string you up and parade you through the town with tar and feathers!"

Prince Akdemir starts to laugh. "Basim told me many times of your humor. I only wish he were here to share this. I make a promise to you that Jason will make a choice when he is ready."

"I mean for Jam-ale to promise not to come onto our property without our knowledge or take Jason, too! He and you must both swear no harm will come to him or us!"

The Prince's eyes blink, but the flicker of understanding is instantly recognizable, and he turns to Jam-ale. Speaking softly to him, they both swear they'll do as I ask.

In an apparent show of loyalty, Jam-ale moves in front of me, where he swings a clenched fist and arm across his chest, bows slightly, and says, "I will protect you and family with my life. My life for yours, always."

Then he moves toward Adrian, reaches for his right arm, grabbing his at the elbow. Looking down at him (he's a head taller than most of us) saying, "You will guard them with your life, or I will have yours." Jam-ale then leans closer saying, "Take care, she has the temper."

Looking up at Jam-ale, Adrian does not hesitate. He grips Jam-ale's elbow in the same manner, responding proudly with, "My life for theirs." Then leans up to say, "I am aware of her temper."

Jam-ale turns to smile at me (there are those beautiful white teeth), then at Akdemir, who then glances at me, and for the first time, I feel included into their secret world of silent gestures.

"Be well, my nephew. Take good care of your family. We will talk soon." The Prince bids us farewell and climbs into his limo as we wave goodbye to him and his entourage.

Adrian squeezes my hand, then tells Jason how proud his father would be if he were here. His cellphone chirps and I know by the ringtone its Levi. Before he walks away, he gives us the status of our situation. Levi will come to Ashwood, as there's more news he wants to share with us. He also releases the CIA agents from guard duty, once word the jumbo jet that carries Akdemir and his group has left the ground.

Levi arrives a few days later, taking Mother into the library to talk with her privately while we say our goodbyes to Larry, as he is officially off our case. We will miss Larry's humor and the easy way he took care of us. He promises to bring his family to Ashwood from time to time. As Larry drives off, I wonder if his wife knows what he does for a living?

About an hour later, Levi and Mother join Jason, Adrian, and me in the living room. Mel and Curlie wondered why the discussion did not include them, but they got over it when I promised to order something they've been wanting.

Mother sits down next to me, her eyes still red from crying. Levi slowly repeats what he told her. My father left a sealed letter and packet of papers in the vault at CIA Headquarters with instructions to open them upon his death. Unfortunately, it went unnoticed until Levi asked his teams to look for anything that might explain the Basim/Ravi Affair.

"First of all, I apologize for not being able to tell you certain things about your Daddy and husband, Ellen. As agents, we have to sift through information that might be classified. We kept their identities a secret, to ensure your safety." Levi says.

"I'm sure you had a good reason, Mr. Levi. Let's hear it."

"It all started when your father discovered the currency hidden behind a wall in his attic bedroom where he lived with the adoptive family who took him in after the war. It was a hiding place for his Uncle Lautaro Ruggeri's stolen hoard. He removed enough not to draw attention."

"Grandpa was raised by gangsters?" Jason says interrupting.

"No, Jason, his adoptive father was legit. He removed the 1934A bills. When Uncle Lautaro found out, he hounded your father to give them back. Not too long after, there was an argument between his adoptive father, Tomas, and his brother, Lautaro."

"We didn't talk about that part of his life," Mother offers. "Now I wish we had. It would have made more sense to us now."

Levi paces in front of the fireplace, then says, "This is going to sound complicated, but hear me out, okay? When your father found Lautaro standing over Tomas' dead body, that's when he fled, and never returned to Argentina. He sought revenge by getting involved with the authorities. Your father kept the money as a failsafe, using it to trap his uncle."

"Excuse me? Are you saying my father had the currency? Then how did it get into the books? Abdul told me that Basim/Ravi did that."

"I'm getting to that. When your parents first came to Chicago via Canada, your father was already a part of the CIA but lacked training. He didn't attend a public college in Argentina; he was there to study certain classes."

"I'm not following, Mr. Levi," Jason says candidly.

"It will make more sense by the time I'm done explaining it, son." Levi turns toward me. "King Basim Abdul Fariq Obagur approached your father, Miss Ellen, when he got the assignment to Saudi Arabia in conjunction with peace talks. That's Basim and Akdemir's father. He asked your father to become his son's protector. Your father gave his word that he would do that at all costs."

"Mother, did you know about any of this before he told you?"

She shakes her head, "No, I had no idea . . ."

"At first, we couldn't see the connection between the documents and the currency. We thought it might be unrelated, but they were so intertwined it was hard to unravel it all, but we did. Adrian, would you like to step in?"

"Certainly, sir," Adrian says. "It seems that many years ago, good old Uncle Lautaro and his men pulled a bank heist that led to his being in possession of the 1934A currency. Uncle Ruggeri traveled to the United States on and off for nearly ten years conducting business this way. That particular bank heist was an unsolved one, and the FBI went nuts trying to find out who did it until we got Interpol involved," Adrian says.

"Thanks, Adrian," Levi says. "This man has been on the FBI's Most Wanted List for years. That's how the U. S. Marshals and the CIA became involved. Your father made up his mind that he would join the CIA and use whatever he had at his disposal to bring his lying, cheating, murdering Uncle Lautaro to justice. It proved harder than he imagined as he disappeared along with the rest of the stash in the attic--and so did his men," Levi concludes.

Adrian takes over. "By then, your father met and married your mother Francesca, and they moved to Canada, where he completed his training. Do you recall what Levi said earlier, about your father being in Saudi Arabia for those peace talks?"

"Yes, but this doesn't seem like it's going to gel."

"The king took your father aside and gave him the original documents found in the books, but your father held some back for safekeeping. That's what we found in the vault, the rest of the documents, and the rest of the currency. They were in the envelope along with the letter to explain everything. We're sorry we didn't find them sooner, it might have saved you some grief," Adrian says apologetically.

Jason shakes his head. "I'm still not getting all this. Why didn't they tell us about it and get it over with?"

Am I in denial? "This is such an unbelievable story, Levi. Like Jason, I don't see the connection. Ravi had part of the documents and part of the currency, and Daddy had part of the documents and part of the currency, but why?"

Levi frowns, "I told you it was complicated. Your father kept part of the documents, in case Basim's heirs needed them. Do you want me to stop, Francesca?"

"No, go on Levi, they need to hear all of it," Mother says softly.

"The king felt that Basim's life would end if he didn't get him out of Saudi Arabia. An incident no one can speak of made it necessary for plastic surgery, altering his facial structure. Here's a photo of him before that. It's hard to imagine what he went through. No one knew about this except five people; the King, Basim, your father, and then later, his brother and his giant sidekick."

Levi hands me two old photographs. Jason comes to sit on the floor near me, taking one he says, "Geeze . . . I can't believe this was Dad!"

It's difficult to see any resemblance to the man I married. In one photo, a young man is dressed in royal attire and has more resemblance to Ak dim than to the Ravi we knew. The second photo is of a man whose face is a mangled mess.

"Who did this to him?" Jason asks.

"We aren't sure, but it's probably why the king wanted him out of the country," Levi offers. "Everyone was told he died of injuries sustained in an accident. No one questioned it when the photo of the beaten man was distributed."

"How would Daddy know that Ravi and I would even marry, let alone have heirs?" As soon as these words leave my mouth, the realization hits me that I was part of the equation from the beginning. "I'm furious to think that Ravi married me to escape his country."

"Ellen, you have every right to be angry," Levi says. "But there's more."

Mother takes my hand. "Ellie, it's not what you think, sweetheart. It's all there in the letter your father left in the vault. Ravi fell in love with you the moment your father showed him your picture. He loved you at first sight and couldn't wait to meet you."

"Your Mother read the letter, and she'll share that with you once I leave," Levi says. "I know it's hard to swallow."

"I never saw those books before I went into Dimmy's library. How could I have picked the same ones the documents went into?"

"Your husband did have two of the books in his possession. Maybe you picked them because they looked familiar, a subconscious thing. My team thinks that the other books were fixed and planted so you would have to take all three of them."

"Maybe your father thought that if Ravi kept the money, he would have something to fall back on, so no one could connect your father to his uncle?" Adrian speculates.

"That's one theory," Levi looks thoughtful. "Another theory I came up with is that if Basim/Ravi kept part of the money and documents, the other half would remain with your father."

"I'm not sure I want to hear anymore, Levi." Tears are rolling down my face as Mother turns to me.

"You need to hear the rest of it, sweetheart. I don't like it either. Go ahead Mr. Levi; tell her the rest of it."

"Your father thought it could be used at some point as a bargaining chip," he says.

"Why would he need that?" Jason asks. "What was he going to bargain for?"

"Good question, Jason. Even though your Grandfather was retired for several years, he contacted the authorities to warn them that Uncle Lautaro was alive and coming after him. He had, after all this time, tracked him to Evanston and he was fearful he would harm one of you."

"Was he responsible for my father's death?" Mother squeezes my hand tightly.

"No, although Uncle Lautaro was a terrible man by most standards, your father had a bad heart, honey," Levi says.

"What did Lenard tell you? Did you get him to admit he hurt my nephew, Danny? That he's responsible for our dead horse? Did he work for the uncle?"

"We told Lenard we apprehended Ruggeri, who it so happens was hiding out in Mr. C's Guest House, quite unbeknownst to anyone. We also told Lenard that Ruggeri named him as the one who performed several robberies, forgeries, and other heinous crimes."

"In his defense, Lenard started singing like a canary," Adrian grins.

"Ruggeri was the one who hired Lenard aka Deter Eckert and Gene aka Thomas Lindner to throw you off the track because they wanted both the currency and the documents. They were convinced that Basim gave them to you for safekeeping," Levi says.

Suddenly, something occurs to me. "This Ruggeri person was the other man with the foreign accent at the restaurant that day. His hands were large as I recall."

"That's right, Ellen. According to his profile, he was large, ate well, and lived as a wealthy man. Ruggeri, who it turns out also hired the woman who got on the plane with Basim/Ravi has lots of connections, everywhere."

Adrian goes on to say that Ruggeri installed Lenard and Gene at the airport to apprehend Basim. "His elaborate plan started to backfire when the plane exploded, and he had to rethink his plan. They knew you were with Basim and wouldn't get on the plane, because the woman told Lenard she made sure you wouldn't. She didn't know the plane wouldn't make it off the runway."

"If Ruggeri was behind drugging me, then how did I get to Saudi Arabia? Why did they have to kill Ravi? What's the connection?"

"That's an interesting story, too," Adrian muses.

Levi lets out a breath, "When Ruggeri discovered you were not in the restroom, the little group panicked. They planned to kidnap you, and hold you until you told them where everything was. But Prince Akdemir's men were already there to protect Ravi."

"It was plain luck you were discovered and taken to safety," Adrian adds.

"If Dimmy's men were there to help, I'm confused. Who blew up the plane?"

"We don't know for sure. It has something to do with Akdemir's enemies," Adrian says. "They want control of the oil wealth. They're a clever bunch, very secretive, not unlike other warring factions around the world."

"That's a completely different part of this story. That's why we couldn't figure it out at first. Many things were going on at the same time. You were caught right in the middle of it," Levi recons.

"So if Ruggeri knew I was not on the plane, he came after the rest of my family and me?"

Levi nods his head, and says, "He was irritated and convinced that if your back was to the wall, you would do anything to get out of it. He was convinced that you knew where the currency was. He orchestrated the sale of Ashwood and tried to manipulate you to use it to pay for things, but you didn't fall for it. When you sold the antiques and won all that money, it made him crazy."

"So the banker was in his pocket too? I'll go along with him being crazy. I'm dizzy trying to make sense of all this. I hate to ask, but is there more?"

"As matter of fact, there is. The government cleared Mr. C of all charges of tax evasion and any wrongdoing. Ruggeri had a hand in that too, and since he turned State's Evidence, Mr. C is more than willing to testify against him and his band of thugs."

"Does that mean he has no claim on the house? Did Dimmy buy the other half of it and it's a legitimate deal? Have we traded one lunatic to have another take his place?"

Adrian smiles that silly grin of his. "As far as Prince Akdemir goes, we don't think you have anything to worry about as he is who he says he is. He does own half of Ashwood Stables."

"Since Gene is dead," Levi continues, "we can't corroborate their stories. Lenard is currently in a holding cell, awaiting extradition to Germany. Something about a non-valid passport, forgery, passing bad checks and a multitude of other charges that will take years for the authorities over there to unravel. The only loose end is the agent called Andrea Simmons, who has gone poof, but we'll keep an eye open for her. Anybody have any questions?" Levi stands up.

"I do. Who is responsible for our dead horse? Does a Mr. Jenkins or a Mr. Lassiter have anything to do with *Didge's* death?"

Levi looks thoughtful. "We don't have an answer for that, Ellen. We're not aware of anyone by those names. Did you check on them, Adrian, did Larry? Of course, you had your hands full. I'll run a check if you want."

"Does this mean we can go back home to Evanston?"

"Yeah, can we have our name back? Can we contact our friends now?" Jason asks.

"No," Levi replies solemnly. "I'm sorry, that would compromise the program. Although Lenard did a good job of forgery, you must remain where you are and follow the same protocols he laid out for you."

"Even though I don't like it, I understand. It's our home now, but what about my sister and her family?"

"Ellen, it would take too many resources to change things back, and frankly your houses are sold, and other people are living in them now. We can't go back and undo this; it's too complex. As for your sister, we're still working on that," Levi says.

"Thank you for all of your efforts, Mr. Levi. We appreciate everything you and your teams have done for us."

"Glad to have helped. We need you to continue here. It's home to you now, isn't it? What about it Jason?"

"Yeah, its home now," Jason says. "We're getting used to it."

Levi looks thoughtful for a moment as Mother blinks back tears. "I'm sorry to tell you that after all you've been through, but this is the way it must be. You are in the Federal Witness Protection Program."

"What did Ruggeri need with the documents? Why would they be so important to him?" Mother suddenly asks.

"That's a good question, Francesca. Ruggeri thought that your husband was in possession of some documents he had stolen in a previous heist, but what he didn't know was that he turned them in at CIA years ago. Ruggeri still believes that the documents you had, were his."

"So the ones Akdemir is so anxious to have are . . ."

"Oh, yes, I have them right here." Levi hands me a delicate bundle. "You'll find these are what Prince Akdemir seeks. You decide what to do with them. As far as the government is concerned, they belong to you. But consider the consequences of keeping them; relinquishing them to Prince Akdemir would be the right thing to do, Ellen."

Adrian says, "You and Jason might want to read the notes attached to them before you do. In case he decides to take Uncle Dimmy up on his offer."

"Fat chance that'll happen, Mr. Adrian," Jason says in a hostile voice as Mother reaches to caress his cheek.

"So you know, it was your father and your husband Ma'am that was honorable to the end. If there are no more questions, it's a long drive back to Langley. Adrian, would you walk me out?" Levi hugs me, then shakes Jason's hand. He extends belated apologies, regrets the oversight in not finding the information sooner, and lingers to hold Mother's hand for a long time.

It's clear from what Levi and Adrian told us that my father loved us all. He was a good man and a better agent than most, and we should all be proud of the legacy he left.

Levi didn't hesitate to say the same about Basim/Ravi. We asked him to convey our thanks to his diligent teams who tirelessly worked on our behalf. Words cannot adequately express our feelings and we will eternally be in their debt. We extended an open invitation to them all to come and stay at Ashwood at any time.

As we try to digest what Levi and Adrian told us, we feel duped and annoyed. Mother hands Daddy's letter to me, and my eyes blur with tears. Reading it through, suddenly all of the events of the past come clearly into focus. Daddy saw fit to explain everything; from the museum in Italy to the amusement park where that awful man tried to take Curlie, all of it because of the horrible man named Uncle Lautaro Ruggeri and Daddy's relationship with Basim/Ravi's father.

Handing the letter to Jason, I open the delicate pile of documents to read Jewel's deciphered notes. "Hum, that's interesting."

I glance up to see Jason's solemn expression. "Too bad we didn't know this before," he says quietly. "Why did Dad keep it a secret? I would have understood."

His grandmother replies, "I'd like to know that one myself, Jason. Certainly would have been helpful. It explains so much!"

"The water, as they say, is over the dam and we can't go back. There's always a reason for things, we don't always know what they are, but eventually, it will make sense."

Adrian strolls in and has a big smile on his face. "Why so glum? Levi left you with some good news."

"Will you be leaving us now too, Adrian?" Mother wonders.

"Yeah, Mr. Adrian, do you have to go now too?" Jason asks.

"That's what I want to talk to your mom about."

Mother excuses herself to make a cup of tea as Jason walks out to the barn.

"What are you going to do with the documents, now that you have them?" Adrian asks.

"I'm not sure. Prince Akdimguy knows I'm not happy with him right now. Jason is still a pawn in all this, and I don't want to force his hand in making a decision he might regret someday."

"I like your new name for him. It fits somehow."

"It looks like he was right about one thing. We all belong to his household, even in death. Abdul doesn't know we have these, so let's let him stew about it for a while, and Jason and I will talk later. He's hurt over the fact his father didn't tell him some important details that could impact his life."

"It's finally over. How does that make you feel, Mrs. Thompson?"

"You think it's over, Mr. Sellers?"

"Yes I do," he says thoughtfully.

"I don't."

"Except for the dead horse part and the stupid stuff that happens at the racetrack, yeah, I think it's mostly over. Oh, except for the part about Prince Wonderful and Jason going to Saudi Arabia, guess it's not exactly over, is it?"

"There is all that. Did the fat lady sing yet, Adrian?"

Adrian looks confused. "What fat lady?"

"The fat lady that sings at the end of the show that signals it's over."

"How can I leave you and the family with all that going on?"

"What are you trying to say, Mr. CIA man?"

"I've been thinking, darling Ellie. Don't you still need some protection here? Some nasty people are still out there that might want to harm your family. I think I'm the man for the job." Adrian may want to stay a few more days because his bag isn't packed and waiting by the door.

"Did I offer you a job, Mr. Sellers?"

"I believe you did, Mrs. Thompson." He changes his voice to a high-pitched whine, saying, "Please Special Agent Adrian B. Sellers, I need you here, and I can't live without you."

"What does the B stand for, bull?"

"You also said my family needs you, our horses adore you, you love Ms. Mona's cooking, and you can't do without me," he grins.

"I said all that?"

"Sure, don't you remember? It was that awful morning Prince Waldorf came a calling at two in the morning. Ah, you don't remember. Here, let me refresh your memory." Adrian pulls me into an embrace, tenderly kissing my lips.

"Oh, now I remember."

"If you won't join me there, Miss Ellie May Thompson, I don't see the point in staying with the CIA."

"I can't join you there, Adrian. I belong here with my family."

"I did promise the big guy to protect you all. I'd work very hard, Mrs. Thompson! You know I can muck out the stalls with the best of them. Can I stay? I already gave Levi my two weeks' notice, and put my townhouse up for sale . . ."

# Epilogue

A thorough investigation into both Mr. Jenkins and Mr. Lassiter's backgrounds yielded some interesting facts. While one is a bully, the other one is merely a nosey neighbor. Agent Levi Johnson suggested that we stay out of their way, if at all possible. He figured what transpired at Ashwood Stables was isolated to our neck of the woods. In the future, please don't hesitate to call upon him should we require his services.

In the meantime, Sheriff Rocky will keep an eye on both Jenkins and Lassiter, but he doesn't hold out much hope of a conviction in the case of our dead horse unless the same thing happened again. Race day medications are an everyday occurrence, and unless we have some way of catching the culprit in the act, it will be nearly impossible to prosecute anyone. And the mystery drug remains—a mystery.

Agent Adrian Sellers said it was time to inform the Virginia Racing Commission about possible indiscretions concerning the issue with Mr. Jenkins' driver, during that hair-raising race our first season out at the racetrack. The formal complaint stated precisely which infractions the driver violated that day. It gave me great pleasure to recite them, verbatim no less, to several members of the commission who conducted a review. A full investigation and reprimand will come down on the guilty party, or parties, according to the rules. Again, Levi said we should let him know should this not be resolved to our satisfaction.

On a much lighter note, Reed and Dr. Jessica announced their intention to marry in the spring. I was caught up in the excitement and suggested they have their reception here at Ashwood Stables. We can put our new paver stone patio and BBQ to good use, as after all, we designed shindigs and hoedowns for that purpose.

What better way to celebrate spring? All the petunias and daffodils will be ready to bloom around the perimeter, and the flowering trees should make quite a statement. The festivities will include little twinkly lights around a tent set up for the occasion. The women of Ashwood have been deep into the food and wedding cake plans, along with the myriad of other details that a wedding entails since Jessica enlisted their help.

Reed and Jessica asked if they could restore the rooms over the garages, which we now refer to as the Carriage House. We hope that the reconstruction will go without a hitch so that they can occupy it after their honeymoon.

In all the excitement, we forgot about the old vault in the basement. It was such a rusted mess that Reed had to take a torch to it. Inside we found Sarah Ashwood's jewelry. We did not notify the Ashwood heirs, as we paid all the back taxes while the house remained empty, so we took possession of them.

Gerald Tillman put the jewels up for bid on his state-of-the-art website page that Reed built, then announced several days later that they fetched a tidy sum. Glen was stunned at this news, as after all, had they been discovered sooner, he and Mona would not have been forced to eat vegetables until they came out their ears.

The tiny key found stuck to the bottom of the old desk drawer in Mr. AJ's office, unlocks a small ornate inlaid wooden box we found toward the back of the old safe. Opening it amid much anticipation, it contained locks of hair from each of the original Ashwood children. Mother suggested that we leave it in the vault for now. After all, some things are better left undisturbed!

Also in the vault were several documents, one of which turned out to be the original title to the Duesenberg. We managed to track down the new owner, and when we handed it to him, he nearly fainted, because it boosted the car's value quite considerably.

Mr. High and Mighty had no trouble sending funds to cover what Mr. C and the other investors owed us as he felt that it was his duty as half-owner of Ashwood Stables. The master suite once set aside for Mr. C is now for His Most Royal Highness and General (pain-in-the-ass), whom we affectionately refer to as Uncle Dimmy. We hope is that they are infrequent visits.

The exquisite Arabian Stallions gifted to us by Uncle Dimmy, are a great addition to our stables. He saw fit to leave one of their costumes in honor of Basim/Ravi, who wore the blue and silver proudly once upon a time. Since *Abbas* and *Husayn* trained in Dressage, Reed advertised that we now give that style of riding lessons.

Uncle Dimmy could not be with us for our Christmas Holiday this year but sent an abundance of expensive gifts. Then he extended an invitation to all of us to join him at the palace any time could get away. We sent him a polite refusal, as I'm not ready to see that place anytime soon. He'll return to Virginia when he can, but we are to carry on without him. It makes us all laugh, what else does he expect us to do?

We decided that when Jason made that false bomb threat, we felt that we needed to replace them. Our anonymous check for $50,000, payable to the local fire department/bomb squad unit should help defray the costs.

The Board of Directors removed Mr. Yancy from the bank in town. It seemed that he mishandled not only the Ashwood property but several others. An indictment against both he and Mr. Allen, the Executor of the defunct Ashwood Estate, will force the authorities to confront our allegations of fraud. During their investigation, they were unable to uncover where the estate money went, and Mother wanted to know if we would ever see any of it. Highly unlikely, Adrian told her; don't we have enough without it?

The children seem contented to live here in Virginia with our extended family, with the promise that Terre and her family will someday be able to join us. My n Mother now has plenty of people to smother with her love and Mona doesn't mind cooking for the lot of us. Doesn't she have the most wonderful kitchens in the world and employers who love her?

With the evil people behind bars, awaiting trial or extradition, it's a good feeling to not worry about anything. We are at peace with the world, as we settle in for what promises to be a Winter Wonderland for our second Christmas here in Virginia. The lights twinkle, the wreaths hang in each window, and the tree takes center stage near the big windows in the living room as the fireplaces are ablaze with a warm glow.

As we make our traditional toasts, we include our gratitude, remembering the Ashwoods. Our success might not have been possible if it weren't for Sarah Ashwood's determination. I'd like to think she's proud of what we've done to bring her vision of the house back to its former glory. I'm convinced it's her spirit that roams the halls because she loved it here so much, she never wanted to leave it.

Jason will one day make a life-altering decision. Will he go to Saudi Arabia and accept his destiny when he turns twenty-one? Or will he settle for college and a career and stay here with us?

Until then, we are content to live in peace with the knowledge that all is right with our little corner of the world; for the time being, that is.

# *Acknowledgements*

I would like to thank all those individuals who were part of our family's experience after my son suffered a traumatic brain injury from an automobile accident. All of you helped in our time of need, and he would not be where he is today if it were not for your tremendous support and prayers.

There are too many of you to name here, but you are our 'angels' nonetheless. You have inspired me to write this book. *The Ancient Whisper* reflects our incredible journey from a tragic accident to self-discovery, through a remarkable recovery, and finally to self-awareness and acceptance.

Although no longer with us, Sylvia I. Richter, encouraged and critiqued this book which facilitated the impetus to write its sequels. Her helpful hints and ideas not only strengthened but enforced the story. It made me go where I have never gone before.

Thank you, to all of you!

# BOOKS AND RESOURCES:

Funk & Wagnall's Standard Dictionary, <u>Ancient</u>. 1969, Volume One, New York.

Hillenbrand, Laura. <u>Seabiscuit</u>. New York, NY: Ballantine Books, 2001.

Horan, Nancy <u>Loving Frank</u>. New York, NY: Ballantine, Books, 2008.

<u>2012 Virginia Fact Book</u>, a statistical guide to the Thoroughbred Industry in Virginia. Prepared by The Jockey Club. 01 July 2012. http://www.jockeyclub.com/factbook/StateFactBook/Virginia.pdf

# WORLD WIDE WEB/INTERNET:

<u>Arabian Costume</u>. 31 July 2012.
http://www.almostranch.com/arabiancostumes6.html

<u>Beginner's Corner</u>. 24 July 2012. http//www.dmtc.com/handicapping/beginners

<u>Books; Collectibles</u>. Moby Dick; Or, the Whale. 21 July 2012.
http://www.alibris.com/booksearch?qauth=Herman+Melville& collectible

<u>Biosphere 2</u>. 23 January 2013. http://en.wikipedia.org/wiki/Biosphere_2

<u>Coupe Brougham</u>. 15 January 2013.
http://www.colonialcarriage.com/item.cfm?id=1097

<u>Currency</u>. 12 July 2012. http://ask.yahoo.com/20051110.html

<u>Cuthbert</u>. 01 August 2012. http://en.wikipedia.org/wiki/File:Cuthberta

<u>Death and Disarray at America's Racetracks</u>. 15 July 2012.
http://www.nytimes.com/2012/03/25/us/death-and-disarray-at-americas-racetracks.html

<u>Duesenberg Model J (1933)</u>. 04 July 2012.
http://www/supercars.net/cars/468.html

<u>Duesenberg Model J. Images</u>. 03 July 2012.
http://www/conceptcarz.com/view/photo/729947,13703/1933-Duesenberg-Model-J_photo

Dulay, Cindy Pierson. *Handicapping How to calculate betting* odds and payoffs. 24 July 2012. http://horseracing.about.com

<u>Dumbwaiter</u>. 29 January 2013. http://www.ameriglide.com/item/ameriglide-express-dumbwaiter.html

Einstein, Albert. <u>Theory of Relativity</u>. 07 July 2012.
http://en.wikipedia.org/wiki/Theory_of_Relativity

Eng, Richard. <u>Examining Different Levels of Competition at the Racetrack</u>. 24 July 2012. http://www.dummies.com/hot-to/content/examining-different-levels-of-competition-at-the-racetrack

FBI. Federal Bureau of Investigation. 25 January 2013.
  http://www.fbijobs.gov/11.asp

First call. 15 January 2013. http://en.wikipedia.org/wiki/First_call

Frank Lloyd Wright: architecture. 13 July 2012. http://www.nytimes.com

Fun horse names. 01 August 2012. http://www.funhorsenames.com/arabian-horse-names.html

Gun laws in Virginia. 12 July 2012. http//:en.wikipedia.org/wiki/ Gun Laws_in_Virginia

Hieronymi DeSvbtilitate. 21 July 2012.
  http://www.ebay.com/item/FIRST-EDITION-MOST-IMPORTANT-BOOK-GIROLAMO

Hack Life, Marc and Angel. Thirty Books Everyone Should Read Before They're Thirty. 13 July 2012.
  http://www/divinecaroline.com/22189/98450-thirty-books- everyone-read-they-re#ixzz20WDzQHtc

Harness Charts from Harness Eye: Handicapping 101.14 July2012.
  http://www.harnesslink.com/harnesscharts.Handicapping

Harness Racing. 01 July 2012. http://en.wikipedia.or/wiki/Harness_racing

History Victorian Inventions. 29 January 2013.
  http://www.innovationslearning.co.uk/subjects/history/information/Victorian/inventions/inventions/toilet.htm

Horse Names. 15 July 2012.
  http://www.angelfire.com/tx2/horsecorral/horsenames2.html

Horse Racing Glossary A-Z, Terminology, Jargon, Slang, Vocabulary. 14 July 2012. http://www.ildado.com.com/horse_racing_glossary.html

Horse Racing; racehorse numbers; assignment of, horse jockey, race horse. 24 July 2012. http://en.allexperts.com/q/Horse-Raing-2248/race-horse-numbers-assiment.htm

How to calculate betting odds and payoffs. 02 July 2012.
  http://horseracing.about.com/cs/handicapping/odds

How to Read the Daily Racing Form. 02 July 2012.
  http://www.turfparadise.com/racingform_how.php

How to Write a Bibliography. 01 October 2012.
  http://www.angelfire.com/ny2/library218/bibliography.html

Interpol. 17 January 2013. http://www.interpol.int

Maps of World. 16 July 2012.
  http://www.mapsofworld.com/usa/states/virginia/virginia-ap.html

Map of Langley, Virginia. 16 July 2012. http://wikipedia.org/wiki/Langley, Virginia

Melville, Herman. Moby-Dick; or, The Whale. 13 July 2012.
  http://en.wikipedia.org/wiki/Moby-Dick

National Racing Compact. 18 July 2012.
  http://www.racinglicense.com/criteria.htm

National Register of Historic Places. 24 January 2013.
  http://www.nationalregisterofhistoricplaces.com

Pari-mutuel betting. 15 July 2012.
  http://en.wikipedia.org/wiki/Parimutuel_betting

Piano. 21 June 2012. http://en.wikipedia.org/wiki/Piano

Racing Secretary. 27 January 2013. http://en.wikipedia.org/wiki/Racing_secretary

Saudi Arabia. 31 July 2012. http://en.wikipedia.org/wiki/Saudi_Arabia

Seabiscuit (2003). 16 December 2003 Universal Studios film.
  http://www.imdb.com/title/tto329575/

Setterbo, Jacob J., Tanya C. Garcia, Ian P. Campbell, Jennifer L. Reese, Jessica W. Morgan, Sun Y. Kim, Mont Hubbard, and Susan M. Stover, University of California, Davis. Can Racetrack Surface Reduce the Risk of Musculoskeletal Injury in Thoroughbred Racehorses? 24 July 2012.
  http://www.vetmed.ucdavis.edu/ceh

State of Virginia Racing License. 15 July 2012.
  http://www.vrc.virginia.gov/racinglicenses.shtml

Strange Are the ways of Communication at race course. 17 July 2012.
  http://www.dnaindia.com/sport/report_strange-are-the-ways-of-communication-at-race-course

Sulky. 01 July 2012. http://en.wikipedia.org/wiki/Sulky

The Jockey Club. 17 July 2012. http://home.jockeyclub.com/silks.asp

TrackMaster Proprietary Ratings Specification, (Harness Racing) 24 July 2012.
  http://www.trackmaster.com /harness.htm

True Lies. 15 July 1994 Twentieth Century Fox film.
  http://en.wikipedia.org/wiki/True_Lies

United States Federal Witness Protection Program. 23 January 2013.
  http://en.wikipedia.org/wiki/United_States_Federal_Witness_Protection_Program

Vintage house plans. 13 July 2012. http://www.archivaldesighns.com/housplan

Virginia Department of Historic Resources. 24 January 2013.
  http://www.dhr.virginia.gov

Virginia Racing Commission. 15 July 2012.
  http://www.vrc.virginia.gov/racinglicenses.shtml

# GLOSSARY AND OTHER INFORMATION:

Across the Board. This is a bet on a horse to win, place, or show. That is three wagers combined into one. If the horse wins, the player wins all of the three wagers, if the horse comes in second, the player wins two of the wagers, if the horse comes in third, and the player wins one of the wagers.

All weather racing. The abbreviated AWT means all-weather track used to describe the conditions on the track on which a race takes place, an artificial surface.

Antique car. 1933-Duesenburg-Model-J is what the author used to describe the car found in the barn, the fastest eight cylinder, with a 265-horse power engine that had flex-pipe headers. It was the most popular American touring or passenger car made at the time.

Arabian Costume. The costume is of upholstery weight velvet that has hundreds of crystal and cobalt blue stones and exotic silver sequins, tassels are heavily beaded. Many pieces go with this costume; robe, headscarf, hat piece, harem-type pants with a blue shirt; horse has matching neckpiece and saddlecloth; ring to match. They can cost about $ 1,425.00 U.S. Dollars per complete outfit.

Arabian horse names. This is where the names of the Arabian Stallions, Abbas and Husayn, came from that Prince Abdul gave to the Thompson's as a gift.

Betting Board. Bookmakers use this board to display the odds of the horses engaged in a race.

Betting Ring. This is the main area at the racecourse where the bookmakers operate.

Betting slip. This is the ticket given to the person placing the wager.

Blinkers. A cup-shaped device used by trainers to cover the sides of the horse's head near his eyes to limit vision. It prevents swerving away from distracting objects or other horses on either side of him, come in a variety of sizes and shapes to allow, as little or as much vision as the trainer feels appropriate.

Biosphere 2. Located near Tucson Arizona, it is an Earth systems science research facility currently owned b y the University of Arizona. Built to be an artificial, materially enclosed eco-system for the possible use of closed biospheres in space colonization.

Bolt. This is a sudden veering off from a straight course.

Bookmaker. The bookmaker is the person licensed to accept bets on the result of an event based on their provision of odds to the customer. (See Sportbook US).

Boxed in. This is the term used when the horse is trapped, between other horses or carts, and may not be able to move either to the left or to the right.

Brougham Carriage. The Frey Carriage Company specializes in America's finest selection of horse drawn vehicles; preserved or restored, starting at $ 12,000.00.

Breeds of horses. North American harness racing is restricted to Standardbred horses. They get their name from "the early years of the Standardbred stud book; that only horses who cold pace or trot a mile in a standard time or whose progeny could do so", and those are the only ones who are admitted into the book.

> A Standardbred horse has shorter legs and a longer body than a Thoroughbred. It has a more easygoing temperament than a Thoroughbred, and more suitable for a horse "whose races involve more strategy and reacceleration than do Thoroughbreds." http://en.wikipedia.or/wiki/Harness_ racing for the entire article and quote.

Breeze. Term that sometimes called breezing; this is working the horse at moderate speed.

Bug boy. This is the term given to an apprentice rider.

Call to the Post. This is the bugle call that plays at horse and dog race tracks, that signals all mounts ( or drivers) should be at the starting gate because the race is about to begin. Once the bugler finishes the tune, there is approximately 5 to 10 minutes before the scheduled start time of the race.

Central Intelligence Agency. (CIA). Other services listed; Office of Intelligence & Analysis, National Clandestine Service: The branch, which is an elite corps of men and women shaped by diverse ethnic, educational, and professional backgrounds.

Chalk player. This is the term used to describe a bettor who wagers favorites.

Champion. There are over 35,000 Thoroughbred racehorses born ( or foaled) each year and every one of their owner's hopes that he/she will have a future champion.

Chief Steward. This is the official from the track, which meets with each driver prior to the first race.

CHP ( concealed handgun permit). Virginia residents have the right to keep and bear arms from government infringement. A concealed handgun permit ( CHP) is required for those over the age of 21 provided they have proper safety training.

Chute. The term for the spot in the homestretch, that allows a longer straight run. Code of Virginia. Legislative Information System. Title 59.1 Trade and Commerce. Chapter 29—Horse Racing and Pari-Mutuel Wagering, etc. These are the rules sited to be violated during a race between Ellen Thompson and another driver.

Colors. These are the racing silks, the jacket, and cap worn by jockeys. They can be generic and provided by the track or specific to one owner.

Colt. This is an ungelded (entire) male horse that is four years old or younger.

CWP. Concealed weapons permit, see CHP.

Combination bet. This is a bet that means the selection of any number of teams or horses to finish first and second in either order.

Cracking pace. This means that when the leader of the leaders of a race runs at a very quick speed. This is usually in the early stages of the race.

Cracker Jack. This refers to the caramelized popcorn that contains a small prize.

Currency; large denominations. The Bureau of Engraving and Printing: largest currency d e nomination ever printed is the astronomical sum of $100,000 series gold certificate made in 1934. President Woodrow Wilson's portrait is on the front of the bills. Other denominations printed: $500, $1,000, $5,000, and even a $10,000 paper bill, considered legal intended only for government used mostly for bank transfers. These were taken out of circulation around 1946 and by 1969, ceased altogether. They are not out of circulation, and collectors who still have them can still cash them in.

Cuthbertina. This is the name given to Curlie, a derivative of the old English word Cuthberta, meaning brilliant, and a feminine form of Cuthbert.

Daily double. A type of wager that calls for the selection of winners of two consecutive races, usually the first and second.

Daily racing form. (Or the daily schedule) A daily listing contains the racing information that includes news, part performance data, and handicapping.

Death and Disarray at America's Racetracks – NY Times.com (study of the incidence of injury to racehorses as well as jockeys.) May of 2010, "race day medications are not allowed" to be administered, shocking in and of itself, the statistics of injury to both the horse and jockey are astounding. Twenty-four horses, on average, die each week at racetracks across America. The authorities do often not examine them, and the bodies either shipped to rendering plants or go into landfills.

Dime. Known as a dime bet and consists of US Dollars at the rate of $1,000, for instance the bet or wager would be $3,000 if a three-dime bet were placed.
Distance. The length of a race. Five furlongs is the minimum, while four ½ miles of the Grand National is the longest. The margin by which a horse wins or is beaten by the horse in front of him. This could range from a short head to a 'by a distance' (which is more than 30 lengths).

Dressage. The fundamental purpose of Dressage is to develop a horse's natural athletic ability and willingness to perform, done through standardized progressive training methods. The horse responds to a skilled rider's effort-free direction, as the rider appears relaxed. Often referred to as Horse Ballet, Dressage is a discipline that has ancient roots in Europe, first recognized as an important equestrian pursuit during the Renaissance Period.

Driver's Meeting. The meeting that takes place with the Chief Steward at a designated time and place to go over the rules. Each driver is notified of this meeting in writing at least one day before the meeting takes place.

Duesenberg Model J. The Duesenberg Model J Dual Cowl Phaeton J243 was a factory demonstrator and was sold to Mr. A. E. Archibald by the Duesenberg New York City branch in the autumn of 1930." It sold in 1990 for the reportedly unbelievable price of $1,760,000 by the last owners' estate.
Favorite. This is the most popular horse in a race, and is quoted at the lowest odds because it is deemed to have the best chance of winning the race.

FIRE DRILL CODES. This is a fictional code that the Thompson family used.
　　Fire Drill= we need a contingency plan.
　　Houston we have a problem = there is a situation.
　　Eagle has landed = we are safe and ok.
　　Horse has left the barn = our target is leaving.
　　Target = someone identified as a threat to us.
　　HOT = FIRE. STAT = get help I'm in trouble.
　　OOG = out of gas.
　　SOS = Help no time to chat.
　　FOG = full of gas.
　　ER = I'm hurt bad. Free popcorn, anything free = lie.
　　CODE BLUE = get everyone to safety.

FBI Special Agents. FBI Special Agents conduct sensitive national security investigations and enforcing over 300 federal statutes. There is a rigorous training program for those who qualify.

FBI Special Agent Cases. Can be any of the following: terrorism, foreign counterintelligence, cyber-crime, organized crime, white-collar crime, public corruption, civil rights violations, financial crime, bribery, bank robbery, extortion, kidnapping, air piracy, interstate criminal activity, fugitive and drug-trafficking matters, and other violations of federal statutes.

First Editions. These are rare and often expensive books sought by collectors. Found on-line, in bookstores, or in the possession of private collectors.

First call. This is a bugle call used at horse races and known as the Call to the Post, can be sounded by a bugle, or a recording.

FTL. Abbreviation for First Time Lasix. This is a brand name (Lasix) for furosemide or furosemides derived from the last six hours, refers to how long it lasts, used for high blood pressure. A quick acting drug usually works within an hour; used in racing to prevent Thoroughbreds and Standardbred racehorses from bleeding through the nose during races.

Foal. This is a baby horse. It refers to either a male or female from birth to January 1 of the following year. All racehorses have the nominal birthday of January 1. A two-year-old born in June and one born in January of the same year are considered the same age. The purpose is to satisfy the conditions of some races in regards to weight carried. The January horse may have the significant advantage of physical development at this early stage in its career.

Furlong. A measure used by trainers to determine how a horse performs. It is 1/8 of a mile [or 220 yards] or 660 feet (approximately 200 meters).

Glock Pistol. The Glock pistol has a polymer frame and metal slide and barrel, which makes it legal to possess.

Graded 1 Stakes. The Triple Crown = the Kentucky Derby, Preakness, and the Belmont Stakes are all Grade 1 Stakes races and champion racehorses compete against the very best in their respective divisions. These also have the richest purses.

Grade 2 Stakes. A cut-below grade 1, attracts good racehorses. If a stakes race has horses in a race that usually run in a grade 1 stakes, the race can be upgraded the following year to grade 1. It can move up or down in grade depending on the caliber of horse that runs in it.

Grade 3 Stakes. Another level down from grade 1, grade 2. Has noticeably smaller purse because of kind of horse it attracts. A keen competition, more grade 3 stakes run larger pool of horses it draws.
Graduate. This is someone who has won for the first time.

Green. This is an inexperienced horse or driver.

Handicapper. Someone who predicts winners in a horserace.

Handicapping. Many forms and methods of handicapping, most common types are class, speed, pace, trip, and computer handicapping.

Handicapping 101. Ellen and her father came up with some rules she could follow when first learning how to wager at the racetrack. The five steps are found online under Harness Charts from Harness Eye. (See specific website under bibliography section).

Harness Racing. A form of horseracing that requires the horse to race at a specific gait; either a trot, or a pace. The horse pulls a two-wheeled cart called a sulky driven by a driver, not a jockey, as in other forms of horseracing.

Harness Racing Rules. Article 14; 112-14-5. Harness racing conduct (a) and (b), 1 through 4 that explicitly explains what is considered grounds for expulsion; 112-14-7; unsatisfactory harness race driving, and 112-14-9 Prohibited acts. (See Virginia Racing Commission).

Hedge. This is a term for covering a bet with a second bet.

Hit the board. This is the term used for horses whose numbers appear on the tote board as first, second, third, or fourth

Hopples/Hobbles. These are straps to connect the horse's legs (on each side), used to aid in supporting the gait of the horse at top speed.

Horse Racing Glossary A-Z, Terminology, Jargon, Slang, Vocabulary. A complete listing of terms A to Z of the most often used jargon, includes slang and vocabulary universally used around the world.

Hub rail. This was a hard rail, replaced in the 1990s that is now a row of pylons or flexible material that marks the 'inside boundary' of the course.

Important Harness Races. 1. The Hamiltonian is part of the Triple Crown of Harness Racing for 3-year old trotters. 2. The Little Brown Jug is part of the Triple Crown of Harness Racing for 3-year old pacers. 3. The Breeders Crown is a series of eight races that conducted on one day at different racetracks each year. First run in 1984, today's purses and awards total $13 million cover each of the traditional categories of gender, age, and gait (pace or trot).

Inquiry. This is a review of the race to check into a possible infraction of the rules.

Investor. A person who bets with a licensed bookmaker. Or a person who is not present at the race but places a bet on the horse(s) engaged at that race with the off-course bookmaker.

Interpol. This is the world organization that helps to locate and arrest wanted criminals who cross international borders.

Jog cart. (road cart). This is a two-wheeled cart for training is bigger and bulkier than a regular sulky, has larger seats so the driver doesn't have to be so agile trying to control both the horse and him/herself.

Length. Measured from the tip of the horse's nose to the start of its tail, usually eight feet. For instance, Secretariat won the Belmont Stakes by thirty-one lengths.

License criteria. (1VAC10-30-40). Determined by the commission, a limited license of application, the integrity of the applicant includes: A. Criminal record; B. Involvement in proceedings in government regulation of horse racing and C. Any other factors related to integrity, which the commission deems crucial to its making, as long as the same factors are considered with regard to all applicants, etc.

Little Brown Jug. The ultimate race for three-year-old pacers. Part of the Breeders Crown series of twelve races that cover each of the traditional categories of age, gait, and gender. It is part of the Triple Crown of Harness Racing for Pacers.

Long odds. This is more than a 10:1 ration.

Maiden race. This is a race for non-winners.

Map of Langley, Virginia. The map used for the location of the fictional town of Jasper, located in Virginia to the real town of Langley.

Mare. This is a female horse that is five years old, or older.

Modern dog cart. These versions have independent suspension and coil springs that give a smoother ride, lighter ones made out of lightweight material such as aluminum help achieve a higher speed than traditional types.

Muddy track. This is a condition of a racetrack, which is wet, but it has no standing water.

National Racing Compact. The National Racing Compact establishes certain criteria to determine eligibility for the National Racing License. A. Licensing Criteria, General licensing standards, 1. Criminal Record, 2. Racing-related Sanctions and 3. Character and/or Integrity Concerns. If these are violated, notification is given.

Neck-and Neck. This is an early term from the 1800s, which comes from horseracing. It describes where the necks of two horses that is in competition; appear to be side by side.

Nickel. This is a $500 wager.

Nolo contendere. In U.S. law, the term means a plea entered by a defendant that does not explicitly admit guilt, but subjects the defendant to punishment, while allowing denial of the alleged facts in other proceedings.

Non-graded stakes. This simply means that it is non-graded. It may be a stepping stone race to a graded stakes race.

Odds. A bookmaker's view of the chance of competitors wins that is, after the amount is adjusted to include a profit. The figure by which a bookmaker offers to multiply a bettor's stake, the bettor is entitled to receive the amount from the bookmaker.

Off the board. This is a horse that the bookie will not accept action on the horse because he is so lightly bet on, and it taken off the betting board.

Outsider. This is the term given to the horse when it's not expected to win and usually quoted at the highest odds.

Overbroke. This is results in a loss for the bookmaker.
Pace. This is the natural gait of many horses. It means that the horse moves its legs laterally, right front and right hind together, then left front and left hind together.

Pace handicapping. Based on turn times of a horse as well as the pace of the race. The theory is that it may allow a horse to come from behind horses that have burned up their speed. A knowledgeable pace handicapper can tell which horse is faster and able to run ahead of the others.

Pacing Races. This constitutes 80% to 90% of all harness races conducted in North America. Pacing horses are faster than trotting and are more important to the bettor because they are less likely to break stride.

Pari-mutuel. A form of wagering, originated in 1865 by Frenchman Pierre Oller, all money bet is divided up among those who have winning tickets, after taxes, other deductions are removed. The most common type of betting involves the prediction of the order of finish for a single participant, could be any one of the following: win, place, show, exacta, perfecta, or exactor, trifecta, superfecta, box, duet, double, triple, quadrella or sweep, etc.

Pathology report. Approximately twenty-four horses die each week at racetracks across America. They are called 'throw away horses' because they are used in the pursuit of larger and more lucrative prizes and they are inexpensive to replace. Their deaths go unexamined and their bodies shipped to 'the glue factory' and landfills instead of to pathologists. Without test results, it can't be determined why the horses died.

Piano hammer. When a key is pressed on a piano's keyboard, it causes a felt-covered hammer to strike steel strings. When the hammers rebound, it allows the strings to continue to vibrate at their resonant frequency.

Photo finish. A photo is taken of the horses as they pass the winning line. When a race is too close to be called, a judge views the photo to determine who has won.

Pocket. The spot on the rail behind the leader and known as the pocket because a horse in that position is said to have a greater chance of placing at least second in a race.

Post position. The position or stall at the starting gate from where the horse starts the race.

Post time. The designated time for a race to start.

Purebred. Refers to horses that have descended from a line of ancestors of the same breed, not necessarily registered in The American Stud Book or a foreign stud book recognized by The Jockey Club and the International Stud Book Committee. Of note here is that a Thoroughbred is a purebred.

Purse. The term that refers to the purse that holds the prize winnings.

Race bike: (formally known as a sulky). The only style allowed used in qualifying heats or harness racing. They are lighter, the seat smaller and harder for a driver to sit on but are more compact and aerodynamic than the training carts.

Race card. This is the program for the day's racing.

Race day meds. This is an anti-inflammatory drug consists of corticosteroids that are given to horses on race days. (Death and Disarray at America's Racetracks) Race Day medications are not allowed yet trainers continue to use them in the major racing, state of Florida.

Racing form. The important part of the information gathering Processes of statistics about previous performances and comments about a horse, also has the expected current performance of a horse.

Race horse numbers. Entries are drawn for each race, for each horse, and put on a separate sheet of paper that's called an entry slip. The number of postposition is also the number that the horse will wear on its saddle towel. Coupled entries are the exception and this will have a 1 and 1A, etc.

Rare and collectible books. This is the list the author used for our heroine Ellen to take out of the library. She chose the first two editions based upon the year and likelihood of their being collectables.
1. <u>Moby Dick; Or, the Whale</u> - Hardcover by Herman Melville (1851) Seller: Argosy Books Current Selling Price is $40,000.00 description: Very Good.
2. <u>Moby Dick, Or, the Whale</u> - Hardcover by Herman Melville (1851) Seller: Bookfinger Current Selling Price is $22,000.00 description: Very Good.
3. <u>HIERONYMI Cardani Medici Mediolanenfis DE SVBTILITATE</u>: First Edition of most important book written about Science knowledge of the XVI Century, describes such ell as God and demons. The author of this book tries to provide scientific formulation but the atmosphere surrounding it is magic and superstition. Current Selling Price is $17,000.00.

Ratings. (CR) is for Class Ratings, based on projected finishing times based on the speed ratings of the individual horses coming into each race. (SR) for Speed

Ratings, calculated in a few steps. (See TrackMaster website for further information.)

Receivership: This is the process, whereby a court appoints a receiver to take custody of the property, business, rents, and profits of a party to a lawsuit pending a final decision on disbursement, tern he property is in receivership applies.

Saudi Arabia. The Kingdom of Saudi Arabia has the world's second largest oil reserves, concentrated largely in the Eastern Province.

Seabiscuit. Passed from owner to owner, purchased by a car dealer, gave his trainer the short in stature Thoroughbred who became one of the all-time favorites during the Great Depression. It is also the story of how a horse with incredible spunk overcame injuries and crooked legs to beat the odds against him as well as an insight about the workings of race stables and jockey's lives.

Seabiscuit. Universal Studios, movie 2003. Actors Chris Cooper, as the trainer, Jeff Bridges, as the car dealer, and Toby Maguire as the Jockey, Red Pollard as the main characters, along with the horse that could; Seabiscuit.

Sleeper. This underrated horse unexpectedly wins a race having previously shown that it may not be able to compete with the others.
Standardbred. Horses, or their progeny, that can trot or pace a mile in a standard time; have shorter legs, longer bodies, a pleasant disposition, can stand up to the rigors of trotting or pacing; than Thoroughbreds.

Stallion. This is a male horse used for breeding.

Starting Gate. The motorized hinged gate mounted on a motor vehicle that moves slowly toward the starting line. The wings of the gate fold up and the vehicle accelerates away from the horses.

Stretch. This is the final straight portion of the racetrack to the finish line.
Sure thing. This is what the bookie thinks will be unbeatable in a race.

Taken up. The term used when a horse is pulled up sharply by his rider/driver because of being in close quarters.

The Jockey Club. The organization dedicated to the improvement of Thoroughbred breeding and racing. Incorporated in February of 1894 in New York City, it serves as North American's Thoroughbred register responsible for the maintenance of The American Stud Book that contains a register of all Thoroughbreds foaled in the United States, Puerto Rico, and Canada. It also includes all Thoroughbreds imported into those countries from jurisdictions that have a registry recognized by The Jockey Club and the International Stud Book Committee. The Jockey Club "is dedicated to the improvement of Thoroughbred breeding and racing and serves as the breed registry for North American

Thoroughbreds.", and the responsibility for eligibility of a horse for a race shall rest with the trainer.

Theory of Relativity. Einstein's theory encompasses two theories, a special relativity, and a general relativity. These concepts introduced by theories of relativity include the "measurements of various quantities" that "are relative to the velocities of observers". This is how space and time can expand. Another concept that time and space should be calculated together in relation to each other as well as a third concept, w h i c h has to do with the speed of light and the idea that it is unchanging, and the same for all observers.

Third on the rail. An undesirable place to be in, known as the death hole.

Thoroughbred. A horse whose parentage traces back to any one of the three Founding Sires; Darley Arabian, Byerly Turk, and the Godolphin Barb. Must be registered in The American Stud Book, a foreign studbook, and be recognized by The Jockey Club and the International Stud Book Committee. No other horse, no matter the parentage, will be a Thoroughbred for racing and/or breeding. A purebred is not necessarily a Thoroughbred.

Ticket. The betting slip or ticket that is received by the person placing the bet. It comes from the bookmaker and is proof of his/ her wager. No winnings can be collected without it.

Tote board. This is the electronic board that is in the infield that displays up-to-the-minute odds. It could also show the amounts that are wagered in each mutual pool as well as other information about drivers and equipment changes.

TrackMaster. Proprietary Ratings Specification, (Harness Racing). This is part of what a serious handicapper needs to fight the daily pari-mutuel battles. It includes speed ratings (SR) calculated for every harness race in North America.

Trot. The term used to describe a horse, which moves its legs forward in diagonal pairs, right front and left hind, then left front and right hind, striking the ground simultaneously.

Trotter. This is the term for harness racing in general. It can describe the specific gait of a trotter, or pacer.

True Lies. James Cameron directed, co-wrote 1994 American comedy/action film starring Arnold Schwarzenegger and Jamie Lee Curtis. The premise is that the husband lives a secret life and the wife uncovers his lies and unwittingly gets embroiled in his capers.

United States Federal Witness Protection Program. The program administered by the U.S. Department of Justice and operated by the U.S. Marshals Service, designed to protect witnesses that are threatened before, during, and after a trial.

Virginia Fact Book, (2012). A statistical guide to the Thoroughbred Industry in Virginia. Sections on breeding, racing auction sales, as it pertains to races.

Virginia State Legislative Information. A). Controls racing, pari-mutuel wagering; system of bets on horse races using electronic machine, totals bets, deducts management charges and taxes, and determines the final odds and payouts. B). Fee Schedule for Permit Holders.

Virginia Racing Commission. In the Commonwealth of Virginia, it lists all fee schedules for permit holders, staff, stables, Corporations, Vendors, Vendor Employee, Groom, pony rider, exercise rider, outrider, owner, trainer, asst. trainer, jockey, rider, apprentice jockey/rider, private vet, jockey agent, authorized agent, as well as blacksmith. This also includes other horse industry related permit types, combination permit for Harness Trainer/Driver, and Combination permit for Harness Owner/Trainer/Driver, and Fingerprint processing fee along with bar-coded picture badge for proof of licensing.

Virginia Racing Commission. ARTICLE 14., No driver in a race shall:
1. "change to the right or left during any part of the race when another horse is so near that, in altering the position, the driver compels the horse following to shorten that horse's stride; or causes the driver of the other horse to pull the horse out of stride, driver compels the horse following to shorten that horse's stride, or causes the driver of the other horse to pull the horse out of stride.
2. jostle, strike, hook wheels, or interfere with another horse or driver. And my personal favorite is the one where it is just plain wrong to or.
3. Cross sharply in front of a horse or cross over in front of a field of horses in a reckless manner so as to endanger other drivers".

Wise guy. This is a serious and knowledgeable handicapper or bettor.

Withdrawn. The term for when a horse is withdrawn from a race (scratched) before it starts. They can be withdrawn because of adverse track conditions or because of illness or injury to either the driver or horse.

# POEMS, PRAYERS, QUOTES, SAYINGS, IMAGES:

Architectural house plans found in this book are not real house plans, and therefore, are not to be used for an actual house. They are included to help guide the reader through the spaces.

Butterfly Image: M.A. Appleby created the image that appears at the beginning of all chapter. It is included with the copyright of this book, and may not be used in any form, unless given permission by its creator.

Deepak Chopra, 16 August 2012. "In the midst of movement and chaos, keep stillness inside of you." (Chapter Ten)

Frost, Robert, 06 May 2012. "In three words I can sum up everything I've learned about life; it goes on." (Chapter Three)

Gibran, Khalil, 10 June 2012. "Generosity is giving more than you can, and pride is taking less than you need." (Chapter Seven)

Guardian Angel Prayer, 06 May 2012. (Chapter One)
https://www.loyolapress.com/our-catholic-faith/prayer/traditional-catholic-prayers/prayers-every-catholic-should-know/guardian-angel-prayer

Hill, Napoleon, 19 September 2012. "A quitter never wins and a winner never quits." (Chapter Thirteen)

Lombardi, Vince, 07 October 2012. "It's not whether you get knocked down, it's whether you get up." (Chapter Fourteen)

Mahatma Gandhi, 19 November 2012 "Happiness is when what you think, what you say, and what you do are in harmony." (Chapter Fifteen)

Mother Teresa of Calcutta, 08 June 2012. "The greatest good is what we do for one another." (Chapter One) and "Kind words can be as short and easy to speak, but their echoes are truly endless." (Chapter Six)

Pope, Alexander, 12 August 2012. "Hope springs eternal in the human breast; Man never is, but always to be blest. The soul, uneasy, and confin'd from home, Rests and expatiates in a life to come." (Chapter Eleven)

Prescott, 14 September 2012. "An obstacle is often a stepping stone." (Chapter Twelve)

Runbeck, Margaret Lee, 9 August 2012. "Happiness is not a station you arrive at, but a manner of traveling." (Chapter Nine)

Tzu, Lao, 03 June 2012. "The journey of a thousand miles begins with one step." (Chapter Four)

Warhol, Andy, 03 June 2012. "They always say time changes things, but you actually have to change them yourself." Chapter Five)

Waitley, Dr. Denis, 07 July 2012. "There are two primary choices in life: to accept conditions as they exist or accept the responsibility for changing them." (Chapter Eight)

Woolrich, Cornell, 02 May 2012. "Time is strange. A moment can be as short as a breath, Or as long as eternity." (Chapter Two)

# Read the National Award-Winning Non-Fiction book that started it all:

***RAISING DAVID AGAIN*** ~ ISBN: 978-1-4984-9873-9
*A Guide To Understanding The Uniqueness of Brain Injury
And How Our Faith Sustains Us*

**Other books by M.A. Appleby:**

**A Whisper of a Mystery Trilogy**:

*The Ancient Whisper*, Book 1 ~ ISBN: 978-0-6929-2129-6
*Whispered Dreams*, Book 2 ~ ISBN: 978-0-6929-2133-3
*Journey of a Thousand Steps*,
            Book 3 ~ ISBN: 978-0-6929-2134-0

# Visit Author's website:
# www.maappleby.com